CHARLOTTE LEVIN

If I Can't Have You

MANTLE

First published 2020 by Mantle
an imprint of Pan Macmillan
The Smithson, 6 Briset Street, London EC1M 5NR
Associated companies throughout the world
www.panmacmillan.com

ISBN 978-1-5290-3239-0

1 3 5 7 9 8 6 4 2

A CIP catalogue record for this book is available from the British Library.

Typeset by Palimpsest Book Production Ltd, Falkirk, Stirlingshire
Printed and bound by CPI Group (UK) Ltd, Croydon, CR0 4YY

Visit www.panmacmillan.com to read more about all our books
and to buy them. You will also find features, author interviews and
news of any author events, and you can sign up for e-newsletters
so that you're always first to hear about our new releases.

For Mum and Dad
The snow

'Unexpressed emotions will never die.
They are buried alive and will come forth
later in uglier ways'
SIGMUND FREUD

*

They all stared.

The group of girls cooing over the fruits of their Christmas shopping trip stopped and slapped each other's arms. The Marrieds ceased to argue and held hands. The Reading Man lost his page.

I stood in the Tube carriage among them.

A young suity-booty City Prick and a Sloane Ranger with a leg-kicking infant on her lap parted ways to expose a seat for me. I don't believe out of politeness. Most likely out of fear, confusion. The fact my light-headed sways made it probable I'd fall their way.

Regardless of the reason, I was grateful, and squeezed my white taffeta-engulfed body between them, while attempting to keep the material under control, which proved impossible as the voluminous skirt overlapped onto them both.

The child, who I could now see was a girl, stroked my dress with her saliva-ridden fingers.

'Look at the princess, Mummy.'

The mother buried her spawn's head into her blazer, clearly wishing to God she'd just got a black cab as usual. However, her utter Englishness forced her to smile at me. I returned a semi-version, but was conscious of my front tooth, hanging by a minute thread of gum. It hurt. I closed my mouth and looked down at the blood covering my chest. It was odd how it had taken more to the embroidery than the taffeta.

Raising my head, I could see in the window's distorted reflection Sloaney and City Prick looking at each other behind me in wide-eyed horror. Though they appeared to be strangers, I'd bonded them. Beyond their ghostly images was the huge High Street Kensington sign. It was telling me goodbye. I remember thinking I'd write a book about it one day. *The Fucked Girl on the Train.*

As we pulled away from the station, eyes screwed and faces twisted with calculations as they tried to decipher what had happened. Was I the jilter or the jiltee? But as you know more than anyone, Dr Franco, people are rarely what they appear to be on the surface. The Marrieds may have in fact been illicit lovers, the shopping girls been out on the steal.

Sloaney pressed her Chanel silk scarf against her nose. It was my vomit-laced veil she could smell. I was tempted to turn and tell her everything. Ask for her help. But I couldn't, because I didn't know her. I didn't know anyone anymore.

She wouldn't have given a shit, anyway. Her only concern being I didn't scare Mini Sloane. I smiled at the kid. It cried.

I was already old news. People stopped gawking, or were doing so more subtly at least. They returned to their arguing, laughing, avoiding. Heads magnetically drawn down to phones. But then came the flashes. There was no doubt I'd feature heavily in conversations that day. Photo evidence was needed. I'd be trending on Twitter.

Reading Man glanced up from his book, *The Seven Habits of Highly Effective People.* Perhaps he was wondering which one my habit was. But then that's what I love about London. Rather than staring, why didn't they ask if I was OK? I was not fucking OK, people. In Manchester, I'd have been in someone's house by then, being handed a cup of tea with six sugars and a Blue Riband.

The Tube slowed to a halt. Earls Court. I could see them on the platform waiting for me.

My tooth dropped onto my lap.

My darling Samuel,

I've never written a letter before. Love or otherwise.

As much as I've been desperate to tell you how much I miss you, think about you until my head spins, my stomach constricts, it was Dr Franco's suggestion that I write.

You must know I intended to join you. I promise I did. But when it came to it, I couldn't. Not now I have something to stay here for. I'm sorry.

It'll be some time before I see you again and I can't stop fretting that I never got to explain myself fully. Aside from the brief, clumsy attempt you allowed me that day. That terrible day. I can't even steady the pen as I write these words.

Anyway, I've decided to take his advice. Tell you everything. From the beginning. My account of it all. My side. Moment by moment. Hurt by hurt. Though Dr Franco insists there are no such things as beginnings. Only the point from which someone is prepared to start telling their story. So I'll start from our beginning. And I promise it will be the entire truth. Something no one else shall know.

*

I often think about the first time I saw you: when they broke the news that Dr Williams had been killed at the weekend.

Dr Harris and Dr Short had gathered everyone into the surgery waiting room, even menials like myself, and Harris relayed the shocking details. 'You may as well hear it from me as there'll only be speculation.' Mrs Williams. An argument. The car that hit him as he ran across the road after her. How he was still alive when the ambulance arrived. How he was dead before they could get him into it. I heard it all. The terrible events. The intakes of breath. Linda blubbing next to me. I heard. But it was you who held my concentration.

You were the stranger among us. Kept your head down in respect. Or was it embarrassment? Your hair fell forward, draping your face in that way it does, and when you glanced up, your eyes, pale, unsettled, unsettled me.

Dr Harris hadn't been speaking long before Linda felt faint. With difficulty, her being built like a walrus, I eased her round the *Country Life*-covered coffee table and onto the nearest section of modular seating, before fetching her a glass of water as instructed.

You stood in the doorway. I could smell you. Lemons. My

hand brushed yours as I passed, but I didn't acknowledge you or smile, merely walked on as if you were a ghost. On my return, you'd moved further into the room, meaning there was no accidental touch.

As I'm sure you'll remember, Linda's reaction was stronger than everyone else's. Possibly even than that of Mrs Williams. It was always obvious she'd had a thing for him. We – Linda, myself and Alison – were responsible for all the doctors' admin, as you know. But Linda coveted Dr Williams's work. I could identify the glint through her cloggy eyelashes each time she had to go to his office. Poor Linda. The 'speculation' was that Mrs Williams was running away because she'd caught him with another woman. Another woman who wasn't Linda. It wasn't just his wife whom Dr Williams had betrayed.

I remember feeling conscious that I didn't look upset enough. Or shocked. Even the unfriendly agency nurses, or the Ratcheds, as I called them, looked emotional. But I was just as shaken and moved by Dr Williams's fate as everyone else. Only, I'd lost the ability to express. As you know, with me, it's all inside. Always inside.

With Linda now settled into a low-grade wail, Dr Harris brought the meeting to practical matters. As a private practice, there wasn't the option of telling people there was a three-week wait for an appointment. He wasn't prepared to lose money, dead partner or not. That was when he introduced you.

I never liked Dr Harris. Mainly because he was a wanker. But also, the way he'd always point – no, jab – with his party-sausage fingers, onto which he'd somehow managed to stuff a ring. I wondered about the woman who'd screw such a man for a nice house and car. I presumed that was her motive. But I couldn't imagine a house or car spectacular enough.

'Constance, I'll draft a letter for you to send out to all of Dr Williams's patients. You and Alison call anyone due to see him today and give them the choice of rearranging with me or Dr Short for later this week or keeping their appointment and seeing Dr Stevens instead. Please encourage the latter.' He summoned you further into the room. 'This is Dr Stevens from our Harley Street surgery.'

Grateful I could now look at you directly, I contemplated the intricacies of your face. Soaked you in. You were the epitome of posh. Everything I despised. Yet I was conflicted about how attractive I found you.

I observed as you pushed your fine-cotton white shirtsleeves further up your forearms, which you folded, unfolded, folded again before daring to draw the long breath that enabled you to speak. Before the words sounded, you broke into a smile, which forced me to momentarily lower my burning face.

'Hello . . . I'm so sorry about Dr W-Williams. I know he was very much loved by you all. Although it's in the saddest of circumstances I'm here, I look forward to working with everyone and getting to know you . . . and the patients.'

You delivered your stilted lines almost perfectly. Aside from that stutter with his name. Yes, I noticed. But I'm sure no one else did. You'd clearly been practising. I suspect out loud in your full-length bedroom mirror. And I could sense the relief once it had left your lips.

Your micro-speech triggered Linda's sobs to start up again

and gather momentum. Dr Harris instructed Alison to call her a cab, and for me to pack up Dr Williams's personal belongings in his office. I didn't want to. The idea scared me. His stuff. But I nodded subserviently, as I always did.

I remained in the waiting room, prolonging the task. Dr Harris had already left for his office. The Ratcheds had disappeared too. Alison was helping Linda on with her raincoat. You were shaking hands and talking in a low, respectful voice with Dr Short. I wonder, were you suppressing a smile at the contrast with his name and his practically being a giant at six foot seven? It always amused me. Stood next to him, I looked like a tiny child. He treated me like one as well.

Throughout all this you hadn't noticed me once.

To further delay going to Dr Williams's office, I headed to reception to pull up his appointments for the day. Alison was shuffling Linda out of the building, passing the responsibility on to a bemused taxi driver. The front door banged shut.

Minus the crying, all was quiet until Alison made her way to the desk.

'I can't believe he's dead.' She leant over the wooden ledge separating us to deliver her whisper.

I feel bad saying Alison was boring. It sounds cruel. But is something cruel if it's also true? Her boringness was a fact. And why do the boring ones talk the most? To be fair, I only listened to around forty per cent of what she had to say, so she may have been riveting for the other sixty. I even preferred the bitterness of Linda and her banging on about getting another thyroid test while tucking into her fourth KitKat Chunky of the day.

'Yes, it's terrible.' I stared at the computer screen.

'I just can't believe it. Dr Williams. Dead.'

'Yes. It's horrible. But . . . well, people die.' I knew it would show itself. My hands trembled over the keyboard, and I was overcome with queasiness.

'So what do you think happened? All sounds a bit fishy to me.'

'I think it was a terrible accident.'

I hoped she'd interpret my taut words as 'Shut the fuck up', yet she continued. 'Hmm . . . I'm not so sure . . . Isn't death weird, though? You're just not here anymore.'

'Don't you think you'd better call his patients? I'm worried you'll not catch them all in time.'

As she joined me behind the reception desk, I stood for her to sit in my chair, believing she'd finished, but no.

'That Dr Stevens is lovely, isn't he? I mean, I love my Kevin and wouldn't dream of looking at another man, but he's very handsome, isn't he?'

'I didn't notice.'

'So they say it was an accident, but Dr Williams's wife – Margaret, is it? – wasn't she—'

The door buzzed.

'That's Mrs Akeem. You'd better shush now,' I said, before escaping into the back in search of a cardboard box.

On entering Dr Williams's room, I'd expected you to be there, but it was pitch-dark. When I switched on the light, it wasn't only the space that was illuminated, it was death. The silence. His things. Just there. How he'd left them on the Friday.

No doubt you'd be aware of that phenomenon: when someone's belongings become both hugely profound and utterly useless at the same time.

The air, hot and clammy, made my nausea worse and I squeezed my stomach for relief. His Manchester United mug, half full with the tea I'd made him, looked lost. A large crumb – I'd guess from the stash of digestives he kept in his drawer – was stuck to the rim. During my interview, he'd picked up on my Mancunian accent. Presumed I was a Man United fan. I was by default, but I don't care much for football. He told me he went to uni there. Lived in Fallowfield. The opposite end to where I was. He was full of nostalgia, yearnings for my hometown, and I'm certain that's why he hired me. A link to his youth and happier times. Or maybe he just liked me. All I know is it wasn't my experience or qualifications. I'd already felt lucky that I'd managed to immediately land a job pulling pints in a dive pub. But I saw the vacancy for the surgery receptionist in a copy of the *Evening Standard* someone had left on the Tube and applied that night on a drunken whim. When he called to offer me the job, I felt for that moment like I was a real person. Worthy of something good. But I soon remembered that I wasn't at all.

I picked up the wooden-framed picture of him and his family, all smiles, and placed it face down in the box. Next, I reached over for the mug, but as I did, the nausea overwhelmed me, and before I'd had a chance to think, I'd run to the sink and thrown up. And again. And again. When it all seemed over, and I gripped the sides of the cold porcelain, breaths heavy, I felt a hand on my back and jumped.

'Oh God . . . I'm sorry. I didn't mean to frighten you. I was just . . . Are you OK? It's a terrible shock all this, I know.'

I faced you. Aware of how I must have looked, I turned back towards the sink and pulled paper towels from the dispenser to wipe the remnants of vomit from my chin before throwing them in the bin. 'Yes . . . yes, I'm fine. I . . . I don't know what happened. I must have eaten something.'

'Are you sick every morning?'

'No . . . God, no. I'm not pregnant, if that's what you're getting at.'

'No . . . I . . . Well, yes, I was getting at that, but I'm a doctor. That's kind of what I do.'

'Honestly, it's nothing. I've probably just got a bug or something. Dr Franco went home with one on Friday.'

'Dr Franco? I thought it was only Dr Harris and Dr Short?'

'Yes, yes, it is. Dr Franco just rents a room here. He's a psychiatrist or . . . psychologist. I always get confused. He's not here all the time, though. He also works with inpatients at some hospital in Ealing.' A strange look I was unable to interpret washed over your eyes. 'Anyway, Dr Stevens, I'd better . . .' I returned to the desk and picked up the mug.

'Alison, isn't it?'

You have no idea how much that stung. 'Constance.'

'Constance . . . of course, Constance. I'm sorry. I'm terrible with names.'

'Alison's in reception.' I took the mug to the sink and rinsed it along with the residue of my breakfast.

'And the office manager is Linda? Is that right? Is that it, then?'

'Yes. Yes, that's right. Apart from the R—' I stopped myself. 'Carol and Janet, the agency nurses. They're just part-time, covering maternity leave. For Rayowa, the proper nurse.'

'Well, thank you, Constance. For saving me from embarrassing myself again.'

I smiled, then turned back towards you, shaking the mug free of water. 'I'll leave all Dr Williams's medical things here, but let me know if you need anything ordering. Stationery or other supplies.'

'Are you feeling better?'

I dared to look at you properly, but your smile caught me off guard. 'Yes, Dr Stevens. I feel fine now. Thank you . . . I'm just embarrassed, that's all. Your first day as well.'

'Yes, I prefer at least a week to go by before the staff vomit in my presence.'

I would have smiled back had I not been so mortified. Instead, I quickly grabbed the box and said, 'I'll let you settle in, Dr Stevens, shall I? Get the rest later?'

You followed me to the door. Held it open like the gentleman I thought you were. It was then I caught your eyes directly for the first time. They were cold in the paleness of their grey. Unnervingly familiar. I turned my head, focused on a bald patch of carpet until you said, 'You couldn't possibly get me a coffee, could you? White, one sugar. Strong but milky.'

I didn't see much more of you during that first day. Not as much as I'd hoped, anyway. Most of Dr Williams's patients cancelled, and I went to your room only twice. Once with the cup of coffee you requested, which had taken three attempts to get right. I was unsure what was meant by 'strong but milky'. I'd made the first too weak, so chucked it down the sink. The second, I was certain I'd overdone the sugar, so remade it with a level spoonful. After placing the third version in front of you, I loitered at the door, waiting for the verdict, which judging by your expression, wasn't very good at all. I was so annoyed at myself for not sticking with the sweeter one.

The second time was with a file you'd requested. You were busy sorting out your desk.

'Hey, Constance. Come in. I'm just trying to make myself feel more at home.'

I'd already noticed that your hand was ring-free, but I still feared that the following day you'd be displaying a photograph of your own.

With the last patient gone, Alison and I tidied reception and prepared to finish for the day. I was hoping you'd leave at the same time. Prayed you got the Tube. But your door remained closed.

Outside, I stopped at the bottom of the entrance steps, breathed in the fresh air before digging in my bag for a desperately needed cigarette.

'You shouldn't be smoking, Constance. Not when working at a doctor's surgery,' said Alison.

Luckily, with the fag now hanging from my mouth, it was too awkward to tell her to fuck off. She lingered as I struggled to get a spark from my near-empty lighter. But thank God, she didn't want to be late for her sewing class, so fucked off on her own accord.

Still determined to get the ciggie lit, I huddled into the adjacent wall and cupped my hand to shield it from the warm breeze. Finally it took. I turned back round and leant against the rough bricks. Closed my eyes. Thought about you as the chemicals performed their tricks.

When I reopened them, there was a face in front of mine that I wasn't expecting.

*

We never talked about Dale much, I know. I never wanted
you to think there was . . . that I had any romantic feelings
towards him. I didn't. Whatever I share with you from this
point, you must believe that. I'd avoided discussing him to
prevent you from enduring unnecessary jealousy. Regardless
of what you did, I'd never want to put you through that.

'I've been calling and texting you all day. Nearly forgot to
process the payment run, I was getting so worried . . . Would
have given Jean yet another reason not to give me the
account-manager job.'

'Oh, have you? I'm sorry.' I removed my phone from my
bag. Although we had to keep them on silent at work, I
would usually check and reply to his messages, which were
generally asking if I wanted to share a pizza or go for a drink
at Connolly's. There were nine missed calls. Numerous blocks
of blue text. I looked up at his concerned face. 'Sorry. I . . .
It's been . . . Dr Williams died.'

'Shit, man, you're joking. Which one's he? How?'

'Run over.'

'Run over? Jesus, who gets run over?'

'At the weekend. It's weird . . . He's the nice one. The
Man U supporter.'

15

'Still, he didn't deserve to die.'

I didn't fake-laugh as I usually would, which forced him to back-pedal.

'That sucks. It's always the nice ones, isn't it? You've remembered about tonight, though, right?' My blankness must have shown. 'The film? I knew you'd—'

'Of course. I have . . . remembered. I thought you meant something else when you said . . . The film I have. I'm looking forward to it.'

'Well, we need to get a move on, then. You know I get all angsty being late and that.'

As I flicked the rest of the cigarette to the ground and we headed off, I heard the surgery door open. I stopped, turned to look. You were oblivious to us. Chatting with Dr Harris as he locked up. You laughed. Forced. I understood. You were holding your linen jacket in one hand and your doctor's bag in the other. Car keys dangled from your fingers, quashing my wish of us ever getting the Tube together.

'Constance, for fuck's sake. What are you doing?'

'Sorry . . . I—'

'Who is that?'

'It's just Dr Harris. And the new doctor.'

'Right. Well, can we go, please?' He tugged my arm to encourage me to move again, causing me to trip on a raised corner of pavement. 'Why are you so clumsy?'

After walking for a few seconds, he said, 'The new doctor looks a right dickhead. Where does he get his hair cut – 1995?'

I wanted to glance back at you once more. I didn't. But noticed that Dale did.

* * *

It was a foreign-film festival at the South Bank and they were showing the only Almodóvar Dale hadn't seen: *Talk to Her*. The last thing I wanted to do was to sit through some sub-titled arty bollocks.

We were informed that the trailers had already started. This was, of course, my fault and he slipped seamlessly into a sullen mood. Before he could argue, I rushed towards the bar and stood on my tippy-toes to get served as quickly as possible. He followed me, once again gripping on to my arm, pulling me away.

'I need a Coke . . . and a snack or something. I'm starving.'

In silence, he escorted me to the corner of the foyer. His eyes flicked from side to side, paranoid and spy-like. Two triangles of blush appeared on each cheek, and his signature stress-sweat seeped from his upper lip. He lifted the flap of his record bag to reveal two small Lidl apple-juice cartons with attached straws and a stack of cling-filmed cheese-and-piccalilli sandwiches that were as sweaty as he was.

'Oh right,' I said.

He dropped the flap back down, wiped his mouth with his sleeve. 'Well, you don't have to.'

'No, that's . . . Cheese and piccalilli is my favourite. Thank you.'

The cinema was fairly empty. Dale marched us to his desired spot – centre middle – then stood back against his chair to let me in. 'Is that OK? I prefer the other person to be on my right.'

I felt him, smelt him, as I squeezed past. We'd never been to the cinema together before. Our hanging-out had mainly taken place at the house or at Connelly's. An awkwardness rose between us. We smiled in unison.

I'd only known Dale for three months at that point. He was already a tenant of the house on Lynton Road when I'd moved in. I'd gone to the viewing in a state of desperation. Dale was at work, but Mr Papadopoulos, the breathless, fleshy landlord, showed me round.

'This would be your bedsit . . . You share bathroom and kitchen with nice young man who live in room opposite. I'm in flat upstairs . . . Very quiet. You can come straight away. Anna, the other girl . . . nice girl . . . left one night and never come back . . . Left me up the shit's creek.'

I wanted to cry as I stared into the damp-smelling room, decorated with greying woodchip, double bed on one side, brown velour sofa on the other. A torn paper lantern hanging from the ceiling. The only thing brightening the place was a lurid green dreamcatcher with dangling pink feathers hanging from the bedhead that I knew I'd be immediately throwing out. Dreamcatchers scared me. My dreams were something I'd never want to be caught. But after the horrors of the previous places I'd viewed that day, and the fact it was available immediately, I was relieved to accept.

I'd not long left Manchester behind, it all behind, and moved into my first London abode. A room in a house belonging to a middle-aged actor called Rupert James. It was 'bijou yet airy', aka minuscule with a window. But Rupert was interesting – colourful, let's say, and I presumed gay. The roll-top bath had sold me. I'd only seen the likes of it in magazines. Above it was a shelf on which sat a skull. I hoped it was a prop from a *Hamlet* production and not his previous tenant.

All went well for a couple of weeks until one day I returned from work to find my bedroom had been cleaned and tidied. Bed made. Dirty clothes picked up. Dirtier knickers ditto. And Blusha, my one-eyed elephant, tucked up neatly under the covers with only her trunk on show. I was uncertain who was being the weirdo, him or me. But I didn't like it. Inside.

Then one evening I went into the kitchen and there he was, smoking an enormous joint and holding an even more enormous glass of red wine, which explained his eyeballs and skin always having a matching crimson hue.

'Constance.' He removed a glass from the draining board, filled it with wine to a level higher than his own and handed it to me.

'Constance, my dear, I need to ask you something.'

It was clear he'd noticed my change since Tidygate. I decided I'd be brave, tell him, politely.

Then it came. 'Constance. Dear Constance. Would you like to fuck?'

'Sorry?'

'Would you like to fuck?'

Floored, scared and unable to think of a more repulsive prospect, I didn't want to make him feel uncomfortable, so I said, 'I'm really very tired, Rupert, but thanks anyway,' then went to my room, locking the door behind me.

In bed, I pulled my knees to my chest, foetal, and squeezed Blusha with more intensity than ever before. Not only because of Rupert but because it hit me. The gradual drip,

drip, drip from which I was running. As I bit Blusha's ear to transfer my pain onto her, I realized I was completely alone. Unprotected. Unloved. If Rupert had added me to his skull collection, no one would have noticed. No one would have cared. That was my new reality. Immersed under the covers, I allowed myself to cry for the first time since I'd left home. This must have somehow carried me into a deep sleep because the clock said 03.07 when I woke to the rattle of my doorknob turning frantically, followed by the thud of a foot kicking against the wood. By 03.09 this stopped. By 04.30 my case was packed, and by 05.00, when I could hear definite snoring from the next room, I left. By 14.00 that day I'd moved into Lynton Road, and by 20.00 Dale and I were friends.

It's hard being friends with someone who doesn't truly know you. What you really are. But he was the only person in the world I had. The only person who cared.

Dale thoroughly enjoyed the film. I thought it was pretentious crap.

We were still arguing about it on the bus home.

'But he loved her,' he repeated for the hundredth time.

'So?' I repeated for my hundredth time, each one increasing in volume, intensity. For that last one I half stood up to say it. 'He was just some nutter who sat watching her, obsessed. She didn't even know him.'

'Not all men can tell a girl he likes her, you know.'

'Then the poor cow is in a coma and he shags her. No, no, rapes her.'

'But he did love her.'

The cycle began again until I broke it with 'Loving someone doesn't excuse everything, you know.'

'You've never even been in love, Constance.'

'So?' This 'So?' was considerably quieter than my previous ones, and I remained firmly seated to say it. 'You haven't either. You told me.'

He turned away. His usually soft marshmallow face stony in the window's reflection.

I sat back and looked out towards the insane, lit-up London that I'd never feel part of. And as I did, against my will, your face strobed my mind.

*

The next morning it was still you who occupied my thoughts.

Not Dale. Not even poor Dr Williams.

Instead of swiping snooze on my alarm with increasing despair, I woke immediately. Facing the wall, for once I wasn't irritated by the tear in the woodchip that exposed a rainbow from wallpaper of times gone by. My mind wasn't darkly drawn downwards, through the mattress springs, beyond the wooden slats, to the suitcase below filled with realities I couldn't face. Once out of bed, I wasn't crestfallen by the disarray of my room. Or the mould that clung to the tiles round the bath when I showered. I even washed my hair and shaved my pits.

I wore a silk blouse that had only ever had an outing for my cousin Margot's wedding. Applied a lick of make-up. Nothing obvious. I didn't want it to be noticeable to everyone, to Dale.

As I snuck out of my room, Dale exited his, feigning surprise at my being there, smiling as if the night before he hadn't slammed his door without saying a word.

I went along with the charade and we left the house, chatting about needing milk and bin day. At the end of Lynton Road, when we were about to part ways, he said, 'You look weird today,' then ran for his bus.

On the hot, stifling Tube, my blouse now ruined by ink blots spreading under my arms, I dwelt on Dale's words. My single atom of confidence melted, I rubbed at my cheeks and stripped the lipstick with the back of my hand.

By the time I'd reached the surgery, I looked more bedraggled than usual. And when Linda glanced up at me, bemused, I was unsure if it was because of my appearance or the fact I was on time. Something I hadn't managed since my first day.

'Are you feeling better today, Linda?'

'Not really. I'm . . . I'm just very sad, to be honest. He was a great man.'

'Yes . . . Yes, he was.' I dropped my head.

The moment hung like smog until Linda broke the silence. 'When you've settled, can you take these files into Dr Stevens for me, please? I find it quite distressing going in there.'

'Of course. No problem. You know, I . . . I can do all Dr Stevens's stuff if you want. It's no trouble. You mustn't upset yourself, Linda.'

She mouthed the words 'Thank you', then performed a succession of fast little nods before running into the back room. I suppose I was expected to follow her, comfort her, but I took the file and headed to your office.

After calling me in, I realized you were on the phone. 'Look, I can't talk about it now,' you said to the caller. I sensed it was personal. A woman. You bit the end of your weighty silver pen. After placing the file on your desk, I went to leave, but you raised your hand to stop me.

'It's nearly two months . . . Well, just get them, then . . . Look, I've really got to go. I'll see you later.'

My stomach churned.

You ended the call, placed the pen in your inside jacket pocket, then smiled as you patted the file. 'Sorry about that. Thank you, Constance. How are you feeling today?'

'I'm . . . I'm fine. Much better, thank you. Dr Stevens, Linda's asked if I can do all your work from now on. She feels too upset to keep coming into Dr Williams's office. So if . . . if you need anything, just ask me. Not Linda . . . or Alison.'

'Oh right. OK. You've not been sick again, then?'

'No. No, I'm fine now.' You looked directly at me, squinted, ensuring I was telling the truth. You cared. 'Can I get you a coffee, Dr Stevens?'

Sitting back in your chair, you pushed your fingers through your hair. 'Constance, do you think they'll ever accept me?'

'Of course. Of course they will. It's just very early days, isn't it?'

'Because I like it here, you know. I do. I prefer it to Harley Street. I can tell already. For a start, I live less than a ten-minute walk away. Not that I've walked it yet, mind. Lazy bastard . . . Sorry.'

'It's OK. You can say "bastard". I don't mind.'

You laughed. I laughed too. Although I wasn't sure what was funny.

'I'm glad, anyway . . . that you'll be doing my stuff.'

You have no idea of the overwhelming delight I felt at you saying this and forced a cough to conceal the evidence of blood surging to my face.

'You really should give up the fags, you know.'

My surprise at you saying that transformed the fake cough into a genuine one, and you handed me a small half-empty

24

Evian bottle from your desk. I unscrewed the lid. Aware I'd be placing my lips directly on top of where yours had been, I sipped. And while doing so, my blouse draped open and I was certain you glanced at my chest.

'I noticed you smoking . . . with your friend yesterday.'

'Oh . . . I . . . He's not my boyfriend . . . just a . . . I will.' I took more water. 'I know I should . . . give up smoking.'

'You OK now?'

I nodded, handing him back the bottle.

'Good. Anyway, Constance, tell me – what are you doing for lunch?'

You probably noticed the sharp intake of breath. I couldn't believe you were already inviting me to lunch.

'Well . . . I . . . It depends . . .'

'Do you ever go out for a sandwich or something?'

'Yes, well, I'm sure I will . . . I mean, I usually do.'

'Excellent. If I give you the money, will you pick something up for me as well? I've got all these patients to swot up on.' You handed me a tenner. 'Something chicken would be great. I'll let you decide.'

Outside your office, deflated, I noticed Dr Franco bounding down the hallway. 'Well, hello, young Constance.'

'Hey, Dr Franco. Are you all better now?'

'I am. I am, indeed. Thank you. Lost a couple of pounds in the process too,' he said, patting his belly. 'But it's truly terrible about dear Dr Williams. I was so shocked. You must all be terribly shocked.'

'Yes . . . yes, we are. It's very sad.'

His tearfulness was magnified under the convex of his glasses and he rested his hand upon my shoulder. 'It is indeed.' He paused, then said, 'Though, sadly, as life goes on, I must get going. I have a patient.' And off he went up the stairs.

I liked Dr Franco. Still do. Despite everything he now knows about me.

The hours up until lunch went quickly. We were extra busy due to the patients who'd cancelled the previous day now deciding they wanted to be seen. Apparently, being rich permits such things.

Finally, able to escape, I headed to M&S. Tesco was closer, but I thought I'd get a higher-quality sandwich for you in Marks.

Once there, I grabbed a basket and within seconds had thrown in Alison's requested tuna sarnie (Linda was on SlimFast) and my egg and tomato. Allowing me time to study the chicken selection.

After much stress, I opted for the last remaining chicken salad sandwich, in a bag rather than a plastic packet, but the lettuce looked decidedly ragged. I asked the acnefied boy filling the crisp stand if there were any more in the back, and after some resistance, he relented, returning with a much perkier one that I was happy to give you.

On the way back, fantasizing about us eating our lunch together in the staffroom, I realized I'd run out of fags, so popped into Mo's kiosk. While waiting for my change, which took longer than it should, as Mo was, as always, on the phone and running a one-armed operation, my eyes scanned the papers next to me. 'Austerity Not Over.' A picture of an elderly woman being evicted from her council house. Then I noticed the date: 26 July.

I'd forgotten.

I'd never forgotten before.

Panicked, I searched for a card. An array of faded drawings with naff proclamations of happy occasions perched in what appeared to have once been a rotating stand. But lack of space and rack rheumatism meant it could barely swing a centimetre side to side. There was only one for a father. An embossed watercolour of a man playing golf. *Happy birthday to the best dad in the world.* I paid for it, along with a book of four stamps, and mouthed for Mo to lend me a pen so I could write the same words I always did. *Happy birthday, Dad. Love, Constance.* Beneath, my number and current address. On the envelope, *MR PATRICK LITTLE*, written in clear block capitals. A stamp.

Aware time was racing, I hurried back to work via the postbox.

A postman was filling a sack with all the mail. I hovered next to him.

'Shall I take that, darlin'?'

I hesitated, placed the card in his hand, then swiftly continued down the road.

'Hello . . . Excuse me, love,' I could hear him shout. 'Miss.'

I didn't stop. But neither did he. 'Woohoo, miss.' He whistled. So shrill that I had no choice but to turn.

'You've forgotten to write the address on it, my darlin',' he shouted.

I ran back to him. Smiling, rolling my eyes. 'I'm such an

idiot,' I said, as I took it back. He handed me a pen he'd removed from behind his ear. 'Oh . . . thank you, but I haven't even come out with the address.'

We laughed. I thanked him. I continued down Kensington Church Street. Turned off onto the High Street, where there was another postbox.

I dropped in the card.

The air was still clammy, though smatterings of rain offered some comfort. The grey sky merged with buildings. Rain came properly then. Heavy. Umbrellas went up around me like mass flowers in bloom. People ran or stayed still under shop canopies. But I stopped. Stood in the middle of the pavement, raised my head, closed my eyes. It felt good. Well, better. Like it was washing things away. And only I would ever have known it wasn't just rain that poured down my face.

I remained there for a few seconds. I think. I don't really know. When I returned to the world, I was so soaked that I pushed back my hair, flat to my head and down my neck like I did in the shower, and ran. Ran like everyone else.

Back at the surgery, my wet blouse was paper-thin, see-through. I stood in reception in what looked like only my bra. Linda was eager to get me out the back. Away from the view of patients, who were somehow all immaculate and dry.

'But I need to give Dr Stevens his lunch.'

'Dr Stevens has gone out on house calls. He won't be coming back today.'

I dried myself in the loo and put on a jumper that a patient had left behind yonks ago. Then I ate my sandwich in the staffroom with Alison, not you. She relayed, word for word, the previous night's episode of *Emmerdale* and complained that I'd actually picked up salmon instead of tuna.

After counting down the minutes to home time, when it was nearly five, Dr Harris asked if I'd stay on and do some overtime, to sort through Dr Williams's paperwork. Reluctantly, I agreed.

Everyone else had gone. Harris remained in his office. I was alone in yours. It spooked me, being in there. The feeling was heightened by the heavy rain. Outside was dark, oppressive. A humongous black cloud hung over West London, like the spaceship in *Independence Day*. The precursor to an inevitable storm. And storms terrified me.

When little, I'd climb into bed with Mum. She'd tell me God was angry at me for some act of childhood I'd committed that day. I'd cling to her, silently praying for His forgiveness. Not stopping until He'd given it.

Except that last time.

It was different that time.

While shredding documents, I noticed you'd left your jacket behind. It was hanging on the back of the door. Expensive. Soft, muted linen. I wanted to touch it. My eyes fell onto the pockets. More shredding. As the noise drilled, I found myself walking across the room. My fingers gently running down the crinkled cotton. I lifted it to my face. Only for a second. Lemons again. My palm traced its pocket. There was something in there. I craved information about you. I wasn't going to look. That would have been wrong. My fingertips stroked the top of the opening. Moved slightly inside. Then an almighty thunderclap shook through me. I stepped away from the door. Looked up, apologized to God and returned to the paperwork.

It was almost eight by the time we left. As Harris locked up, I attempted to open a brolly that had been resting in the corner of the stationery cupboard since I started working there. I waited for the offer of a lift. At least to the station. It never came. Because he was a wanker.

We said our goodbyes and walked in opposite directions.

The brolly was about as useful as a child's skirt on a stick. Dipped at the front, not only did it fail to prevent me from getting wet, it created a guttering effect that directed the water straight into my face. However, a few seconds into the battle, I heard Harris calling. I stopped and turned. There was no way he'd really let me walk in this, and I was over-come with guilt at always thinking he was a wanker.

'Don't be late tomorrow – we've got a lot of stuff to get through.'

Heading towards the Tube, I tried to ignore the deafening thunder and electric sky. The streets were empty. Practically post-apocalyptic. It wasn't just the storm. A girl had been attacked nearby a couple of weeks prior and my imagination was in overdrive.

Too nervous to contemplate the cemetery cut-through, I took the longer route to Kensington High Street. Desperate for civilization, I picked up speed, but it was still a ten-minute walk away.

As I passed a row of elongated town houses, a cagouled man appeared at one of the doors with a beautiful greyhound.

The dog looked as nervous as I was. The man nodded his head in my direction but didn't say hello or mention the monsoon. We were still in London, after all.

Although happy to encounter another human, one who didn't appear to be a rapist or killer, my imagination didn't quit. Instead, in my head, I played out the following day's interview with that man. The last person to have seen me alive. I'd cast him as Anthony Hopkins. The policeman was Tom Hardy. I played myself, grey, open-eyed, slit throat. A red rose placed on my chest. The first victim of a serial killer seemed better somehow. The greyhound barked once in the distance, immediately followed by whimpers.

I abandoned the useless brolly in someone's wheelie bin, then turned into the last side street before the main road, which was darker than the others. The downpour turned biblical. I could barely see ahead, so took shelter under the pillared entrance of the mansion block I was passing.

After flicking rain from my face, hands, hair, I lit a fag and watched the water bounce off the pavement, until a noise louder than the downpour made me jump.

A car was coming to a violent stop on the opposite side of the road. A hundred nails on a blackboard. I wasn't sure what kind of car it was – I'm not a car person – but even I realized it was beautiful, classic.

Just as I made out the shape of a man and woman through the steamed windows, there was a scream. I shat myself and was about to grab my phone when I realized the woman was screaming the words 'But I love you, I love you' over and over. I patted my heart and pulled hard on my fag to soothe myself, then watched the show.

It was mainly angry muffles. No clarity at first other than the odd words such as 'love', 'selfish' and 'bastard' from her. And 'done', 'mental' and 'calm down' from him. This went on for some time until her explosive 'You're such a fucking shit.' She got out. Her door remained open and light burst from inside, creating silhouettes. I couldn't see her properly, but she was tall, elegant. She stepped away from the vehicle, then returned to it.

'I've been such a bloody idiot.' She was crying.

'Well, go back to him, then. Nothing's stopping you,' said the man.

She dipped her head back into the car to shout, 'I hate you.' Door slammed. This shocked the rain into lessening.

She was walking up the road then, prouder than her words had made her seem. The rain ruining more and more of her perfect hair. The clip-clop of her heels echoed. Percussion to her whimpers. Whimpers not dissimilar to those of the greyhound.

Does this sound familiar to you?

With the downpour less torrential, I stepped into the open air and took the last pull of my fag before throwing it on the pavement to sizzle to its death. But then came another slam. The man was outside the car now. His arms outstretched on the roof like he was being frisked by an imaginary policeman. His head facing the ground. His body wet.

It was you.

Flustered, I returned to my shelter and watched as you viciously kicked the front wheel, yelling, 'Fuck,' before running up the steps and disappearing through a huge black door.

Like you said, so near to work.

I stared up at your building. The lights went on in the first-floor windows. I imagined you in there. Furious. Tearing off your soaked shirt. Thinking of her.

And already I didn't like it.

*

For the remainder of the week, whenever my mind wandered towards romantic notions about you, I forced myself to focus on your negatives. From the microscopic particle of spittle that flew from your mouth and landed on my arm when we discussed Mrs Jamison's scan to the once-white-now-grey crumpled hanky you'd repeatedly pull from your trouser pocket because of your 'bloody hay fever'. And on the Thursday you gave me the gift of wearing a salmon-pink jumper around your shoulders.

All may have remained that way, had the following not happened on the Friday.

I was gagging for the weekend, even though I knew it would involve a PlayStation tutorial from Dale. Linda had left early for the dentist, and Alison had taken a day's holiday to climb Mount Snowdon with her rambling club. Both Dr Short and Dr Franco had said their goodbyes a while back. Harris's last patient had left some time ago, but he was lingering in his office as always, and you were still in with Mr Brown after a peculiarly long time.

Unable to go home until all patients had left, I tidied reception and gathered my belongings for a quick escape. At five twenty, when I was considering popping out for a desperate fag, Mr Brown finally emerged, unresponsive to my smile or small talk. But I soon regretted mumbling 'Rude' under my breath as I turned for the stapler, because when I went into his file, I saw the diagnosis for colon cancer. I wonder if he's still alive.

When I went to your office to ask permission to leave, your head was in your hands. I was unsure if you were angsting over Mr Brown or *her*. You looked up at me, your smile as phoney as my own.

'Yes, of course . . . If you've done everything Dr Harris wants you to do?'

I nodded.

'Well then, get off with you. Enjoy the weekend.'

As usual, the first hit of nicotine made everything better. Aside from my cough. Pausing at the top of the steps, I closed my eyes, relished the sensation. My head light with chemicals, I gathered my senses and set off towards the station.

It's difficult to relay exactly what occurred next, as it happened in simultaneous fast forward and slow motion. I'm unsure if I made a noise. Or swore. But I recall my arms circling the air one moment, then the next my legs buckling beneath me. Immediate pain dispersed through my ankle, and my cheek burned against the abruptly met slab of cold pavement.

Dazed, I looked beyond the bottle top that brushed my lashes as I blinked towards my bag and its scattered contents. Just able to make out my phone, a Tampax and the Crunchy bar I'd searched everywhere for the previous night.

I'm not sure how long I was down, waiting for someone to come to my aid, but no one did, so I pushed myself up to reveal grazed, bloody palms, ingrained with tiny stones and particles of dirt.

A car sped past. My already pounding heart accelerated faster than the vehicle. Several attempts to stand ended in failure. The agony when I tried to put weight on my right foot was unbearable, making me want to chuck. Shock subsiding, tears came.

After hopping towards my bag, and managing, with difficulty, to bend down and retrieve both it and the contents, I turned back, and noticed the culprit. That same bastard bit of pavement I tripped on with Dale.

Gathering my remaining energy, I hopped back towards the steps and levered myself up the flight, the handrail acting as my crutch, then pushed the door open and called out your name. It must have been loud. Perhaps hysterical. As within seconds both you and Dr Harris were standing in front of me.

'What on earth, girl?' said Harris.

You placed my arm around your warm neck. Dipped to even our heights. 'Constance, what the hell has happened?'

'Did it happen in here?' said Dr Harris.

I shook my head and gave in to the sobbing. 'Outside, on the pavement.'

'OK. Good . . . Well then, there, there . . . you poor girl.' He turned to you and said, 'Will you see to her?' Then disappeared back into his room.

'Come on. Let's look at you.' Cheek to cheek, an uncomfortable tango, you manoeuvred me into your office and lowered me gently onto the patient's chair. It was strange being in such proximity to you and I was overwhelmingly self-conscious.

'So, go on. What the hell did you do?'

I attempted to stop crying, though my words remained staccato. 'I . . . I don't know . . . My foot, it's . . . killing me . . . It was . . . the fucking pavement. Sorry.'

'That's OK – you can say "fucking". I don't mind.' You smiled. A smile I knew you wanted me to reciprocate, as if you were attempting to pacify a scriking child. I obliged. You pulled tissues from the box on your desk and handed them to me. Until then, I'd been oblivious to the string of snot hanging from my nostrils. I quickly wiped it away, hoping to erase it from both our memories as well as my nose.

It was then you crouched in front of me. Undid my laces with care. Gentle. Slow. You removed the shoe, like a reverse Cinderella, exposing my sock and the hole in its toe (which definitely never happened in *Cinderella*). Then you peeled that off with precision, making me wince as it disturbed the bruised skin.

I fixated on you the whole time. Concentrated on you concentrating.

'Oh dear,' you said.

My stare was broken and I glanced down. My foot was already bluing and looked as though an egg had been inserted under the skin. Tears rose again.

'Don't worry – I've seen worse.'

Your cold hands cupped my heel. *Cold hands, warm heart*, Mum would say. My self-consciousness increased. I hadn't been touched for so long. And it wasn't just anyone's touch; it was yours.

Following your commands, I attempted to flex, point and wiggle my toes. None of which I could do successfully. Or at least not without experiencing pain I wasn't prepared to inflict on myself. You pushed up the bottom of my trouser leg, but it refused to budge past the ankle.

'You'll have to take them off,' you said.

I was convinced I hadn't outwardly shown my anguish at this request, but you followed with 'Don't be silly, Constance. I'm a doctor.'

After turning away, you gathered various items into a steel tray. I undid my zip. Pulled them down. It proved difficult, as I had to remain seated, and accidentally brought my knickers with them before immediately whipping them back up. I sat there. Stretching my shirt as far over my thighs as I could, noticing how your hair was more unkempt at the back, the bottom strands matted with sweat.

You turned back round, with the pretence it was a coincidence I'd finished undressing. Once dropped into your chair, you wheeled yourself over.

'OK . . . let's see what's going on here. Can you straighten your leg for me?'

You stretched it towards you, my calf in your hands. The sensation trickled towards my inner thigh. You were unaware of my reddened face as your fingertips pressed my pale flesh, inch by inch, downwards from my knee. With each application of pressure, you asked if it hurt. It didn't, until you reached my ankle and I made it clear with an almighty 'Jesus, yes.' You remained silent, focused. Didn't make eye contact with me once.

Snapped from your trance, you pushed your hair off your face. 'OK, I think it's just bruising and swelling on the knee, but I'm not sure if you've broken your foot or not. It could just be a bad sprain and ligament damage, which believe me, can be as painful.' Your tone was professional. 'Let's clean up your cuts and grazes quickly, then get you to hospital for some X-rays.'

'What? I . . . I really don't want to go to hospital . . . It's fine.' I stood. Then sat again, realizing that I was both half naked and the pain still immense.

'Sure you are. Look, you've got no choice, I'm afraid. You can't ignore a potentially broken foot.'

'I . . . I don't like hospitals.'

You didn't respond but turned my hands over to expose my damaged palms and placed them on your knees. We were even closer. I could smell coffee on your breath. Your hair draped your eyes as you cleaned my grazes with an astringent wipe. It stung, but I didn't flinch. Only watched as you cared for me.

'Can I get a cab on the work account and pay it back? I can't afford—'

'Don't be silly. I'm taking you.'

I went to thank you but couldn't speak, because without warning, you were pushing my fringe away from my face and touching my cheek. I stopped breathing. Until I realized you were once again cleaning my skin. I wasn't even aware I was hurt there. The antiseptic was cold. Your lips so close. They dropped open slightly. Urging me to cover them with mine.

The murky sky and rain meant I hadn't noticed your car was metallic pale blue the first time, or, more importantly, that it was a convertible. The top was down, exposing the beautiful

39

navy leather interior to the people who stared in awe as we crawled through the rush-hour traffic. Yet you were so blasé about it.

'I've never really seen a car like this before. What is it?'

'A 1966 Austin-Healey 3000.'

'It must have cost a fortune.'

'My father gave it to me.'

'I love it.' I mentally compared it to Blusha. The most precious gift my father gave to me.

'So do I.'

After that interaction, you remained quiet for the entire journey. Appeared nervous. And I wondered why. In contrast, the novelty of riding in such a car calmed me, distracted me from the foot pain and the anxiety associated with our destination. I daydreamed we were heading to the seaside for a picnic. That in the boot was a huge hamper filled with champagne and posh titbits like strawberries, olives, fancy bread and my mum's favourite Gouda. You'd lay before us a woollen checked blanket, which would bellow as it caught on the soft breeze. Then we'd eat and laugh, and tell each other our deepest secrets before we'd kiss.

Arriving at St Mary's, the dream evaporated and my anxiety returned with force.

I hadn't been inside a hospital since Manchester. And I'd vowed never to enter one again.

You pulled the car into a forbidden area and went to collect a wheelchair. After chivalrously seeing me into it, you instructed me to stay put while you parked up.

I tried to remember the list of negatives I'd conjured up about you, but I couldn't. It was a pointless exercise, anyway.

You can lie to other people easily, but it's impossible to lie to yourself.

After lighting a much-needed fag, I took in the building's vastness. Forced my mind to accept that inside, as babies were being born, people were also dying. Some already dead.

I took out my phone. Six missed calls. All from Dale. I called him back.

'Hey. It's me. Sorry.'

'Where the hell are you?'

'I had a fall . . . but don't go crazy – I'm fine, but I may have broken my foot.'

'Oh, you're joking. Well, where are you? I'll come now—'

'No, no . . . I'm fine, honestly.'

'But you can't be on your own.'

'I'm not . . . I'm not on my own. Dr Harris is with me. Look, I've . . . I've got to go – they're calling me in.' I pressed the red circle and blew the guilt into the air with my smoke.

An ambulance pulled up nearby. Paramedics opened its doors and wheeled some poor bastard out on a stretcher as they urgently babbled medical terms, most of which were foreign to me, except the word 'stabbing'. I turned away, my heartbeat rapid. But, thank God, I saw you coming to rescue me.

Inside, I gave my details at reception. Citing Dale as my next of kin. They asked for my GP, but I hadn't even signed up with one yet.

'I'm her GP,' you interjected, and gave them your full name. Dr Samuel Stevens.

Sam-u-el.

* * *

You'd gone to fetch us some tea. Alone, I scanned the waiting room. It was a typical line-up of London all-sorts. Bearded hipster with an ice pack on his arm. Farrow & Ball couple constantly checking the forehead of their little girl, who was clearly well enough to keep running around. I prayed she'd stay away, so I didn't catch whatever it was she had. Then a man in a football kit sat in the row of chairs right opposite. The white towel he held against his head was gradually turning red. I tried to look away, but he was too near to avoid, and as the scarlet blot grew, I felt my own blood drain towards my feet.

'Hey, are you OK?' You were standing next to me holding two flimsy plastic cups. 'Machine only, I'm afraid.'

I extended my tense hand out to retrieve mine, noticing you clock the bleeding man.

'Are you cold? Let's move away from the door,' you said, and wheeled me to the other side of the waiting room.

With the man out of sight, I sipped on my tea to raise my blood sugar, as you advised.

'You know, a fear of blood is common. It's physiological.'

'Yes . . . I've always been like this. Since a kid.'

But I hadn't. I hadn't at all.

I learnt a lot about you during that hour. Some of which I hadn't already found out from the internet. The fact you'd moved into your flat a year ago. Another family heirloom. Your father wanted to sell it, but you convinced him to keep it because you loved the Georgian architecture and huge windows. It still looked like you'd just moved in – bare walls, no curtains (though you hated curtains). It still didn't feel like home. Nowhere had felt like home for a long time. You missed your brother, who had emigrated to New Zealand, you believed to escape your father, whom you both hated.

'Why would you hate your father?'

'Oh . . . it's complicated.'

You tried to read a classic novel every month. Currently *Great Expectations*. You watched too much TV and played poker every Tuesday night at your friend Paul's house. It was the only time Tanya, his controlling wife, was out of the way, as she visited her parents Monday through to Wednesday because they were old and losing it, but you wished it happened on Fridays because you don't get in until well gone eleven, which wasn't ideal for school nights.

'Every Tuesday? You must be a good player by now. Show me your poker face.'

You did and I laughed. Then employed my own to disguise how appealing I found it.

You loved to travel and detailed some places you'd been. Thailand was your favourite destination. Followed by Peru. I told you I hadn't been anywhere apart from Benidorm and London. Unless you count Llandudno.

'You should come out to Thailand with me. You'd love it, I swear.'

You know, Samuel, you really shouldn't say things like that to people. Not if you don't mean them.

'Can I let you into a secret, Constance?'

I nodded. Unable to look you in the eye.

'I don't like hospitals either.'

I laughed. 'What do you mean, you don't like hospitals? You're a doctor.'

'I know. You're right. I was just trying to make you feel

better . . . Anyway, enough about me. What about you? What about your folks?'

A nurse shouted my name.

As you know, it wasn't broken. Just badly torn ligaments and bruising. I was gushing words of relief as you wheeled me down the corridor, my crutches in hand. But as we approached the exit, a tall, blonde female doctor was walking towards us and you hurriedly turned off down a side corridor and stopped.

'Where are you going?'

Your breathing was heavy above my head. 'Sorry . . . sorry. That was a friend of my ex and I didn't want to deal with her, sorry. We split a couple of months ago, but I swear she's gone crazy, Constance . . . Won't let it go. We keep going round in circles. God knows what bullshit she's said about me.'

'Oh no, I'm sorry. Well, maybe you'll get back together?'

'God, no. I just want her stuff out. I think the only thing we agree on now is that we hate each other.'

I was glad you were behind me, unable to see the delight overtake my face.

The drive back was quiet. But unlike before, we were both swathed in calm. The tiny clock inserted into the walnut dash said it was nearly ten. The motion lulled me into a hazy tiredness and so I rested my head against the back of the seat.

You turned on the radio. 'Do you mind? It relaxes me. I'll keep it low.'

It was classical music. I had no idea what. I thought I hated classical music, but it turned out it relaxed me too. We listened in silence. I was so comforted, being with you, that I almost nodded off, until you said, 'I was lying when I said it was to make you feel better. I really don't like hospitals.'

I pushed myself up straight, opened my eyes but didn't look at you. Sensing allowing you to talk was the right thing.

'My mother . . . she died . . . in a psychiatric hospital . . . when I was fifteen. She was there for just over a year. The constant visiting, the walks down the corridors . . . Now the smell of those places makes me . . . I don't know. She wasn't mad, though. My father . . . she . . . she'd react to his womanizing. He deserved it. But she loved him, you see. And was, I don't know . . . inconvenient.'

'So he put her there?'

'He's a top neurosurgeon. All the Stevens men are doctors. Whether we hate hospitals or not. Obviously, though, as a GP, I'm a terrible disappointment.' Your laugh that followed was tinged with hysteria. 'Anyway, he followed the procedures, but . . .'

'That's horrible.' In that moment everything made sense. Why our souls were magnets. 'Did she kill herself?'

'No, no, nothing like that. She just died. They didn't know why. Sudden adult death syndrome, the coroner concluded. But everyone knew why, really.'

'That's . . . I'm so sorry, Dr Stevens.'

'Hey, I think "Samuel" now. Especially after telling you that. I'm not sure what made me blurt it out in that way.'

I did. I knew.

'Oh, this is beautiful.' You turned up the volume. 'Shostakovich. Symphony No. 5.'

I nestled back, closed my eyes. Thinking about what you'd told me. Confided in me. And you were right – the music was beautiful. Fitting. I've since bought an old vinyl record of that piece. And others. I play them when I can't sleep or am stressed. Which is often. Along with our song, of course.

Everything was perfect in that moment. It made me want to share about myself. Though I kept my eyes shut to say it.

'Mine died in April.'

'Sorry?' You turned the volume down.

'My mum . . . She died in April.'

'Constance, that's so recent . . . I didn't . . . I'm so sorry. But you've only been here since April? Is that why you—'

'She had cancer.' It wasn't a lie.

The car stopped. I presumed at lights, but I still couldn't look.

You searched for my hand. Squeezed it. 'What about your dad?'

I shook my head.

'Brothers or sisters?'

I shook my head again.

'Oh, Constance. Well, you've got me. We're friends now, don't you think?'

I dared to open my eyes and moved my finger to touch yours. The lights turned green. You placed your hand back onto the wheel and we drove again.

'Does anyone know about your mum?'

'My housemate knows.'

'No, I mean like Harris or Franco. You should speak to Dr Franco.'

'No. Why? No . . . I'm fine.'

Before you could talk about it anymore, ask me questions, I leant forward and turned the volume up again, then sat back and closed my eyes. This time, so you couldn't see me, I faced the passenger window.

Shame washed over me when we arrived at mine. I'd grown used to the sink and car parts in the garden, but I saw it through your eyes. Sat in your expensive car. Knowing about your grand flat. And I was pissed off with Mr Papadopoulos and his lazy-landlord ways.

You parked in the nearest spot and switched off the engine. We sat for a moment in darkness before turning our heads towards each other.

'Well, thank you, Dr Stevens.'

'Samuel.'

'Samuel.'

The leather creaked beneath us. Time stopped. Only starting again when you said, 'Oh God, I need to get you out, don't I?'

I looked through the window, back towards the house, for signs of Dale. 'No, I'm . . . I'm fine from here.'

'Don't be silly. I'll walk you to the door.'

'No, honestly . . . I need the practice.'

'Well, I must help you get out at least. Even the able-bodied can't get out of this bloody thing.'

Before I could argue, you were already outside, opening

my door, lifting me up. I fumbled with my bag, which you took from me and placed across my body like a pageant-queen sash. 'Well, at least let me watch you. Make sure you get in.'

It felt like an eternity as I clumsily made my way down the front path on the crutches. When I finally reached the door, I scrambled in my bag for the key. Before I'd located it, Dale was standing in the light of the open doorway. I turned towards you, but you were back in the car.

'You poor sod. Here, let me help you.' He fussed around me, making everything more difficult. 'Don't you worry – I shall be your nurse slave. Hey, I've bought the new *Call of Duty* for us, so you won't be bored being laid up.' As he shut the door, I felt our severance. 'That wasn't Dr Harris. You said Dr Harris was with you.' He lifted my bag over my head.

'Did I? I don't think I . . . I was in agony, Dale. Sorry . . . I meant Dr Stevens.'

'Well, it's easily done,' he said, smiling, but as he turned away, I noticed his grin drop in the hall mirror.

*

My weekend consisted mainly of killing.

Dale's mandatory *Call of Duty* marathon was only made bearable by the serene haze produced by codeine and paracetamol, plus the constant stream of tea and snacks he brought me.

But by Sunday afternoon I'd had enough. Putting down my metaphorical foot by pretending I had a migraine, which I'd timed for the start of a *Marple* I hadn't yet seen.

He did turn off the PlayStation, but he also insisted I needed to lie down in dark quietness, meaning I never got to watch the *Marple* after all. But that wasn't the worst thing. That came once I'd settled in bed with the lights out.

He appeared, a silhouette in the doorway. 'I've got something for your foot – some arnica. It's great for bruising.' Before I could object, he'd walked in. The light folded away as the door closed. I could feel him sat on the edge of the bed. 'It'll bring it out quicker.' He pulled the duvet aside and took hold of my ankle.

I reached up to put the lamp on.

'No, don't do that. It's not good for your head.'

I slid back down.

'I wasn't told to put anything on it, though, Dale.'

'Just relax and close your eyes. It really works. Mum used it on us all the time as kids when we fell over.'

I did close my eyes, but I wasn't relaxed at all. I heard the ointment spurt from the tube. His cold, gel-coated hands slowly caressed my foot.

'How does that feel?'

'Sore. It's sore to touch, Dale . . . I think it's best if you leave it.'

'But it'll help all the—'

'Please.'

He stopped. Nothing happened for some time. Black silence, broken eventually by the sound of the top being screwed back on.

'Thank you, though.'

'Sure . . . I'll leave you be,' he said, and left.

An hour later I woke with a genuine headache.

Groggy, I pushed myself up and switched on the lamp. I was desperate for the loo, so forced myself out of bed and took hold of the crutches resting against the wall. On standing, I allowed my foot to take a little weight, like you told me to. Thank goodness the swelling had reduced and it no longer felt impossible.

On my way back, hearing the familiar shooting and explosions coming from Dale's room, I shuffled over there and knocked. No answer. Presuming he couldn't hear, I opened the door.

'Hey,' I said.

'How's the head?' He didn't look at me. His top teeth bit down on his bottom lip as he straightened his arms, and pressed, pressed, pressed.

'It's still there . . . I fell asleep.'

'Yes, I noticed.'

'Oh . . . Oh right. What are you having for dinner?' An explosion made me jump.

'Had it.'

'Oh . . . Is there anything I could have?'

'Not really.'

'Right. Well, I guess I'll order a pizza, then, or something.'

'OK.'

I pulled the door to, then stopped halfway and said, 'You know, I think the arnica's really helped. Thank you.'

He paused the game, turned to me. 'Actually . . . I think I may have a pizza left in the freezer. You go back to bed and I'll bring it in to you.'

Once in my room, I took more painkillers, smoked a cigarette and turned on the TV. Flicked through the wasteland of shite. An old *Nigella*, a soft-focus shot of her sucking her finger free of kumquat jam. A penguin documentary that prompted an emergency channel change because of the impending death of a chick. People already humiliated by having the bailiffs round enduring further humiliation by having it filmed. Flick, flick, flick.

Then my heart was stabbed.

Though near the end, I instantly recognized it: *Brief Encounter*.

I was fifteen.

Mum had begged me to bunk off school to keep her company. Insisted we stayed in our nightwear, had a pyjama party. Me in my faded Winnie the Pooh nightie. Her in an old dressing gown adorned with a mismatched belt and fag-burnt lapel. She flitted to and from the kitchen, carrying a variety of bowls and plates filled with crisps, biscuits and lumps of cheese. Each time she left, I watched the small section of matted hair on the back of her head. With each entrance, her breath smelt stronger and stronger of vermouth.

'*Brief Encounter*'s on, Connie. Please, Connie . . . watch it with me. I won't enjoy it without you.'

Reading its summary in the TV guide she'd thrust in front of me, I didn't fancy it at all, despite its five stars. But I humoured her and watched.

As always, she felt compelled to commentate. Telling me how the film reminded her of a married woman she once knew called Norma who met a man at Knutsford Service Station every Sunday while she was on the way to visit her mother. Norma was rumbled when her neighbour filled up with petrol at precisely the wrong moment. The boring story made me want to watch it even less. I fixed my vision directly on the TV. Engaging with her was lethal, or else the chattering would never stop.

She kicked off her slippers, lay on the sofa. I was on the floor at her feet. These were our usual positions. I could have used the armchair, but it was Dad's, so I never did. No one did. It remained pristine as the sofa grew threadbare.

Ten minutes into the film, her speech became more sporadic, less lucid, and finally there was silence as she passed out.

To begin with, I thought *Brief Encounter* was so terrible it was hilarious. The way they talked, the corny expressions.

But soon my giggles switched to a blank face, watching intently while mindlessly wolfing crisps and cheese. I hung on every word. Every tiny, tragic moment.

You know that last scene when they're saying their good-byes in the buffet? Knowing they wouldn't see each other again. When he tells her how desperately he loves her?

And she replies with doe-eyed despair that she wants to die.

I turned to my mother, snoring, drunk, alone. Her delicate wrist touching the arm of the empty chair beside her. And for that moment I understood.

'It's a bit burnt around the edges.' Dale had entered carrying in a tray, upon which I could see was a pizza, a glass of Coke and the glistening foil of a Tunnock's Teacake. After placing the drink on the side cabinet and laying the tray on my duvet, he perched on the bed next to me.

'Thank you. I like burnt, you know that.' I carefully knocked off the ash from my fag and pinched the end, saving it for later.

'What are you watching?' he said.

'I wasn't . . . I was just . . .' I turned off the TV and lifted a slice of pizza to my mouth, conscious of him hovering over me.

'I'll pop a bit more of this on, then, if it's helping.' He removed the tube of arnica from his pocket.

'Oh . . . thank you, but you can leave it on the side – I'll do it. You don't want to be touching my horrible foot.'

'No, it's OK. You eat your pizza.'

I told myself it was fine. That he wouldn't take long. That

he was only trying to help. While massaging my skin, he talked about *Call of Duty* and a film he wanted me to watch. I feigned interest. Swallowed the dough with difficulty. Wanting every aspect of what was happening to be over. Then it was, because once again you saved me.

'Who's that ringing at this time?' he said.

'I don't know. I don't recognize the number. But it's only seven thirty, Dale.'

My heart rate increased tenfold when I heard your voice. Foot aside, I could have skipped around the room. You were enquiring about the sprain, but it was more than that. You wanted me to know you cared.

I must have sounded so flustered. Could you tell? 'It's . . . it's . . . a lot better, thank you. I'll start walking on it more tomorrow.' You told me Dr Harris had passed on my number when you'd informed him that I wouldn't be in for a few days. Hoped I didn't mind. You had no idea how much I didn't mind.

I desperately wanted to talk to you longer. And I'm sorry if I came across as rude or ungrateful. I wasn't. I wasn't at all. I was so happy, but it was Dale. Lingering. Static. Listening to my every word. As our conversation wrapped up, he put the top back on the tube and stood to leave. I said goodbye to you and ended the call. He stopped at the door, requiring answers.

'Dr Stevens. Just seeing how my foot is doing.'

'Oh right. That's so nice of him. Anyway, at least your headache seems to have lifted. You should eat up before it gets cold,' he said, and left.

Able to feel my excitement in his absence, I took a bite of

pizza and turned the TV back on. And there it was. Taunting me. That scene. The pain of lost love. What it can do.

My thoughts flashed to my mother. Forever haunting me.

I'm going to play Shostakovich's Symphony No. 5 now. Hopefully, it will help me slip away and erase the image that has invaded my mind once again.

*

I made it back to work on the Thursday. Off the crutches but sore-footed and limping. I couldn't bear being cooped up any longer and all I could think about was seeing you.

I got the bus in. It took almost twice as long, but involved less walking, and when I'd envisaged being on the Underground, my breathing shallowed and I imagined being buried alive.

After snagging a window seat with 'Jan loves cock' etched in the glass, I watched the other humans, wondering what it was like to be them, not me. And I thought how much Mum would have liked it. Riding a London bus. We always took the bus at home. Smirking, as we telepathically knew we'd both clocked specific people, then talking about them once we'd got off.

Until that day.

When she thought she saw the green suede of his jacket swagger down the street.

Banged her hands against the window. Pushed the people out of the way to get to the exit. Pressing each bell she passed, again and again and again. How the driver wouldn't stop. And the passengers tutted and cussed until silenced by her screams.

From that day she only looked outwards. Quiet. Watchful. Searching.

I'd arrived only twenty minutes late, though Linda wasn't quite as impressed with my achievement.

'Thank you for joining us, Constance. How's the foot?'

'It's like I'm walking on a hundred tiny razor blades. But you know . . . I didn't want to let you down.'

'Right . . . Well, thank you.' She resumed the pretence of reading a document.

'Hi, Constance.' Alison waved at me like an overexcited child, sunkissed from her mountain climb. My heart sank. She'd have so much to tell me.

Cranking up the limp, I walked around reception to my seat, surprised by the scent of a new white orchid on the front desk. Why does everything remain the same, day in, day out, but if you're away for even a short space of time, things are different? Or perhaps we don't notice change when we're part of it. I never noticed the change within me.

'So, what do I need to know?' I asked Linda.

'Nothing, really. Dr Harris is in his office. Dr Short is on a house call. Mr Copeland is just waiting to have some blood tests with the nurse. Dr Stevens has a couple of patients booked in, but then he's off to the Harley Street practice. Alison's working on this report for . . .'

I tried to appear as if I was still listening, but her words became noiseless and my insides twisted.

When her mouth stopped moving, I said, 'Why is Dr Stevens going to Harley Street?'

'Don't ask me. It's not my job to know why . . . So you need to go into this file Alison's working on, then join her in adding all the—'

'Sorry, Linda. I . . . I need the toilet . . . Sorry.'

When passing your room, a woman with a crusty-nosed child exited. She smiled. I somehow managed to return a warped version, then continued down the corridor with the full intent of going to the ladies'. But I stopped, turned and limped back towards your door.

My knock lacked confidence. When you called me in, I noticed the room contained less of Dr Williams. His certificates had been removed from the wall, exposing rectangles of original crisp white paint. You hadn't replaced them with yours, which added to my concerns.

'Constance . . . hey . . . You're back.' You finished scribbling in your diary, then put your pen down and looked up at me.

'Yes . . . well, I didn't want to let people down.' I thought perhaps you'd offer me a seat.

'And how's the foot?'

'It's OK . . . You know . . . still bruised but getting there.'

'Well, these things take time, unfortunately. Use it, but don't overdo it.'

'Yes . . . yes, I will.'

An uncomfortable silence hit.

'Well, it's good to have you back.' You took your pen in hand once more, jiggled it between your fingers.

'Thank you. So . . . so Linda says you're going to Harley Street this afternoon?'

'Yes, they're struggling without me, apparently.'

'Right. So you're going back to work there now?'

'Oh no . . . At least, I hope not. It's only for a couple of days, they said.'

I controlled the extended expulsion of air from my lungs. 'OK . . . That's nice . . . that you can help them out.'

Once again you scrawled onto the pages. 'Anyway, I had better get on. I've got a patient coming in.'

'Of course. Sorry. I just wanted to say hello . . . and thank you again for last week. So, thank you, Dr Stevens.'

'No need to thank me, Constance. I'm a doctor – that's what I'm supposed to do.' You spoke down towards your desk, muffling your words.

'OK, Dr Stevens.' For the second time I waited for you to correct me. Insist I called you 'Samuel'. You didn't. Merely stopped writing and turned. Fixed a smile. But it wasn't warm like the smiles we'd shared that night. It was a smile that said the conversation was over.

I tried to work as best I could, pasted on a cheerful demeanour, but couldn't stop going over and over the night of the hospital. The change in you. And I had no choice but to begin a new list of negatives, which started with the rogue wiry nasal hair I'd noticed would poke out when you held your head at certain angles. I reached into my bag for my phone to add this observation to my notes but dropped it back in immediately when surprised by the unusual presence of Dr Harris looming in reception. His face even more humourless than usual.

'Girls, can I have a word, please?'

Alison and I stopped what we were doing. Linda was already not doing anything to stop.

His tone was softer, quieter than usual. 'We've got a date for the funeral. Three weeks today, 25 August. So, I think it would be right and proper if we all attended and showed our respects.'

'Of course,' said Linda, her voice breaking.

Alison echoed her. I mumbled something. I don't know what. I was only aware of the word 'funeral' obsessively repeating in my head. *Funeral. Funeral. Funeral.* I appeared still, composed, but my hands were shaking behind my back.

'Now, it's in Kensal Rise, so that's easy for us all, and it's at one o'clock . . . So this is what I propose: we have morning surgery. Last patients should be booked for midday. Then we'll organize cabs for half twelve . . . Linda, can you arrange this, please?' She nodded. 'I should imagine the whole funeral and cremation will be done and dusted, if you'll excuse the terminology, around one forty-five. Then we'll go on to the wake, which is at a hotel in Kensington.'

'Very good, Dr Harris,' said Linda, jotting the information into a notebook.

'But . . . and there is a "but", I'm afraid. Dr Stevens won't be attending the funeral, as . . . well, he never even met Dr Williams, and I can't close the surgery. So he'll be here the whole day as usual. And a nurse, of course. Which means, I'm afraid, one of you will have to return after the service to cover reception in the afternoon. Which sadly means not coming to the wake. Now, I think that—'

'I'll do it, Dr Harris.' I raised my hand like an eager

schoolchild. 'I can forfeit the funeral as well if it makes things easier.'

'Oh . . . well, that's very kind, Constance. I was going to suggest . . . as you've been here the shortest time . . . but excellent. And no, no, no, I wouldn't dream of you missing the funeral, don't you worry. I know Dr Williams was most fond of you.'

The only time, ever, Dr Harris had been nice to me, and he didn't realize that he wasn't being nice at all. Regardless, I thanked him for his shitty, misplaced kindness, before he returned to his office, Linda in tow.

Back at my desk, I was unable to concentrate. My mood darkened, stress increased, and I could feel cortisol spreading throughout my body. Your dismissiveness towards me, the fear of attending the funeral, the story Alison was telling me about joining a rambling club with Kevin. And when I thought it couldn't get any worse, Linda returned and pulled her chair up next to me.

'Constance, can I have a word?'

I turned towards her, deadpan.

'Dr Harris is coming in on Saturday to finish these reports and update the database and needs one of us to work for half a day. Now, Alison and I have already spoken . . .'

I looked at Alison, who moved her head nearer to the computer screen, pretending to be oblivious.

'And we think it's only fair you did it as you've been off this week.'

'Off sick.'

'Well, you hurt your foot, yes . . . but it makes it a much longer week for us two . . . and I have my cycling club, you see, on Saturdays, and Alison, well, she's got to—'

'Fine. OK, I'll do it,' I said, unable to cope with hearing about Alison's plans for the weekend. And my brain couldn't even process the words 'Linda' and 'cycling club' being in the same sentence.

'Thank you, Constance,' said Alison. 'It's just that Kevin and I are—'

'It's no problem, Alison, really.'

A grim atmosphere hung for the next hour. We all intently got on with our work. In silence. The only talking that took place was with patients. This new way of working meant I had at least finished the report, but as I walked over to the printer to collect the sheets, my pulse quickened as I noticed you coming towards the desk.

'Hello, ladies.'

From the corner of my eye, I could see Linda and Alison greeting you with syrup and giggles. I, however, kept my head down, cool, calm, counting the printed pages.

'I'm off to Harley Street now for the remainder of the day and won't be back till Monday. So can you take messages and ring me there if urgent?'

'Will do, Dr Stevens. See you next week,' said Linda.

'Bye, Dr Stevens. Have a nice weekend,' said Alison.

'Thank you. You too. Bye. Goodbye, Constance.' You projected your voice.

I looked up, slow-blinked, deeply unimpressed. 'Yeah, sorry . . . bye.' Then immediately returned my eyes to the papers and shuffled them intently, ensuring you understood that I was more interested in the sheets than your departure.

You left, and I was satisfied I'd deflected some of my earlier humiliation back onto you.

Being in the surgery on a Saturday was, frankly, weird and perturbing. It was cold in there. Even smelt different. Five minutes after I'd arrived, Harris plonked a cardboard archive box full of files onto my desk and instructed me to either update the database or erase if they were no longer a patient/dead. Even *Call of Duty* was preferable to that. The only thing that made it bearable was that as the surgery was closed, I was allowed to listen to the radio.

I came to terms with the fact that the only way through this was to work my bollocks off. Get it done as fast as possible, then escape. So I did. I worked harder than I'd ever done before. Which went totally against my nature. It was made marginally easier with the aid of Frank, Lesley Gore, Aretha . . . The sounds of my childhood. My life. My dad, blurred-faced, playing along on the guitar. Mum dancing in the lounge, laughing. Bending down, holding my tiny hands, wiggling me from side to side.

Despite the crappy work, I enjoyed being there. That parallel world within my mind.

Even Harris seemed impressed with what I'd achieved and told me to have a tea break at eleven. By half twelve I'd done so well I was singing along to Dusty Springfield, finishing off my last file.

Then there was a knock at the door.

I stopped. Confused, I looked towards Dr Harris's room

in case he was expecting someone, but he didn't emerge. The knocking came again. This time harder, longer.

Presuming someone had got the wrong address, I went over to open it. As I pulled inwards, my free hand automatically shielded my eyes from the blinding sun. And so it took a moment for me to realize that it was you.

'Oh . . . thank God you're still here.' You walked in past me as I opened the door fully.

'Is everything OK, Dr Stevens?'

It wasn't the 'you' I was familiar with. It was a sweaty, dressed in shorts and damp T-shirt, exposed muscular legs 'you'.

'Apart from being a total moron, yes, I'm fine . . . I . . .' You could barely get your words out. Placed your hands on your hips and leant forward. 'Sorry . . . stitch . . . I thought I'd do something positive this morning . . . Got up, went for a run. I haven't run for ages . . . clearly. So I do five miles—'

'That's good—'

'Yes . . . five bloody miles. I make it home . . . thinking I was going to die . . . which, as a doctor, means there was a lot of evidence to back it up—'

'Do you want some water?'

You nodded, your energy for speaking used up. I hurried to the kitchen, letting the tap flow, so it was cold enough for you.

When I returned, you took it off me and gulped it all. Wiping the excess from your mouth before running your fingers through your wet hair, revived.

'And so I make it home, barely alive . . . then realize I

hadn't taken my bloody keys with . . . Didn't have my phone.'
You handed me the empty glass.

'Oh no . . . Shall I call a locksmith?'

'No, no. Thank God I always keep a spare in my desk. It's
not the first time I've done this: I have form. I'm so bloody
lucky that Harris was in today . . . Thank fucking Christ,
eh?' You headed towards your office. I followed you. 'Why
am I such an idiot, Constance?'

'I don't know, Dr Stevens.'

I'm sorry for that. I didn't mean it the way it sounded.
Though I don't think you were listening anyway, as you
continued babbling.

'I asked someone for the time . . . then regardless of the
heart attack I was already having, I ran here too, to catch
you. Constance . . . can you open up for me? No keys.' You
smiled, but your face flooded with blood and irritation.

Once inside, I was desperate to get back to my computer
to finish up, in the hope that we could leave together, but
you kept talking. Mainly to yourself, but it felt rude to walk
away.

'Right, well, I'm certain I put it here.' You scrambled inside
the top drawer of your desk. 'Oh, for fuck's sake . . . don't
tell me that I— Ah . . . yes . . . Thank you.' You lifted the
two keys that hung from a red plastic fob and kissed them.
'Sorry . . . Thanks, Constance. Where's Dr Harris? I'd better
pop my head round.'

You dropped the keys into your pocket before lifting the
bottom of your T-shirt to wipe your face. I tried so hard not
to look at your stomach.

* * *

It was one o'clock. I'd finished everything, so I knocked on Dr Harris's door to ask permission to leave.

I'd interrupted your talk. Harris was sat back in his chair, chubby hands clasped behind his head. You were leaning against the filing cabinet. Molecules of sweat covered every inch of your exposed skin. I imagined zooming in on them like a photographer. Perfect spheres filled with your natural perfume. It wasn't exactly lemons you exuded that day, but neither was it something I could add to my negative list.

'Yes, yes, you get off, Constance. I didn't realize the time. And thank you for today. I'm suitably impressed with all you've done.'

I felt a twinge of something unfamiliar. Pride, perhaps. I didn't dare look up as my face grew warm. To conceal it, I turned to leave.

'Wait for me, Constance . . . I should get off as well, Bill . . . but yeah, let's look into that properly next week.'

You had no idea how happy walking with you made me.

Good things come to those who wait, Mum would say. Usually when I'd grow impatient at her taking forever to pack the shopping at the till in Morrisons. Or when she'd forget to make the cup of tea she'd offered two hours previously. Situations that never truly fitted the phrase. But as I hobbled side by side with you, it was finally relevant.

'Should I run ahead and get the car? Drive you to the station?' you asked, looking towards my limping foot.

'No . . . no, I'm fine. It's doing me good. Just slow down a bit.' It hurt like crazy, but I didn't care. My joy overrode the pain.

It was so easy between us, wasn't it? How we talked. The seamless flow of conversation. From the fact you were wearing uncomfortable socks, to how men shouldn't wear Lycra, to you having run a marathon in your late twenties.

'I can't even run for the bus,' I said. 'At school, I once came second to last in the annual cross-country race. Only beating Mathew Sims, who'd broken his foot and did the whole thing on crutches to raise money for Cancer Research.'

You laughed. 'You crack me up, Constance.'

I dug into my bag, pretending to search for something so you couldn't see the happiness on my face.

The junction of Church Street had arrived all too quickly and I was forced to stop.

'OK . . . so which way are you? Because I can either cut through the graveyard, which is quicker, or go down Church Street, which is longer but less scary.' I was pleased at my acting. There wasn't a hint of my knowing where you lived.

'How's the foot?'

'It's fine, actually. I think the walking is helping.' I smiled to block out the throb.

'OK, that's good. Why don't you come the Church Street way with me, then? You can tell me more about your sporting prowess.'

As we continued, our bodies gravitated towards each other and my hand brushed yours on more than one occasion. I lit up inside when you laughed, head back, free, as I recounted the story of how I had to be rescued from the climbing-frame section of the Sports Day assault course because my arm got tangled in the metal.

We were approaching your road.

'This one's me,' you said.

'Oh right, well this is my route to the station too.'

'Of course . . . You know, I'm glad this has happened. It's shown me how bloody near I am. I'm definitely going to walk to work from now on.' Did you notice my joy when you said that? Imagining all the stories we'd share.

When we turned the corner, two lads in their late teens, wearing grey trackies and interchangeable faces more suited to the estate back home than this leafy idyll of West London, were on bikes, propping themselves up against the wall of the first house. You pretended you hadn't seen them as we walked past. Talked about how you were desperate for a shower. I replied about being more of a bath person, but we were both conscious of their presence. They laughed, loud, towards our backs. Forced, attention-seeking laughs. Again, we ignored. Talked. Until one shouted, 'She looks like she's got a nice tight pussy, mate.'

You stopped. Then I stopped. You looked at me, not them. I was certain you didn't want to do anything and were seeking my approval not to.

I gave you what you wanted. 'Ignore them,' I said. 'They're idiots.'

'OK . . . No, no, you're right.' You walked on. I followed your lead. 'Anyway, I'm sorry for all the sweating.' You tried to spark another conversation.

I dryly answered, but neither of us was concentrating and everything became awkward and strange until you slowed to a standstill.

'This is me, but I don't want to leave you while they're knocking around.'

I glanced over at the boys, who were mounting their bikes. 'I think they're going now,' I said under my breath.

Like your car, the town house that contained your flat was more impressive in the sunlight. The door wasn't the black I'd taken it for but racing green. I turned towards the canopy of the opposite mansion block I'd sheltered under that night. That too appeared different, swankier. I almost slipped up by saying so, but was thankfully saved by the sound of cycles whizzing past.

'Thank Christ for that,' you said.

We watched as they wheelied down the road. Waiting until they became nothing but the tiny specks of shit that they were.

'I'm sorry about that, Constance.' You placed your hand on my shoulder.

'It's not your fault there are idiots in the world.'

'I know, but I should have said something, maybe.'

'No, no, don't be silly.' But you should have, Samuel, you really should.

'Why don't I drive you to the station from here?'

'No, honestly. I'm practically there now. By the time I'd got in the car, I'd be climbing out again.'

'I know, but— Hello!' You weren't addressing me anymore but shouting and waving at someone behind me. I turned to see it was an old man, coming up the other side of the road with a bag of shopping, waving back. Your focus returned to me. 'He lives in the flats opposite. Seems a right character, bless him. Anyway, Constance, what I need is a nice long, hot shower.'

You looked directly into my eyes. Were you using the words

provocatively? I couldn't sustain the contact and stared down at the pavement.

'Yeah . . . sure . . . Enjoy . . . I'll see you Monday.' When I brought my gaze back up, you were already running up the steps to the front door. At the top, you held up the keys and did a thumbs-up. I laughed. Then you were gone.

After rummaging in my bag for a fag, I lit up, took a long, hard drag and tried to contain my excitement at the return of your friendliness towards me. Exhaling, I watched the old boy trudge up the road and was in a dilemma as to whether I should cross and help him. But as he neared, I could see how sharply dressed he was, with his bright red V-necked jumper and camel trilby, and sensed any offer of assistance could offend. Instead, I nodded and smiled, then headed off towards the station. As I did, I saw them in the distance. The shits. Cycling back up the road.

My first instinct was to phone you, but there was no response. I tried again. It rang out. I climbed the steps to your door but realized I didn't know your flat number. Though, thankfully, it all became irrelevant, as they once again shot past and disappeared around the corner.

Relieved, shaken, I came down the steps, my cigarette wobbling as I returned it to my mouth. But I'd only taken a few strides before I heard the click, click, click of bicycle chains behind me.

I dropped my head, carried on.

'Did he dump you?' The words came from my left.

I could hear the squeak of the wheels adjacent to me, but I didn't stop, look. Just prayed that would be it. That if I ignored them, they'd get bored, fuck off again. But the noise increased before coming to a halt as they straddled their bikes on the pavement a few feet in front of me. I stopped. Stayed still. Glanced back at the old boy, now approaching the canopied entrance of his flats.

They separated. They were now aware of him and it was my fault. I looked round in despair to see one of them slowly riding towards him.

The other closed in on me. Metal between his legs, toes on the ground, he walked the bike my way. Stopped inches from my body. Up close, his skin was dry, pallid.

'Were you crap at blowjobs? You can practise on me if you like.' His hands gripped the handles like a kid pretending to ride a motorbike.

I looked straight into his bloodshot eyes.

'Hey, I don't like being ignored,' he spoke from his cracked lips.

My heart pumped so hard I felt it in my ears. 'I've . . . I've already called the police.'

He laughed. 'No, you haven't. I'll come quickly, don't worry.' Leaning in, he removed the ash-heavy cigarette from my fingers and smoked it.

I attempted to walk around him, but he blocked me with his bike. 'Please . . . please leave me alone.' I looked back towards the canopy. Old Boy was about to climb the steps, unaware that Shit Two had abandoned his bike on the pavement and was behind him. I closed my eyes. Willed you to help. Anyone to help.

'Hey, Granddad. Have you bought me something nice?' I could hear.

'Tell your friend to leave him alone.' But I'd barely trembled out my words when Old Boy was pushed over and sprawled against the steps, his hat cascading down towards the pavement along with a waterfall of oranges and a jar, which smashed, then oozed a thick black substance.

'Sorry, Gramps . . . I didn't see you there.'

Both shits laughed.

'Is that your granddad?' Shit One asked.

An orange rolled into the road.

I turned back to him. 'Please leave us alone . . . The police will be here any second.' Words were difficult to form. I was devoid of saliva and didn't have control over my mouth. Over any part of my body.

'What you talking about, sexy? He's helping the aged.'

I looked over again to Old Boy, wincing as I watched him try to scramble to his feet, crying, a trainered foot pushing against his back, and I could feel a monster forming inside me.

'Samuel,' I shouted. Loud, desperate. But you didn't appear.

'He's dumped you, babe.'

'Dr Stevens.' Nothing. 'Please, please . . . just leave us alone.'

His face moved closer. Too close. I smelt weed on his breath. He threw away the cigarette butt and with his tobacco-scented knuckles wiped the tears now tumbling over my cheeks.

'Please just let me pass,' I said, barely audible.

His yellow, sticky fingers slid down my face, down my neck. 'Your tits are amazing.' Past my collarbone, under my shirt. I froze. Stood there as his dirty, clammy hand slipped into my bra. 'So, do you spit or swallow?'

I closed my eyes. Asked Mum to save me. And remembered. Spying on her and one of her strangers through the banister with the missing post. Laughter, dancing, Bob Dylan, 'It Ain't Me, Babe'. His hand up her skirt. How she said no. And no. And no.

Then snap.

When I recall what happened next, it's as if I'm describing a film, a violent film, not reality. Telling a story that happened to someone else, not me. Because I don't remember punching Shit One in his face with such force he fell to the ground, bike on top of him, wheels spinning endlessly. But I did. I know it happened because I watched him down there, clutching his bloodied nose. Even the red drips didn't affect me, break my fury.

'You hit me . . . I can't believe you hit me . . . you fucking little whore.'

And I don't particularly recall running over to Old Boy either, though I must have done because I was somehow pulling Shit Two away from him by his hood. Kicking him, kicking him. 'Leave him alone. Leave him alone.' I didn't stop. Couldn't stop. It seems strange. That I did that. Me.

They were back on their bikes then. 'You're a crazy fucking bitch.' And even when they were riding away, I was chasing them. No limp, no fear. The only thing stopping me, bringing me back, was the sound of the siren.

Two officers escorted me and Old Boy, whom I'd now learnt was called Edward, up to his flat. With the adrenaline drained from my body, I was juddering, crying. The policewoman comforted me. My legs, boned and filleted, my foot throbbing, she acted as a support to lean against.

'I was doing national service at their age. Little bastards,' said Edward.

My tears stopped when he switched on the light in his hallway. No one was prepared for what it exposed. It was impossible to know where to look first: the huge old metal diving helmet on the sideboard, the sunglasses-wearing stuffed squirrel with a cigarette sticking out of its mouth next to it or the hundreds of bizarre knick-knacks that surrounded them.

'Excuse the mess.' He led us down the hallway and disappeared into the lounge.

We all followed him with wide-eyed wonderment, like we were entering Willy Wonka's chocolate factory.

'We've been through all this, young lady, and I don't even know your name,' he said, dropping into a floral beat-up wing-backed chair that produced a plume of dust as he landed.

'Constance,' I said, scanning the huge wall of books before my eyes came to rest on a one-armed mannequin wearing a black bobbed wig, grass skirt and coconut bra.

Edward must have noticed me looking, as he said, 'That's Ursula. The only woman in my life, and how I like it . . . Now, Officers . . . Constance here is a hero.'

'No, I'm not.'

'Don't you listen to her – she bloody well is.'

'Mr Seymour, if you feel up to it, we need to go over what happened while we wait for the paramedics.' The officer's radio crackled. A muffled voice came through. She excused herself, then talked into it.

I've no idea what she said, because the sounds sent me back home. To Manchester. To that day. The room distorted. Slow motion, I looked down at the line of splattered blood across the white of my shirt. My legs weakened, vision dimmed, and I felt my knees bend beneath me.

'Are you OK, Miss Little?' The male officer propped me up. 'I've got paramedics coming – don't worry.'

'Yes . . . yes, I'm fine. I felt a little dizzy, that's all. I'm fine. I have to be somewhere, though – will it take long?'

Edward and I answered their questions succinctly. At least, I told them all that I could remember. They said our accounts matched that of the neighbour who'd called 999.

'Though you shouldn't have put yourself at risk like that, Miss Little,' said the male officer.

The policewoman agreed, then smiled at me, like I was her hero as well as Edward's, before saying, 'So, medical backup is on its way, to check you both over.'

'No, they are not, young lady. I'm fine. I'm old, not made of paper. You see, this is why I like Ursula – she doesn't fuss. Now, you've asked your questions, and it's not like you'll actually do anything, and there's a programme about the Berlin Wall starting soon, so if you wouldn't mind . . .'

'I really am fine as well,' I said. 'I just need to go.'

'No, no, Constance. You must stay and have a cup of tea with me.'

'Bloody useless they are,' said Edward, once I'd seen them out. 'It's not their fault, though, is it? It's all the bastard cuts.' He pointed to a leather chair near the window. 'Sit for a minute, gather yourself.'

I politely obliged, still jittery, desperate to leave. The seat squeaked beneath me.

'Let me get you a nice sweet cup of tea.' As he pushed himself up, his breathing rattled. Climaxing in a cough on reaching a standing position.

'Are you sure you won't get seen by a doctor? My friend lives opposite and I—'

'No. Absolutely not. I gel with doctors even less than I do with the police. Now, milk and sugar?'

'No . . . I . . . I really should be getting home, Edward. If you're OK, that is? Is there anyone I can contact for you? Get to come over?' I also stood and we lingered awkwardly in the middle of the room.

He took a silk paisley handkerchief from his trouser pocket and wiped his eyes beneath his glasses. 'Well, how about another time? Let me thank you properly. I'll get some biscuits in.'

'Yes . . . yes, I'd love to,' I said with no intention of doing so.

My phone rang from within my bag. It was you.

'Sorry. I need to take this.' Turning away to answer, I faced the window. And there you were. I could see right into your flat. How your handset was sandwiched between your ear and neck crook, as you were putting your arms through a T-shirt.

'Sorry, Constance. Did you call a bit ago? I was in the shower. Is everything OK?'

I suppose I should have mentioned that I was watching you, but I didn't. Only briefed you on events as you towel-dried your hair, stopping as the shocking incident unfolded. Then you said the words 'Come over to mine.'

When the call had ended, I tried to contain my excitement. 'Sorry about that, Edward.'

'Well, I can't thank you enough, darling girl.'

'Please . . . stop thanking me. I don't know what happened, where it came from . . . but I'm no hero, I promise you. Here, take my number – for if you need anything.' I removed an old receipt from my bag and used the pen that rested on the paper that straddled the arm of his chair.

He thanked me, folded it neatly and placed it in his back pocket as we walked side by side through the hall towards the door.

'I still can't believe it, you know – how you swung into action like that. I bet you never thought you'd react that way in a million years.'

His kind eyes creased as he laughed. I laughed too. Though it was fake. Because I should never be shocked by what I'm capable of. Not when I'd already done such a terrible thing.

You buzzed me in and I stepped over the threshold. Crossed into your world.

The entrance hall was grander than Edward's, with its polished black-and-white-checked floor and imposing stair-case. Sweeping, curved marble, drawing my eyes upwards towards the opulent chandelier that hung ominously above my head. Such a contrast to the bare low-energy bulb in the hall at Lynton Road.

I gripped the wooden banister that perched on top of the ornate black wrought-iron balustrade, my clammy hands leaving prints which disappeared like invisible ink. The climb seemed never-ending. Especially as my foot had fully returned to its previous sore state. When I finally reached the landing, I held on to the rail to catch my breath, leaning over to view the spiral below, testing my vertigo, touching distance from the chandelier, until the rail inched forward and I stepped away, unsteady, my heart feeling as if it had slipped over the edge.

'Be careful, Constance.' I turned and moved towards you. The smell of your cleanliness hit me. 'The residents' committee needs to get it fixed, but often as it is with rich people, no one wants to pay . . . Come here, you.' You pulled my head towards your chest and hugged me.

It was so unexpected that every one of my muscles tensed. My rigor mortis arms longed to slide around your waist and under your T-shirt. When I finally gained the courage to return the gesture, you released me and held the door open for me to enter.

'I can't believe it, Constance . . . I feel so bad.'

I suppose you wanted me to tell you not to. That there was nothing to feel bad about. But I didn't. We should all get to endure the guilt we deserve.

The pale parquet of the landing continued through your hall, which was the polar opposite of Edward's, with its gallery-white walls and strategically placed black-and-white framed photographs. As you guided me past the metal console table, displaying the lamp that looked like twisted white paper, I was showered in shame. Remembering you'd seen where I lived.

Even with the stylish lead-up, my eyes widened when we reached your lounge. You hadn't mentioned it was akin to a music video. You know the ones. A white grand piano in the corner and muslin curtains billowing into the room. 'Ebony and Ivory' meets 'Imagine'. Except there was neither a piano nor curtains. Just two vast windows that stood almost floor to ceiling, dramatic and bare. It was, however, as empty as you'd described, with only your sofa – grey, of course – the beaten-up leather club chair, TV and shelves filled with books and CDs. Other framed arty photographs and prints, which hadn't made it onto the wall, rested against the perimeter. It wasn't like a home. Not a home I'd lived in. I'd walked into the pages of a lifestyle magazine.

'I did tell you it looks as if I've just moved in. I'm a man – what can I say?' You gestured me further into the room. 'Come on, sit down. You'll be in shock.'

Limping towards the sofa, I noticed your eyes squinted, scrutinizing me. 'You've got blood on you. Are you hurt?'

Your words triggered the urgent need to get it off me. 'It's . . . it's not mine.'

'Oh God, it's not the old guy's?'

'No. I . . . It was the boy . . . One of them fell and smashed his nose on the pavement.'

'Well, karma or what? I swear to God if I had the chance . . .'

I'm glad you stopped. It would have been embarrassing, you lying to us both.

'Why don't you borrow a T-shirt or something? You don't want some toerag's blood all over you, especially with your phobia . . . Oh, actually, come through here.'

I followed you back through the hall, unsure of where you were taking me.

You turned to check I was in tow. 'Is your foot hurting?'

'Yes, I . . . I was running on it. I don't know how.'

'Adrenaline. I'll have a look in a minute.'

You opened a door. It was your bedroom. Your oversized bed, staring at me. Where you slept, dreamt, touched yourself. Air heavy with citrus and, I believe, sandalwood. Your checked boxers strewn on the floor. Intimate. Any mask of formality between us evaporated.

A little like when as a teen, round at my friend Claire's, the daughter of our geography teacher Mr Reynolds, I'd crept into his bedroom on the way to the toilet and seen a DVD I shouldn't. Though it wasn't really the same, because

I didn't yearn for Mr Reynolds. He was disgusting. As I'm sure was *Missionary Impossible 2*.

You opened a door of the fitted wardrobes that clad the wall. 'Here, have a scan and take anything you want, anything. It's Laura's, the ex's – stuff she still won't bloody collect.'

You thought you were being nice. But you weren't. It was a cupboard filled with clothes of someone you once loved. And you'd given her a name.

'Seriously, I don't give a shit – take anything you want. She's lucky I've not binned it all after two months. My theory is, she still wants it here . . . Why can't women ever let go, eh? Anyway, have a rummage . . . apart from in the big box.'

'What's in the box? Sorry. I shouldn't—'

'It's my mother's . . . Anyway, I'll leave you to change into whatever you decide.' You pointed towards another doorway at the back of the room. 'Use the bathroom to clean yourself up. I'll make us some tea.'

Once you'd left, I inspected her clothes, which included a Lanvin sequinned dress, a velvet Chloé jacket and a black silk Dolce & Gabbana skirt. Things I could never afford without robbing a bank and she couldn't be arsed to pick them up. It's a different world, isn't it? One I'd foolishly thought I could be part of.

I pushed back the hangers in irritation, exposing the box. The forbidden is always so tempting. Like Mum's diaries used to be. Yet now, locked in their case, a ghost beneath me as I slept, her words begging to be read – I couldn't even contemplate.

I closed the cupboard and returned to the lounge. 'It's

really kind of you, but I feel a bit strange taking her things. Would you mind if I borrowed an old T-shirt of yours instead?'

Alone, I sat on the edge of the bed and pulled on the old faded black T-shirt you'd given me. I lifted the bottom half against my face and sniffed. Disappointingly, it was freshly washed. But I thought of all the times it would have been next to your skin, and now it was next to mine. As it often still is. I'm wearing it right now, as it happens.

I used the time alone in there to properly take in the room. Switched one of the trendy copper side lamps on and off and opened the copy of *Great Expectations* where your bookmark was inserted. Not far in.

> *'Do you know what I touch here?' she said, laying her hands, one upon the other, on her left side.*
> *'Yes, Ma'am.' (It made me think of the young man.)*
> *'What do I touch?'*
> *'Your heart.'*
> *'Broken!'*

I closed the book and went to wash myself.

Now accustomed to the poshness of your flat, I was unsurprised by the fancy mosaic-tiled bathroom and huge sink which sat like a bowl, in a way I'd never seen before, on top of a wooden cupboard. I immediately removed lids from your potions, sniffing them one by one like a sommelier. Inspected your heavy silver razer. Ran my nail across the teeth of your comb. But once I'd stared into the mirrored wall, I was distracted by the speckles of blood on my face, of which I'd been unaware. I blinked. To make the image disappear. Then scrubbed away the traces, so the next time I dared look, my face shone with rawness as I patted myself dry with your towel, still damp and full of you.

When I returned to the lounge, you were sat on the sofa. Loose-limbed, relaxed. Two mugs of tea rested on a magazine to protect the floor.

'Better?'

I nodded.

'Come and sit down.'

I did as I was told. Kept a polite distance. Wanting to be closer.

'Sorry – it's probably cold now.'

You lifted your mug, which was white with a large black letter 'S' on the front. As I turned mine to take a sip, I noticed it had the letter 'L'. I swivelled it back around.

'Actually, I think I've got some biscuits.' You placed the tea back down and stood. Carried on talking as you left the room. 'Oh, and get prepared so I can look at that foot on my return.' Then from the hall you shouted, 'You like chocolate, right?'

'Yes . . . if it's milk?' I bent to undo my laces. 'Trousers as well?'

'Of course.'

Removing my shoes, I was thankful Dale had 'sorted me out' when I was laid up, as this time my socks were without holes. But I still suffered the same discomfort about removing my trousers. Against my nature, I folded them neatly next to me, then pulled at your T-shirt, bringing it over my knees and distracting myself by eyeing your wall of CDs. No one used CDs anymore. I stood to have a proper look; then I heard you returning and dropped back onto the sofa.

'I've even put them on a plate. Are you impressed?'

I smiled.

'I'll let you have first pick— Oh . . . sorry, Constance. I didn't mean . . . You only needed to take off your shoe.'

I froze, apart from my eyes, which moved side to side, helping me compute the shame. Once registered, I grappled to put my trousers back on. 'I . . . I'm sorry . . . I did ask you, and you said—'

'It's not a problem.' You were laughing.

As I sucked in my stomach to zip them up, I also sucked in tears. I didn't know where you were or what you were doing because I couldn't bear to look at you.

'Oh, come on – don't get upset. I don't care . . . I'm still a bloody doctor. It's funny, that's all.'

I reached for my socks, tucked inside my shoes. 'I should go anyway, Dr Stevens. I promised my friend I'd—'

'Samuel . . . But you can't go . . . Constance, chill, please. You need to calm down first, after what's happened . . . and I don't mean you stripping for me.' You laughed again.

I pulled my shoes nearer. 'No, I've got to go—'

'Constance . . . Constance, it was a joke. Sorry . . . I'm not funny. Please. Seriously now . . . I need to check your foot before you go anywhere.' Your tone changed, and you placed your hand on my shoulder, gently pushing me down towards the sofa. 'It was my fault. I thought you only asked about the chocolate. I didn't hear you ask about the trousers. And it really doesn't matter.'

You were already kneeling in front of me. My foot held within your soft hands. They weren't cold like the first time. No warm heart. And I hated how your touch soothed me as you manipulated, evaluated.

'Is that hurting?'

I nodded.

'You're shaking.' You pressed my sole/soul, then with both hands began rubbing, gently, in opposite directions. 'Your foot's freezing. It's fine, though. You were running on the bruising, so it's going to hurt, but no actual damage has been done.' You released it and placed it down on the floor. It pulsated with new warmth. 'I'll get you another tea,' you said, collecting both our cups.

Once you'd left, I sat for a moment, awkward. Then to distract myself, I crossed the room to investigate your CDs. Ella Fitzgerald, Jeff Buckley, Johnny Cash, Aretha Franklin, Chopin . . . The list was endless, the collection enormous. Aside from the latter, I smiled at our common ground.

'Choose something if you want.'

I jumped.

'Sorry. I always seem to be scaring you . . . Only if you want to, of course.'

'No, I . . . I was just surprised, that's all . . . You've got a lot of CDs.' I limped back over to the sofa and picked up my shoes.

'Why don't you leave them off? Relax, sit down. I think you're still in shock. Here, I thought this might help more than tea.'

I sank into the sofa as you handed me a wine glass and poured into it a burnt-amber liqueur from the bottle you carried. I sniffed the contents. The potency snatched my breath and made me cough.

'It's a good brandy, that. It'll relax you, warm you up. Sorry, I'm a heathen and don't have the correct glassware.' You smiled, as if you remembered that the person who lived in a house with a sink in the garden wouldn't care about such things.

I allowed it to wash across my lips, then licked them. 'It's very strong,' I said through a wheeze.

'Have a few sips. It works, I promise . . . Look.' You swirled the heavy liquid, which clung to each part of the glass it touched, then took a large gulp before blowing imaginary fire from your mouth. 'See . . . relaxed.' You pulled a silly face like you were entertaining a child.

I copied, feeling you watch me. 'It's still so strong.' It almost stole my voice, but I enjoyed the burn as its warmth enveloped me.

'It's just normal brandy. I promise. Keep taking tiny amounts . . . You'll feel better soon. Shall I pick something, then?' You were at the shelves, glass in hand, your finger tracing a line along the CD spines. 'I bought the majority before the whole download thing . . . but there's nothing like having something physical, don't you think . . . something to hold?'

Your fingers stopped. You turned to me and smiled, then faced the shelves once more, removing a disk that I couldn't see, then placing it in the player. 'I reckon you're a Blondie girl, hey?'

Before I could say anything, I'd identified the intro to 'Heart of Glass'.

You turned back towards me. Your smile dropped. 'Constance, what's wrong?'

I'm not sure how I'd appeared to you, but I suspect I'd whitened to the colour of your porcelain sink.

I somehow summoned the words 'Do you mind if we put on something else? This reminds me of my mum.'

You mumbled apologies as you fumbled with the buttons, until, thank God, it stopped and my heart functioned once again.

'Dr Stevens, I should maybe go.'

'Samuel . . . No, no, I'm sorry.' You pulled another CD from the wall and quickly inserted it. 'This is nice and soothing.'

It was Nina Simone.

'I recognize the voice, but I don't know this song,' I said, as you sat back down next to me. Sipped more brandy and nodded for me to do the same.

'I thought people your age preferred R&B. You know, someone featuring someone else.'

'How old do you think I am?'

'Younger than me.'

'I'm twenty-six.'

You smiled, raised your eyebrows. 'As I say, younger than me.'

You didn't disclose your age, but I already knew. You were thirty-seven. Your birthday, 12 February.

Time flowed as freely as the brandy.

We'd talked nonstop after that. Do you remember the ease? Discussing Nina Simone and music in general. How your mum was a fan and was lucky enough to have seen her live in Paris. 'She was something unworldly, Samuel – she'd say.' I told you how I'd always wanted to go to Paris. Imagined myself flouncing around the Champs-Elysées in clothes I wouldn't dream of wearing here.

'Well, maybe you will,' you said. 'Though I can't imagine you flouncing anywhere.'

Aretha Franklin was singing, and I was immune to the brandy burn. I may have been slurring. Was I? My glass seemed to be frequently empty, frequently filled. We giggled at unfunny things. I smoked a fag, but you'd made me hang out of the window. It was dark. I searched for Edward's flat. I'd forgotten about him already, what happened. I imagined him sat waiting for me with an unopened packet of Garibaldis. A moment of sober worry, guilt, which left as quickly as it arrived.

I was back on the sofa. 'I'm sorry, but it's too cold there – I'll have to have the next one right here.' I popped a fresh fag into my wonky drunken lips.

You looked at me disapprovingly, then sang along with Aretha. 'R-E-S-P-E-C-T.'

'Fine. I won't, then,' I said, and went through the motions of smoking it unlit.

Then you said, 'You know, you remind me of someone, Constance.'

'I do?'

'Someone I used to know. Isabella . . . my first love . . . Whoa, this brandy *is* really strong, isn't it?' You emptied the dregs into your mouth. 'I noticed that first day at the surgery how much you were like her, and I felt compelled to blurt it out . . . but then I thought it was inappropriate. And you were vomiting, of course. It's probably still inappropriate, isn't it? Is it?'

'No . . . no . . . I don't think so.' My face burned. 'The brandy,' I said, touching my cheek.

You took my hand in yours. 'See, it's made the shaking stop . . . I feel a bit drunk now, you know,' you said. 'Do you?'

'A bit.'

My hand slipped from yours, and you poured more brandy into your glass, then mine, then rested your head on the back of the sofa.

'We get on well, don't we? It's funny, isn't it? How some people just . . .' You clicked your fingers. 'You don't know why . . . but it's there . . . like a knowing. Do you think it's because of our dead mothers?' Your hand returned to mine. The sensation carried through my body.

'I . . . I don't know.'

'Nah, I don't think it's that.' You turned your head, looked at me. 'It's just there . . . because that's what happens with certain people. Connection. And it's a rare and wonderful thing.'

I wondered if I was so drunk I was imagining it all. If it was one of those frequent dreams I'd have about you, when I'd wake, stomach flipping. Or if it *was* happening, perhaps I was misunderstanding all you said.

Etta James was singing 'At Last'. In that moment I knew it had now become our song. You looked at my eyes, my mouth, my eyes. I remained silent. Silent, as you removed the glass from my hand and placed it on the floor. Silent, as you brought your face so close the alcohol on your lips took my breath away. Silent, as you placed your hands either side of my head.

Silent, as we kissed.

Did it feel different to you? Than with anyone else? When you were inside me. When your eyes bored into mine. My hair wrapped around the hand you pulled it with, causing pain, beautiful pain. Did you feel it? Our bond. I never told you this, but when I came, when I dragged your salt mouth to mine as I came, that was the first time it had happened with anyone but myself.

Did you feel it too? When we lay on our backs, fingertips touching. Breeze from the open window cooling our stomachs. You did. I know you did.

And do you remember? How when I shivered, you pulled the duvet over me, kissed my goosebumped skin, stroked my hair. We shared a cigarette and you said, 'So anyway, Constance, who was your first love?'

I didn't reply. Merely blew smoke into the air and watched the white strings infiltrate the atmosphere. Because we both know the answer to that, don't we?

It was you.

*

For the next three weeks, every thought, feeling, was consumed by you.

Meeting you. Touching you. Kissing you.

I enjoyed the thrill. The excitement of the show. Remaining professional. 'Of course, Dr Stevens . . . Yes, Dr Stevens.' But when alone, with the excuse of a coffee or a file, which I'd place on your desk, brushing against the skin exposed by your rolled-up sleeve, leaning forward, heart rates in sync, I'd feel your hot breath against my ear, whispering, 'I wish I could have you right now.' If interrupted by Linda or a patient, I'd switch. 'Yes, me too, Dr Stevens. I'll do that for you as soon as I can.'

Whenever able, we'd arrange our trysts, which, as you know, only ever took place in your flat. I'd either walk and meet you there or sometimes, if you had the car, you'd pick me up halfway. It was strange that now we were close, intimate, we couldn't walk together as before.

'You know you can't tell anyone about us, Constance. Not your housemate, anyone. If we got found out, we'd both be in the shit.' I'd always nod in agreement, but the truth is, inside I didn't agree, didn't understand. Surely even Dr Harris understood love.

As instructed, I didn't tell Dale. I never wanted to anyway, yet I wasn't entirely sure why. Although, I recently saw a documentary about female prisoners and a psychologist said we all subconsciously know the whys of everything we do.

To make the process easier, I never stayed over at yours. 'You know I'd love you to, Constance, but it'll only make him more suspicious. If he's your friend, he'll be asking who you're with, won't he? You don't want to have to look your friend in the eye and lie, do you? And if he fancies you . . . well, he'll want to know even more.'

I scrutinized you for signs of jealousy, of you dreading that was true. But you were using your poker face as a mask of pride. I instantly defused your anxieties. 'He . . . he doesn't . . . He's just a friend . . . But I'll go home soon, don't worry.' And so I did. Every time. Except that one Friday night.

We'd both fallen asleep after sex. Well, you had; I'd only pretended. I watched you the entire night. The way your breath fluttered a strand of hair that had fallen across your face. How you placed your hand on your pulsing heart, the other behind your head in surrender. You looked so peaceful and innocent. I positioned my head next to yours and took a lovely photo of us together. For once without you immediately making me delete it. I wish I still had that photograph, and it angers me that I don't. But I can still see it. When I close my eyes, just before I go to sleep.

The next morning I imagined we lived together. Rising early to make your breakfast. Do you remember? How you complained I'd boiled your eggs too long. 'I prefer just cereal,' you said, throwing them away. So I fetched you some cornflakes instead.

On the way home, I popped into Boots and printed off our photo before deleting it. I wasn't stupid. I knew it was too risky to keep on my phone. Anyone could accidentally catch a glimpse.

I told Dale I'd bumped into an old friend from school, Mary Feely. Touchy Feely, as she was known. Said I'd seen her at High Street Kensington Station and she'd just moved to London. I wasn't even sure if Touchy was still alive. I'd heard through the grapevine she had MS or something. Anyway, I told him we'd got drunk together, that I crashed at hers and my phone had run out of juice.

'It's got forty-five per cent,' he said, when I'd placed it on the kitchen table.

'Jesus, Dale, who are you – Poirot? Mary's flatmate, Jenny, who's a teacher, lent me her charger in the morning.' I added the specific details to make it more convincing. I learnt that from Mum. Although, when she'd elaborate on how she hadn't had a drink, she wasn't convincing at all. I left the kitchen, indignant, upset, which I also learnt from her.

Once in my room, I dragged the dusty case from beneath the bed. Coughed as I disturbed the particles. The label from our one holiday abroad, Benidorm, was faded and torn. I unclicked the stiff locks, lifted the lid. They were all there. Colourful and sad. I looked beyond them, blanked them out and concentrated on making a space in the corner where I placed our photograph.

* * *

The days we didn't connect, like the Tuesdays when you were at poker or at the weekends, I missed you terribly. I'd spend them with Dale to keep him satisfied that our friendship still existed. We went to the cinema once, I think. I can't remember what we saw. There was no space in my head for anything other than you.

However, amid all the happiness, there was one of our rendezvous that I didn't enjoy at all. That time we ate pizza as 'Purple Haze' blasted out. I leant over and removed the string of cheese that clung to your chin and said, 'I wish we could go out one evening at least, get a nice meal somewhere.'

'Constance, doctors aren't supposed to fuck their receptionists, you know.' You pointed to the last slice of pizza in the box. 'Are you eating that?'

I shook my head. You tilted back yours and eased the triangle, point first, into your mouth. Chewed with your lips apart. The pulping of the reddened dough made me want to retch. Though not as much as what you'd said. How you'd said it. But I convinced myself it was born from the same frustrations I had.

Then came the day of the funeral.

We were all dressed in black. Apart from you. You wore your pale blue shirt with the bottom button missing, and a minute iron singe on the collar, of which you were probably unaware. I'm sure you remember what I wore, because I noticed you trying not to stare at me in my mum's black skirt and the fine-weave blouse I hadn't realized was slightly see-through when I'd panic-bought it for the funeral from a charity shop.

Immersed in our relationship, I'd successfully pushed the funeral towards a secluded area in the back of my mind. But once it had arrived, hurtling towards the forefront, it brought with it reactions that I couldn't disguise.

'Are you cold, Constance?' asked Alison. 'You're shivering.'

'Yes . . . It's not as warm as it has been, is it?'

I was desperate to talk to you. For you to ease my nerves. But you were busy with patients. Then the opportunity finally arose when you asked if I could quickly grab Mrs Randall's referral letter before I left.

Placing it on your desk, I let the blouse drape open near your face. Waited for your whisper to infiltrate me.

'Thank you, Constance,' you said formally.

I turned, presuming Mrs Randall was behind me. But no one was there.

With the surgery closed for lunch, we gathered in reception to await the cabs. You remained in your room. A hushed atmosphere spread. Any words spoken were muted, sombre. Dr Franco sat with Dr Short. Alison was still behind reception. Linda stood talking to Dr Harris, the tissue in her hand becoming more crumpled with each moment. She was dreading it as much as I was. Albeit for different reasons.

I sat alone. Distracting myself by leaning over the glass table and scanning the covers of the *Country Life* magazines. (Flicking through one felt inappropriate somehow.) '£18 Million House'; 'What Really Goes On In Private Members' Clubs?'; 'How to Draw Dogs'.

'This can't be easy for you, Constance.' Dr Franco was taking a seat next to me uninvited.

I turned to him, smiled. 'No. It's a sad day for us all.'

He rested his fingers upon my shoulder. I resisted the urge to shrug him off and accepted the discomfort. 'Dr Stevens told me . . . about your mother. So recent for you . . . and no support network.'

I reached for a magazine, turned its pages. 'Yes . . . I'm fine, though, Dr Franco.'

'Please don't be upset with Dr Stevens. He was only concerned and thought you may benefit from talking with someone. With me. As do I . . . Now, before you say, I know I charge disgusting amounts of money, but the truth is, my chat with Dr Stevens highlighted how I hadn't taken on any pro bono clients for some years. As a struggling student, from a world very different to the one that I now inhabit, I made a pact with myself that I always would, and frankly, Constance, I'm ashamed. So I assure you it would be for my benefit just as much as yours.'

He was wrong. I wasn't upset with you. In fact, I was suppressing a grin at how much you cared.

'Thank you . . . Really, thank you. That's a very generous offer . . . It's just that I don't need to talk. I'm fine. Honestly.'

'"I'm fine" is one of the most misleading phrases ever to be uttered, I find. It's just a chat. No harm, hey?'

I attempted to avoid his eyes, but he caught hold of mine and wouldn't let them go, nodding, until I said, 'OK . . . Well, thank you, Dr Franco. If you're sure.'

'Excellent,' he said, rising. 'How about tomorrow lunch?'

'OK, yes. That's very kind of you.' He patted my shoulder and left me to return to Dr Short.

I already felt guilty, knowing that everything I'd tell him would be a lie.

Driving through the cemetery gates, we followed a trail of amber leaves, fallen from thinning trees to reveal a spectrum of grey, ranging from majestic tombs to simple crosses overlooked by crying angels. I remember thinking how even the trees here died before their time.

As we drove at a sedate pace, I imagined beneath the car's wheels the extended tangle of bones and earth, woven by worms and roots, as we moved through the hovering souls.

Sandwiched between Alison's inane chattering and Linda's cries, I observed the crowd of mourners huddled beneath the grand arches of the crematorium. Kissing cheeks. Shaking hands. Wiping tears. The hearse at their centre, shiny and open in preparation.

It's funny, isn't it? How we'd all have been horrified if a blackened, putrid Dr Williams was on display instead. Our loved ones may be concealed by an overpriced box made palatable by lilies and shiny brass handles, but inside, they're decaying, disappearing. The person you need. The person who'd be alive if not for you.

I know you find such ideas laughable, but some believe the dead show themselves in white feathers floating from the sky. Or snow. But Mum wasn't a feather. Or at peace enough to be snow. She was fallen leaves, swirling, uneasy, as I walked the path. It wasn't a comfort. Her watching me there, knowing she was checking if I'd make it to the end.

As we approached the building, I'd managed to break free from Linda and Alison, and somehow found myself directly behind four emotionally restrained pallbearers in matching black suits heaving the coffin upwards. The effect slightly ruined by one lad's brown shoes and the uneven dip caused by his diminutive height.

I held back. Allowed the family to take their correct positions. First a fragile Mrs Williams, then their two daughters. The teenager comforted her little sister, who sobbed with each solemn step.

The rest of us remained mute, kept our heads down, followed, as the muffled melody of 'Fly Me to the Moon' floated through the air.

I made it through the service by thinking of you.

As the celebrant, who resembled an off-duty Elvis impersonator, delivered his insincere speech, I imagined your delighted face when telling you I'd be able to stay over that evening. When Dr Williams's brother recounted the story of how his sibling was destined to become a doctor because aged six he'd amputated the arm of his Action Man, I imagined our afternoon ahead, alone, together. During his sister's reading of that deluded poem which pretends it's like the dead are only in the next room, I thought about us kissing openly in your office. And for the most difficult part, when the curtains drew around the coffin to Mama Cass singing 'Dream a Little Dream', the pain was so sharp, so intense that I closed my eyes and imagined you deep inside me.

Everyone left the building. Except, ironically, Shit Elvis. The majority would continue their lives as before. Others would never be the same again.

Standing outside, surrounded by the chattering about the poignancy of it all, it became apparent no one had arranged a cab to take me back. So I lit an urgently needed cigarette and began the long cemetery route towards the exit. As I walked, the leaves gathered momentum and swirled angrily around my feet.

Back at the surgery, I rushed straight to your room to find the door closed. Pressing my ear against the wood, I deciphered the voice of a female patient, so returned to reception and checked your appointments. Miss Sampras. Miss Sampras was unusually pretty, and I didn't like the thought of her cavorting around in her bra, breathing in and out for you, dropping her lips open as you asked her to make sex noises while looking down her throat.

She was in there far too long for comfort, and when she finally emerged, I couldn't even raise a smile towards her. Thankfully, once her notes came through, I saw her ailment was a fungal toe. No one finds fungal toes alluring.

Determined to see you before the arrival of Mr Parker, I rushed to your office, not even bothering to knock.

'Sorry, Constance – I didn't hear you knocking. How was it?' You relaxed back in your seat, your shirt undone a button lower than usual. Had you released it for the benefit of Miss Sampras?

'It was horrible . . . as expected.' I sat upon your knee like a little girl. And I felt the upset drain away as you swung the chair side to side.

'Oh well . . . it was brave of you to go. Well done.'

'I've got some good news, though,' I said.

'Oh yes?'

'I told Dale I'm going back to the wake and staying at Alison's, so I can sleep over tonight.'

The swinging stopped. 'Oh right. I can't tonight, unfortunately. I said I'd meet Paul in the Castle after work.'

It was surprising even to myself how quickly I wished to cry. 'But I . . . Couldn't you meet him tomorrow instead?'

'I don't think that's very fair, do you? Jesus, Constance.'

'Sorry . . . I . . . It was just an opportunity for us to—' The buzzer made me jump.

'That'll be Mr Parker,' you said. 'You'd better let him in.'

Mr Parker overstayed his welcome. Your next patient had arrived before he'd finished, and so the overlap continued all afternoon. Ratched One left, with an unfriendly goodbye. And it was five thirty by the time Mr Hammond, your last patient, was done and I could finally bolt the door behind him.

I headed to the ladies'. Mussed my hair, pinched my cheeks. Undid my blouse, washed my bits. Wincing as I wiped myself dry with the scratchy paper towel. I then decided to remove my knickers completely and stuff them into my pocket. It was all I had. It was all she'd ever used.

'What are you doing?' you said as I locked your door behind me.

You were still sat, pen poised above a prescription. I walked over to you, slow, unflinching.

'I've got to finish signing these.'

I hitched up my skirt, straddled you.

'Constance . . . stop it . . . We can't do anything here.'

But your words were futile. You were already kissing me.

Your fingers frantic, searching beneath my skirt. Myself, so relieved, content, that I'd successfully changed your mind.

Sat on your desk, skirt ruched around my waist, bra undone, I watched you hoist up your trousers, button your shirt. After you came, you hadn't kissed me as usual but reached for the patients' tissues and dried yourself off in silence.

You stared at the scattered manila files, escaped documents and a now-open box of paper clips on the floor. 'We need to clear this up.'

Squatting, you collected the clips with your right hand, dropping them into the cupped palm of your left. You didn't look at me. Not as I slid off the desk, pulling down my skirt. Not as I removed the knickers from my pocket and sheepishly put them on. Not as I fastened my bra before kneeling to help you.

'That shouldn't have happened.' You finally looked at me as you poured the clips from your hand into the box. 'Do your blouse up, will you.'

Standing, I fastened the buttons as requested, though my fingers were fumbling and uncooperative. 'We could pick up a curry or something? Get some wine?'

Your lips curled and your eyes squinted. 'What are you talking about? I've told you, I'm going out tonight.' You stood too. Threw the box onto the desk. There was the sound of tinkling metal as several paper clips ricocheted back out. You bent down again, the redness of your cheeks travelling south towards your neck, and you began gathering up papers.

I copied you. My eyes flitting upwards towards your face.

'I . . . I know you did . . . Sorry. Is that Mr Parker's file? This belongs with that.'

You snatched the letter from my hand, causing a paper cut to my finger, which I sucked to stop the sting.

'I'm not doing this, Constance. Having you make a massive issue because I want to go out one night with a friend.'

'I . . . I'm not. I—'

'Look at the bloody mess. We shouldn't have done that.'

'It's OK. No one else is here. No one will know.'

I attempted to hug you, but you turned and threw the file onto the desk. 'But I know, for fuck's sake.' Newly replaced pages flew out with the force. A sheet floated back to the floor. You didn't retrieve it. Just dropped into your chair, which rolled backwards with the motion, and covered your face with your hands.

I didn't know what to do. How to stop you worrying. All I could think was to gather the remaining evidence from the floor.

Then do you remember? How you changed so suddenly. At least, I thought you had.

'I'm sorry . . . I'm sorry, Constance. Come here.'

I followed instruction. Allowed you to pull me onto your knee, alleviating my concerns.

'I'm a shit . . . I'm such a shit, Constance . . . You know I'm very fond of you, don't you?'

Fond.

Still I smiled as you pressed my head to rest against your shoulder, stroked my hair.

'But it shouldn't have happened.'

I closed my eyes, nestled deeper. 'We'll tidy it up. No one will ever know, and we'll never do it again.'

You kissed the top of my head. 'You're so adorable. I meant us . . . It should never have happened. You deserve better than me, than this.'

I didn't move.

Didn't punch away your hand, which continued to caress my hair. Didn't speak. Breathe. Scream.

'Constance? Say something.'

I slid from you. Stood. 'But I . . . I'm happy with it like this. I didn't mean . . . Please, I'm sorry. I know I talk about going out and things, but I don't mind not doing . . . honestly, I don't.' I watched your head tilt back, your eyes covered with your palms. Uncertain what was happening beneath them. 'And I know I say I'd like to stay over, but I wouldn't . . . I mean, it's not important. We don't have to be like other couples, do we? However things need to be, I'm fine with it, Samuel. I . . . I don't mind.'

You dropped your hands and sat forward. 'Other couples? Constance, come on . . . We were just having fun.'

It's embarrassing to think what I did next: collecting up wayward biros that littered the desk and returning them neatly to the pen holder. Desperate to make everything as it was before.

'I mean . . . I'm not capable of more. Even if I wanted to be.'

'You said it was a rare and wonderful thing . . . our connection.'

'Connection? Did I? I don't think I . . . There's one fallen under the desk . . . There, by the wire . . . No. To your left . . . left . . . That's it. Look, you're a really great girl, but I think it's done now. I mean, it had to end sometime, didn't it? Everything comes to an end sometime. And that was definitely a memorable ending, don't you think? We should just go back to how it was. We can still have our banter and things . . . be friends.'

Tell me, Doctor, when you were training, did you ever remove the heart of a donated body? Place it on the slab next to them? Dissect it? Rip it apart?

I stood still, mute, as the room spun around me. Until I heard myself say, in an unrecognizably weak voice, 'Please don't.'

'Oh, come on now . . . Don't be one of those, Constance. You're so much better than that.'

I didn't cry. Wouldn't cry. I held the tears until they almost choked me.

'Look, I'm going to be late and need to finish up. Why don't you go and shut down reception? Then we can get out of here.'

So I did. Somehow. I finished inputting Mr Hammond's notes. Turned off the computer. Washed up the mugs.

Soon you appeared in reception, bag in hand. 'Ready?'

I nodded. Put on my coat. Collected my bag.

You didn't notice my inability to speak. That no blood circulated my face. That I couldn't look at you.

We stood a foot from each other. You dropped your bag and followed with your head. Then pulled me towards you, hugged me. I breathed in hard. To take a part of you away with me.

'You're so great, Constance. Most girls get all . . . you

know . . . crazy when you end things, but I knew you'd be cool.' You released me.

I smiled, turned towards the door.

'Hey, we should get a sandwich at lunch tomorrow,' you said. 'Jesus, I'm gagging for that pint . . . What you up to this evening?'

'I'm . . . I'm not sure.' I barely heard myself, so I doubt you did.

Outside, at the bottom of the steps, we said goodbye and parted ways. I walked away, my head held high, not out of pride but in order to keep me upright. I'd not got very far when I felt you next to me. I stopped. Tried not to crumble with hope.

'Constance . . . look, I know I don't have to say this, but still, obviously, no one can . . . you know . . . find out about anything happening between us, right? It would be bad. For both of us, I mean.'

It didn't matter that I hadn't responded. 'You're the best, Constance. I'll see you tomorrow.' You walked away, then turned back to shout, 'Let's definitely get that sandwich.'

I walked, eyes glazed. Smoked. As each cigarette ended, I began another. I was a robot. And you'd pressed a button that released immeasurable pain. I couldn't stop. Couldn't cry. Faster and faster and faster I strode the streets. When I reached the Tube, to my surprise, I passed it by. Carried on. To fuck knows where. Just walked, walked, walked until I eventually hit a filthy dead end. Facing a high brick wall with the word 'tosser' sprayed in red. A rat scurried from a nearby bin and disappeared beneath an abandoned sofa supporting a bowing mattress.

Instead of turning back round, I lit my last fag, threw the empty packet onto the sofa. Heaved. There were too many to cope with. Feelings. All with nowhere to go. I approached the wall. Placed the fag in my mouth, left it there. And then I prayed to God for release as my fist hit the bricks.

I still have the scar. I'm looking at it as I write. So small compared to the ones that cannot be seen.

*

I was still drunk as I rode the bus to work. Broken, numb. The vodka's odorous molecules bounced back into my face when I breathed against the window.

I'd woken early, the sky barely lit, to the smell of TCP and the sound of snoring.

After sliding my arm around your waist, I'd opened my blurry eyes and watched your hair flutter as you exhaled. But it wasn't you. It was Dale. And I had no idea why.

Crispy velour itched my neck as I shifted down the bus seat to snag some physical comfort, instantly ruined by a school lad bouncing into the space next to me, knocking my bandaged hand.

Feeling queasy, I closed my eyes and attempted to block out both the annoying rustling of the boy's anorak and the loud banter with his mate behind. Their voices triggered fragments of the night before. The Castle. Drinkers. Raucous, laughing. Amy Winehouse, 'Back to Black'. Searching for you. The barman's startled eyes when he clocked me. Scanning myself in the lager pump's reflection. Black mascara-stained sockets. Blood from my hand now smeared across my cheeks from wiping away tears. Your absence. *I'll wait a bit longer.* Getting drunk. Not drunk, smashed. The desperate middle-aged perv in an Eighties leather jacket. 'Why don't I take you home?'

'Why don't you fuck off?'

You never showed. And considerably less intoxicated, remembering, I was nothing but thankful that you hadn't.

But the point is, you lied, Samuel. You lied.

Aside from Harris, the light shining beneath his door, I was the first to arrive.

I headed straight to the toilet, splashed my face and used loo roll to remove the smeared remnants of funeral make-up from under my eyes. Combing my hair with my fingers, I vowed that from then on, I'd always carry a brush like a proper person.

I hung on to the sink through a moment of swimming nausea. This induced another memory fragment. Throwing up. On Dale. His horrified expression as the acidic potion splashed his jeans and new Converse. Being ordered to sit on the bed like a naughty girl. Hot black coffee. Him removing my shoes.

'Now get undressed.'

His presence as I did. Tucking me in. Bathing my hand with TCP. It stung. He bandaged it. Slowly, carefully. Crying.

'What's wrong, Constance?'

My lies.

'It was the funeral. It brought it all back.'

'You've got me . . . You'll always have me.'

Linda, disgruntled I'd beaten her into work, waxed lyrical about the 'lovely send-off'. How the hotel was 'grand without being ostentatious'. I nodded. Made the correct noises. But the whole time I was focusing over her shoulder, waiting for you.

'It was only for us close friends and family anyway, really . . . so probably best you didn't come . . . What's wrong with your hand?'

I was about to invent a story when the door opened. I recognized the tip of your shoe and pivoted, knocking the stapler on the floor. When bending to pick it up, I stayed there longer than required, eyes glued to my knee.

'Morning, Dr Stevens. I was just telling Constance about how lovely the wake was.'

'Oh, I'm pleased to hear that, Linda. Though I can't deny I avoid funerals whenever possible.'

Did you say that for my benefit? To remind me of our core bond.

I felt you leaning over reception. 'You couldn't bring me in a coffee, could you, Constance?'

In the kitchen, I was back to day one. Nervous, unable to get the colour right, accidentally double-sugaring and having to make it again from scratch. Once satisfied, I poured some out into the sink to prevent my jitters from causing it to swill over the edge.

As I walked to your room, another memory was triggered from the previous night. Dale's dank fingers stroking my face. Pretending to be asleep. His shadow over me. His breath. Garlic. Beef Monster Munch. His lips touching mine. Me turning over. Fake sleeping groans. Praying. Waiting for the shadow to leave. Relief as it lifts and turns.

* * *

You were writing in your notebook when I entered. No acknowledgement. I quietly walked over and placed the mug in front of you.

'Thanks, Constance.' You caught sight of the bandage and put down your pen. Bothered to look at me. 'Oh no, what have you done now?'

'I fell over.'

'Again? You're very clumsy, aren't you?'

'It's fine. I've put TCP on it.'

'I want to see. Sit down.'

I did as I was told. You wheeled over to me, took my wrist in your warm hands – *Warm hands, cold heart* – and unravelled the dressing.

'So how did you fall this time?'

'I'm not sure.' You smiled at me, expecting more of an explanation. 'I think I tripped on my laces and knocked my hand against a wall.'

'That could only happen to you, Constance.' You removed the last bit of bandage. 'It looks like you've given someone a left hook.'

I looked down at my exposed hand. Blue-black knuckles crisscrossed with red. 'I didn't, though.'

'I was joking . . . I mean, if you were going to punch anyone, it'd be me, right?' You stood and crossed the room to gather antiseptic and such into a dish.

Once again I watched you. That unruly section of your hair. Your shoulder blades slicing beneath your shirt. We'd come full circle.

I'd planned to keep quiet, but with your back to me, I developed bravery.

'So how was the Castle? Did you have a nice time?'

You paused. Then moved again as if you'd been affected by a PlayStation glitch. 'Yeah . . . yeah . . . It was good. It was pretty quiet in there, so it was nice just having a beer, catching up, you know.'

And there it was. The additional detail for legitimacy. You weren't even skilled at it.

You turned to me with the dish. I smiled.

As you wiped my hand, it carried me back to that day. And it was too much. Too painful.

'I must get on. Linda will go mad.'

'Well, I just need to put a fresh bandage on and then you're free.'

Free. It was as if you were gloating.

I was about to snatch my arm away when you said, 'I'm . . . I'm so sorry about yesterday, Constance.'

I tried not to appear startled but couldn't stop myself from exhaling a long breath. 'Oh God, Samuel. So am I.'

Your lips were unnecessarily close as you pressed the gauze against my broken skin. I was certain you wanted to kiss me, though knew you wouldn't. Considering why the whole issue started in the first place. You wound the bandage and my hand already felt better, secure.

'You're such a special person, you know, Constance. You understand me . . . and that's so important.'

You're such a worrypot, Mum would say. And she was right. I'd done it again. Fretted unduly. So inexperienced that I couldn't even identify a lovers' tiff.

'So are you. Special to me, I mean.'

'Thank you, Constance . . . That means a lot. It really

does.' You smiled and your eyes moistened. The bandage completed its final cycle and you tore off tape to secure the end. 'And I know you're going to meet someone great. I just know you are . . . Sorry, did I hurt you then?' I'd pulled my arm away. Stood. 'Is the bandage too tight?'

'It . . . it stung a bit, that's all. I'd better get on with my work. Thank you.'

'Sure, sure . . . but before you go . . . I'm so sorry, but let me give you this.' You delved into your pocket and brought out a twenty, then a ten-pound note, which you pressed into my uninjured hand as you whispered, 'Look, I can't tell you what to do . . . but obviously we were . . . well, unprepared yesterday . . . I know I didn't . . . you know . . . inside . . . but not using a condom was . . . Well, we don't want any disasters to deal with, do we? I'd write you a prescription, but it's too risky.'

I scrunched the notes in my fist. 'No . . . of course. I'll go to the chemist after work.'

'Thank you. Obviously, I'd take it myself, if I could. Hey, let's get that sandwich at lunch, shall we?' My legs wobbled as I turned. 'Whoa, are you OK there? I forgot about the whole blood phobia thing.' You pointed to your own knuckles.

'Yes . . . I'm fine. Thank you.' I made it to the door, fingers grappling for the handle, stability.

'Constance.'

I turned to look at you.

'Thanks for being so great about everything.'

* * *

Tell me, Doctor, when people die of a broken heart, does it always happen fast? I know it happens. Takotsubo cardiomyopathy. You mustn't be surprised that I know things. I know lots of things now. But I wonder if heartbreak can also cause slow, drawn-out deaths. Over months, years. Perhaps that's why your mother died. It was why mine died. She had cancer, yes. But really, she'd been dying for twenty years. Since that day. That weird day.

After leaving your office, I'd somehow kept it together. Switched off. Didn't cry. Though I was glad of the relief from pretence when Linda sent me into the stationery cupboard to check stock levels. I couldn't think straight, let alone count bloody prescription forms, but when I returned with a list of fabricated numbers, Dr Franco was waiting for me in reception.

'Oh . . . Dr Franco. I'm . . . I'm sorry . . . but I . . . I can't do today after all . . . Dr Stevens wants to go through something with me during lunch.'

Linda took the list from me. 'What are you talking about? Dr Stevens has just this minute left. He's on home visits for the rest of the day.'

Sat in Dr Franco's vast consulting room, engulfed by the soft leather seat, staring over at the books and certificates that laced the walls to avoid his dark, full-of-concern eyes, I felt like I could have died of takotsubo cardiomyopathy. I didn't. But I still often wonder if I will.

'Now, I don't want you to feel worried or nervous, Constance. It's only a chat. A friend who wants to help if I can . . . You don't even have to stay.' He moved an antique wooden chair with a red velvet seat from near his desk and placed it a few feet away from me before sitting, smiling.

I was going to politely decline. Say it was very kind of him, but I didn't feel comfortable talking about it. Then he said, 'So how are you? How was yesterday?' And my face must have betrayed me because he followed it with, 'That good, eh?'

I dropped my head. Wanted to tell him. Someone. Not about the funeral, about you. Ask him what to do. How to get you back. That's all I wanted. He'd know. That's what they do, these people, isn't it? Decipher minds. And if you can do that, know how people think, you can get them to do anything.

'Why don't you start by telling me about your mum?'

I stared up at him. 'What do you mean? Like what?' My foot tapped an anxious rhythm on the worn Persian rug and I pressed my knee to make it stop.

He unfolded his arms and turned to retrieve a pad and pen from his old leather-topped desk. 'Just so I remember things . . . Nothing formal, don't worry.' Then he looked at me in expressionless silence. Waiting.

I didn't want to think about it. Her. So instead, I wondered how old Dr Franco was. I'd always presumed he was in his sixties, but when I observed him closely, the skin on his face was smooth, line-free, and I suspected he was one of those people who'd always looked like an old man. Even as a kid.

His desk clock ticked like a bomb. Staring back down to my fiddling fingers, I thought I could play the game. Endure the excruciating awkwardness. But I'm ashamed to say he won. I told you they can get you to do anything.

'She died in April. Cancer. What's more to say? Life's shit. It happened . . . No point talking about it . . . It won't change anything.' I glanced up to check his reaction. I'd said it so many times that even I believed it.

He twirled his pen like a baton, then scribbled words about me. It was unsettling. The scratching of the nib grated. In what other circumstance is it acceptable that someone writes secret notes about a person in front of them?

'Look, I don't know why I'm here, to be honest, Dr Franco . . . I was being polite because it was so kind of you . . . but I'd really rather not talk about it.'

He stopped writing and placed the pen in the crevice of his pad. Removed his glasses and folded the metal arms neatly inwards before laying them next to the pen. 'OK, OK, Constance. I understand. You can leave whenever you wish. As I said, it was just a chat.'

That's why understanding minds is so powerful, manipulative. He knew that part of me I didn't even know myself. The part of me that wanted to stay.

A few moments ticked by.

'What was your mum's name?'

'Angela . . . Angie.'

'Like the Rolling Stones song?' he smiled.

I looked at him suspiciously. He'd delved further with his mind worms than I'd expected. The song would often play on loop in our house. Dad would take her by the hand and they'd slow-dance in a way I've not yet experienced but hope to one day. Though back then, I'd pull out my tongue in disgust. Dive into the sofa cushions to hide my horrified yet excited face.

'Yes, that's right. It was played at her funeral.'

'Oh . . . I'm . . . I'm sorry.' He returned his glasses to his face. Embarrassed. At least, I thought he was. But he carried on. 'And what was she like?'

'Like?'

'Yes . . . Tell me about her. How would you describe her?'

'I don't know . . . She . . . she looked a bit like me, I guess. A tad taller, though.' He waited for more. 'And she was funny, without knowing it . . . always getting her words mixed up or saying daft things. She was much prettier than me. Not that she thought so . . . not since . . . not for some time. But you know . . . she was fun. We laughed a lot. When she wasn't sad. Or drunk.'

It was strange how soothed I was. It dawned on me that I never talked about her. Only repetitive thoughts. No one even knew her. Or cared. I'd tried to avoid it all so much she was almost a figment. A ghost I'd become afraid of. But she was my mum. My mum.

'She sounds like someone I'd have liked to have met.'

As I smiled, I caught sight of the clock. I'd only been in there fifteen minutes. My leg pulsed again. Up, down, up, down. It concerned me that if I stayed any longer, my guard might drop too much.

He returned to making notes in his pad. I felt more comfortable with it this time. Almost curious. Until he said, 'Why was she sad?'

'What?'

'You said she was fun when she wasn't drunk or sad. What do you think made her sad?'

I shrugged. 'I suppose some people just are, aren't they?'

He paused and looked up at me with his hooded eyes. Again waited without a flicker.

'I don't know . . . She just was. That's all . . . since Dad. Even when she wasn't, it was only a window. I'd lose her again at any moment.'

'Since Dad?'

'Sorry, Dr Franco. I . . . I realize I didn't bring any lunch . . . Sorry. I need to get a sandwich or I'll have to go all day without eating.'

'Oh . . . that's a shame. But just stay a couple more minutes if you can. Tell me, why was your mum sad about your dad? Did they divorce?'

I dropped my head and clenched my teeth. 'No.'

'Oh no . . . Did he pass away too? Did something happen to him?'

I was wrong. It wasn't comforting at all. I didn't like it. Loathed the way he rummaged inside me, regardless of how good it felt to bring her back. My hands pushed down into the plush hide of the chair to help me stand.

'I don't know what happened to him, all right. We never did.'

London. A city with a population of nearly nine million and there was I, weaving souls, avoiding bodies, a stranger to them all. The story goes that when I was born, my parents called me Eleanor, after 'Eleanor Rigby'. A couple of days later they changed their minds, concerned I may fulfil her prophecy. Instead, they named me Constance after my grandma, who was decapitated in a car accident when my dad was only five years old. For some reason, they didn't mind me fulfilling that prophecy. Not that it mattered. I was already Eleanor. No one can escape their destiny.

After joining my troops for the Friday-night commuting battle, we stormed the Tube station as our opponents attempted to leave. I found myself behind a particularly annoying man, shuffling along, typing into his phone, oblivious to other people. Instead of politely, patiently following his snail pace, as I ordinarily would, I pressed my undamaged fist into the hollow of his back, while thinking of you, him, her, Dr Franco when I shouted, 'I don't want to do this. It's pointless,' and his annoyingly calm reply: 'I understand, Constance. Shall we say a week on Monday?'

The man turned around. Brow furrowed. I probably would have felt bad at that point, had he not also had a ridiculous handlebar moustache. 'I'm so sorry – someone was pushing into me,' I said.

Surviving the scrum, holding on to the yellow pole inside the carriage, I wondered how many of us squashed in there felt as isolated as I did. Loneliness isn't reserved for the elderly at Christmas, like John Lewis would lead us to believe. It had nothing to do with the nine million people at my fingertips. It was about not being truly seen, connected to another. The day I met you, I ceased to be lonely. And I didn't want to go back to being so again.

Costcutter was far too bright. Armed with a little extra money after having bought a cheaper morning-after pill, I made a dash towards the booze aisle but was distracted by a buy-one, get-one-free Jaffa Cakes stand displayed under a hypnotic flickering fluorescent tube. I threw four packs into the rusty basket.

Aside from me, Mum's best friend was Martini. Or Martin, as it became known between us. She needed him. Just like she needed Dad. On good days she'd say, 'I haven't spoken to Martin today.'

'Well done,' I'd say, followed by a misguided moment of optimism. Until something occurred. Be it a small thing: a bill, forgetting to buy milk when she went to the shops or seeing a happy couple on TV. Then it would change to 'Martin and I have things to discuss.' And I'd lose her to her bedroom.

I didn't buy Martin. Because I despised him for what he did to her. I opted for a litre of Vladimir instead.

The tired-of-life woman on the till packed my Jaffa Cakes,

forty fags and Vladimir into the plastic bag I'd begrudgingly purchased. She glanced up at me for a second, her eye carrying a glimpse of disgust. Or perhaps she was wondering if there were any Jaffa Cakes left for her. Either way, I somehow felt the need to justify myself.

'I'm having a party.' She said nothing, forcing me to add, 'It's my birthday, so I'm having a party.'

'Thirty-six pounds ten,' she said.

Back home, the silence from Dale's room reminded me that he was visiting his parents and I was relieved to be alone and free to finally surrender to my anguish.

I changed into your T-shirt and lay on the bed with Jaffa Cakes to my left, Vlad to my right and Blusha on my chest, unleashing tears to our song, 'At Last', on loop. Imagining you were listening to it too, regretful, thinking of me. Only swapping it occasionally for Martha Wainwright's 'Bloody Mother Fucking Asshole'.

In a short space of time I'd consumed nine fags, half a pint of vodka, emergency contraception and a full pack of Jaffas. I felt damaged and relished the comfort in that. The room spun. I turned onto my side to steady the world, regurgitating liquidized orange jelly into my mouth, which I swallowed back down before circling in and out of sleep, until woken fully by my phone pinging next to my head. The noise brought with it an injection of hope. My drunk-and-disorderly fingers inputted the wrong PIN three times. When I finally unlocked it, there it was. *Domino's, any size pizza for £9.99 weekend special.*

I couldn't return to my sleep. Felt sick. But had to hold

it in for three hours or the pill wouldn't work. I was unable to settle. Didn't know what to do with myself. The feeling was so overwhelming that I needed to replace it with something else. Something worse.

I knelt beside the bed. Dipped underneath into the filthy darkness, reaching to feel the handle of the suitcase, my drunken brain pounding against my skull, and pulled. Click left, unlock. Click right, unlock. Opened the lid. I sneezed in response to the inhaled dust.

Although the picture of you, us, was the first thing I noticed, that wasn't my weapon of torture. The diaries were all there. As always. The last one on the top. The one I feared the most. The one I needed to read yet couldn't even bring myself to touch.

Various colours, differing sizes. Some had the dates on. Others labels. I picked one up. *Journal of Angie Jones.* It was backed in pastel floral wallpaper. Jones was her maiden name, so it was an old one.

I closed my eyes and chose a page at random. *Went to see Flashdance with Michelle tonight and now I want to get my hair permed* . . . I shut it. Couldn't do it. The loops and swirls of her writing. Her voice. Her ghost. It went back in the case. Click left, lock. Click right, lock. And I pushed it even further back under the bed than before.

As I re-emerged, a knock at the door startled me, causing me to bang my head against the frame. When I looked up, rubbing my crown, Dale was standing in the room.

He walked over towards me, dropping his bag on the floor halfway. 'What are you up to?'

'Nothing . . . I . . . I was just sorting some stuff out.

You're back early?' I remained on my haunches, unsure of how much of a state I looked.

He flopped onto the bed. 'Yeah, well, you know the drill. Mum's a control freak, Dad's a bigot, and I'm a huge disappointment . . . Is that vodka?' When I managed to stand, he was holding the bottle in his hand like a disapproving parent. 'You're trashed again, aren't you? Why are you trashed on your own at home?'

I snatched the bottle from him and placed it under the bedside table. 'I'm not trashed. I've just had a bad day, that's all.'

He dropped back onto the duvet. 'Yeah, well, we all have, but there's no need to be an alchy about it.'

It's funny that after all the things that had occurred, it was those words that finally broke the dam. 'I'm not a fucking alchy . . . Don't say that . . . You shouldn't say that.'

Forty-per-cent-proof tears stung my face. Strings of snot and saliva quickly formed. I watched Dale's horrified expression as he stood, grasped that I was crying.

'No . . . no, I was only joking, Constance. I'm sorry . . . What's wrong? Talk to me.' He engulfed me in his arms, rocked me back and forth, kissing my hair.

My instinct was to shrug him off, but I soon gave in to the sensation. It was warm, comforting.

'Hey . . . come on . . . Tell me what's wrong.'

I had two choices. The truth or a lie. So I did the right thing.

'It was the funeral . . . It's brought everything back. I miss her so badly, Dale.'

Not a lie. Just not the entire truth. But you know all about that, don't you?

I unglued my wet face from his shoulder. 'They all leave me. Everyone I love.'

He drew back, took hold of my arms and jolted me to look at him. 'Hey . . . not me. I'm not going to leave you.'

'You say that, but—'

'But nothing.' He entwined his little finger around mine. 'Promise.' He smiled.

When he left to get changed, I noticed the empty pill box that thankfully he hadn't and folded it up, small enough to hide inside an empty cigarette packet on the side. I then contemplated moving over to the couch, but I didn't want to leave the small comfort of my bed, so I switched on the TV and lit a fag, coughing as the smoke entered my fragile body. Dangling over the side, I retrieved the bottle for one last swig before his return, which left me feeling sick again. Checked my phone. Nothing. My mind returned to searching for you in the Castle, and a new torturous idea that you were instead at your flat having sex with a better-suited posh girl. I dragged my hands, harsh, over my face to erase the image. Took another gulp.

When Dale returned, in his 'comfy garb', he threw himself on the bed between me and the wall and said, 'For fuck's sake, we're not watching *Murder, She Wrote*.' So we put on *Blade Runner*. He had to watch it a few times a year and hadn't since June apparently. I didn't care what was on: I couldn't concentrate. My thoughts were only of you. Agonizing. Yet forbidden to be expressed. Like the last scene in *Brief Encounter*. Where she's sat in the armchair and her husband is so happy to have her back. She cries in his arms. But he is unaware that the tears are not for him.

Dale moved Blusha out of the way and gestured for me to rest my head on his chest. Tentatively, I complied. Surprised at the comfort it induced. Exhausted, drunk, I finally relaxed. My eyelids dropped further with each exhalation.

Then he said, 'You know . . . I thought you were seeing someone. And that perhaps it was over.'

I didn't move. Didn't lift my head. 'What do you mean?'

He too remained still. 'The past few weeks . . . I just . . . I just got it in my head you were seeing someone.'

'Why would you think that?'

'I don't know . . . You were . . . different, I guess. You didn't come home—'

'I was with a friend from school—'

'Yeah . . . yeah . . . I know. You said. So, are you?'

'What?'

'Seeing someone?'

I pushed myself up, turned to him. You would have been so proud of me because I looked directly in his eyes and said, 'No . . . no, of course not. You're my best friend. If I was seeing someone, don't you think you'd be the first to know?'

He covered his face with his hands. 'You're right. I'm sorry. That's what upset me – the thought that you hadn't. I know I've been a bit funny lately . . . That was why. I'm sorry . . . and there you were having a really shit time and I was up my own arse.'

I lit a cigarette. 'I promise you I'm not seeing anyone.' Rephrasing it eradicated some of the guilt. Another truth-lie. Except it wasn't, really. It was now just the truth.

Tears crept up on me again.

'Hey . . . I didn't mean to—'

'No, no, it's fine. I'm just drunk.'

But it wasn't that. It was because I was a terrible person, and I never used to be.

He grabbed a roll of toilet paper off the side, wound some around his hand and passed it to me. 'You know, I'm not being truthful.'

I took the paper, confused, and blew my nose.

'I've made out that I'm upset because I thought you hadn't told me you were seeing someone . . . and I was. I mean, that would be upsetting, but—' He stopped.

I was meant to coax it out of him but didn't. I remained mute, head down, wrapping the tissue around my finger. Because I sensed what he wanted to say, and I didn't want him to say it.

'OK . . . fuck it. The truth is, it . . . it felt horrendous. The thought of you being with someone.' His eyes searched for approval, but I just blew my nose again and withdrew my gaze from his, my eyelids descending slowly, focusing on my hands tearing at the screwed-up tissue.

It was so very long, the silence. Loud. After some moments within its deafening boom, he stood. 'Right . . . well, don't I feel the dick . . . ? Erm . . . yeah, I'm not really in the mood for *Blade Runner* tonight, if that's OK?'

It was then I'd intended to say something. At the very least tell him he wasn't a dick. But by the time my lips had emerged from their coma, he was halfway out of the room. 'Dale . . . I—' The door slammed.

I followed him. Knocked on his door. Knocked again. Nothing. Tried the handle, but it was locked.

'Dale . . . come on . . . Please let me in.'

Then there was the sound of explosions, firing of machine guns, the death throes of shot zombies, but no response.

I was back to being alone.

Being Eleanor Rigby.

*

It's impossible to know what course we'd take in life if we hadn't met certain individuals. I was unaware, but you'd altered me. You, a catalyst who had, by definition, remained unchanged.

Dale had disappeared. I heard him leave on the Saturday morning, and he never returned. Even arguing with his parents was preferable to facing me. I shan't pretend I wasn't glad. I needed the space to drink and smoke, alternate between hope and despair.

On the Monday morning I'd woken in the despair mode. Leaving me no choice but to call in with feigned food poisoning. But by ten o'clock, after an hour, pacing, un-settled, I'd returned to hope. Desperate to see you. And by eleven I was standing in reception, a puffy-faced wreck.

'I'm feeling much better now,' I declared to the bewildered faces of Linda and Alison.

It was midday and I still hadn't seen you. Each of your patients arrived early, a conveyer belt of illness, leaving no gap I could take advantage of. When Linda and her prying eyes went to the toilet, I checked the system for the rest of your appointments. Mrs Hall, Mr Pinner, then, thank God, a break.

Mr Pinner was in with you longer than the allocated slot. He didn't even look that ill.

Despite being unable to concentrate, I inputted patient details in order to appear busy to Alison, who was killing me with stories about her new NutriBullet.

'I know what you're thinking – it's the same as any other blender.'

'That's not what I'm thinking, Alison.'

Finally Mr Pinner emerged. I took his debit card and smiled dutifully as he gave Alison a run for her money with his chat about the orchid. It was a Miltonia. Did you know that?

Once he'd left, I was collecting up the paperwork to complete at my desk when I clocked you. I stayed put. Despite my somersaulting stomach, I continued with the notes on the reception desk, my back to you, seemingly unaware of your existence, waiting for what was to surely follow: a request for a coffee or a file. The corners of my mouth flickered upwards as my prediction came true.

'You couldn't make a copy of these and bring them in to me, could you, Alison?'

My mouth dropped. The somersault ended with a crash.

Still I continued writing. Pressing so hard I ruptured the paper, tattooing the wood beneath.

On hearing the buzz of the printer powering up, I turned to see Alison standing next to it, pages edging out, inch by inch.

'I like to add melon to the kale one. As a sweetener.' She

removed each sheet from the machine. Ordered them in her hands. When the last one spat out, she placed it at the bottom of the pile. 'I'm going to try a smoothie tomorrow, banana and strawberry.'

'I hate strawberries. They make my face swell and could kill me.' I grabbed the pages from her. 'I'll take these, Alison . . . don't worry.'

I did knock but didn't wait for the invite before entering.

You were on your computer, engrossed in someone's notes. 'Thanks, Alison. Pop it on my desk, will you.'

As I gently placed it down, the familiarity of your scent both comforted and upset me. However, I mustn't have carried much of an aroma myself, because you continued to gaze at the screen, oblivious. I didn't leave. I stood there. Patiently.

'Is everything OK, Alison?' You finally turned your head. Blood surged to your cheeks. 'Oh, Constance . . . I didn't . . . I thought you were . . .'

'No.'

'Is everything OK?'

'I wondered if we could talk?'

You swivelled your chair to face me. Interlaced your fingers and placed the ankle of your right leg onto the knee of your left, revealing the blue polo player of your red Ralph Lauren sock. 'Of course. What would you like to talk about? Did you take the pill?'

'Yes.'

'Thank you. Well, it was for your sake just as much as mine. So what would you like to talk about?'

As you sat there, cocked-headed, foot wagging, waiting

for me to speak, I felt ridiculous. Smaller than the molecule of crust resting upon your eyelash.

'I . . . well . . . I—'

'I'm quite busy, Constance.'

'I just don't understand.' The words were out there. Bouncing pointlessly around the room.

'You don't understand what?'

I dropped my head. 'Why . . . why you'd say those things, then change.'

'What things?'

My throat clamped. 'That . . . that we . . .'

'You're mumbling now.'

'That we were connected and . . . and that it's a rare thing.' I looked up. Watched as you dropped your head back, revealing a shaving cut on your throat.

'Why are you bringing this up again?' you said to the ceiling. Or God. Was it to God?

'I just don't understand,' I whispered.

You took a long intake of breath, then exhaled loudly. 'OK . . . OK . . . I can't believe we're still doing this, but I'll answer you because I'm a decent guy, and don't like seeing anyone upset, but I don't want to have to answer it again, OK?' You continued as if I'd nodded in agreement. Your face was mapped with red. 'Good, OK . . . I think you're a great girl, and we did connect, or get on or what- ever . . . We still do. But at any point did I say it was more than just a bit of fun? Look, I'm . . . I'm sorry if you believed otherwise. Honestly . . . I'm a straight-down-the- line guy. If I'd thought for one minute that you did or . . . or had any . . . feelings, I would have nipped it in the bud instantly. OK? Is that fair enough? You really have to let it go now.'

I looked into your unblinking eyes. 'So you jeopardized your career, my job, for a bit of fun?'

Your foot dropped to the floor with a thud and you leant forward, placed your hands together, like you were praying, deep in thought. Then you sat up and said, 'Is it going to be a problem, Constance? Us working together? I hope not. Because I enjoy working with you. Really, I do.' You looked at me in a way I'd never known before. Cold.

'No . . . no, of course not . . . I'm sorry.'

'Hey, it's fine. Friends?' You extended your hand for me to shake.

I slowly walked towards you and met it with mine.

'Excellent,' you smiled, gripped. 'Now . . . you couldn't get me a coffee before Mrs Charles arrives, could you?'

It felt as though five o'clock would never come.

While you consulted in your office, not thinking about me, I could do nothing but obsess over you. I'm sure as far as you were concerned, that should have been it. As a doctor, you may have been knowledgeable about the aorta and the ventricles, but you seemed unaware of the real workings of a heart.

When home time finally came, I waited for you outside. To walk with you. Attempt to at least articulate myself better.

As soon as the fresh air hit, I pulled out a fag. Luckily, Linda and Alison didn't wish to linger, so said their goodbyes and left. I headed down towards my usual corner between the steps and the wall. My hands clammy as I rehearsed what

I might say, pulling hard on my cigarette until it depleted, pacing like a deranged tiger in one of those shitty concrete zoos.

The door opened above. I held my breath. Pressed my back against the wall. The sound of soles against the stone of the steps. A hand on the rail. I exhaled. It wasn't your hand. I recognized Dr Franco's gold pinky ring. Once he'd reached the bottom, he walked in the direction of the surgery car park around the side of the building.

I relaxed. Not completely, but enough to breathe and begin another fag. Although it made me nauseous, I needed the assistance.

Once again the door opened. I could sense it was you this time, and I was right. I pressed myself back against the wall. Your buffed, unworked fingers slid down the rail. You were talking. No one else was in view, but as you neared, I could see your headphones were in and realized you were on the phone.

'Yep . . . definitely. Not the green one, no, the other one. OK, so the one on the opposite side, then. The big one. The Wheatsheaf, I think it's called. Yep . . . Friday . . . about seven. OK, Jimbo. Cool . . . See you there, mate . . . You'd better bloody not, you arse . . .'

Engrossed in your conversation, you hadn't noticed me at all.

You were already heading down the road. Unsure of what to do, I set off behind you. Held back, waiting for you to end the call. We hadn't got far when you pocketed your phone, and I took a huge breath before shouting, 'Samuel.' Nothing. 'Samuel.'

The white of your headphones still peeked through your hair. You were no longer talking, so it must have been music that filled your ears. I was uncertain what to do. In hindsight, I should have run up and tapped you on the shoulder. But I stayed behind you. Dropped back further. And as we walked together but not together, I felt something in contrast to the diminished husk you'd reduced me to in your office. Close to you without you knowing. Observing your walk. The slight dip when you dropped onto your left foot. The back of your hair floating in the breeze. Your hand reaching into your pocket like it always did. It was strange how it both excited and relaxed me. I was your invisible shadow. And I felt powerful.

You reached the cemetery. The point at which I should have torn myself away. But I didn't. It was all so easy to continue on your heels. Until you stopped. And I stopped. Heart thumping, I ducked into a driveway, terrified you'd turn and see me. But you were just pausing to fiddle with your handset, then walked on again. As did I.

Once on your street, I didn't cross with you. I made it to Edward's block and stepped under the canopy. My body flat against the pillar, my head turned towards you. An elderly Hitchcock blonde, with unnecessary sunglasses and headscarf, was being pulled by an overenthusiastic Labrador towards your flats. You reached the door at the same time. The dog sniffing you, tail swishing. You patted its head, made indecipherable small talk with Tippi Hedren before unlocking the door and holding it open for her to enter first. Then it shut. And you were gone.

I stayed there for some time. Staring up towards the light

of your flat. Unable to see you, though comforted by your proximity.

Yet it wasn't enough. It would never be enough. But then I remembered about Friday. That there was always the Wheatsheaf.

*

It had been some time since Dale and I had ventured to Connelly's, though nothing about it had changed. I don't think anything about it had changed since the 1990s. We chose the shithole as our local purely due to laziness and economics. It's hard to say what specifically made it a shithole. Perhaps the strip lighting, or the dated mahogany furniture covered in foam oozing burgundy velour, or the clientele: football supporters and ageing alcoholics, the two inter-changeable. Or perhaps it was Gavin, the psycho landlord.

After an awkward walk from the house, Dale held the door open for me to enter.

'All right, babe?' Gavin greeted me as we walked towards the bar, his arm draped over the Foster's pump, exposing his McDonald's tattoo.

I smiled sweetly to avoid being put on some kind of hit list and gave Dale a tenner to get the drinks in, the first step in my bridge-building process.

While heading to our usual spot in the corner beneath the broken wall-mounted TV, I noticed the pool table was free. I'd hoped we'd have a game, break the ice. Dale loved pool but lacked any skill, so I figured he might hate me less if I let him win. The previous player had possibly attempted the same technique. The reds had been potted; the yellows remained. Or they could have just been crap at it. Like Dale.

I didn't think he'd agree to the outing. He'd been avoiding me for days. Staying out late, leaving before I woke. Knowing he was slipping away scared me and I needed his friendship back.

You'd been at Harley Street since Tuesday. They were down a couple of doctors apparently, so I hadn't seen you at all. You didn't answer any of my calls. Never returned them. Not that I'd coherently planned what to say even if you had. Except on the Wednesday when I was eating lunch in the staffroom, zoning out to Alison's grain-by-grain, fold-by-fold recipe for an eggless chocolate cake and my phone lit up with your name. Elated, I nearly choked on my ploughman's baguette.

'Hey . . . hi,' I said, getting up and leaving Alison mid-sentence.

No words greeted me back. Only strange beeping noises and the mumbling of voices.

'Hello . . . hello.' Then I realized it was a pocket call and you were at a supermarket self-checkout.

'We should have a game,' I said as Dale returned with our drinks.

He dropped the change onto the sticky table and shrugged before sitting and supping his pint. The removal of the glass uncovered a froth moustache in place of his usual sweat one.

I sipped on my vodka and Coke, ignored the tension, pushed on through. 'So you're doing OK, then?'

'Yeah, all right.' He stared straight ahead. Picked up his beer again.

'So work's OK?'

'Yes . . . You've already asked me that.'

'Sorry. *Call of Duty*?'

'At the Nazi zombies.'

'Oh good . . . good.' I gulped half my drink. 'So, do you fancy a game of pool, then?'

I could see a minute twitch beneath his eye. He could never turn down a game of anything.

'If we have to,' he said.

We transferred the dire atmosphere to the other side of the pub and he racked up the balls. I filled the silence by vigorously chalking my cue.

'You break,' he said.

When the white barely disturbed the colours, he didn't laugh as he ordinarily would, or joke about my comparison to Paul Newman in *The Hustler*.

It turned out I didn't have to let him win. His sheer determination not to engage created such focus that he was thrashing me.

I was happy to remain in the uncomfortable void, but near the end of the game, I was taking a shot and he said, 'So tell me, Constance, are we going to talk about the other night or what?'

I miscued. The white ball bounced into a pocket. 'Two shots to you,' I said.

He didn't move. Held his cue like a staff.

'I think you should go for that one there, Dale. If you go for the one over the pocket, you'll pot the black.'

'Yes, but it may bounce off the pocket and then I'll still—

Oh for Christ's sake, stop talking to me about the game, will you? Did you not hear me?'

A scolded child, I perched my cue against the wall and followed him with my drink to the tiny table tucked in the corner. We sat on the low stools, positioning ourselves to avoid touching each other's knees.

'You first,' he said.

My legs mirrored what was going on inside. Twisted. Numb. Not wanting to knock him. My only hope being if Gavin flipped out and we'd have to save people's lives. 'I . . . I don't know what to say, though, Dale.'

'Fine . . . I'll start, then.' Instead of doing so, he supped his pint.

I followed suit with my near-empty glass.

'Fuck . . . OK . . . The thing is, Constance . . . we've been friends for a little while now—'

'And our friendship is so important to me.'

'Sure, to me too . . . but, well, the fact is . . . I don't think of you as just a friend anymore.'

Though hardly a surprise, now the words were projected into the universe, I couldn't look at him, never mind reply. I tilted my glass in search of vodka. Only ice remained, so I desperately dug some out with my fingers and sucked on it.

'You see . . . you don't say anything . . . It's so bloody frustrating and I can't work out if it's because you're shy—'

'I . . . I just—'

'Because there's no need to be shy.' He uncurled his fingers from his glass and reached for my hand. Held it. *Cold hands, warm heart.*

I dared to look at him, smile.

'So, you *are* just being shy?'

'No . . . I . . .' I shook my head. My eyes apologized.

His hand released mine to grasp his beer once again, which he then gulped until only white froth slid down the sides. This time, there was an unmistakable slam.

'It's surely been fucking obvious from day one?'

'What has?'

'You know exactly what I mean.'

'I . . . I thought we were friends. That you . . . you were my friend.'

Elbows now resting on the table, he dropped his head into his hands. 'I am . . . I . . . like being your friend . . . Actually, no . . . I don't.' He let out a strange laugh, looked up at me.

I crunched down on the ice in my mouth.

'In truth, I fucking hate it. I hate having to pretend. I hate that I want to kiss you . . . touch you.'

My lips unintentionally contorted as he said the words. His eyes filled with hurt.

'Are you guys playing?' a man in a Chelsea shirt that barely covered his protruding belly shouted over to us from the pool table.

'We are, yes, sorry,' I said.

'No, no. We're done, mate.' Dale put on his jacket and emptied the last dregs into his mouth.

'What are you doing? Are we going?'

He did that laugh again. And before I could gather my bag, follow him, the door of the main entrance was banging shut.

* * *

It was thrashing it down.

I spotted him. Walking, brisk, a way up the road, his jacket now held over his head. Already soaked, I ran to catch up. Each step a jump into a puddle.

'Dale,' I shouted. 'Dale, please.'

A car drove past, drenched me even more. I closed my eyes and caught my breath before gathering myself to belt out the third call: 'Dale.'

He stopped, turned and pounded back down the pavement towards me. To an observer, it would have appeared so romantic as we raced towards each other, met in the middle.

'What, Constance? What do you want?'

Rain trickled inside my mouth. 'I . . . I want us to be friends.'

He closed his eyes, sighed. All was still for a moment. Then he pulled me towards him. As we hugged, I felt everything relax. I smiled into his chest, relieved. Exhaled against his wet T-shirt.

'Look, Constance, I'm sorry . . . I think I should leave . . . move out.'

I removed myself from his embrace. That feeling happened in my stomach. The internal explosion. The panic. My one friend leaving me. Being left.

'What do you mean? You can't . . . Why? You . . . you said you'd never leave me. You pinky-promised.' I held up my little finger in the hope he'd hook on to it. But he lifted his palm to his forehead, losing the grip on his jacket, which splashed onto the ground.

'Jesus, Constance. Not everything is about you, you know.'

I bent down to pick it up, but he pushed my hand away and retrieved the saturated rag, shook it.

'Are you done?' He looked at me, wanting me to say things I couldn't say. 'OK . . . OK, Constance . . . Well, *I'm* done.' He turned, shaking the jacket once again, knowing it was futile, a time-filler.

And all I could do, despite the anxiety rising inside me, as if the rainwater was overtaking my body, covering me, inch by inch, was watch him walk away.

*

It wasn't the first time I'd been to the Wheatsheaf.

During those few stifling days in the early summer, Dale and I had wandered in, enticed by the two-for-one Pimm's offer. But it looked different as I observed it from the opposite side of the road, pulling on my third cigarette in a row, anxious, excited, preparing myself for you.

I still hadn't seen you. Nor had we spoken. I'd abandoned any further attempts at calling. Harley Street had claimed you, and my concerns that you'd stay there were growing.

The one benefit of your absence was that it heightened my confidence in the plan. My presence may surprise you, the coincidence floor you, but any suspicions would be quashed by the fact there was no way I could've known you'd be there. To enforce this, I arrived early. So if anything, it would've been you who appeared to be following me. The only flaw to all this was that I'd be alone. But I'd decided that good old Mary Feely was supposed to be meeting me. 'I'm worried about her,' I'd say. 'It's not like her to not show up, and she's not answering her phone.' That reminds me. I really must find out if Mary is dead or not.

I'd already changed from my work clothes in the toilets of another nearby pub. Determined to make an impact, make you see me differently, grown up. Like Laura. This involved wearing Mum's stuff, not my own. Her pointy black heels, tight red dress. When I came to London, most of the items thrown into my two suitcases belonged to her, not me. I had no choice but to let go of the house contents, but clothes, clothes are different. They're still the person. Carry their essence. Though some were merely pieces of material, cuts of leather. I left those with ease. But others, it was as though she was still alive. Wearing them, yet invisible. And when I'd pulled up the straps of the dress, positioned my foot into the well of the shoe, she was with me. Or perhaps I became her. All I know is, when I'd stared into the mirror in the toilets of the Rose and Crown – voluminous hair, make-up strong – it wasn't me.

Heaving open the door of the Wheatsheaf, I was relieved to find the place was already murmuring with after-work drinkers and was reminded of the abundance of areas and alcoves where I could watch, hide.

At the bar, I took my position next to two shiny-headed middle-aged men wearing shirts draped with loosened ties and ordered myself a vodka and Coke.

The nearest man elbowed his friend, then turned to me, smiling, twenty-pound note in hand. 'Can I get that for you, sweetheart?'

I paid the bartender. 'It's OK, thanks . . . I'm meeting someone.'

'Not a John, by any chance?' They both laughed as if it was the funniest thing in the world, but I didn't understand and had no idea who John was.

Drink in hand, I couldn't get away quickly enough and headed over to the large table on the raised section towards the back, in order to get a clear view of the main door.

Sat, waiting, heart near exploding, barely able to control the glass enough to direct the liquid into my mouth, the reality of what I was doing hit me. How insane it suddenly felt. But I reasoned with myself and reapplied my lipstick. Because ultimately, Samuel, you gave me no choice.

The place soon filled up, obscuring more and more of my vision. The atmosphere hummed with enjoyment, laughter. Heads back, arm slapping. People with their friends. People had friends.

I forced myself to restrict my sips, knowing that being drunk wouldn't help me. But I was finding it difficult and would have happily been on my third.

Then I waited.

And waited.

Seven arrived and left without any sign of you.

But at seven twenty came a stroke of luck.

A group of dolled-up young women, carrying a variety of glittery gift bags and gaudy parcels, approached the table. They infiltrated the area, claimed the seats. I was about to make some sarcastic 'Sure, no one's sitting there' comment when the long-haired brunette in the blood-flow-restricting dress picked up a previously un-noticed plastic 'reserved' sign between her gem-encrusted talons and said, 'Well, it must be this one . . . She did say at the back.'

Realizing my mistake, I stood and was about to apologize

when a woman with envy-inducing candyfloss-pink hair asked if I was there for Jen's birthday.

'No. I . . . I'm sorry. I'll get out of your way.'

She smiled through her annoyance at my accidental gate-crashing, so I embellished as I climbed over a chair to escape: 'I'm sorry . . . I didn't realize it was reserved. I was meeting a date, but I think I've been stood up.'

Her expression changed. 'You're joking.' She turned to the brunette. 'Did you hear that, Kate? She's been stood up by her date.'

'Oh what? That's awful . . . I'm so sorry, darling.'

'Don't get Kate started,' said Pink Girl.

'No, don't get me started . . . They're all arseholes. Fucking hate the lot of 'em. What's your name, hon?'

'Constance.'

'Hey, everyone, shush a minute . . . This is Connie. Some arsehole's gone and stood her up.' The gang mumbled their condolences.

My eyes filled. The earlier realization reinforced. I wanted to go home. Remove my facade.

'Hey, don't you be crying over the wankers, Connie . . . You stick with us for the night, darling . . . Jen won't mind, will she, Kate? If Connie joins us? We can't let a bloke just leave her hanging like that.'

'No, you stay with us, Connie. Was it Tinder?'

I nodded.

'Well, he'd be twenty stone heavier, ten years older and have commitment issues, so you stick with us – you'll have a much better time.'

Ordinarily, I would have bolted. I wasn't part of their

world. Had nothing to say to them, no common ground apart from my dress, which wasn't even mine. But it was the perfect scenario for being there. I was out with my friends. Like a normal person. So I took it as a divine sign. Approval.

Before long I'd been invited to other events: Shelly's barbecue and a shopping trip followed by tapas. All lovely gatherings I definitely wouldn't attend. Even the birthday girl welcomed me in, once she arrived. I endeared myself to her by buying her a pina colada, complete with umbrella and sparkler. It was all quite touching, really. I was unused to being around women in this way, but it was nice. Though I didn't see that at the time. I was only concerned with you.

It was nearly nine. The place was heaving. A myriad of people, none of them you. I'd made attempts to search, but you were nowhere, and each time the girls pulled me back to sink more Jägerbombs and sing songs from *Frozen*.

There was talk about going on to a club. The effects of the alcohol had mutated from fun to maudlin. The disappointment overwhelming. Barely able to focus, I broke free to stagger to the bathroom.

Waiting in the queue, I caught myself in the mirror. A stranger. A black-eyed, smeared-lipped stranger. I left the line and went over to the sink, yanked a wad of paper towels from the dispenser and wet them under the tap. Wiping my stupid face clean of the futile attempts at desirability, I realized it was her. Mum. Looking back at me. The mess in the dress. Lava rose inside and I threw the sodden ball of paper at her image, gripped the sides of the sink, dropped my head and shouted, 'Fuck,' into the plughole.

When I turned around, I was faced with a wall of staring women.

'I've been stood up, OK? And it's my birthday.'

'Purple Rain' played as I dug around the work clothes stuffed in my bag in search of my fags and battled back through the fun and frolics.

Pack in hand, I looked up towards my goal, the exit. Then I blinked, long, hard. The song slowed. I thought I was so intoxicated I'd imagined it.

You.

Leaning casually against the wall of an alcove. Your shirt half untucked. Swaying. Eyelids drooping. Talking, laughing with your two friends, who looked like they'd just stepped out of a Tory conference.

Someone jostled me from behind. Squeezed past, carrying drinks over my head. Sticky liquid dripped onto my deflating hair. I remained rooted, unsure of what I should do. Unsure of what I wanted to do. But soon the choice was taken from my hands.

You'd put your empty pint glass down on a shelf and headed towards the direction of the bar. My direction. Slow motion. And as you neared, your eyes widened, your head jerked back in shock. Then there you were, standing right in front of me.

'Hey . . . Constance . . . What are you doing here?'

I smiled, my lips snagging on my teeth as my mouth drained of saliva. People pushed past, but we defied the current. You'd raised your voice above the music, but I didn't reply.

Presuming I hadn't heard, you dropped your head, placed your warm mouth against my ear. 'I said, what are you doing here?'

I closed my eyes, inhaled the alcohol on your breath. Wanting to turn and kiss you. The tingles when your words brushed my flesh had been born of something mutual. I knew they were. I felt it. The electricity running two ways.

Now my turn to speak, you dipped your ear towards my lips.

'I'm just here with friends,' I said, pointing towards the real people I didn't even have to make up. 'What about you? What are you doing here?'

You held both arms out in an exaggerated shrug. 'Fuck knows.' You laughed at yourself for a moment, then said, 'You look nice.'

I needed to hear the words again. 'What? Sorry? What did you say?' I bent my neck further, not just to listen but to expose more flesh. More of my scent.

'I said, you look really nice. Very sexy.'

We swapped again, like Europeans kissing cheeks. 'Oh . . . Oh right . . . Thank you.'

I noticed your eyes linger on my chest. Then you closed them for a few seconds, bit your lip.

Neither of us spoke for a moment. I wanted to stay there forever, but my purpose was complete. You'd seen me again. Differently. *Always leave them wanting more*, Mum would say, after she'd already given too much.

'Well, it's good to see you, Dr Stevens . . . I'd better get back to my friends now.' Bravely, I stepped away, then felt a clamp around my wrist.

'Hey . . . come on. Don't "Dr Stevens" me . . . Stay, talk to me.' As if you'd forgotten what you'd done. How you'd not responded to my calls. Yet I allowed you to walk me, hand in hand, to another alcove by the fruit machines.

It was happening. What I'd dreamt of, prayed for. We were standing so close. You, holding my hand, inspecting it like a precious gem.

'Hey, I'm . . . I'm sorry I've not called you back . . . Arghhh, you look so hot tonight . . . When did you get so hot? I'm . . . I'm a fuck-up, Constance . . . you know . . .'

Is it possible to be equally thrilled and offended? Because I was. I should have told you I needed to get back to my friends. Made you work harder. But you leant in, your nose nuzzling into my neck, and it felt so much better than all the pain.

Beyond your shoulder, I could see your mates looking over, pointing, laughing. You placed your lips onto mine. We were back together, kissing. As natural and right as it always was. And it all seemed so silly then. The tears, the hurt, the distress.

You led me outside. Aside from the clutch of people standing around smoking, it was cool and still, in contrast to the rowdiness indoors. My hand gripped yours.

'Let's share a fag,' you said.

Adrenaline was sobering me up, but I couldn't suppress my smiles, the happiness that emanated from me.

The music and laughter from inside were muffled and distant. My ears rang with the quiet. I lit a cigarette and handed it to you. After your first drag, you coughed.

'You really shouldn't smoke, you know,' I said.

You laughed and tried again. 'It's your fault – you're a bad influence on me.'

As the smoke bellowed from your lips, you threw me a sideways look.

'What?' I asked.

You handed back the ciggie. 'Nothing. Just I've missed you.'

I've. Missed. You.

I wanted to scream to the sky I'd missed you too, but I smiled and said, 'You're drunk.'

'Fucking hell, you're right . . . You're always right, Constance, you know that? I am drunk . . . but you know what they say? Many a true word . . . Shit . . . That's jest . . . But I have – I've missed you.'

'I . . . I've missed you too,' I dared.

The pub doors flew open. A group of revellers spilt out. Their unwanted, noisy world infiltrating ours. I looked down at my aching over-arched feet as we stopped talking, waiting for them to disappear. Defended our bubble.

Then you said, 'Come here . . . I want to show you something.'

With your arm draping my shoulders, you walked me down the side of the building. It was difficult for me to keep up in her shoes. The heel tips were wearing down, uneven, and I nearly went over on my ankle.

'Where are you taking me?'

'Shhh.' You placed your finger over your mouth.

We turned a corner. It was devoid of light. Some kind of alleyway. I giggled, but it was almost pitch-black and I became disorientated.

'What? What are you showing me? I can't see a thing.'

Your hands slid around my waist, and you pushed me against the cold brick wall, your mouth hovering over mine.

'You really like me, don't you, Constance?'

I nodded, then realized you couldn't see me. 'Yes . . . I do.'

You wrapped your arms around me, hugged me tight. We swayed, my head nestling into your chest. Lack of vision accentuated your smell, the usual citrus mixed with booze and tobacco.

'But why? Why do you like me so much?' you whispered.

I released my arms and copied your earlier exaggerated shrug. 'Fuck knows.' I laughed, but you didn't join in, and the silence told me you were seeking a genuine answer. I returned my arms to your body. 'Well . . . you're handsome . . . and funny—'

'I can't hear you.'

'I said, you're handsome and funny, and we have things in common, and . . .'

'And?'

'And we have a connection.'

'Is that it?'

'And . . . I don't know . . . Being with you just . . . It makes me happy.'

We stayed there. Locked together in silence. Consumed in the strangeness, I wanted the embrace to last an eternity.

But that wasn't what happened, was it?

'What about me? What do you like about me?' I asked.

No words came. Only the sharpness of the wall against my back as you kissed me. Harder than before. Harder than ever before. When you gripped my hair, your nails dug into my scalp. Do you even remember? Do you remember what happened when you were pressing up against me? I wanted it to happen. I think. But I was also scared. In the dark. You were pulling up my dress. It was tight and difficult, and I had to help you. I heard the rustling of a condom packet being torn open. You were carrying a condom. You didn't know I'd be there, but you were carrying a condom. The bricks grazed my flesh as you pulled my knickers aside and pushed inside me. I couldn't look in your eyes, connect, because I couldn't see your eyes. But I kept saying to myself, *It's OK. He wants you again . . . He wants you.*

It didn't last long.

There was the sound of you removing the condom and pulling up your zip. Your shoes clacked against the concrete as you took a few steps away from me. Then there was the noise of you heaving, followed by the splash of the contents against the floor.

'Sorry . . . sorry, Constance . . . Hey, we've gone full circle. You now have to ask me if I'm pregnant.' You laughed.

I tugged down my dress. My finger got caught in a tear at the seam.

'Are you OK?' I asked.

'Yes. Yes, sorry . . . I'm a bit trashed. We should go . . . You ready?'

You escorted me out of the alley. As the world became lighter, I felt exposed, but you were kind and put your arm around me as we walked back towards the pub. I could now see the tear, so removed my bag from my shoulder and held it against my hip to cover it.

As we approached the entrance, your two friends were there, shoulders lifted, jigging as if cold.

One of them saw us approaching and pointed. 'Oy-oy, Sam,' he shouted over.

I smiled, nervous about meeting them. Then, when we were about twenty feet away, you stopped.

'Look . . . I'm going to have to go.'

I was confused at first, thought you were replying to your mate but hadn't said it loud enough. My teeth chattered. 'Oh, I . . . Can I come with? I think my friends will have left now.'

'I wish you could, but it's boys' night . . . They'd go ape-shit. You know how it is.'

I nodded. Smiled. But I didn't know. I didn't know at all.

'Here . . . take this and get a cab home.' You handed me thirty quid. I accepted it like a hooker.

'Samuel, you bastard,' shouted your other friend.

'It was good to see you, Constance. Really. I'll see you Monday.' You appeared suddenly quite sober. As was I.

You walked away. Then your steps turned into a sprint, which ended with you jumping onto the back of one of the Tories, like a good old boys' rugger scrummage. I stayed rooted. Cold and aching. Watching as you were being piggy-backed down the road. The same road from which I'd earlier observed the pub with so much hope.

*

I watched a documentary last night. I do things like that now. It was about the rivers in India that are so polluted they both give life and take it away.

You were my toxic river.

I hadn't seen Dale all weekend. Then on the Sunday evening I received a text saying he was staying with his parents for a couple of weeks. I tried not to let it ruin everything, scare me. Told myself that he'd return as if nothing had happened, loving me as my friend. Wanting it to all go back. I decided to enjoy the freedom of thought his absence brought. The joy of starting things up with you once again.

When Monday finally came, I sat at my desk, clean and prettied up. You arrived late, unshaven with bloodshot eyes. Stomping through reception, you brought with you an atmosphere that put me on edge. Seeing me didn't soften you at all.

'Sorry I'm late . . . Constance, could you bring me a strong coffee, please?'

You disappeared without waiting for my reply. It was a demand, not a request. And something defiant inside prevented me from jumping up to fulfil your wishes. I continued to type a letter for Dr Harris, and as I was finishing it, my rebellion was encouraged to last longer by him bringing me another.

'Girls, can I speak to you all a moment?'

We stopped what we were doing to give him the attention he required.

'You'll probably be surprised to know . . . that I'll be turning fifty in a couple of weeks.'

I wasn't surprised; I was astonished. I'd had him down as being at least sixty.

'Mrs Harris is insisting that we have a bash to commemorate the milestone, and I'd very much like to invite you to join us. It's only at our house, nothing fancy. That's in Chelsea, so not far . . . next Saturday, the seventeenth. I'll send over the address to the reception email. OK . . . well, I don't wish to keep you.'

Linda and Alison excelled with their sycophancy. 'Oh, that's marvellous, Dr Harris . . . Thank you, Dr Harris . . . Let me crawl up your arse and live there, Dr Harris.'

Then I realized you'd be going too, so joined in. 'That sounds lovely, Dr Harris.'

My spirits raised, I decided it was now time to make your coffee.

'Thank you, Constance. You couldn't just pop it there, could you?' You gestured to a space on the desk, beyond your diary, and sat back to watch me walk, place it carefully. 'And then can you shut the door.'

I did as I was told, excited for the return of our clandestine interactions, whispered secrets.

'It was good to see you the other night,' you said.

'Yes . . . yes, you too.'

You puffed your cheeks and blew like you were slowly extinguishing birthday candles. 'What a crazy night . . . I'm still suffering.' You took a sip of the coffee and pulled the same unimpressed face you did on that first day.

'Sorry . . . You said strong, so I put a bit more—'

'No . . . no, it's fine . . . thank you.' You smiled, but I didn't believe it. 'Listen, Constance . . . I'd have liked to have been able to chat longer, but you took your time, and now Mrs Rose is due any second. I just wanted to say . . . Well, I . . . I was pretty wasted on Friday . . . as I think you were too . . . and I . . . Well, I can't remember much of what happened . . . and . . . Wow, this is embarrassing, but . . . we . . . we didn't kiss, did we?'

I tried to compute what you'd said. Thinking I must have been confused, misheard. But you continued talking while removing files from the open bag lying at your feet.

'I do remember you looking very sexy, though. So it wouldn't be entirely my fault if we did kiss.' You smiled again, as transparent as an insect's wing. 'But we're in such a good place now, I'd hate to fuck up our friendship in any way.'

I latched on to the door handle behind my back for stability and finally sourced words. 'So . . . you . . . you really don't remember?'

Your head hung over the files that now lay on the desk. Your fingers pushed through your hair. 'Oh God, we did, didn't we?'

You swivelled to face me fully. Looked right at me. I

attempted to search inside you, extract the truth from your concerned face. But I couldn't.

'Yes. Yes, we kissed.'

You blinked, long, drawn out. 'Well, we can't blame ourselves, I suppose . . . We were drunk . . . These things happen. But I am sorry for potentially jeopardizing our friendship like that.' You held out your hand. 'Still friends?'

There was a knock at the door.

I wanted to take my palm and slap you across your smiling face, but instead I placed it softly into yours.

'Come in,' you shouted.

The door opened to expose an uppity face.

'Mrs Rose. Good to see you. Please take a seat.'

As she moved across to the chair, placed her beautiful tan Birkin bag on the floor, you picked up the coffee. 'Constance, actually, you couldn't remake this, could you? I didn't like to say, but it's a tad bitter.'

Back at my desk, after taking in the improved coffee, I appeared calm as I quietly inputted the notes that lay before me.

Inside, I was feral.

An alternative-reality film rushed my mind in which I burst into your office, threw the coffee over your head, told you what we really did, you did, smashed things, and before I left, stole Mrs Rose's bag.

I remained in this state for the rest of the morning. So consumed that I'd forgotten about my meeting with Dr Franco at lunch.

*　*　*

The chair felt comfier this time, but I refused to allow myself to sink completely into the soft leather and tried to ignore the small box of tissues he'd positioned on the table next to me.

Once back in his seat, he shuffled papers, hitched up his trousers and crossed his legs to expose the small Superman emblem on his royal-blue sock.

'So, how are we doing, Constance?'

'Good. How are you?'

I'd hoped I'd keep him talking, use up the time, but he said, 'I'm very well, thank you . . . So, you were telling me about your dad when you had to go last time.'

The fury I felt at my not remembering and cancelling the appointment escaped through my tapping foot. 'You've definitely got the best room in the building, you know, Dr Franco.'

'Thank you. It is indeed lovely when the sun streams in.'

I focused on the wall of floating dust particles, illuminated by the slice of light beaming through the window. That's what happens in a room like that. Hidden dirt is exposed.

'So, you were going to tell me about your father?'

'I already did.'

'You mentioned you didn't know what happened to him?'

'No.'

'Well, why don't you tell me about the last time you saw him?'

'I was only six.'

He eased back into his chair and placed his pen on his pad.

'I mean, I was only six, so . . .'

'So you don't remember it?'

'Well, I . . . I suppose I do . . . I . . .'

He paused again. This time removing his glasses, expressing his willingness to wait.

So I told him. As I'm about to tell you. To help you understand.

She was cooking. Real food, like she did back then. A Sunday roast. Beef and Yorkshire pudding. My favourite. I salivated as the smells floated into the lounge, where I lay on the floor watching cartoons. Our dog, Alfie, pawed my back as I repeatedly swatted him away, scolded him. It wasn't Alfie's fault. I was already sulking because I'd not long asked if I could have a packet of crisps.

'Don't be ridiculous, Connie. Dinner will be ready soon.' She was having none of it, didn't understand how hungry I was, how much I liked beef and Yorkshire pudding, and would still eat it no matter what.

Dad was upstairs playing his guitar. He'd practise for hours on Sundays. I heard him tell Mum once it was the only thing he had left of himself. She said, 'For Christ's sake, Patrick, that ship's sailed.'

He was my pop star. I'd always request the song 'In the Gateau': *As the cream dries . . . where the chocolate and cherries are . . . a chubby little baby falls . . . In the gateau.* It'd make me giggle beyond my control. The image of a baby falling into a giant cake was too much. It wasn't until I was seventeen, listening to the radio in my room, and the DJ introduced a song by Elvis called 'In the Ghetto' that I realized he'd just changed the words. That our song never really existed.

Mum was in a strange mood. I think she'd been crying. I'd heard her in the bathroom earlier. And the night before. And the night before that.

They hadn't argued for a long time. Not since we came back from holidaying at the caravan in Llandudno with the Parkers and their daughter, Marsha. I liked Marsha. She was seven and taller than me. We collected hundreds of pebbles and shells in a bucket together on the beach. Counted them in the evenings. But after the holiday Mum said I couldn't see Marsha again because Mrs Parker was a whore.

A religious programme followed the cartoons. I wanted to turn over but was worried God would be angry with me. So I rested my head on Alfie's tummy and drifted off to sleep with him, until I was woken by Dad stroking my hair.

Rubbing my tired, prickly eyes, I pulled myself up from the floor. Alfie had woken too and was jumping all over Dad.

'Good boy. Good boy, Alfie,' he said, until it got too much and changed to 'Get down. Get down, Alfie.' He obeyed, like the good dog he was, and dropped to the floor, flat, his eyes the only part of him moving. *Doing his Princess Di look*, Mum called it.

Dad dropped to my level and pulled me in for a hug. The softness of his suede jacket tickled my cheek. I could see his guitar behind him, perched against his chair. I hung from his neck like a monkey, giggling, 'Stop it . . . stop it,' as he kissed my head all over. 'Will you help me colour in?'

The kisses ended and he released me. 'I've got to go, Connie.'

'But I want to do colouring.'

'I can't, baby. I can't.'

As he stood, I played our game. Where I'd latch on to his leg, refusing to let go, and he'd walk around with me clinging to his ankle. I'd laugh until I'd nearly wet myself, and he'd pretend he couldn't find me. 'Where's Connie?' he'd say. 'Has anyone seen Connie?'

But he didn't say it this time. Didn't play along.

Mum emerged from the kitchen, wiping her brow with a manky tea towel. Mascara smudged beneath her dimmed eyes. 'Dinner will be ready in half an hour.'

'Right. Thanks,' said Dad.

'Oh, and we've run out of Bisto. Could you pick some up while you're out?'

'Sure.'

'Where are you going?'

'For a walk.'

'Right . . . Well, dinner will be ready in half an hour.'

He dragged me over to her. I looked up between them. 'Angie . . . I'm . . . I'm sorry.' He lifted her chin and kissed her lips.

'Me too, Patrick . . . I really am.' She swiped across her eyelids with a twisted corner of the towel. 'Let go of your dad, Connie.'

'No,' I snapped.

A loud sizzling sound filled the room. She took a moment to realize what that meant, then said, 'Shit,' and ran into the kitchen.

'Come on, Connie, get off now. I've got to go.' He looked down. A looming giant.

'No.'

Bending his knees, he crouched in front of me. 'Connie . . . I've really got to go.'

'No.'

Then something strange happened. He dropped his head and cried. The same way Mum would. Pushing his fingers through his thick, oily hair as he sobbed.

I didn't know what to do. I'd never seen him cry before. So I just watched him.

'Please, sweetheart.' He looked at me with such a sad expression that I released my tiny arms and let go of his leg.

Once free, he kissed me on the forehead and rose. He wasn't crying anymore. Said nothing. Didn't look at me again. Merely picked up his guitar and left.

We ate our roast in silence. Without gravy.

Mum placed her knife and fork down every few minutes and phoned him. Growing angrier each time there was no answer.

Once we'd finished eating, she called other people. Each conversation ending with the words 'Thanks anyway.'

After feeding his dinner to Alfie, she cleared the table as normal and did the washing-up.

Knowing she needed company, I fetched my colouring book and worked on my blue rabbit. After sitting opposite me, she reached into her apron, pulled out her packet of cigarettes and lit one up, while I squeaked the felt-tip, back and forth. She didn't cry. Or talk. Or tell me how good my bunny was. Just smoked and smoked and smoked until I felt nauseous from the thick, stale air.

* * *

She put me to bed early that evening.

When tucking me in, she didn't mention him, yet we both knew he wasn't coming back. My heart pushed against my chest. Stuffed with things it would carry forever. But I didn't cry. Didn't want to make her sad.

Once she'd left, I grabbed on to Blusha, who looked at me like the dumb elephant she was, and I took one of her eyes between my fingers and twisted and twisted until it was in my hand and cotton bled through the hole. And then, then I cried.

Dr Franco put on his glasses and scribbled in his notepad. 'That's difficult for you to talk about, isn't it, Constance? It felt like you'd become that little girl again.' He gestured towards the box of tissues, which I refused to use. 'How does it make you feel? Talking about that day?'

My hands were crossed over my chest, pushing. 'I . . . I don't know.'

'It must have been hard for you. A little girl losing her father like that and never knowing why. Then your mother so tragically.'

I looked up at him, smiled. He was supposed to know things but was clueless.

'So tell me. What have you taken away from what happened? What beliefs did young Constance create from this?'

I didn't need to be in that stupid room to think about that. I'd always known the answer. But I humoured him. 'Well, I suppose . . . everyone I love leaves me.'

'Is that what you think?'

'That's fact. And it's my fault.'

'Constance, you're not to blame for any of that. Not your father leaving . . . not your mother's death.'

I laughed again and swiped a tissue from the box. Twisted it around my index finger.

'You were a young child—'

'But it *was* my fault, Dr Franco . . . It all was.' The tissue seemed to have magicked into confetti, which I let fall upon my knees.

'Why do you say that? What would make you think it was your fault?'

'Did you not listen to what happened?'

'I did. I listened to everything. And there was nothing that showed me it could be your fault in any way.'

'Can I go, please? I need to get a sandwich.'

'Of course.' He sat back, closed his book.

I didn't move. Aside gripping on to my ponytail with both hands.

'Constance . . . I want to help. If there's something you think you did as a young child that made your father leave, it might be good to say.'

'For Christ's sake . . . I let go, OK. I let him go.'

I stood. The tissue fragments floated to the floor. 'I'm very sorry for shouting, Dr Franco, but I really do need to be going now. It's bad for me not to eat anything.'

'Of course. I understand.'

I didn't look at him as I retrieved my bag, collected the tissue pieces, but I could feel his gaze upon me right until I reached the door.

'Constance . . . I hope we can talk again, and that you have taken something from today?'

Poor Dr Franco. I envisaged him being quite worried about me when I left his room. Though he needn't have been. As I strode down the corridor, through reception, into the freedom of the cool air, I felt so much clearer. Not because my guilt had been alleviated but because it cemented what I already knew.

If you love someone, never let them go.

*

From that point on, you acted as though nothing had happened.

When asking for a coffee or requesting a file, you behaved as though we'd not recently kissed each other's lips, that you hadn't been inside me, squeezed my half-naked body as it beat against the jagged brickwork of an alley wall. Hadn't looked me in the eye and told me you missed me. So I had no choice but to accept you really didn't know.

I never disclosed the truth. Fluctuating between thankfulness for you not remembering me in that humiliating way and uncertainty it even happened at all.

I performed my role with aplomb. You would never have known that when my eyes opened each morning, you were my first thought. That accompanying that thought was an agitation which increased throughout the day. How every non-intimate conversation you led cut me, diced me.

And you had no idea that after we'd say goodbye at the end of each day, I'd follow you home.

Initially I'd convinced myself it was accidental. That I was merely having a cigarette in the corner by the steps. That you happened to be leaving and I was too slow to catch you up. After all, I was only walking home, taking the same route.

It was perfectly acceptable. If you'd turned around, I would've smiled, explained how you hadn't heard me shouting due to your headphones. But after a few times I didn't need to convince myself of anything. Because I didn't care.

I needed it.

In the same way I needed nicotine.

I often question what I gained from seeing you perpetually walk away from me.

There was of course the ability to be close to you. The comfort your proximity provided. The luxury of being able to concentrate, analyse your every movement, every stroke of your hair, tilt of your head. Wondering what music you were listening to. If it was our song.

And there was something else. Something I hadn't accounted for. Unlike when you were rejecting me – requesting coffees, files, fucking me in alleyways then forgetting – it was me, not you, who was in control.

But how quickly we develop tolerance to our drugs.

Initially I was content with hiding against the pillar of the opposite flats, watching as you'd disappear through your door. The exercise completed, finished, like a stamped-out cigarette. But soon it became harder to leave. Staring up at your window, I'd wonder what you were doing, where you were doing it. Desperate to see. Frustrated I couldn't.

It was then I realized that I needed to increase my dose.

*

Edward's flat was even more eccentric than I recalled.

I hadn't absorbed it in its entirety the first time. Smoking squirrel, the diving helmet and Ursula were as I'd remembered, although dulled by an additional layer of dust. But somehow, previously, I hadn't noticed the terrifying shark's skeleton jaw that hung above the mantelpiece, where you'd expect the elderly to house a fake Constable. And even more disconcertingly, I realized I was standing upon a real tiger-skin rug.

Sensing my disapproval, he said, 'Don't you worry – I killed it with my bare hands when it attacked me.' I laughed politely, but his straight face left me unsure if he was joking.

He was so delighted at my visit that I resented the guilt it created. His crinkled face was warmer, friendlier than on our first encounter. Though to be fair he hadn't just been attacked by a youth.

'I'd got biscuits in just for you, Constance, you know, and not eaten them for all this time because I knew you'd come.'

'Garibaldis?'

'No . . . no . . . sorry. They're custard creams. Would you have preferred Garibaldis?'

'No, no, not at all. Custard creams are perfect.'

He gestured for me to sit. 'I'd just boiled the kettle as well. I must have known.'

I remained standing, feeling the need to justify myself. 'I'm really sorry for not coming sooner. I've had lots on, and, well, time goes so quickly.'

'You mustn't apologize. I was a young man only but yesterday, so am all too aware of how time can slip away . . . Anyway, I knew you'd come eventually.'

The air was claggy with the stench of fried bacon. He must have noticed my nostrils twitching because he picked up a canister of air freshener from the table next to his chair and squirted fake flowers into the room. 'Just had my dinner. Anyway, dear girl, you sit and I'll get the tea.'

Instinctually I began to offer to make it, then stopped myself and sat as requested. Exactly where I wanted to be. Planned to be. In the chair next to the window.

To my annoyance, Edward remained in the lounge, small-talking about a turn in the weather and how he'd wanted to get Jaffa Cakes, but they only had these weird strawberry ones. 'There's nothing Jaffa about a strawberry, is there? Terrible idea . . . terrible.'

I smiled, nodded as he wittered on. But all I could think about was you.

Finally, after the obligatory 'Is a Jaffa Cake a cake or a biscuit?' discussion, he left the room and I was able to turn to the window.

Tranquillizer injected into my veins.

There you were. Sitting on the sofa, staring at the television. Wine glass in hand, filled with red. Changed into your old David Bowie T-shirt. I recalled its touch, velvety and worn. Watching you intently, I analysed every laugh, every movement, until the percussion of tinkling spoons against crockery broke my trance.

His distorted, quivering hands placed a rose-trimmed cup and saucer, a bowl of sugar lumps and a small matching plate piled with biscuits on the table next to me. I thanked him, though my words fell quiet against the sound of his breathlessness, akin to someone having climbed Everest. The wheezing lessened once he'd dropped into his chair, and I attempted to speak again.

'Thank you, Edward.'

After sipping the tea, grease coated my lips. I suppressed a gag, imagining the cup languishing in a cupboard since the 1950s.

'It's still a little hot,' I said, wiping my mouth with the back of my hand and returning the cup and saucer to the table. 'So anyway, Edward, how've you been?'

'Well, you know. The same as always . . . Don't forget the custard creams. Come on.'

I took a biscuit, trying not to look at the state of the plate beneath. 'And how's that?'

'Good . . . I'm good.'

I understood his lie.

He removed his glasses and brought them down towards the paisley handkerchief on his lap. It was obvious he could no longer see as he rubbed them clean. I turned away. You were on the phone. Who were you on the phone to?

'How about you?' he said.

I returned to looking at him as he raised his glasses back to his face.

'Me? I'm . . . I'm good too, thanks.' I smiled. And he stared at me, without saying a word. Making me so uncomfortable that I resorted to taking a sip from the filthy cup.

'You have a lot of interesting things, Edward. A lot of . . . things. How does someone ever get to own a smoking squirrel?'

'Oh, Cyril? I've had him since the sixties. He came from a tobacco shop on the King's Road that was closing down. The bastards were going to throw him away, so I saved him from certain second death.'

'I see . . . Well, there's so much it's hard to know where to look.'

'It was my mother's fault. Well, isn't everything? She was an actress . . . theatre mainly . . . Collected artefacts from her tours around the world. Always had an eye for the most wonderful things. "The items we own must either be a thing of beauty or tell a story," she'd say. And so that's the rule I've stuck to. And let me tell you, Constance . . . there's been a lot of stories. Obviously, sometimes they're both. Like with dear Ursula.'

'What's the story with Ursula?'

'Ah, now, not all stories are meant to be told.' With the hanky, he wiped his magnified eyes underneath his glasses. 'I'd like to show you something, Constance . . . You help yourself to more biscuits.'

Seeing his struggle to rise, I went over to help him, to be greeted by his hand tapping me away. 'Don't be bloody ridiculous . . . What do you think I do when I'm on my own?'

I apologized and returned to my seat. Turning, so he didn't

feel the pressure of me watching him. You were still on the phone. Laughing. Sipping on your wine. Enjoying the conversation far too much. My stomach curdled, so I refocused on Edward, shuffling towards the huge cabinet and pulling down the back of his risen jumper, which exposed his purple crackled skin. As he rooted in one of the cupboards, I stood and rested my hands against the windowpane, hoping to improve my vision by blocking the sunlight.

'It's here somewhere. Please bear with me, darling girl . . . and eat as many biscuits as you like.'

'No rush, Edward . . . take your time.'

I hadn't seen you move, but you'd disappeared and were no longer on the sofa. Then you reappeared, lifting the sash window of your bedroom, minus your phone, and perched on the sill smoking a cigarette. You'd always told me you didn't really smoke. Only took puffs on mine. Another lie? Or were you thinking of me as you inhaled?

'What's so interesting?' Edward made me jump.

'Sorry . . . I . . . I was just seeing if it looked like it was going to rain.'

'And is it?'

'No . . . I'm not sure . . . Oh wow, what's that? Edward, I think someone's parrot has escaped.'

He laughed. 'It's a feral parakeet. Have you not seen them before?'

'No . . . A what?'

'Feral parakeet. They're parakeets that escaped and bred and bred and now adorn the trees and skies of London.'

I pressed my nose to the glass, following the direction of its flight, to see a mass of them perched in the cherry tree next to your flat. 'That's so weird . . . They look strange being there.' Although genuinely fascinated by the tropical birds, you stamping out your cigarette into an ashtray distracted me. 'They don't belong here,' I said.

'Well, they do now . . . Anyway, enough about the birds. I want to show you something.'

I was back in the room. Edward was standing in front of me holding a photograph. His shakes more pronounced than previously. Appearing to be nerves rather than age. He extracted his hanky again from his pocket, dabbed his face. 'Come round this way . . . Have a look.'

I did as I was told. It was a black-and-white picture of a girl, laughing, on a beach, ice cream in hand, breeze through her hair. A perfect example of captured joy.

'Who is it?' I asked.

'So, there's nothing familiar?' His voice was raised, excited as he stabbed at it with his finger.

I went to take the picture from his hand for a closer look. He let go, reluctantly.

'You mean the beach? I'm afraid I've only ever been to Llandudno.'

'No . . . no, not the beach, the face.' His eyes widened, like a charades player growing frustrated at rubbish guessers.

The girl was pretty with plaited hair. Broad smile. Her dress could have been floral, although it was hard to tell because the print was so small. But there was nothing remarkable about any of it. Nothing familiar at all.

'Sorry, Edward. I'm not sure what I'm looking for. She's lovely, though. Who is it?'

He took the photograph back off me, returned to his chair

and dropped. 'There was so much going on the day we met. I didn't realize it at first.'

I sat too and had a biscuit. Allowed his befuddled ramblings to emerge. Trying to appear interested and not look over to you.

'It was when I woke the next morning that you were my first thought on opening my eyes. I saw your face but realized it was her face.'

I coughed as a crumb flew down my windpipe. 'Sorry. I . . . I don't understand.'

'That's my daughter . . . in the picture . . . Amy.'

'Oh right, I see. Do you see her often?'

He shook his head. 'She died four weeks after that picture was taken.'

I replaced the half-eaten biscuit onto the plate. 'Oh, Edward, that's . . . I'm so sorry . . . How? She was so young.'

'A stomach infection. Can you believe it? A stupid stomach infection. It wasn't fair. Not fair at all. And here am I, alive all this time, old and useless.'

'You mustn't say that . . . What about your wife?'

'We weren't . . . We divorced not long after. She wanted to carry on as before . . . How can you carry on as before?' He wiped his eyes with his hanky. 'See . . . decades later it's still the same. Riding so near the surface that a picture can take you back to day one.'

'I'm so sorry, Edward . . . I really am.'

He threw the photo onto the table next to him and it skidded on the floor. I picked it up.

'And now look at you, Constance. Here, in my room. I

thought you'd be able to see it . . . how much she looks like you.'

The hairs on my arms prickled. I scrutinized the picture. Her dimpled smile, freckles. Other than long, dark hair, she bore no resemblance to me at all, but I said, 'Oh yes . . . I can see it now . . . I can see what you mean.'

His face lit up; his eyes moistened. 'It's uncanny, isn't it? I know it takes a bit of looking, but once I saw it . . . and the way we met. It was as if it was meant to be. A sign.'

I smiled but suddenly felt quite strange. Claustrophobic. He was looking at me with such misplaced affection. Like I was an angel. The answer to his pain.

I nodded towards the cuckoo clock hanging next to the window. 'He'll be springing out any second,' I said. 'I didn't realize the time . . . I'd better be going . . . I'm meeting a friend on the other side of town in an hour.'

'Oh, Colin never springs . . . He died in there many years ago . . . and he's ten minutes fast. Constance, I do hope I haven't—'

'No, no . . . you haven't anything. It's been lovely.'

He attempted to push himself up.

'No . . . no . . . Please. I can see myself out. You stay put.'

I collected my bag from the paw of the poor tiger.

'You will come again, though, won't you? When you've got more time?'

I looked towards the window. You were back on the sofa, the television flashing light onto your face. 'Yes. I will. I promise.'

*

It was the evening of the party.

Dr Harris wasn't just a wanker; he was a rich wanker.

His address turned out to be a huge town house in a nook of Chelsea where the likes of me were suspected burglars. Though, today I was more 'hooker'. I was her again. In her black stretch dress this time. Same crippling shoes. The heels so worn that raw metal scraped against the pavement. Hair bigger. Make-up stronger. I couldn't find my lipstick anywhere, so in a brave moment bought a Barry M one called Pillar Box Red. All the entrapments that had worked previously. But extra. Except I was more self-conscious this time, because there would be people who knew the other Constance, and my confidence dwindled with each pinching step. And as I clung to the iron railings that caged the immaculate pansy-lined private square, the centrepiece to the white mini palaces, greyed by twilight, clutching the bottle of some French Red le Plonk I'd bought from Costcutter, I lacked conviction in my choices.

I surveyed the street for your car, thinking how even in such an exclusive area, it would stand out for its rarity and beauty against the boring Audis and Mercedes. Then it dawned on me that you'd be drinking and I wouldn't get the prior confirmation I'd hoped for that you were inside. If I'd known for certain you weren't, I would have bailed. Gone home and downed the wine myself. But there was no way of knowing without entering the unknown.

I viewed the film of elegant people through the bow-windowed cinema screen. Each elegantly holding elegant cut glasses, under a stupendously elegant chandelier. Laughing elegantly at what were undoubtedly elegant jokes.

I practised a titter of my own. Unaware of the Dalmatian-walking man coming towards me. I smiled. It wasn't reciprocated.

After crossing the quiet road with as much grace as the shoes would allow, I walked under the pillared entrance and ascended the steps. The security light came on as if I was an actor on stage, under a spotlight. I was. I stood for a moment staring at the oversized glossy black door. Then once my breathing levelled, I pressed the bell.

A woman dressed like a breakfast-television presenter opened the door. Though smiling, she viewed me with wonderment as to why such a person would be on her door-step.

'I'm Constance . . . I work with Dr Harris.'

'Oh, of course . . . Hello. I'm Cecelia . . . Bill's wife. I think we may have met at poor Peter's funeral.' She looked me up and down like I was shit on her shoe. Yet I still had nothing but admiration for her. She did live with, and, even worse, shag her husband.

She took the bottle from my hands. 'Oh, how lovely, thank you.' Though we both knew it would end up in a stew. 'Would you like some champagne?'

I'd barely nodded before I was being handed a glass by a young waitress who was way more refined than me.

Mrs Harris escaped me with an insincere 'Sorry, Constance, would you excuse me a moment? Do go in and make yourself at home.'

Yes. Of course. Because this was so like my home.

I necked the champagne faster than was acceptable. My glass was near empty by the time I'd reached the lounge.

Alison's desperate wave greeted me from across the room and I weaved through the overpriced saccharine colognes and perfumes to reach her.

'Oh my God, Constance, I hardly recognized you. Then I said to Kevin, "Kevin, I think that's Constance over there" . . . and it was you. Didn't I, Kevin?'

Kevin was so nondescript I can't even recall his face. He nodded and raised his glass.

'Sip it slowly, Kevin . . . He's driving,' she said, looking at me. 'You've not met Kevin, have you, Constance?'

'No . . . but I've heard so, so much about you.'

He nodded and raised his glass again. And I, at last, understood why Alison never shut the fuck up. She was used to having to be both sides of the conversation.

'So, who's here?' I asked.

'Well, Dr Harris is around somewhere. I've already wished him a very happy birthday . . . and he said, "Alison, you are so sweet." And Dr Short was here a moment ago chatting to Dr Franco, and Linda is around too. Her husband, Graham, well, he . . .'

My mind drifted for some time until I heard '. . . and Dr Stevens was in the hall when I arrived . . .'

I continued listening as if those words had no impact. Hadn't caused my heart to double-beat. Kevin had unfortunately found his voice and I pretended to be interested in his story of how they almost ran out of petrol on the way there because he wouldn't stop at the Esso garage that had once refused a 'perfectly genuine' twenty-pound note. It must have been a great comfort to Alison. Knowing there was someone in the world more boring than her.

I excused myself. Tilting my glass for them to see its emptiness.

'Already? You are funny.' Alison laughed and slapped Kevin's arm.

As I made my way through the Tories, I was faced with Dr Harris's fat back. Out of politeness, I tapped his jacket. 'Hi, Dr Harris. Happy birthday.'

He turned, performed a cartoon double-take, then thanked my tits. I escaped him by asking directions to the toilet.

Legs crossed, I tried the handle of the door in a hallway off a hallway, but it was locked, and I could hear more than one voice laughing inside.

I noticed Mrs Harris walking in my direction, carrying what looked like joss sticks, but in hindsight would have been unlit sparklers. 'Oh, Catherine dear, why don't you use one of the upstairs loos? Second door on the right . . . We don't want any accidents.' I wondered for a moment if my gold-digger theory was incorrect and it had actually just been a case of wanker meets wanker.

The chattering of silver spoons quietened as I climbed the

lush cream-carpeted staircase. I stopped halfway to check each shoe in case I'd stood in some dog shit or something on the way there. No faeces. Only the ghost of the Primark sticker.

I imagined for a moment it was our house. That the Farrow & Ball-coated hallway was where you'd greet me when you'd return from work and I'd be coming down the stairs after getting our baby off to sleep. You'd be carrying beautiful flowers – tea roses, tipped pink, to show how much you loved us and would never leave.

At the top, temptation surrounded me. Door after door willing me to open them. See how this kind lived. I knew which one the toilet was. *But what if I accidentally went to the second on the left instead? An innocent mistake. No harm.* My fingers rested on an incorrect heavy brass handle and I pressed down slowly, pushed. It betrayed me with a squeak as it opened into a pastel bedroom cut directly from one of the *Country Living* magazines in reception. As perfect as the rest of the house. Untouched. Sterile and unlived in. I pushed the door wider and with tiny, quiet steps entered the forbidden space.

'Are you being naughty, Constance?'

I unavoidably squealed. 'Sorry. I was just looking for . . .' I turned.

It was you. Laughing at me.

'Now, we both know you were having a nosey.'

'I . . . I wasn't. I couldn't remember which room she said the toilet was in, that's all.'

You tapped your nose. 'Of course.'

'Did you follow me?'

'Now, why would I follow you? I was in the coatroom. Thought I'd lost my phone, surprise, surprise. Thankfully, it was in my jacket pocket.' You held it up. 'Did you not bring a coat, Constance? You'll catch your death wearing that.'

'It's got sleeves.'

Perhaps you were drunk? The way you came so close that our bodies almost touched. How with one finger you stroked the flesh that spilt shamelessly over the top of the dress.

'Why do you keep making me want to kiss you?' you whispered in my ear.

I snatched a breath and closed my eyes. Awaited your lips to touch mine. But the sound of a toilet's flush made me reopen them, and when I did, you were much further away and leaning against a section of wall between two doors.

A sturdy blonde emerged. A younger Mrs Harris clone. Not quite breakfast-TV presenter. A weather girl, perhaps. She smoothed the fabric of her cerise tailored dress. I noticed how she sucked in her bulging belly. 'Oh, you waited for me,' she said, more plummy than royalty. I didn't connect the jigsaw at first. Then I realized she was talking to you. And for some strange reason touching your arm.

'This is Constance, one of the receptionists at the surgery. Constance, this is Fiona.'

'Constance, I bet you've got lots of stories about this one.' She placed her manicured hand on his shoulder.

'Yes . . . yes, so many . . . Excuse me . . .' I pushed past you both and went in the toilet, slamming the door. Threw my head back against the wood, shut my eyes and tried to regulate my breathing. Reason with my mind. She could have been anyone. I was fucking paranoid. But the effects on my body had already happened, and I'd barely got my knickers down before I'd emptied myself.

Downstairs, I grabbed another glass of champagne from a wandering tray and headed to the buffet area at the back of the lounge. It was no 'paper plates, cheese and pineapple on toothpicks' affair. It was an M&S advert. Not just a buffet. A wanker's buffet.

I couldn't face enquiring about vegetarian options so filled my gold-rimmed china plate with a hunk of artisan bread and safe leafy salad. While chewing on the heavy dough, hoping it would soak up the alcohol, I felt a tap on my shoulder. My stomach overturned, thinking it was you. But it was her. 'So . . . go on, then . . . What's he like to work for, Samuel? Sorry, I mean Dr Stevens. It must be weird for you, me calling him Samuel.'

I forced more bread into my mouth. 'Not really.' I chewed slackly, watching her lips squirm at my gob full of white paste.

'Is he a good boss?'

'He's not my boss.'

'Well . . . well, you know what I mean.' She picked up a plate and dolloped practically every dish onto it.

'No, not really.'

'I mean . . . is he nice . . . to the staff? You know what they say – when dating a man, check how he treats the waiter as that shows more about the person than how he's treating you.'

The bread stuck in my gullet and I spoke in a deep voice. 'You're . . . you're dating him?'

'Oh no . . . No, we've only met tonight. So not yet anyway.'
She laughed. I didn't. 'Well, go on . . .'

'Go on what?'

'What's he like?'

'I . . . I think he's still in love with someone.'

'How would you know that?' Her face warped with
contempt.

'It's just what I . . . you know . . . what I heard, but I
don't really know. I'm just one of the receptionists.'

'Yes . . . yes, exactly.' She looked at me in a way I recognized. A look that said I wasn't good enough. That I looked
cheap. That I didn't belong there. That I was a feral parakeet.

A waitress offered up more champagne. I downed the
remains of my glass and swapped it for a new one. Fiona
looked at me with even more smiling disgust.

'Oh no . . . I really shouldn't,' she said to the waitress.

And I couldn't help myself. 'Oh, but you must. They now
say it's fine to have one or two glasses when you're expecting.'

'I'm not expe—'

'Oh no . . . Oh my God, I am so sorry.' I touched her
arm and glanced at her tummy. 'I don't even know why I
. . . I'm always putting my foot in it . . . I'm so sorry.'

She put down her plate and reached for a glass from the
waitress's tray. We stood in silence for a minute until she
said, 'I've . . . got to . . . I should . . . I've just seen a friend,'
and left both me and the room.

I too wanted to flee but couldn't bring myself to leave you.
You were in the corner surrounded by a gaggle of toffs.
Holding court. They laughed at your jokes. You were relaxed,

your shirt untucked. Not thinking of me, wanting to find me. I should have left and stopped the torture. But I couldn't do it.

It was nine o'clock, and for half an hour I'd been forced to talk to Linda and her husband, Racist Graham, about topics such as why they were convinced I'd soon die if I didn't eat some meat, their new hot tub and how Nigel Farage was the only one 'telling it like it is'. I perched on the edge of a claret velvet chaise, nodding politely, my feelings about Linda vindicated. Any grains of guilt I had for hating her evaporated into the air, along with Graham's spit, which sprayed out with each offensive utterance.

Across the room, I saw you in deep discussion with Dr Harris. I tried to lip-read while enduring Graham's story about the supposedly unfriendly Muslim man on their street. I couldn't decipher your words, but I was scared you were being talked into a permanent return to Harley Street.

In contrast, you didn't look over my way. Not once. Didn't feel my presence. Want to save me.

At nine thirty I could bear it no longer. Your conversation with Harris had ended some time ago and you'd now disappeared. I had to find you. Talk to you.

I excused myself from Adolf and Eva, determined to corner you, but as I was heading for the lounge door, the lights went off and Mrs Harris was wheeling in a trolley on which perched a huge candle-lit cake with crackling sparklers. The guests began to sing. 'Happy birthday to you. Happy birthday to you . . .'

Dr Harris took centre stage, repeating, 'Thank you, thank you, all,' as the room sang off key. It took forever for him to blow out the fifty candles. At one point I thought he might die before extinguishing the last flame.

You'd disappeared.

Dizzy with champagne and frustration, I needed to escape for a while, gather myself and have a fag. I slipped away as everyone cheered and pretended Harris was a 'jolly good fellow' when I'm sure they too thought he was a wanker.

As I neared the lounge door, I encountered Dr Franco, who tried to make small talk through the hip-hip-hooraying. We both politely gave up and I mouthed I was going outside for a cigarette. I caught him looking at my dress. Not in a lecherous way. In a way that indicated he knew it was all a facade.

Outside was bliss. As the door shut behind me, and I stood in the spotlight once again, I wondered if I would even go back in. The night air was cool. The breeze kissed my skin, covered me in goosebumps. I enjoyed the shivering.

I crossed over the road to see if there was a way of getting into the garden square, but the gate was locked, so I returned to my earlier observation spot, rested against the railings and lit a fag. The interior of the house appeared brighter in contrast to the now-blackened sky. But I couldn't watch that show anymore. I was separate from them. Different. Instead, I perched on the narrow rim of concrete holding the metal fence in place. Slipped off my shoes to circle my poor bruised feet and closed my eyes, enjoying the nicotine and my freedom.

They jolted open again to the sound of Harris's door slamming. The security light switched on.

And there you were.

It wasn't just you, though, was it? She was draped on your arm, laughing like the moron she was, as if you were hilarious. But you weren't hilarious, Samuel. You were not funny at all.

My breath locked high in my chest. Had I been standing, I think I would have keeled over. You didn't see me. Not because it was dark but because you were so busy kissing her, touching her. Pressing yourself against that fucking belly.

Swaying, you took her by the hand. She wasn't even drunk. She was just posh. A party girl. That's what they're called, isn't it? Whereas if she was poor, she'd be a slapper. Was I just a slapper to you? How were you not aware of me in the shadows? How could you not sense such hurt happening so near to you?

You walked away. Hand in hand. On the same side of the road as me. Oblivious. Laughing, kissing, laughing. I knew what that walk meant. I'd been on one oh so recently, hadn't I?

Without warning, I threw up on the pavement between my legs. It sizzled on the concrete. Once I'd raised my head, I'd lost you in the darkness.

The merriment continued through the window. The world still turning. Like it always does. I didn't cry. I didn't even want to cry.

I retrieved my mother's spattered shoes and scrambled in my bag for a tissue. There wasn't one, only a Costcutter receipt, which merely smeared the vile juice from one part of the shoe to the other and which I then had to discard on the ground. A snapshot, in this lovely part of London, that showed me up for what I was.

On the Tube, I stared at myself in the window opposite. My ghost. Her ghost. We were the same. To others, I'm sure I appeared blank, lifeless, but inside were images of the two of you I couldn't erase. Images I'd created. You kissing her naked body. Fucking her from behind. A perverted movie I couldn't switch off.

I'd fully intended to go home. You must believe me.

It was at Ealing Common that the shift happened.

I climbed the steps of the station and stopped midway. A man tutted at me for blocking his exit. But I didn't care. Didn't move. Didn't give a shit about anything other than what you'd done. And as I stood, people passing me by, it rose from my blistered feet and spread through me like a wildfire.

There was no conscious journey between standing there and standing outside your flat. It was trance-like. Hypnotic. Can you sleepwalk while awake? You'd know, Doctor.

I leant against your car, looked up at your window. The lounge light was on. I couldn't breathe. Knowing what was going on in there. Drinking. Talking. Kissing. Listening to music. *Our* song. Her sitting where I should have been sitting. Lying where I should have been lying.

I lit a cigarette. Took an elongated pull. Do you have any idea how you'd made me feel? Do you understand now? The inner force that pulled the metal striker wheel of my lighter towards your car like a magnet? What made me press hard, deep, into the metallic paint? Silently screaming, until my possessed hand stopped the contact.

I couldn't look at what I'd done and removed my shoes for a quicker escape. With my bare feet on the cold concrete, I was diminished in every sense. I should have just walked away. And I would have done, had I not foolishly glanced up at your window one last time.

The lounge was now black. The bedroom shone with the familiar soft glow of your copper lamp. The images played stronger, more vividly. Your sweaty bodies. *Stop*. Smashing against each other. *Please stop*. Melding together in ways I knew. *No*. Her hair laced through your hand, your mouth on her mouth. *I can't bear it*. On her tits, on that fucking belly. *Please make it stop*.

The shoes dropped to the ground. My hands felt for my head. Each finger grappled chunks of my hair, tangled in tight fists. As you'd be doing to her. I released the matted locks and bent down to retrieve the shoes. Rose again. The left one swung off my index finger. The right gripped by the middle of the arch. The metal-tipped spiked heel faced the side window of your car.

And I shattered it.

Like you'd shattered me.

*

By the time I'd put my key in the door, I just needed to sleep. To wake on a different day. Shut it out. The unmistakable sound of breaking glass triggering windows to light up around me. Not yours. You were too busy. Me hiding under a monstrous Range Rover, inhaling dirt from the road, until prying eyes returned to bed and I could run to safety, barefoot, holding on to my shoes, my sanity.

As I entered the hall half dead, I was surprised, delighted, by the distorted sound of a TV coming from Dale's bedsit. After the initial relief at his return, finally having my friend back, I once again removed the shoes from my grazed, soiled feet and tiptoed towards my room to ensure he didn't see me in such a state. Filthy. Oil and dirt smeared on every visible part of my skin.

Despite my efforts, he opened his door.

'Jesus. Good night?' He soaked in the mess. 'Where've you been? What the hell happened to you?'

'It's . . . it's a long story . . . A party.'

'A party? What was it? The annual Chimney Sweeps' Ball? Why are you always bloody injured or in a total state whenever you go out?'

'I . . . I fell.'

'Down a chimney at the Chimney Sweeps' Ball?'

I dropped my head. 'Trust me, you don't want to know.'

'Oh, but I do. It's fascinating.' He raised his arm and leant against the door frame.

'So you're . . . Are you back now, then?' But as I looked beyond him into his room, I noticed cardboard boxes in various states of construction scattered around the floor.

'Actually, there's something I've been wanting to ask you—'

'What's going on? What are the boxes for . . . ? Are you really going?'

He took my cold, greasy hand in his. I wanted to cry. It was the kindest he'd been to me for some time.

'Constance . . . are . . . are you a member of *Fight Club*?'

I pulled away from him.

'Sorry . . . I know . . . I know . . . The first rule is you can't talk about it, but—'

'Are you really moving out?'

He looked down and rubbed his nose with his finger, spoke to the floor. 'I . . . It's for the best.'

'It's not. It's not for the best . . . I don't want you to.' I couldn't look at him.

'Jesus, Constance . . . you've left me no choice.'

My eyes fixed on the hinge of the door, but I could see he'd stopped leaning. He was drifting backwards into the room. My words barely formed a whisper. 'Please, Dale. Don't leave.'

The interlocking metal of the hinge twisted as the door shut.

*   *   *

I removed her dress. Put it with the red one in the dirty linen basket. Naked, I was at least free of the physical connections to the evening.

In the shower, I stood under the scalding water, watching the grey liquid fall at my feet. Scrubbed shampoo so hard into my scalp that red appeared under my nails. Knowing I'd never be clean enough.

Back in my room, I dried myself off apart from my hair and threw myself into bed. Pulled the duvet over my head, burying myself in a safer world. Terrified at the possibility of police visiting soon. Squeezing Blusha and kissing the hole where her eye had once been. Until, thankfully, my brain cut off and I fell asleep.

The scream of metal on metal like a rusty machine grinding to a halt.

It was outside our house on the estate. They were all out. Those people who'd avoided me. Cath and Ian next door, George from number six, the Patels. She was wearing the black dress. Her arms slung around a lanky, moustachioed man, whispering hollow honey into her ear. They gathered and watched. I used the small knife. Scratched and scratched and scratched the white car. She giggled as the man's hand disappeared under her dress. I stepped back to view what I'd done. They all applauded me. Until the claps slowed to silence as red paint dripped from the marks.

I woke, breathless. My room pitch-black. Hair still wet from perspiration as well as the shower. I wiped my hands across my belly to remove some of the sweat, then switched on the lamp, which I didn't think I'd turned off. The bulb had blown.

The erasure I'd tried to achieve with sleep hadn't worked. It was all still there. Pounding my mind. What I'd done. What you'd done. What Dale was about to do.

I prised myself out of bed. Felt around the wall for the main switch, then searched the floor for my dressing gown and headed to the kitchen for some water. Light shone through the gap under Dale's door. I was aware more than ever of the security that brought me. And the panic I felt at losing it.

In the kitchen, I kept the tap running in an attempt to get rid of the usual metallic taste. Filled a glass and gulped it down. Then filled another to take to my room. The air cooled my sweat and I was shivering. But it wasn't only from the chill. It was the physical manifestation of anxiety.

As I made my way to my room, I remembered that night at Rupert's. Holding on to Blusha. How I'd felt. The aloneness I'd felt. And I knew I was returning to that.

I'd intended to walk on. I did. I swear. But somehow I'd stopped and was knocking on his door. He must have known it was me but delayed opening it to make me suffer.

'What's up?' he said.

I didn't know what to say at first. But when he looked at me, so cold, distant, as if he'd already left, I knew there was only one way I could stop myself feeling like this.

'OK,' I said. 'OK.'

*

Everything changed after that night.

For a start, I was Dale's girlfriend.

If I am about to tell you this, you cannot judge. I'd accept judgement from those whose relationships only ever had pure love at their core. Where no other dynamics have ever entered the equation. Not security, or money, or filling holes left from other losses. Not sex on tap or biological time bombs. Loneliness. Duty. Status. Not for the sake of the children accidentally or purposefully conceived. From those people, and God, I'd accept judgement. But not you.

Besides, I had approval.

When you'd called me into your office on the Monday after the party, I was so terrified I could barely make the journey from my desk. My legs belonged to someone else. My mouth, spit-free. I had no choice but to visit the toilet first.

In the confines of the cubicle, sat on the cold seat, my insides falling from me, I closed my eyes, put my hands together and did something I hadn't done since my last night with her. I prayed.

Dear God, I know I have done some terrible things, but if

you let me get away with this one act, I will promise to be good from now on. I promise to let Samuel go. Amen.

'Close the door, Constance,' you said. Your chair faced the entrance, awaiting my arrival.

I hung on to the handle to stop me falling over and gently pressed the door shut, prolonging the turn towards you.

'Did you have a good time on Saturday?'

I nodded.

'Yes, me too. Sorry I didn't get to speak to you much. I had to leave early . . . Had a callout from a patient. An emergency.'

I remained silent. The guilt of your lies forced you to embellish. 'No one you know . . . a Harley Street patient.' You turned to your desk and opened a file. 'Are you OK, Constance? You look a bit peaky.'

'Yes . . . I've . . . I've just not been sleeping very well.'

'I could give you something—'

'No . . . I'm fine. Thank you.'

You turned back round, looked right at me. 'You'll never guess what I encountered Sunday morning, though?'

I held your eyes. My face motionless. My throat so constricted that I had to squeeze out the single word, 'What?'

'My car. It'd been keyed. All down the side and the window smashed. And we both know who it was, don't we?'

I placed my hand on the filing cabinet to steady myself. 'We do? I . . . don't—'

'Course we do.'

The room caved in around me. The walls spun. I was too bad even for God. I had nowhere to go, nothing I could do other than to beg for your forgiveness. 'Samuel . . . I can't—'

'Bloody hell, Constance, you're really not with it this morning, are you? It was those delinquents on the bikes back again. Must have been. The bloody bastards. I spoke to the police, explained all about them, but they didn't give a toss, obviously.'

The relief made me even more unstable, which I disguised by casually leaning against the cabinet. 'Oh yes . . . of course. It must have been.'

'I mean, the attitude of the police was outrageous. There're no CCTV cameras anywhere. Can you believe that, Constance? In Kensington. It's a joke. It's as if someone who has a nice car should expect something bad to happen to it. Some kind of punishment for success. That's the world we live in: little twats vandalize my car, but somehow it's my fault for having worked my bollocks off to buy it.'

'I thought your father gave it to you?'

Your eyes glazed with fury, yet you remained composed. 'Jesus, Constance, whose side are you on?'

'Sorry. I—'

'Anyway, I only called you in to request you phone the garage, please. The insurance has prearranged with them, but I need to book in an appointment. I'd do it myself, but I'm busy working hard, you see.' You handed me a piece of paper with a number on it and smiled, but you didn't mean it. Your face flushed from the nerve I'd touched.

But nothing could take away the relief of the second chance I'd been given. Outside your office, I couldn't contain my tears.

'Thank you,' I whispered towards the ceiling. And so I had no choice but to stick to my word and let you go. Move on.

Kissing Dale wasn't as repellent as I'd predicted.

He was gentle and not as generous as I'd expected with his saliva. Although, the residue from his sweat moustache did carry a saltiness I hadn't experienced before.

The problem was, any activity that involves closed eyes enables imaginations to wander elsewhere. I'd tried so hard to lock you away and had almost succeeded, but one day, when Dale was kissing me outside our front door, I dropped back off the step, hurting my foot.

'Oh God, it's not a hospital job again, is it?' he said.

And that was it. You'd invaded my thoughts and remained there as his lips locked back onto mine, making the whole thing more enjoyable.

From then on I allowed you into my mind only. Thoughts couldn't harm. Only acting on them. However, even with those musings, sex with Dale was difficult.

I'd put it off for as long as possible. Initially saying I wanted to take things slowly. Then pretending I had my period. Then when the phoney one was reaching its end, my real one arrived.

But a couple of weeks in we'd been to Connolly's. He was drunk, I was relaxed on brandy (to remind me of you, of course), and it seemed as good a time as any to get it out of the way.

'I can't tell you how long I've wanted this.' He lifted my jumper off over my head, then smoothed his hands around my back. Although he stopped kissing, his mouth remained over mine as he concentrated on blindly unhooking the clasp of my bra. His breath hot, tainted with beer and cheese-and-onion crisps. Feeling his impatience, I reluctantly reached up behind and assisted. He searched beneath the bones. My bones.

'What's wrong? You don't seem very—'

'Nothing . . . nothing. Let's move over here.'

I led him to my bed, then turned and said, 'Actually, let's go to your room.'

'We're here now.' He lurched towards me.

'But it's so much nicer in your room.'

'OK . . . OK, sure.'

'You go . . . I'll see you in there in a minute.'

Dazed, he gathered up his shirt, which I hadn't even realized he'd removed. 'Hurry up, though.' His face glowed red. I smiled at him till he left.

Alone, I sat in silence. *It's just sex. That's all.* Reached under the bed for some Dutch courage from Vladimir. Russian courage. Then removed my jeans and knickers. Washed down there. Put on some clean ones, put my bra back on properly and covered everything up with my old towelling robe. Then I grabbed my fags and lighter, and made my way to his room.

I hope it's not uncomfortable. Me telling you this. Like it was for me with Fiona. Painful. A knife repeatedly stabbing into my stomach. I'd never want anyone to feel like that. You were the one I loved, remember. That's why all of this happened.

* * *

197

He was in bed when I entered. His *Star Wars* duvet wrapped around his leg, like he was spooning Darth Vader. His naked stomach melted towards the mattress. The sixty-watt bulb of the ceiling light blasted out reality in abundance.

'Can I turn this off?' I asked, hovering in the doorway.

'I want to see you.'

'Well, can't we put the lamp on?'

'The bulb's gone.'

'Oh. Well, I could take the one out of mine.'

'I've just remembered I got a load of bulbs ages ago that were on offer at Poundstretcher . . . there in that bottom drawer.' As I went to open it, he said, 'Actually, no . . . no, don't do that. Let's put the lava lamp on. That works.' He nodded his head towards the sofa. At its side, on the floor, was a lava lamp with the wire wrapped around it.

'Isn't it just easier to—'

'No . . . Let's use that.'

When I picked it up, my hands became coated in sticky dust. He took it from me, unravelled the wire with great concentration, unplugged the existing lamp and replaced it with the rocket.

'It takes a bit of time for the blobs to start moving,' he said, his belly wobbling as he settled himself back on the bed.

When I turned off the main light, the turquoise glow was a stark shock.

He patted the mattress. 'Are you not going to take that off?'

'It's cold.'

'I'll warm you up.'

I slipped under the covers, but he pushed me away. 'You'll have to climb over . . . This is my side.'

Once I'd reached my designated spot, I winced as the cold wall pressed against my back.

I removed my robe underneath the duvet as if changing clothes on a beach, then slithered further down the bed. He followed me. Faced me. Kissed me. The damp skin of his chest touched mine. Then his stomach. Then his thighs. I could tell it was all going well for him as he pressed himself against me.

'What's this doing back on?' He attempted to unhook my bra once again but was on his own this time. I refused to assist with the embarrassment.

When he finally defeated it, he held it up, arm straight like he'd pulled Excalibur from the stone, before flinging it to the floor. Then, without warning, he threw off the covers. Exposed me. My nakedness. I couldn't stand it as he stared. You'd do that sometimes, wouldn't you? But it felt so different with him. Awful. To make it stop, I pulled him towards me, and with him, the covers, lifting his chin to force his eyes onto my face. Then I felt uncomfortable him even doing that, so I kissed him to force his eyes to shut.

He was soon lying on top of me. This was it. The big one. Except it wasn't big at all. After some condom-fumbling, he was in me. We moved out of sync. I closed my eyes. Imagined you through the heavy breathing and 'Oh, Constance . . . I'm fucking you.' But it wasn't you. It was Dale. I prayed he'd come prematurely. I'd comfort him. Say it was fine but with a slight edge to my tone like it wasn't really fine and feign disappointment. It wasn't happening quickly enough, though, so I had no choice but to fake it. I'd barely begun my performance when, thank God, he bolted and distorted and shuddered before saying, 'Oh fuck.' Then slid away from me.

We lay there. Staring at the ceiling. His arm blindly sought my head and clumsily stroked my hair. I sat up and searched for my robe to get the pack of fags from the pocket and put one in my mouth.

'You can't smoke that in here, remember,' he said.

I removed it and popped it back in the packet.

He rolled over to face me. 'Hey . . . that was amazing . . . How about you? Did you—'

'Yeah, course. Couldn't you tell? Sorry – I'm just going to have a few puffs of this in my room.'

'Hurry up,' he said, turning over.

Once out of the bed and within the comfort of the robe once again, I stood for a few moments, still, quiet. Listening to his breathing grow deeper and deeper until it morphed into a snore.

So that's how it went. My new life. My new boyfriend.

At work, I remained distant from you, professional. Your ego resisted the change initially.

'You're very quiet, Constance. Are we not friends anymore?'

'What? No . . . everything's fine.'

Though you knew it wasn't. And I couldn't help but relish the pull I'd created towards me. My increased power. Until you'd learnt to accept our new way of being. Stopped asking me. Trying. And the tables had turned once again.

After work, to maintain my pact with God, I'd either go

home immediately or if I stopped for a fag, I'd make myself visible. Say goodbye to you in a manner so casual it was as if you worked on the checkout at Costcutter. On those occasions, to avoid temptation, I'd wait until you were out of sight before setting off. Always walking through the cemetery, no matter how dark it had become, even if there was thunder and lightning.

I lived like that for a month. The season changed. It was cold and harsh. Darkness came earlier each day and lightness arrived later each morning. But I was proud of myself. I'd broken the spell. Your spell. Like Johnny Cash, I walked the line.

And I'd like to think it would have remained that way. If that Tuesday, when having my after-work cigarette next to the steps, I hadn't answered a call from a withheld number.

*

'Is that Constance?'

'Yes . . . hello. Speaking.'

'Hello, Constance. This is . . . It's your father.'

My vision hazed, legs weakened. The sound of a finger circling the rim of a crystal glass rang in my ears as I slid down the wall, ending with a jolt on the brutal pavement.

'Constance? Constance . . . are you there?'

'Dad . . . I . . . I can't . . .' A laugh morphed into tears. My joy too much to articulate. I hugged my knees against my chest. 'Daddy . . . I knew you'd find me.'

'Constance? Constance, can you hear me?'

'Yes . . . sorry. I just . . . Yes, I can hear.'

Voices mumbled in the background. He told someone to leave him in peace.

'Dad, are you there? So, you . . . you got my card? I can't believe it . . . Where are you? Are you—'

'Constance . . . sorry, Constance,' he whispered. 'This is Edward.'

I'm uncertain I remained conscious. I heard his words, but they were abstract, meaningless.

'I'm in hospital, and they won't let me out unless someone is looking after me . . . and I found your number in my trousers and so I told them I'd call my daughter . . . and . . . I wondered if you could be so kind as to just go along with it. Only to get me out of here. Then you can leave me be. I'll be fine once I'm home . . . Constance? Constance? Can you hear me? I'm at St Mary's, Lewis Lloyd ward . . .'

I dropped my hand. The faint call of 'Constance? Constance?' skidded across the ground. After pulling myself up to a standing position, I stumbled to pick up the phone. When I returned to the wall, I pressed my cheek against the freezing brick, my mouth forming a silent scream.

'Are you there? Constance?'

I lifted the handset to my ear. 'I hope you die in there, you stupid old fuck.'

The Lewis Lloyd ward was on the other side of the hospital to where we'd spent our special night. When passing the entrance to A&E, I stopped and smoked a fag in one of the abandoned wheelchairs while reminiscing about us. Avoiding other hospital memories. The dread. The day they operated on her, and the four hours I couldn't breathe after she'd kissed me and walked down to surgery. I didn't even know patients could walk down to surgery. That's not what happens in films.

Disinfectant fumes stung my cried-out eyes. I pressed the buzzer outside the double doors of the ward. It took so long to get a response I jumped when the loud noise unlocked them. I had no idea if Edward was still there, or even if my vileness had killed him. A lanky nurse stood behind the reception desk, unwrapping a Quality Street, which she'd plucked with angular fingers from the tin next to a grubby fan. She chewed while watching me dispense the antiseptic gel onto my hands. I did it twice, to prove my thoroughness. *No germs. Must avoid the germs.*

'I'm here to collect Edward Seymour.'

'It's visiting time. You can go through anyway.'

I thanked her and walked down the corridor, only to turn back once I realized I didn't know where I was going.

'He's got a side room. Room four,' she said, sensing my ignorance. 'Second on the right.'

He was asleep when I entered. Mouth dropped open. A pale blue knitted blanket pulled up under his chin, which had sprouted a beard. Even with the additional cladding, his face appeared thinner. A copy of the *Guardian* lay folded across his belly. I picked up his pen from the floor, as quietly as possible, uncertain whether to sit and wait or wake him. I wasn't even sure why I was there. Other than guilt. The fear of another death on my conscience.

I chose the waiting option. But as soon as the back of my legs touched the uncomfortable plastic of the chair, he snorted and opened his eyes, which widened with surprise when he saw me.

'Hi. How you feeling? What's wrong with you?'

'A bout of pneumonia.'

'Oh God . . . I'm sorry, that's awful.'

'Awful? I contracted malaria when I was posted in Africa. This is nothing.'

He attempted to push himself up and I rushed over to help him. 'What are you doing here, anyway? Come to finish me off?'

I expelled my last remnants of anger by forcefully plumping

his pillows. 'No . . . no . . . I'm sorry about that . . . I should explain.'

'I had no right to call on you – you're right. You don't even know me. I am merely . . . What was it? A "stupid old idiot".'

'"Fuck" . . . It was "fuck" . . . But anyway, I didn't mind you calling on me. It's just—'

A petite mousey-haired nurse wheeled in a machine. 'Hello, Teddy. How you doing? How was the beef stew?'

'Well, Nina, it was like a boiled tramp's boot, marinated in Bovril.'

'Oh, Teddy, you crack me up.' She laughed and looked at me with a *what's-he-like?* face. 'Right, let's get you checked.'

'Should I leave?'

'No, no, you're all right, love. So, you're Teddy's daughter?'

'No . . . I'm . . . I'm like his daughter, but no.'

'I was going to say . . . you look a bit young. No offence, Teddy.' She inserted a gun-like thermometer in his ear and waited for a beep. 'Gone right down. Reckon you're on the mend, fella. Now, let's do your blood pressure.'

He volunteered his arm. 'Again? Jesus Christ.'

Nina talked over the sound of compressed air as the cuff tightened. 'Though saying that, Mick Jagger's still at it, isn't he?'

A long beep emitted from the machine as it released his limb. Edward glanced at the figures, which I personally have never understood.

'Perfect, see. Constance here has come to take me home.' He looked at me with pleading eyes.

I nodded and smiled at the nurse. 'Yes . . . hopefully.'

'And that's been OK-ed, Teddy, has it?'

'It has indeed, Nina. By the decision-maker. Me.'

She gave a friendly but disapproving look, gathered the wires attached to the machine and walked out while addressing me. 'You'll need to get the go-ahead from Mr Wolf, the consultant, when he does his rounds.'

After a short, sharp disagreement between Edward and Mr Wolf, which climaxed with 'Get back to me when you've reached puberty, Doctor', he was given the green light to go home. I made it very clear to both Edward and Mr Wolf that I'd only be able to check on him after work, and I couldn't keep it up for long. But Edward had decided, and that was that.

'For the record, I honestly didn't mind you calling me,' I said in the cab on the way home.

'You could have fooled me.'

'Oh my God, I'm here, aren't I?' I stared towards the Magic Tree dangling from the driver's rear-view mirror, checking if he was the nosey type, but he was insultingly disinterested in our conversation. 'It . . . it was because you pretended to be my father.'

'But I only said that to shut them up—'

'I know . . . I know you did, but . . . he's . . . he's been missing since I was six. I've been searching for him ever since . . . and I thought I'd found him, that's all. But I'm sorry . . . for what I said.'

'Well, no . . . my goodness, no. I'm the sorry one . . . Missing in what way? On purpose or—'

'You know . . . vanished. Fucked off. Went to get gravy

for the Sunday dinner and never returned. That kind of missing.'

'I . . . I don't know what to say.' And he didn't say anything for a while. We rode in silence, until he turned to me, furious. 'I don't understand how anyone could leave their daughter behind like that.' He sniffed and looked out of the window. Placed his fragile hand on top of mine. 'Well, firstly, you know you still should never wish anyone dead. If only to protect oneself from the guilt, should they take your advice. And secondly, sometimes I really am a stupid old fuck.'

His flat smelt damp and was freezing. He'd only been in hospital ten days, but it already felt unlived in.

I put the heating and kettle on, then quickly tried to cosy up his bedroom by placing a water bottle inside the faded covers of his bed. Edward perched himself on what must once have been beautiful, but was now a shabby, sage velvet chair, grumbling about the hospital food. 'I'm telling you . . . even if you were well when you went in, you'd be dead after that shepherd's pie.'

'You haven't tasted my cooking yet. You'll be booking yourself back in.'

It was strange that moment. Oddly comforting, looking after him.

'So, I'll pop in each day after work. Check on you . . . get your shopping. I can't keep doing it, though.'

'You're a good soul, Constance.'

I smoothed the ripples in his blanket. 'No . . . no, I'm really not.'

He pulled himself up to stand and felt in his trouser pocket.

'Here, take this money and get these cut for yourself.' He handed me some notes and two Yale keys. 'Save me getting up to let you in if I'm having a kip.'

By now he looked wan and exhausted. After some struggle, I managed to get him into bed. Both of us relieved as he sank into the mattress.

'Nothing like your own bed, is there?' His eyes fought to stay open.

I picked up the handset from the side table. 'This is dead. I'm not leaving you without a phone. Where do I charge it?'

I deciphered the faint word 'lounge' as he drifted off to sleep.

In the hall, I called Dale.

'So who is this guy?'

'I've told you, he's not a guy – he's an old man. What's the matter with you?' I headed towards the lounge, so Edward couldn't hear.

'I know he's an old man . . . well, so you say—'

'So I say?'

'But surely he has family who could . . .' His words blurred in my ear.

Because there you were.

I walked over to the window, a moth. You, my flame.

You were alone. Selecting a CD and removing it from the case. You lifted your jumper and rubbed your back, then brought that hand up to your head to push away your hair. I wondered what music you'd picked. Was it romantic? 'At Last'? My guess, by the way you then sat leisurely and closed your eyes, was that it was classical. Shostakovich, perhaps.

And I must have been in your thoughts as you sipped your wine, foot swaying. Remembering our drive home that night.

My free hand pressed against the cold, damp pane.

Like an ex-heroin addict, after one small hit I was hooked.

'Constance? Constance, are you even listening to me?'

'Sorry, Dale. I've . . . I've got to go. He's calling me.'

I placed the handset onto its base, then sat in the chair. Settled back. Slipped off my shoes and fixated on you. And the truth is, it felt right. Honest. Nothing had changed. It had all been a pretence. Wanting to be over someone is not the same as being so.

Nearly an hour had passed when I finally tore myself away and looked at the defunct cuckoo clock. Despite it being ten minutes fast, it was still getting late, so I reluctantly rose and removed Edward's phone from the charger to take back to his room.

I hadn't intended to, I swear. I tried to resist but couldn't help it.

My finger pressed '141', then your number.

'Hello?' you said.

I remained silent.

'Hello?'

I watched your mouth shape the words that transmitted into my ear. It was intimate, sensual.

'Is anyone there? It's a bad line. I can't . . .'

Could you hear my breathing? I was unable to prevent it from fluttering in front of the mouthpiece.

'It's me,' I whispered so low I could barely hear it myself.

And so it was official. My pact with God was broken.

*

No longer the need for restraint, the following day I wore the silk blouse that had summoned your eyes towards me in the first place. On the Tube platform, free from Dale's watch, I gently dabbed on a diluted version of Pillar Box Red and applied some mascara. My stress melted away, without the requirement to suppress my thoughts, feelings.

You arrived at work, a little dishevelled as if you'd overslept. I smiled, long and slow. Willed you to look at me properly, see me like you used to. But your sleepy eyes remained glued to the message Linda had placed in your hand and you merely wished us all a generic 'good morning'. Lumping me in with them. It was most disappointing. Until, just before lunch, you returned to reception carrying a file. 'Can you make a copy of this for me, please, Constance?'

Me. Not Alison. Me. I took the folder from you, gazing right into your eyes. I understood the unspoken perfectly.

Soon you were leaving for Mrs Carter's house call. She was so rich she didn't ever have to lower herself to come into the surgery, even for an in-growing toenail. 'I'm going straight on to Knightsbridge to see Mrs Johnson after, so

I'll be a couple of hours. Thought I'd kill two birds with one stone.'

'Hopefully not,' I replied.

You laughed. As did I. And we were connected once more.

I observed as you struggled with your coat. I hadn't seen it before, and it looked new. Heavy and luxurious. I imagined its woollen arms wrapped around me.

'I forgot to ask, did you sort your car out, Dr Stevens?'

You turned up your collar and smiled. 'I did, thank you for asking. She's all sorted. You'd never have known it had happened.'

And so everything was wiped clean.

At lunchtime I refused Alison's offer to share her heated-up moussaka that good old Kevin had made the night before using his grandmother's recipe. Aside from not eating meat, I had to get Edward's keys cut and pick up his shopping, which included tinned prunes and Bovril. Why are other people's shopping lists so bizarre?

I fastened up my coat. Except for the missing middle button, strands of cotton in its place, shaming me with every outing. All morning the icy air had forced itself in with each opening of the door. Bringing with it windswept, ruby-cheeked patients sighing with relief at finding themselves in the warmth of our reception. In preparation, I searched for Edward's keys in my black hole of a bag, and when I finally found them, I put them in my pocket to prevent any faffing in the cutter's. Then I took the copied papers to your room, in case you returned before I did.

Nervous, excited at the thought of entering alone, my

hand gripped the handle of the door. I took a deep breath before opening it but was stopped by the sensation of fingers tapping on my back. I whipped around.

'Dr Franco . . . You gave me a heart attack.' My hand reached for my chest to calm myself.

'Sorry. Sorry, Constance. I presumed you'd heard me bounding down the corridor.'

'No . . . sorry. I—'

'It's been a while. I was thinking about you today. We haven't had one of our chats for quite some time.'

'No . . . no. I suppose not. But you're busy – you mustn't worry about me.'

'Oh . . . Do you not want to?' The way he looked at me denoted that this was a serious question and I needed to answer accordingly.

'Yes . . . yes, I really do,' I replied.

'Oh good, good. I'll have a nosey in my diary. Let you know when I'm free.' Then to use his own term, he bounded up the stairs.

I hadn't been alone in there since I'd cleared Dr Williams's stuff. It was dark, unsettling. Still carried his ghost. Aside from dead bosses, there was something so satisfying about being inside your life without your knowledge. I scanned the area. Nothing unusual, just your regular doctor things. I stroked your navy suit jacket, which you'd left behind, hung on the back of the door. Sniffed the sleeve. Remembering the scent you'd once left on me. On your desk was a mug of half-drunk tea which you hadn't asked me to make. I touched the outside. It was still warm, and I slowly weaved my fingers through the handle and brought it to my lips.

Covering exactly where I imagined yours to have been. It was nowhere near as nice as the ones I made you. Because no one else cared about getting it right, like I did.

Catching sight of the clock, I became conscious of the time, so quickly replaced the mug, rubbing off the lipstick I'd forgotten I was wearing, and dropped the file onto your desk before turning to leave.

Then I remembered I needed to attach a note as, once photocopied, the colourful pie chart had transformed into a dark grey circle. I allowed my bag to fall to the floor and grabbed the stack of Post-its next to your open diary.

It was then I did the first of two things. Both of which were bad. I tried so hard not to, but before I knew it, I was flicking through your diary. Mrs Carter . . . Mrs Johnson . . . I turned the page. There was an entry that just said, *Sarah*, and a phone number. I found myself scribbling it down onto one of the Post-its, tearing it off the block and placing it in my pocket. My heart quickened as I then wrote the note I'd intended. *Page four. Pie chart didn't* . . . The pen died on me halfway through the sentence. Frustrated, I grabbed the only other biro in the holder. As you had your fancy pen, you were probably oblivious to the fact none of them worked. This one was even worse, making only an inscription. I rolled it angrily in my hands. Scrubbed it across a page to encourage ink, but nothing. So I opened the drawer. Scrambled around the elastic bands and medical gadgets. Then I saw it. The bright red of the plastic fob. The spare keys that had brought us together that day. I put it out of my mind and continued my search.

Eventually I found a chewed-up 5B pencil near the back. I shut the drawer and completed the message, the words thick and shiny. When finished, I opened the drawer once more. Just to drop the pencil back in. Nothing more. But there it was again. The fob. Bright and goading. And no sooner had the pencil dropped back in than the keys were clinking in my pocket next to Edward's.

Linda tapped an invisible watch when I arrived back. I was late due to Edward's complex and annoying list. I had no idea where any of the items were in the supermarket as I flustered down each wrong aisle, growing ever more conscious of the now duplicated keys in my pocket and the wrongdoing that the overly chipper Timpson man had helped me commit.

Alison was still stuffing her face in the staffroom. Unfairly unreprimanded. Quizzing me about Edward's shopping.

'You know, once when I was about nine, I ate too many prunes and—'

'Sorry, Alison, I really want to hear this, but I've got to do something for Dr Stevens.'

'Oh, that's OK . . . I think you can guess how it ends, anyway.'

As I rushed back towards your office, vaguely aware of Linda's voice calling my name, I noticed that I must have forgotten to switch the light off in your room as the bright line shone beneath the door.

'Constance? Constance, hang on a second.' Dr Franco was coming down the stairs. I stopped, though my heart continued at speed. 'I'm afraid my diary is rather full at the moment, but how about the 29th of this month? Shall we say at one?'

'Yes. Yes, that's great. Thank you. I'll put it in my phone.'

My clammy fingers circled the keys in my pocket.

'You look stressed. Are you OK?'

'Yes . . . yes. I'm just a bit late back from lunch.'

He tapped his nose like it was our little secret. 'I shall look forward to our chat,' he said, and carried on down the corridor as I entered your room.

'You didn't knock. You really should knock, Constance.' You were standing over your desk patting paperwork, picking items up only to put them straight back down again.

'Sorry. I—'

'Did Linda send you in to help look for my phone?'

'Yes. Yes, she . . . No joy, then?'

'What's wrong with me, Constance? On one hand, I'm a doctor who can literally save people's lives, and on the other, I'm a moron who constantly leaves things behind . . . It's the second time this week.'

The keys scratched against my thigh as if possessed. You sighed before throwing a heavy medical journal down on the desk. Then you opened the drawer.

'Do you ever put it in there, though?' My voice cracked.

'No . . . no, I don't . . . but where the fuck is it?' You slammed it shut again and I let out a loud breath.

'I presume you've called it?'

'I'm not fucking stupid. It's on silent . . . I'm supposed to be at Mrs Johnson's in ten minutes.' You looked down. Scratched the back of your neck. Embarrassed, I presumed, hoped, by the way you'd spoken to me.

As you'll remember, I joined in the search. Down on the floor, crawling on my hands and knees, looking in every cranny, while you watched.

With no sign of it anywhere, I stood again and went over to your jacket on the back of the door. 'Have you checked these pockets?' I patted the material, unleashing your after-shave. 'It's in here, I think . . . Shall I?'

You stomped over and fished out the phone. 'Oh my God. I love you, Constance.'

I. Love. You.

Joy burst from my heart and spread through me. I wanted to say something back, but you carried on talking. 'I was wearing my coat, wasn't I? Of course. Jesus, I'm such an idiot. Anyway, I've got to dash. I'm late.' You searched in your trouser pocket. 'For Christ's sake, now what have I done with the surgery car key?' I pointed to it on the desk. 'Thank you, Constance. You're the best,' you said, grabbing it. Then you pushed past me and rushed down the corridor, unbothered whether I was following or not.

I put my head out of the door to check you'd gone, shut myself back in the room and with great relief returned the keys.

Carrying Edward's shopping made shadowing you after work a bit trickier.

So as not to lose sight of you, I refused to stop and adjust the plastic-bag handles now embedded into my hands. Instead I continued through the slicing pain. Kept the same distance throughout.

Until you picked up your phone.

It was clear you weren't searching for songs as usual. You'd removed your earphones and were talking to someone on the handset.

I sped up to gain more information. Conscious of the bags rustling as they knocked against my legs. Your free hand gesticulated, and the rare glimpses of your face showed you didn't look happy at all. Your features, screwed-up, tense.

The call lasted around ten minutes. Almost the duration of our walk. My mind searched for who could be on the line. Initially fixating on Fiona. Then I remembered your diary entry. Sarah. You hung up with such fury that the phone slipped from your hand onto the pavement. I froze as you stopped to retrieve it.

When you turned the corner into your road, I didn't follow. I held back, dropped the bags on the ground, releasing my white-striped numb hands, which I shook to bring back the circulation. Despite pins and needles, I lit a cigarette and smoked, giving you time to get inside.

Once I'd inserted the key into the main door to Edward's, it barely moved a millimetre side to side. After cursing the man from Timpson, I realized I'd been using yours by mistake. Guilt triggered, I unzipped the rarely used inside pocket of my bag and dropped them into the darkness, out of sight. Out of my mind.

'Hello, darling girl.' Edward was reading in bed when I entered. His room was depressing and carried illness in the air. He removed his reading glasses before placing the American Civil War book across his chest.

'How are you feeling?' I asked.

'Well, I think my dream of being an Olympic triathlete is over.'

'Hey, don't be so negative.'

'You made me laugh. You're a miracle worker. Though it was an internal chuckle, so there's work to do yet.'

I lifted the shopping bags. 'I'll just sort this out and get your soup.'

Considering my room was a perpetual slobbish embarrassment, it was strange that Edward's grimy kitchen upset me so much. There was little difference between the dirty pots piled next to the stagnant sink water and the supposedly clean ones sat on open shelves or hanging from hooks. Filth dulled the orange of the Sixties flowered tiles to a tan. I didn't understand why I cared. Why I couldn't bear that he lived that way. But I had a once-in-a-lifetime urge to clean, to make it nicer for him. So, once Edward was all set up with his food, I pushed up my sleeves, put on some ancient rubber gloves that I found under the sink and got stuck in.

Don't think that I wasn't continuously aware of your proximity. Imagining what I was missing. I was every bit the addict waiting for a hit. Yet there was enjoyment in the anticipation and so I remained focused on what I needed to do.

As I saw the change, colours coming to life, I wondered why I didn't do it more often. Cleaning. There was something therapeutic in the monotony. Genuine joy from witnessing results. I pressed my hand hard against the tiles. Scrubbing with the sponge, left, right, left, right . . . dipped the sponge back in the bowl. Left, right, left, right. The repetitious hypnotic action glazed my eyes. I fixated on a tile. A stubborn stain. But as I stared, the tile changed shape and colour. Turned white. And suddenly I was scrubbing away at bloodstained grout.

The sound of a plate smashing to the floor propelled me back into the room.

'Is everything OK in there?' Edward shouted.

I tried to sound normal. 'Yes, fine . . . How's the soup?'

'A little like diarrhoea.'

I bent down and collected the pieces of brown-rimmed ceramic into my useless fumbling hands and winced at the noise as it tumbled into the bin.

'I'm ready for my prunes now.' Edward was dabbing the corners of his mouth with a spotted silk handkerchief as I entered the room. Compared to the newly spruced kitchen, his bedroom seemed even more cluttered and dusty.

'So, Edward, what's the story with that car battery on top of the wardrobe? I presume it's not in the beautiful category.'

'Ah . . . well, dear Constance, I never said the system wasn't flawed.'

'It's ridiculous – you need to get rid of some stuff . . . Anyway, I've cleaned the kitchen a bit,' I said, picking up the empty soup bowl.

'What? Well, you shouldn't have.'

'I had to. It was rank.'

'I like it like that.'

'No, you don't. You'll like it now.'

When I brought him the prunes and custard, I enjoyed how his eyes lit up. Though I watched nervously as he crammed them into his mouth.

'For Christ's sake, be careful of the stones. I'm not going back to hospital.'

'Thank you for the advice. Yet I've managed to eat prunes for over eighty years without dying yet.'

'Right, well, I can't watch. I'm going outside for a cigarette.'

'Outside?' He wiped a globule of custard hanging from his beard. 'Just hang out of the window, dear girl.'

'I'm not sure—'

'Don't be stupid. I'll not inhale it from here. I can barely breathe in at all – do you think I can suck it up from the lounge? Though I thoroughly disapprove. You should bloody well pack them in.' The spoon dropped back into the custard.

'OK, I'll do that. Use the window, I mean.'

The thought of seeing you energized me, and I needed the distraction from the episode in the kitchen.

The sash window was so stiff I almost gave up trying to open it.

'Give it some welly,' Edward shouted, which led to a cough.

When I eventually pushed it up, the cold air punched me.

I lit the beautiful stick. Then, fearful you would see me, I concealed myself with the dusty curtains and leant against the windowsill next to a macabre clown figurine complete with glass balloons.

Sitting there, I had one of those thoughts. You know, when you worry that you'll jump without really wanting to. So I held on to the curtain for safety.

It wasn't long before the show began.

You came into view with only a towel around your bottom half. Hair wet. When you threw yourself down on the sofa, you appeared to be talking without your hand raised to your ear. At first, I thought perhaps you were using Bluetooth. But it wasn't that, was it? There was someone with you. Someone out of my view. And you wouldn't be half naked with your legs spread in a towel for one of your mates.

Smoke caught on my throat, making me gag.

Your head was in your hands, your legs wide. You stood up. Walked around. Shouting, pointing to the person, woman, off screen. Passionate hand gestures. Intense face.

I heard Edward coughing. 'Can I get some water, Constance?' His voice crackled.

'Yes . . . just . . . just hang on a minute.'

'I think I'm choking.'

'You're not choking.' It was so difficult to tear myself away, but I dropped the remainder of my fag in the ashtray.

After a few sips of water, Edward's cough subsided completely. I was almost annoyed that he wasn't choking.

'I've left my fag in the ashtray. I'm going to go and finish it.'

'Slave to them,' he said.

You were nowhere. I gave up concealing myself with the curtain and hung out of the window for a better view. There was no sign of you. No sign of anyone.

I stubbed out the husk of the filter and lit a fresh smoke, barely placing it between my dry, anxious lips when the main door of your flats flew open. And there you were. There she was. Fiona. Crying and screaming, 'I can't believe you're doing this to me.'

You stood at the top of the steps, still in your towel. You must have been freezing, but you seemed oblivious to the temperature as you grabbed her arms, told her to calm down.

That you were sorry, but you just couldn't be with anyone right now. That if you'd thought for one minute she'd developed feelings, you would have nipped it in the bud immediately.

I would've laughed had it not hurt so much. Listening to your patter. Your lies.

She was still crying. Can you believe I felt sorry for her? Knowing what you were doing to her? How it felt. Though I didn't cry when it was me. Wouldn't cry. Did you even register that?

She attempted to rest her head on your chest. But you gently took her by the wrists and widened the space between you both. She slipped her hand away and to my delight swiped it with force across your stunned face.

You looked around to see if any neighbours had witnessed your pathetic show. The funny thing was, I saw Tippi Hedren coming down the road. You didn't. You thought it had all gone unnoticed.

As Fiona ran off crying, you looked towards the skies in fury. I ducked out of view, dropping my fag on the floor in the process and knocking the clown figurine off the sill.

'What the hell have you done?' Edward shouted with difficulty.

'I'm . . . I'm so sorry, Edward. It's the clown . . .' The fag had singed Poor Tiger so I stroked his head, apologizing, before stubbing out the cigarette and going to the bedroom to confess.

'I'm so sorry . . . It's broken.'

'What is?'

'The clown thing on the windowsill.'

'What clown thing?'

'The clown figurine. With all the balloons?'

He looked at me blankly.

'You don't even know you've got a clown figurine, do you?'

'Well, there's quite a lot of stuff in here to remember.'

'Well, there's one less thing now.'

When I returned with the dustpan and brush, you were back in your flat. Dressing in the bedroom. Tracksuit bottoms, I think, and a T-shirt. You didn't appear upset. Almost unaffected by what had happened. You disappeared again, emerging a few minutes later, carrying a bowl and spoon into the lounge. I guessed cereal. You guzzled it and wiped dribbles from your chin. I was forced to leave you as I swept the glass. The clown's grinning face stared at me, intact, surrounded by the shattered multicoloured shards. When I stood with the weighted dustpan, I watched you turn on the TV. You sat back, eating, watching, not a care for Fiona. For anyone.

You slowly placed the bowl on the floor and answered your phone. Whoever the caller was, they made you smile, laugh. I observed you throughout the conversation. Timed it by the dodgy cuckoo clock. Six minutes. They'd amused you for the duration. Your head thrown back, fingers running through your hair. I found it hard to believe that Fiona could have brought you round so quickly. Then I remembered Sarah.

Needing to walk away from you for a moment, I carried the dustpan into the kitchen and disposed of the clown on top of the broken plate.

Edward had fallen asleep, so I gently removed his glasses and placed them on the bedside table. Took the phone handset and switched off his light.

When I returned to the lounge, you were back to stuffing your face and watching TV. With Edward's phone, I blocked the number and dialled.

Looking confused, you picked up the call. 'Hello?' you said. 'Hello?'

I remained silent.

'For fuck's sake, Fiona, is this you? If it is, please fuck off and get a grip. We weren't in a relationship. Just let it go.'

It wasn't me who put the phone down this time. It was you.

With confirmation that Fiona wasn't the mystery caller, with frenzied hands I removed the folded Post-it from my pocket and dialled Sarah's number.

It rang once. Twice. Three times.

'Thank you for contacting Everton Car Insurance—'

I ended the call. Rushed over to the window. Slammed it down and pulled the curtains shut.

*

Knowing Fiona had been eradicated, I became more positive. Regained my purpose. Our romantic reunion. Concentrated on ways to bring you back to me. Laid to rest all that had gone before. Forgave you.

One Saturday Dale suggested we went for a coffee on Chiswick High Road. Which was unusual considering he'd rant about the prices they'd charge when it would only cost twenty pence to make at home. But that day, he was adamant, and I wasn't going to argue as I welcomed time away from the bedsits.

It was pleasant being out. Though Christmas was already in the shops and triggered mixed feelings. The dread of the first one without her and the amusing memories of the ones we'd had.

The cafe he chose was cold. Not helped by the shiny metal chairs, which sent shocks through my flesh.

We sipped our cappuccinos. Played the role of a normal couple.

'You know we've almost been together two months now, Constance?' He slurped the froth, then released the cup to reveal a whitened top lip. 'It feels longer, though, doesn't it? But I guess we were together way before any of that really, weren't we?'

'Yes . . . I . . . I suppose so.'

'But I reckon anniversaries are based on the first time a couple makes love.'

My throat closed, causing me to choke on the coffee. After the cough subsided, I croaked, 'Dale . . . don't say that out loud.'

'I'm sure everyone here knows about lovemaking, Constance. You're so childish sometimes.'

Embarrassed, I smiled at the windswept woman leaning over a high chair and encouraging a plastic spoon into her crying baby's mouth.

'She definitely does,' he said under his breath, folding and unfolding his hand in a cutesy wave. It stopped crying and stared at him. 'I hope that'll be us one day,' he said.

'What? Me feeding you puréed vegetables?'

'Funny. No . . . having a baby. Though obviously we'll marry first.'

I stood. 'I'm just nipping to the loo.'

He took my hand. 'Thank you, Constance.'

'For what?' I twisted awkwardly back towards him.

'For, you know . . . being you.'

He looked at me with desperate eyes. Wanted me to say something meaningful back.

'That's OK,' I said, and slid my hand from under his.

On my return, he was surprisingly upbeat. 'Let's talk birthday presents.'

'It's not for a few weeks yet.'

'Yeah, I know, but—'

'Well, I was thinking of an urn or a nice box for her ashes.'

'Not for your mum's birthday, for yours.'

'That's . . . I meant mine.'

He laughed. 'You can't get an urn for your birthday. Anyway, it doesn't matter. I already know what I'm getting you. Something you'll love.'

'I . . . I don't really want anything . . . Honestly, don't worry. We didn't do birthdays, Mum and me. They were only a few weeks apart so one would usually have to borrow off the other for presents, so it seemed pointless.'

He squeezed my hand and smiled before picking up a copy of the *Guardian* from the table next to him and passing me the supplement.

We flicked through our respective publications in silence. Each time someone entered or left the cafe, they let in the raw air and I became uncomfortably cold, concluding I may as well be freezing outside but with the added joy of a cigarette.

'I'm just going to pop and get some fags.'

He didn't look up, only stroked my arm as I stood to leave.

Before reaching the Tesco Express, I was seduced into going inside a shop called Annie's, which was filled with quaint delights I couldn't afford.

Tracing my fingers over a cool glass case full of delicate jewellery, I wished that the angel-wing pendant at the back was Dale's present. She loved angels. But at ninety-five pounds, I knew my wish would remain just that.

I dragged myself away from both the silver and the suspicious gaze of the sales bitch and wandered over to the small wall of cards, immediately being drawn to a beautiful water-colour of roses with *Mum* on the front. It was her first birthday since she died and I was dreading it. As I'm sure, unlike Dale, you'd have understood.

I'd lied about our not celebrating birthdays. We always did. It'd just be the two of us, of course. There was no one else. In the early years I'd overdose on cake and watch her descend into alcoholic numbness, and in the latter years we'd fall there together. How was I expected to celebrate the day she gave me life when she no longer had hers?

Trying to put it out of my mind, I scanned the other designs.

It was then I saw the card.

Rough, thick, cream-coloured paper. On the front, in a swirling black font, it said, *Whatever our souls are made of, his & mine are the same.* Underneath in smaller writing, *Emily Brontë, Wuthering Heights.*

When rushing back to the cafe, my purchase pushed inside my bag, I almost forgot to stop at the Tesco Express for the cigarettes. Stood in the queue, I picked up a small bag of Lindt chocolate balls for Dale, to counteract my guilt.

That night, once Dale had fallen asleep during an episode of *CSI*, I went to my room and extracted the card. I was unsure what to do with it. Obviously, I couldn't just write a message and post it to you. Thinking of my options, I slumped onto the bed, distractedly flicking through the magazine that Dale had stolen from the cafe for me. And it was after an article on whether snails offered the answer to anti-ageing that I noticed a review of Samuel Beckett's *Endgame* at the National.

I'll admit I did have my doubts about writing a message to you using kidnapper-style lettering. I wasn't insane. But there it was. Your complete name. Telling me it was what I should do. Approval.

The card burned a hole in both my bag and mind for the remainder of the weekend, which was mainly spent watching Dale killing zombies and tidying my bedsit after him shaming me. 'Jesus, Constance. You're not a teenager anymore, you know.' Shoot, shoot, shoot.

On the Monday I was aware of its existence the whole day. Fearful it would somehow fall out onto the floor. 'Who's Samuel?' I imagined Alison would say. Then her eyes would widen, her hand block her mouth. But that didn't happen. It remained tucked away. My exquisite secret.

When I followed you after work, aside from the harsh wind, all was soothing. Your earphones were in, your collar up, hair billowing, and I was full of joyous anticipation. Like a child about to give their first gift.

Catching up with Edward about the events of our respect-ive weekends, I was delighted he seemed so well. Reminiscent of the Edward I'd met that first day, feisty and diamond-eyed.

Despite the happiness this brought, as I sank into what we now referred to as 'my chair', I couldn't concentrate on his words. I did try to appear interested, and avoid looking at you, but I was too aware of you wandering around your flat.

'I watched a documentary on Saturday, and, Constance, did you know that NASA have discovered stars that are cool enough to touch?'

'No . . . no, I didn't know that.' I supped on my tea, myself light years away. Which in hindsight was a shame. I really am interested in touchable stars.

I waited with him as he chomped down on his bacon sandwich. 'Now, Edward, did you know . . . that pigs are the closest species genetically to dogs? Except they're more intelligent.'

'Is that so? Well, I've eaten quite a few dogs as well and I can tell you they are nowhere near as delicious.' He noted my look of horror and laughed. 'Darling girl . . . I didn't realize: it was in Vietnam.'

Unable to deal with Edward's canine-eating confession, I made my excuses to leave early. Outside, I placed my hand in my bag and held on to the card. Looking up, I could see your light was still on, but I was anxiously aware that you could head downstairs at any moment. Regardless of the risk, I was about to cross over when Tippi Hedren came down the road with her panting Labrador. As she climbed the steps with her key in hand, I lost my nerve and headed off, weighted with disappointment and with the perilous item still in my possession.

The following day I brought Edward a vegetarian lasagne as punishment for the dogs. He was up, dressed in a pale green jumper I hadn't seen before, a colour that drained the blood from his face, and his prior perkiness had given way to a sour mood.

He clashed his cutlery against the plate. 'What the hell is this dry crap? Just because I'm interested in astronauts doesn't mean I want to eat their food.'

After insisting he needed to eat more greens, I noticed you leaving your flat. Poker night.

'Well, let me tell you, Constance. Your pallor is no advert for eating vegetables.'

Edward was soon tired and pasty-looking.

'If you saw yourself right now, you're not a great advert for bacon,' I said, tucking him up in bed. I brought the layers of heavy blankets up to his chin and stroked the hair off his forehead. The sensation instantly soothed him.

Eyes closed, he felt for my other hand and gripped it tight. 'I'll eat less of the pigs for you,' he said.

Once more I stood outside clutching the envelope. This time, determined.

The brutal wind wrapped my hair around my face, suffocating me. Freeing myself from the tendrils, I looked around for other life within the darkness. There was no Tippi Hedren. There was no one.

I performed the procedure like a ballet. The glide across the road, the ascent of the steps, the raising of the large brass letterbox, the smooth insertion that led to the delicate drop, the turn and departure.

With each action the thrill increased.

Lying in Dale's bed, him snoring next to me, I imagined your return home. The initial dip to retrieve the card from the floor, followed by the surprise at your name pasted, grey, on the front. You'd begin to open it, then stop yourself. Pulse racing, you'd run up to your flat, craving privacy. Door shut. Lights switched bright. Keys clanking into the bowl. With anticipation you'd tear the envelope, then slide out the card. Opening it slowly. Palpitating heart.

This was written for us, you'd read. My words pasted tiny and disjointed. Fluttering stomach. At first, you'd be confused. Then after, when it had sat with you for a while, and you'd undressed, cleaned your teeth, sunk into your soft, rumpled sheets and the beautiful feeling of your body suspended upon your mattress, you'd turn to the card, now propped up on your side table next to your clock, and you'd feel warmth from your bare feet upwards and smile, basking in the love of a stranger. The list of names, possibilities, running through your head again and again until that moment before you reached to switch off your lamp, when your mind lingered on one name predominantly. The one you hoped it was. Constance.

*

The next day all remained the same.

Your eyes didn't glint knowingly towards mine. Dishearteningly, you didn't hint at having received the card or that you'd hoped it'd been sent by me.

All that effort. All the love I'd poured into it. Into you.

I tried to be content with just following, watching. Remaining strong and not making silent calls. But like Mum with Martin, the smallest thing can hurl you into the comforting arms of addiction.

It had been a particularly bad day. Harris was even more of an insufferable prick than usual. Red-faced and spitty, he'd told me to 'pull my socks up' because I'd forgotten to call Mrs Wheatley about her results. And when I'd finally left Wankerville, I called Dale on the way round to Edward's to moan about Harris, but all I got was, 'Well, you did forget to call her, I suppose' and 'I can't believe you're still visiting this Edward guy. I think you need to sort out your priorities.' It didn't dawn on him that I was. That I actually preferred being with Edward than him. That my visits had transformed from duty to want. That I enjoyed spending time with him, and, by default, you.

When I arrived, Edward was in the lounge, sat in his

233

creased, faded dark blue and red paisley pyjamas. The top button missing, his grey chest hairs searching through the gap. His crumpled red spotted hanky hanging from the loose breast pocket.

'You got dressed for bed early.'

'What? Oh . . . oh yes. I did, yes.' He couldn't look me in the eye. 'I think I'd like to go to bed now, Constance.'

'I need to make you something to eat first.'

'I've already eaten.' Again he avoided my gaze. I recognized that lack of eye contact. What it meant.

'You need to eat something, Edward.'

'I'll see myself to bed, then.' He pushed himself up, the effort extracting all breath from his lungs.

'Here . . . put your arm around me.' I bent down to offer myself to him.

'Stop fussing, for Christ's sake. Stop trying to make me infirm.' His face flushed at the embarrassment of his raised voice. I straightened myself and watched him in silence. He managed to stand. Remaining still for a moment, as if to wait for his blood to once again navigate his veins. 'Well, thanks for popping in, Constance.'

'I'll stay . . . make sure you're settled.' I was addressing his curved back, shuffling out of the room.

When I could no longer see him, I dropped into my chair. For once not thinking of you, but listening to his huffs and puffs as he made it into bed. Sounds she'd make. Weak, fragile. Master of trickery with her smiling and 'I'm fine's.

And I didn't like it. How it made me feel. What it brought back. I needed something to counteract it.

It was just the usual at first. Dialled your number prefixed with 141. Walked over to the window and watched as you picked up the phone.

'Hello?'

Silence.

'Hello? Look, take me off your call list. I'm not interested.' You dropped the handset on the sofa before bending, I presumed, to untie your laces.

I meant for that to be it. I swear I did. I was done. Satisfied. I even turned and headed for the door. But as I did, the feelings gnawed at me. Took hold. Made me think of things. See things burnt on my eyelids as I blinked. Images of her from that day.

It wouldn't have happened if I'd had to input the digits individually.

The redial button made it so easy.

I returned to the window, pressed again.

'Hello? For fuck's sake.'

The line died.

You threw the handset down onto the cushion next to you. Put your feet up on a new glass coffee table that I hadn't known about. This disgruntled me further. I wasn't part of your private life anymore.

I pressed the button again. This time it rang out and I watched you ignoring it, ignoring me. Pause. Then again. You were staring at it. Cross-armed, cross-legged. Your one visible socked foot moving up and down anxiously. I wanted to tell you that you needn't have worried. That it was only me.

I pressed it again.

And again.

And again.

I couldn't stop. I wanted to. Believe me. But the more you ignored me, the more I needed your acknowledgement.

Until finally you picked up.

'Who the fuck is this? Hello? Hello? Whoever this is, stop calling me.' You lowered your hand for a moment. I waited for the line to go dead, but you raised it back to your ear. 'Fiona, is this you? Is this you, Fiona? It is, isn't it? You fucking nut-job . . . Oh my God, if you don't stop this, I'm going to report you to the police.'

I ended the call.

Stepped away from the window. Jelly legs causing me to stumble. My heart thumped against my ribs. Once again my hypnotic state was over and I threw the phone onto the chair like a hot smoking gun.

*

For the next couple of days I could think of nothing else.

I avoided your eyes and presence. Terrified of triggering a moment when you'd look at me and it would all suddenly click. Realize it wasn't Fiona at all.

It was around two on the Friday, as I was filling in Alison's charity-walk sponsor form (for which I could only afford a fiver instead of a tenner like everyone else), when I thought the dreaded moment had arrived.

You were about to leave for a house call. I hoped that you'd not come back and all would be forgotten by the Monday. Alison said goodbye to you. I concentrated on the form as if oblivious. As you walked towards the door, I could feel my anxiety leaving with you. But it returned, reinforced, when you turned back around and headed over to the reception desk, with a summoning finger, calling my name.

I dropped the pen onto the sheet and, though petrified, magnetically responded to your request.

'Yes, Dr Stevens.'

You slipped a piece of paper into my hand. 'I almost forgot . . . I've got a new number. Can you tell the other girls as well?' You didn't notice the paper pulsating between my fingers, and must have misinterpreted the outward evidence of my internal panic for curiosity, as you whispered, 'It's a long story . . . Can we catch up after work?'

I nodded.

You smiled, then counteracted our intimacy with a loud 'Goodbye, Alison. See you in a couple of hours.'

As you can imagine, I was in a swirl for the rest of the day. Intoxicated on a cocktail of excitement and fear. Unsure if I'd imagined it. Got the wrong end of the stick. Or perhaps it was a trick and I'd been caught out. But I chose to focus on your smile, which indicated that I was safe.

Dead on five you came into reception, coated up, and said goodbye to us all. I took this as confirmation of my insanity and felt the disappointment resume. Then, when no one was looking, you mouthed, 'Meet me up the road.'

It was the first time we'd walked side by side for so long.

We were propelled back to the beginning. The ease, the friendship. I playfully touched your arm and joked that the wind had given you a Bobby Charlton.

'You're twenty-six. How do you even know Bobby Charlton?'

'Erm, hello? I'm from Manchester.'

I braved asking what you'd wanted to talk about, but you said you'd tell me when we were warm, inside somewhere. As I nodded, my teeth chattered. Do you remember? How your woollen-clad arm encased me, rubbed my shoulder, until that ten-pound note flew from your pocket, taunting you as it danced away whenever you got close. When you finally caught it under your foot, saying, 'I've got you, you bastard,' you were oblivious to my dropped smile. I was so content that I knew it was no longer enough for me to walk behind you.

On your suggestion, we went to the Wheatsheaf. You didn't mention the 'kissing' we did there. Not even as a crude joke. Just referred to it as somewhere we 'both knew'. When we walked past the alleyway, nothing even registered on your face. Whereas I flinched at the image of my bare body bruising against the brickwork.

Inside, the place was much quieter than the previous time. Like a different pub. It was still early doors and the Friday-night shenanigans had not yet begun. I opted for a battered leather sofa in a purposely chosen cosy alcove, as you ordered our drinks from the lone barman reluctantly slicing lemons. I watched your every movement. The exaggerated dip into your pocket for money, your attempts to straighten out your hair.

Then I remembered Edward. He was expecting me, and I hadn't turned up. I mimed with my finger that I would just be a minute and went outside to call.

'Hey, I'm so sorry, but I've had to meet a friend who was upset about something. Are you OK? Have you got stuff in to eat?'

'Don't you be worrying about me. Go see to your friend, darling girl.'

The guilt made me light a fag. 'Are you OK, though? You sound a bit shit? The phone's beeping again – make sure you put it on charge.'

'I'm fine. A nurse came today . . . Maxine. Wonderful, she

is . . . She's an artist as well as a nurse. We had a lovely chat about Klimt.'

'Oh . . . oh, OK.'

'She's going to come regularly now. To check on me.'

'Oh . . . OK. Well, that's good . . . I already check on you, though.'

I waited for him to reply but realized the line was dead and I'd been talking to myself.

You were sat at the table in front of two large glasses of brandy, not the Coke I'd requested. Noticing my confused frown, you said, 'I know, I know, but I thought you needed warming up.'

Was it all part of the plan? To infiltrate my mind with memories of our first time. My body with alcohol.

'So, what was it you wanted to talk about?'

You laughed and stared into your glass, swirling it repeatedly. 'Blimey, can't wait to go, eh?'

You have no idea how much I wanted to be strong. Say I had somewhere to be. 'No, no, not at all.'

You sighed, returned your glass to the table, remained with your head down, distressed. I was unsure what to do. Like I was with Dad that day. I know what I wanted to do. My hand hovered behind your head, wanting to touch you.

'What's up?'

'It's nothing. I . . . It's just . . .' You looked back at me, desperate. My stomach lurched at the fear you'd confront me after all. You breathed out, long and slow. 'There was a woman. Way before . . . you know . . . before us, I mean.'

I sipped my brandy. Suppressed both the surge of happiness

at your use of the term 'us' and the anger at the lie you'd just told.

'It was a one-off thing. I . . . I didn't even fancy her . . . She was just there.'

I was just there too, Samuel. I was there. 'Where?'

'What do you mean?'

'Where did you meet her?'

You picked up a beer mat and swivelled it between your fingers, eyes averted. 'I don't know. At a party somewhere. It . . . it was ages ago . . . I can't even remember.'

I waited for you to continue. Encouraged you to squirm.

'We had a rubbish drunken shag, and to keep her happy and not feel used, I took her out a few times and then ended it like I knew I would do all along . . .'

I took a gulp. Waited. For you to either finish what you were saying or to realize your insensitivity, describing what you'd also done to me. Except you didn't even take me out to prevent me feeling used. I poured more alcohol onto my fire. When I looked at you, it wasn't just your face that was blurred by the influx of brandy but the line between love and hate.

'But now she . . . she . . .'

'I can't stay long, Dr Stevens. I'm meeting my boyfriend.'

I delighted in your face. Your flaring nostrils and widened eyes. 'Dr Stevens again, is it? OK . . . Sorry. I just really wanted your advice . . . So you have a boyfriend now?'

'Yes. Yes, I do . . . Advice?'

'Well . . . I'm . . . That's great . . . I'm really pleased for you, Constance.'

I smiled through your corrosive words. 'So, the advice?'

'Oh yes, well, this woman . . . She hasn't . . . Well, she just can't seem to let go, Constance.' You used your agitated hands to smooth your hair.

'Is it Laura? You've already told me that about Laura. That she couldn't let you go.'

'Did I? No . . . no . . . it's not Laura . . . It's someone else. She keeps ringing me. I swear she's crazy.'

'So another woman can't let go either? What do you do to them?'

You looked right at me. Eyes wide open, as if to prove your innocence. 'Nothing . . . I swear. You know me. I'm not like that. I didn't lead her on or promise anything, but she keeps ringing me.'

'And saying what?'

'Well, that's the thing. Nothing. She doesn't speak . . . She's just there. I can sense her.'

'Sense her?' I sipped my drink to hide the blood surging to the surface of my skin.

'I can feel her on the other end of the line. Not saying anything.'

'Oh. I see. Maybe there's a fault on the line—'

'I know it sounds crazy . . . but I promise you she's at the other end.' You picked up the beer mat just to throw it back down again.

'And how do you know it's her?'

Would it shock you to know that I was no longer scared? Or embarrassed? That I didn't feel shame or guilt? If anything, I was empowered. The way you glanced down. Unable to keep your fingers still. How I'd made you feel powerless.

'I just do . . . There's no one else it could be.'

I tipped the remaining dregs into my mouth.

'You knocked that back quickly. Can I get you another?'

I firmly placed the empty glass on the table. 'But why? If it was such a long time ago that you got together with her, why are you so sure she's the culprit?'

You shot me a puzzled look, then remembered your lie. 'Oh, well, she was just strange from the beginning, clingy. Immediately after sex you could tell she thought it was something more than it was, you know? It's so silly . . . I can't believe she's got to me. So stupid . . . It's just freaking me out a bit . . . Sorry . . . Sorry, Constance. I just knew you'd be someone who I could talk to about it. You understand things . . . me.'

I placed my hand on top of yours. It felt so good, comforting, touching your flesh, hearing you say I understood you. But another part of me imagined folding in my fingers and digging my nails into your skin.

'Hey, it's OK. Do you want me to talk to her? Woman to woman?'

Your eyes lit up with the idea. Then you remembered that I couldn't because I already knew her and you were a fucking liar. 'No . . . no, I think that would make it worse. I've changed my number now, anyway. Threatened her with the police. I don't see how she can call me. Though . . . I didn't tell you everything.' You pulled your coat onto your knee from the seat next to you and fished into the pocket. Your hand emerged with the card I'd so lovingly addressed to you. 'She also sent me some psycho card.' You threw it on the table with such disregard.

'Psycho?'

'Yeah, look at it. An anonymous card. But look at the envelope and inside. It's all cut-out letters . . . really fucking scary.'

I felt tears rise. I hadn't meant for it to seem like that, Samuel. And had at least hoped you'd liked the quote.

You placed your hand on top of mine this time. Not because you'd noticed my upset but for me to soothe yours. 'Constance . . . do you think it's me? I mean, do you think I somehow inadvertently make them crazy?'

'Well, they can't all be crazy, Samuel. Maybe you upset them in some way.'

'But I'm a nice guy. I don't set out to hurt anyone.'

I stood, unsteady. 'I feel a little light-headed from the brandy. I'm going to get a Coke. Do you want anything?'

When I returned with my drink and a packet of crisps to soak up the alcohol, I sat down and said, 'I've been thinking . . . I'd relax about it now. If she knows the number's not working, and you mentioned the police, she'll definitely stop.'

'You think so?'

'I do . . . I really do.'

'Thanks, Constance. I knew you'd make me feel better about it all. You calm me.'

I smiled.

'You know what? I'm not going near a woman again unless I truly have feelings for her.'

I tried to think of something worse you could have said, something more hurtful, more cutting, but I couldn't.

'Do you want some crisps?' I pulled open the packet and ripped the foil apart with my teeth.

'Anyway . . . sorry, Constance. I'm so selfish . . . How are you? So, a boyfriend, eh?'

'I'm OK, thanks.'

You sat back, smiling, watched me as I ate the crisps. I felt so self-conscious I could barely swallow. 'What?'

'No . . . no . . . I shouldn't . . .'

'Tell me.'

It was then you moved away the coats wedged between us. Sidled closer and whispered, 'Well, I . . . I shouldn't say this, but I really don't like that you've got a boyfriend.' As soon as the words entered my ear, you stood. 'Sorry . . . sorry . . . Ignore that. I shouldn't have said it. I'm going to the loo . . . Ignore me.'

Alone, I drank my Coke with the pretence that your words hadn't set me alight. That they weren't the words I'd fantasized about hearing. Words that were now cemented deep in my head, my heart. Impossible to ignore, regardless of your instruction.

'Shall we get out of here?' You'd returned and were reaching for your coat.

I silently agreed and did the same. Unsure of your intentions as I buttoned up. 'Don't forget your card.'

'No, thank you. They can throw it . . . Gives me the bloody creeps.'

I smiled. 'Good idea,' I said, allowing my scarf to slip from my fingers.

Outside, bitten by the cold, we headed down the road. I stopped, raised my hands in exasperation. 'I've left my bloody scarf inside. I thought I was extra cold.'

'You're as bad as me, Constance. Let me—'

'No, no, don't be daft. I won't be a sec.' Before you could argue, I was running back towards the entrance.

Inside, I mingled with the two couples settling into our seats, apologizing as I dipped under the table.

'It's my scarf . . . I left my scarf.' I re-emerged, head full of blood. 'Sorry . . . and this . . . I forgot this as well,' I said as I pushed my arm between the men's bodies, sliding the card off the table and into my bag.

Outside your flat, you asked if I wanted to come up for coffee.

I did think about Dale. Of course I did. But should we deny ourselves happiness if it presents itself? A happiness that for me had been so rare.

When you lay upon my body and moved inside, when you kissed my mouth hard, with each rough jolt I replayed what you'd said – *I'm not going near a woman again unless I truly have feelings for her.* And I thought how silly it was that those words had hurt me so intensely. When, as we lay there hand in hand, I realized they were in fact the proof of how you felt.

*

The whole weekend I was awash with love.

My joy impenetrable. Nothing could pierce it. Not being in the red the day after payday. Not the guilt about Dale. Not the trip to Sainsbury's when he made us wait for an age by the chilled section to ensure we were first on the scene for the new yellow-stickered clearance items. Not Edward's unreasonable grumpiness on the phone because he wouldn't have any Bovril until Monday. Not even your silence.

When Monday finally arrived, I awoke at six, in Dale's bed, listening to his elephantine snores, his body encased in most of the duvet, which in turn exposed my shivering body to the early, frosted air. But I was lofty with excitement at seeing you again in a few hours. Still high on my perch.

Then I remembered.

It was her birthday.

It's funny, grief, isn't it? How you die with them. Whoever you were before has gone. Your ghost walks the earth. You look the same, sound the same, but are not the same. You don't breathe oxygen the way you did before. You negotiate life under an ocean. Drowning as you do your shopping, drowning as you ride the bus, drowning as you go to work.

You can't live with this, you think. No one could live with this. It's unliveable.

Then there are moments when your head rises above the water. You find something funny, laugh. A glimpse of your previous self. Until you are submerged once again. Guilty for your brief ability to breathe.

Over time the water levels drop.

First you tread water; then you swim; then you wade; then you are paddling; until finally you are walking alongside a stream. It flows next to you. Wherever you are, whatever you do, however happy you're feeling, it's there.

But sometimes, be it a song, a crumpled shopping list found in a coat pocket, an anniversary, their birthday, your birthday, Christmas, hearing the theme tune to *Coronation Street*, which you've avoided ever since, the stream becomes a river, becomes an ocean and you are drowning once again.

I should have been making her breakfast in bed. Eggs. Scrambled with a dash of milk, as she liked it. A mug of builder's brew. A fashion magazine on the tray. An expense she couldn't normally justify.

'Oh my goodness,' she would have said. 'Does this mean I have to do this for you in a few weeks?'

'As if,' I'd reply, and she would look at me with her *don't-say-that* face, then would shovel the yellow crumbs into her mouth, tapping with her free hand for me to get in next to her.

To distract me from the pain, I thought about you. In doing so, I remembered the card and removed myself from Dale's bed. Soundless. Put on my dressing gown and crept to my room.

Kneeling on the unhoovered carpet next to the bed, I grabbed my bag and pulled it towards me. Extracted the card. Then searched into the darkness underneath with my arm and dragged out the case, disturbing the dust once more. After pressing a few times to dislodge the rusted left lock, it opened. I tried to avoid the diaries. Just concentrated on placing the latest souvenir with our picture. Safe from prying eyes. Enjoying the feeling of having part of you with me.

Despite the comfort I felt from my growing collection, I was still drawn to her last journal. Like a tarot card on which your mind fixates because you know it holds all the answers.

Inhaling a sharp breath, I dared to lift it out. Wiped my now damp cheeks and the droplets that had fallen to darken the cover. I turned to the last page. It was blank. Turned one backwards. Still blank. Another. And another.

Then there it was.

My beautiful Constance, I'm so sorry—

'Are you OK?'

'Sorry, Dale . . . I . . . didn't mean to wake you.'

'What's going on?'

He was coming towards me, dragging his feet and rubbing his eyes. I shut the diary and threw it on top of the heap. Closed the case, checking the dodgy left lock was secure and pushed it back under. 'Nothing . . . I . . . I just really want to get an urn for her ashes. For my birthday. I really need an urn.'

'What's in that case?'

'Nothing . . . Just things of Mum's . . . Nothing.'

He knelt by my side and pulled me towards him. Hugged

me. I know it sounds selfish, but I wanted it. Needed it. 'Hey, come on. It'll be OK, I promise you . . . All I want is to make you feel happy and safe. Not like this anymore,' he said.

And for that moment I believed him. Thought perhaps I'd got everything wrong. That maybe she'd sent him to me. If I could just love him in return.

But it doesn't work like that, does it?

Being at the surgery was a struggle.

A stressed-out Linda informed me you were at Harley Street and Dr Short was also absent due to a 'family issue', meaning we had to ring and cancel patients or advise them there would be a wait.

I told Linda I had cystitis, so I could keep skiving off to the loo for a cry.

But swollen eyes and vacant looks didn't deter Alison's jabbering about her sponsored walk and how she raised nearly £300 for cancer. Like that would help.

On one of my trips to the toilet, I texted you. Said I'd been looking forward to seeing you. Was disappointed you weren't there. You didn't respond. So I tried calling when on a sneaky fag break, but it rang out. Though I guessed you'd be busy.

Later, at Edward's, I couldn't stop looking towards your blackened windows in the hope of your return before I had to leave.

'Are you OK, darling girl? You're very distracted today.'

'Sorry, Edward. It's just . . . it's my mum's birthday. I've been a bit upset, that's all. It's crazy really. It's no different to any other day.'

'Is that so?' He pushed himself up off the chair before huffing his way over to a drawer in the huge cabinet and pulled out a yellowed vintage shoebox. I followed him.

'Push that stuff to the side,' he said, gesturing to the pile of papers and unidentifiable machine parts covering the dining table. Doing so exposed previously unseen shiny mahogany, which I couldn't help but stroke. 'Oh, this is lovely. You really must clear—'

'Yes, yes . . . never mind that.' He placed the box down.

I focused on the multicoloured, bruised skin of his hands as he lifted the lid.

'Crazy, you say.'

Inside was a mass of white envelopes of various sizes. A name scrawled on each. When I dipped my head towards the box, I realized they all said, *Amy*.

'If you're crazy just being sad, how bat-shit does this make me?'

I wanted to open one, but he didn't offer, so I didn't ask.

'Every birthday I write her a card. Tell her I love her. That I may be joining her for her next one.' Embarrassed, he scrambled for the lid and replaced it. 'You're right, though,' he said. 'It is ridiculous.'

I moved closer to him. Dropped my head onto his chest. 'No . . . no, I promise you it's not at all.'

He reached his arms around me, bony and cold. Kissed the top of my head. And I felt a comfort, safety, that I didn't want to end.

We remained there, within our private thoughts. Lost.

Swaying. Until he said, 'This better hadn't all be because you've forgotten my Bovril.'

You didn't return that evening before I had to leave Edward's, but to my relief, you were back in the surgery the next day. However, it was so busy I didn't get to see you for the entire morning. Dr Short was still off, so you were booked in with patient after patient. All became hectic, including an incident with the unhinged ex-model Ms Kemple who was waiting for her appointment with Dr Harris. She looked as if she was attending her own funeral and declared herself as 'dying of the flu'. When informed there'd be a delay, she burst into tears, shouting about how terrible she felt and that she didn't have her late lover, George, to look after her anymore. Linda ordered me to fetch her a cup of tea. Which I did, while remaining as distant from her and her germs as possible. Even more so when I had to collect up the empty mug, which she'd stuffed with a contaminated tissue. Another example of money and manners being unconnected.

With everything so chaotic, I didn't get to your office until lunch.

'Constance. How are you?' You glanced at me for a second before turning back to your computer to resume working.

'I'm . . . I'm good, thanks. I tried to call you yesterday, but I guessed you were busy.'

'Ah yes, sorry . . . I didn't have a minute to myself.' You lifted a sheet of paper. 'You've not seen my pen anywhere, have you? Christ knows what I've done with it.'

'No . . . sorry.' You mouthed the words you'd begun to

type. 'I'm meeting with Dr Franco in a minute, but do you want to get a drink later?'

Finally you tore yourself from the screen and turned to me. Your eyes missing their target.

'I'm busy tonight. It's poker.'

'Ah yes, of course . . . Sorry, I . . . Tomorrow, then?'

'I'm just . . . I'll be busy for a while, Constance, to be honest.' Which was funny, as you didn't know the meaning of the word. Your lips formed a condescending smile. And the realization dropped onto me. Like lead from the sky.

'Sorry, Constance, I really need to finish these notes. I've not even had chance to have a drink yet. You couldn't get me a cup of tea, could you? I'm trying not to have so much coffee. And tea's your northern girls' forte, isn't it?'

In the kitchen, my heart beat an angry rhythm. I placed my arms either side of the sink to gather myself. Swallowed back down the fury. When able to breathe properly again, I stared at the washing-up that they presumably expected me to deal with. Put on the rubber gloves and ran the tap. When the bowl was full, I filled the kettle for your tea and went to wash a cup. Rage bubbling inside me like the Fairy Liquid in the sink. But there was Ms Kemple's mug on the side. Looking at me. And before I knew it, I'd lifted out the snotty tissue, wiped it around the rim and dropped in a fresh bag.

Back in your room, I placed the tea on your desk.

You didn't thank me until you'd taken a sip, then sighed. 'Hmm, lovely. See, I told you.'

'Did I make it right?'

You blew onto the liquid, then slurped again. 'Perfect.'

You turned back towards your computer. Dismissing me without words.

'Before I go, Dr Stevens, can I just ask you, how long do flu germs last on something?'

'Flu germs? Well, it depends. On hard surfaces, they can last up to twenty-four hours. Why?'

'I was just wondering.'

I went to leave. Then you said, 'She's stopped, by the way . . . Glenn Close . . . Not heard a peep. So all is good again in my world.'

'Excellent,' I said, and left.

They say there's a fine line between love and hate. But I don't think there's a line at all. They're the same thing. What we love we hate for loving. What makes us more vulnerable than love? What hurts as much? It's a tightrope that we walk. Wavering from one side to the other. Desperate to keep our balance. But sometimes you can't. Sometimes it tips and there's nothing you can do.

'On the day you die, do you think you know when you wake up that morning?'

I was nine years old when I asked her the question. And I'd waited three hours to get it out. Death, including my death, had become an obsession. The nuclear bomb, a hand hovering over a big red button, terrorist attacks, spontaneous combustion – all a continual worry. And I'd instantly freeze at the mere mention of 'the Big C'.

'Maybe Dad's dead? Maybe he knew he was going to die that day?'

She reached the bottom step. Stared at me, glassy-eyed. 'For fuck's sake, Constance.'

As if testing the temperature of the sea, she placed the tip of her big toe on the floor. As usual, the water was too cold and she quickly retracted her foot and took herself back up the stairs.

Near the top, on the step with the missing banister post, she stopped and said, 'The fact is, you never know what's round the corner in life, good or bad.' Then tripped on the last step, gathered her dressing gown like a nappy between her legs and disappeared back into her room.

*   *   *

Dr Franco had once again managed to get me talking, exposing.

After leaving your office burdened with both guilt and anger, I wished I'd had the foresight to cancel. But when in that special room, I was lulled into bringing her alive.

'And what is it about that particular memory that sticks with you?' He then scribbled intently in his book.

I appreciated his notes now. It showed someone was listening. And there was importance in what he heard.

'I don't know.'

'OK . . . Let me reword that. When I asked you for a memory about your mum that sticks in your mind, why do you think that's the one that came to the fore?'

'I don't know. Her tripping after saying that. It was funny.'

'So it's a funny memory for you?'

'No. Not really.' I crossed and uncrossed my legs. Attempted to make myself comfortable, knowing nothing would.

'How did it feel having your mother always being drunk in her room?'

'It was just how it was.'

'But how did it make you feel?'

Words snagged on my throat, which led to uncontrollable coughing. He stood and calmly went to a table in the corner, poured a glass of water from a jug and walked back to hand it to me, smiling.

With each swallow, I swilled the emotion back down.

'Better?'

I nodded, keeping my breaths measured to prevent it happening again. Hoping he'd move on. Respect that I obviously didn't want to talk about it. But he eased back in his chair and waited. Waited. Waited.

'It made me angry, I guess.'

'And how did you express this anger?'

'I didn't.'

'Ever?'

'No . . . Well, sometimes I'd pour her Martini down the sink. If she was too pissed to remember she'd just bought it.'

'Then what would happen?'

'She'd buy some more.'

His gold-rimmed glasses slid down his nose and he pushed them back up with his hairy fingers as his other hand made notes. I'd never noticed how gorilla-like they were before.

'That must have been very frustrating for you.'

'As I say, it's just how it was.'

He smiled, before resting his pen in the centre dip of his pad. 'Constance . . . what do you think happened to your father?'

I resented the question. He had no right. A darted look showed my disapproval, but he remained unperturbed. 'I've told you – we never knew.'

'Have you ever tried to find him, contact him?'

'No . . . I . . . Kind of. I post him cards.'

'You've written to him?'

'No, no . . . I just post cards with his name on the envelope. Inside, I put my address and number in case it makes it to him somehow. Why would I write to him if I hadn't found him?'

'Well, it can be cathartic sometimes – to write it all down

without giving it to the person. But what does your gut tell you? Do you feel he's alive?'

'I don't know, do I?'

'Would you rather it that way? That you never know? Say if he'd passed away?'

I pulled my face at the stupidity of the question. 'Obviously, I'd rather not know.' My mind changed on the note-taking. It was grating. Intrusive.

'OK . . . And why is that?'

'Why on earth would I want to know he's dead as well?' I uncrossed my legs, allowing my knees to freely jig up and down.

'Because you may feel it would be better to have that closure, move on. Let go of the anxiety of never knowing.'

'Move on? You don't move on when they die.' I noticed for the first time how he held his pen awkwardly. Like he hadn't been corrected at school. It was irritating, and I had the urge to snatch it from his hands and throw it across the room. 'People need hope, Dr Franco. However small that hope is.'

He removed his glasses and looked right at me. 'That is . . . That's very true, Constance.'

I noticed that he glanced over at the clock, and I was relieved. Expecting him to call time.

'So, going back to your story . . . Do you think we know on the day we die? What about your mum?'

I stood. 'Can I get more water, please?'

He gestured for me to help myself.

When I reached the cabinet, I remained with my back to him and said, 'I think she did, yes.' Staring at the glasses and ornate jug, I had the same urge to pick them up one by one and smash them through the elongated window. I turned around. 'She was ill. It was obvious. Like it always is with cancer.' I walked back to my chair and sat, unable to look at him. Aware he'd sensed my angry tone, I focused on one of his certificates on the wall behind his head. 'She was exhausted . . . could hardly speak, was on loads of drugs.' He was writing those fucking notes again. Judging.

'Did she die in hospital?'

'No . . . no, she didn't. She was at home.'

'That must have been hard for you?'

'I'm . . . I'm sorry. Can we talk about something else?'

He leant forward, making it impossible not to look at him. 'Constance, often the things we find the most difficult to talk about are the things that talking about can help us with the most.' I didn't flinch. Stared him out. He relented, sat back. 'So, what would you like to talk about?'

'I'm seeing someone now . . . a man.'

He swung his glasses between his fingers, by their arm.

'Well, tell me all about it.' His tone changed. His face reddened. And he spoke like we actually were 'chatting friends'.

'Well, I don't really know what to say. He's a doctor . . . Oh, no one you know – don't worry. I met him in my local pub.'

'Well, Constance, I'm . . . I'm very pleased for you.' I detected a glint that he wasn't. 'And you feel meeting someone has helped you during this difficult time?'

'Yes . . . yes, it has. His mother died too, you see. We have a special connection. It's a rare and wonderful thing.'

'Well, then that makes me happy, Constance.' And I think he meant it. That I'd been mistaken about the glint.

As soon as I stopped talking, I couldn't bear what I'd said. I was embarrassed by myself. Wanted to go back in time. Rewrite history. Just like you did about what happened in the alleyway of the Wheatsheaf. I tried to change the subject.

'She didn't want to live anymore. That's how I knew she was going to die.'

He was about to say something when a loud buzzing noise infiltrated the room. 'That's my next client, Constance . . . I'm so sorry. But I hope we can continue this?'

'I . . . I'm not sure it's necessary, Dr Franco. I'm feeling a lot better about things now.'

His forehead crinkled. 'Well, that's your decision to make, but I hope you change your mind. I feel like we're just getting somewhere.'

'OK . . . I'll . . . I'll think about it.'

But I knew the 'somewhere we were getting to' was the one place that I couldn't go.

*

You were on catch-up for the rest of the day and I barely got to see you. But this was a relief rather than a disappointment. Even when I followed you home after work, it was done out of habit rather than desire, and carried a resentment that you'd reduced me to this once again. In the end I hung back and had a fag, let you walk on ahead.

However, my mood was bolstered when I entered Edward's and he greeted me in the hallway, a rattling tray between his hands. 'I've made us tea and biscuits. Are you impressed?'

'I am – look at you.' Blood filled his cheeks and there was a perkiness I hadn't seen since my first visit. Had he not been so breathless, I would have been delighted.

I took the tray from him and carried it to the lounge as he walked behind me. 'What did the nurse say today?'

Waiting for him to reach his seat, I placed his cup and the plate on his side table and held on to mine as I sat and leant the tray against my chair. He was still making his way across the room, wanting to talk but unable to do both in unison.

'Take your time, Edward.' I turned to the window. There you were in your bedroom. Freshly showered. Spritzing your scent. Even for poker night. Loving yourself.

He finally dropped into his chair, making a noise as if

the action had winded him, and waited for his breathing to settle. 'She said I'm doing marvellously . . . Insisting I see the doctor this week, though. Before you start nagging the hell out of me, I've agreed. She's been amazing, Maxine. It's the least I could do for her. She's really put herself out for me.'

'Sounds like you won't need my visits anymore. Not with wonderful-actually-getting-paid-to-do-her-job-yet-apparently-putting-herself-out-so-much Maxine.' I bit down on a fig roll.

He picked up the paper that lay folded on the arm of his chair. 'Don't be so bloody ridiculous. I'll always need your visits, Constance.' He put on his glasses. 'I live for your visits.'

I turned towards the window, not for you but so as not to expose how much that meant to me. 'Well, if you want me to still come over, you'll need to improve on your tea-making. This is the worst brew I've ever had.'

We sat in silence as he scribbled on the crossword grid and I looked out, observed. You were applying product to your hair. You hadn't done that before. I preferred it soft, natural.

After a while I stood to gather the cups onto the tray. And when I next glanced, you were leaving the front door hurriedly. Then you got into your car and drove off.

On the way to the kitchen, carrying both the tray and the empty feeling I always had when watching you came to an end, I felt a period drag in my stomach. After dumping the tray, I returned to the lounge to get my bag. Edward was talking as I entered.

'A deliberate act of betrayal?'

'Sorry?'

'Seven down. "Eat cherry pie as a deliberate act of betrayal"?'

'I'm terrible at crosswords.'

'Nine letters. Begins with "T".'

'I don't know . . . Treachery?'

'Treachery. No, it's not . . . Oh, it is right. An anagram of "eat cherry". Well, you're clearly better at them than you think.'

I headed to the toilet. Another room scrubbed and disinfected by my own hands. As suspected, my knickers were stained, though thankfully nothing had seeped through my trousers. I unzipped the inside pocket of the bag to retrieve my emergency tampon. I couldn't find it at first. My fingers were circling something cold and hard.

Your keys.

I extracted them. Remained on the toilet for some time, clutching them so hard their teeth dug into my palm.

'Are you putting the kettle on?' shouted Edward.

'Yes,' I yelled back.

I didn't return them to the bag. I dropped them into my trouser pocket.

As I made Edward a cheese-and-pickle sandwich and an acceptable cup of tea, I deliberated about what to do with the keys. Reminded myself how wrong it was to have them. Concluded I should return them to the bag forever or throw them away. Yet I did neither.

'Is that going to be enough for you?' I said as I placed the sarnie on the arm of his chair.

'I don't even want this.'

'You've got to eat, Edward.'

After trying to prise out of him when he was planning to go to bed so I could get him settled, tuck him in, he finally said, 'I'm not a child. And besides, Maxine said I'm able to sort myself out.'

Trying not to feel hurt, mumbling under my breath about Maxine, I settled for filling a hot water bottle and secretly placing it between his covers, then left him to it.

Outside, at the top of the steps, I lit a cigarette and watched the white swirls evaporate into the freezing air. I checked my phone. It was coming up to seven, so I dialled Dale.

I'd planned to say I'd be home soon. Honestly I did. But it was as if the keys had taken possession of my brain, willing me to use them, and the actual words I spoke were, 'He's not good at all today, sorry. I won't be too long, but I've got to see him into bed . . . I will, yeah . . . He's seeing one this week . . . Well, I'm sorry. What am I supposed to do?' While talking, I'd crossed the road. Gravitated towards your flat. And by the time I'd hung up, I was standing on your top step.

I flicked away the fag and crushed its corpse with my foot. Checked I was alone. Forgetting to breathe as I lifted the keys from my pocket with an unsteady hand. Then consciously inhaling, exhaling, before inserting one into the lock and twisting.

The door creaked open, inviting me to step over the threshold into your world, then clunked shut behind me like a locked prison cell.

I stood, taking in the hall. Now tinged with trespass, it was grander, foreboding.

My shoes squeaked against the polished tiles as I nervously walked over to the stairs, taking care not to slip as I ascended the curved stone. Reliving the last time. How you'd grabbed my hand when I'd misstepped, almost toppled backwards. Pulled me towards you, whispered sweet lies into my ear.

At the top, I bent forward with smoker's lungs and guilty heart, before gathering myself to follow the trail of parquet floor. Stopping once to glance over the handrail. Checking for witnesses. That there was no one hanging around the flat opposite. Until nauseating vertigo forced me to step away.

I was outside your flat.

The polished brass '4' stared at me. Familiar, encouraging. And I did it. I slid in the second key. It opened oh so easily and I pushed into the darkness.

The door slammed behind me. Announcing my presence throughout the building and plunging me into black.

There was no reason for me to know where the light switch was. You'd always led me in. Led me astray.

I stroked the wall with the flat of my hand until *flick*. The addition of light enabled me to breathe once more.

The silence was unsettling. The sheer strangeness of being there. I half expected you to be sitting in the lounge with a glass of wine. You'd call out my name any minute. Tell me to listen to our song. But of course you didn't. Because you weren't there. It was just me. Alone. In your flat.

As I followed the path of the hallway, your scent intensified.

265

The aroma of shampoo and body wash filled the air. Spiced and warm. I inhaled deeply to take you in.

I don't want you to think I didn't know it was wrong. I did. But my desires outweighed that. I told myself I was doing no harm. And I wasn't really. It was a building. Bricks and mortar. Things. That's what I was violating. Whereas you had violated me.

Switching on the lounge light revealed nothing spectacular at first glance, other than an open CD case on the floor and the 'S' cup on the new coffee table. Angular metal and glass. Highlighting how I didn't even make it into the lounge the previous time.

I surveyed the room like a detective at a crime scene. Not touching, contaminating. On closer inspection, the cup was half filled with tea; the CD, Tom Waits, *Closing Time*. An album that makes you think of people, regrets.

The TV remote lay on the sofa. I stared at it, memorizing its exact position. When satisfied, I picked it up and turned it on, activating the booming commentary of a football match. I was pleased it wasn't porn.

I turned it off again to reinstate the silence. Then with utmost precision replaced the remote on the exact same spot. Except, it wasn't as easy as I'd anticipated, so I made a mental note to take pictures in the future, like the continuity person on a film set.

I almost forgot myself and went to sit. Then remembered how soft the feather cushions were. How they'd mould into our bodies. Do you remember? That time on the sofa? I do. Often. I thought about it at that moment too. I'm thinking about it again now.

Next was the kitchen. Were you perhaps depressed? There was a build-up of washing-up. No pans. Only bowls and cups. Remnants of the cereal I'd often see you shovelling into your mouth. I was concerned you weren't eating properly.

Magnets attached various papers and to-do notes to the front of the fridge. Your calendar was marked with several entries. You'd already turned it to December. The 12th: *Get MOT*. The 14th: *Dentist*. Other boring chores. Secured under a separate heavy grey pyramid-shaped magnet was the back of an envelope with *Milk. For God's sake, remember the milk!* I opened the fridge. Your note had worked. Inside was a small organic full-fat milk, a bottle of Peroni and a wooden circular packet of Camembert, which stank, making me retch. It was pleasing you had no imminent plans for entertaining.

I moved on to the room I'd saved till last. Your bedroom.

Standing in the doorway, I took in the scene. It was almost the same as when I'd last been there. Lying in the rumpled bed. You next to me. Consumed by each other.

The ghost of you was everywhere. The sheets, ruched, carrying your sweat and skin. Your imprint. A glass of water on the bedside table. Dirty boxers abandoned on the floor.

I perched on the edge of the bed. Gently. *Mustn't disturb.* Dropped my bag on the floor and slowly, deliberately lowered myself onto my side, my head gravitating to the pillow until it rested there. Breathing in. Breathing you in. Closing my eyes. Then jolting them back open as my phone rang loud against the silence and wrongdoing.

I pulled myself up to sitting. The pillow moved with me and I panicked that once again I'd failed to remember the exact positioning. Already forgetting my own new photograph rule. The ringing wouldn't stop. I dug into my bag, located it and picked up the call.

'No, no, I'm fine. I've just run from the other room, that's all . . . I'm not whispering . . . I don't want to disturb Edward . . . Yes, I'm leaving now.'

Once the call had ended, I frantically repositioned the pillows and smoothed away my existence from the covers. Thankfully noticing a rogue hair that had detached from my head and lay weightless on the cotton pillowcase. I held it up between the tips of my fingers, then dropped it into my bag.

As I retraced my steps, checking, turning off lights, checking, I noticed the silver of your pen peeking from beneath the bed. I bent to retrieve it. It was heavier than I'd thought, solid. Felt expensive. You didn't even know what you'd done with it. Were as careless as if it had been a Bic biro. So I dropped it into my bag too.

Funnily enough, I'm using it to write this. It's lovely and smooth, though sometimes its weight makes it hard to grip and I have to shake back the circulation in my hand. Especially as it's so cold in here.

Light grew through the crack as I slowly opened the door. Eventually I felt brave enough to check for life. All was clear.

The hallway seemed starker than usual. Or perhaps I felt more exposed. I hung over the dodgy handrail. Vertigo again. I was safe to go, so ran down the stairs, concentrating on not missing a step yet remaining focused on my escape. Not stopping until I was running, running, down the road.

*　　*　　*

You're probably shocked.

Disgusted with me.

I don't blame you. So was I, at first.

But by the time I was on the Tube, sat among the Normals, who probably hadn't just committed a crime, the guilt evaporated.

I didn't feel bad. More . . . exhilarated. Like when people skydive for the first time. Terrified, on the verge of tears, unable to take the leap until they're pushed into the clouds. Then at the bottom, as they breathlessly gather themselves from the tangled silk and string, the first words that come from their mouths are 'I want to do it again.'

I found myself willing the week to rush by. For Tuesday to be here once again.

Never wish your life away is what Mum would shout when we'd had one of our rows and I'd spit out my desperation to be eighteen, to get out of there, be free of her. In hindsight, it was an ironic thing for her to say. And when I woke the day after my eighteenth birthday, I got up, ate the stale crisps left over from our little party and continued my life exactly as before. It turned out I didn't want to be free of her after all.

On the Thursday, you still hadn't arrived by nine and I became worried that you'd called in sick with the flu and Linda hadn't told me. But at ten past you rocked up, fit and well, pulling an *eek* face about Mrs Lloyd, who was waiting for you, then asking me for 'one of those special northern teas'.

This time I took it in good humour. I was newly content, less angry. Being inside your home had connected me to you once again. Given me back some control. As did my growing little collection of items in the case. It all made me part of your life. Albeit you were unaware.

In the afternoon I brought you another perfect sweet tea. You were at the sink, washing your hands, and I'd barely placed the mug on your desk when your phone vibrated next to your printer. My eyes strained to view the caller, but you were already drying yourself with paper towels and throwing them from a distance into the bin as you made your way over.

'Thank you, Constance,' you said. Dismissing me. You picked up the handset looking flustered. Your Adam's apple moving prominently, indicative of a gulp.

I know I should have left. But the way you blushed when you said, 'Oh . . . well, this is a surprise.' The way you swung side to side in your chair nervously. I had no choice but to knock over the tea.

The hot liquid formed a lake on the desk before waterfalling onto the floor. You frowned. Were furious. Tried to remain calm to your special caller, only uttering response words such as 'OK', 'Sure', until you finally said, 'I can't really talk now, though.' I pretended to be oblivious. Act like my only concern was to sort out the mess.

You picked up an old biro you'd been resorting to. Not to write with but to chew playfully as you swivelled the chair away from me.

Like that first time in your office, I knew. It was more than personal. It was a woman.

I ripped paper towels from the dispenser, then walked back, squeezing the stiff blue sheets within my fist, and mopped up the spillage. Witnessing the flush of your cheeks. The pink cotton of your shirt pulsing with your quickened heartbeat.

Yet to you I was invisible. The maid in a period drama.

'OK . . . Well, as you know, I like good news.' You produced a series of idiotic self-conscious laughs.

I swallowed hard. Mouthed, 'I'm so sorry,' as I pointed towards the mess. You didn't engage. Merely fake-smiled at me and waved your hand, in a way that said, 'Don't worry, Constance – leave it.' Or more accurately, 'Please just fuck off.' I returned the smile. Played the fool you took me for. Your stupid laughs continued.

'Oh my God, do you remember . . . ? Oh Jesus. Yeah . . . Yeah . . . OK. Sure . . . How about next Friday, then? Just a quick one, hey? Sorry, sorry . . . I couldn't resist.' Stupid laugh.

And so you arranged to meet a woman. In front of me.

For the remainder of the day I could concentrate on nothing else. My insides were a tumble-dryer of varied emotions. None of them good. My mind full of questions. Who was she? What did she want to talk to you about?

I couldn't even face following you home after work. Knowing I'd despise being behind you, jaunty and upbeat. So I left dead on five without even a pause for a fag and strode determinedly to see Edward.

He was in bed when I arrived. Pale. His lips tinged lilac. 'You look awful. I thought the doctor was coming today?'

'Charming. You don't look so marvellous yourself.' He smoothed the blanket, unable to look me in the eye.

'Edward, the doctor?'

'He said I was fine.'

He leant over for his Shackleton biography, which perched on the old brass carriage clock on the bedside table, and as he spent all his energy dragging it over to his chest, his reading glasses fell to the floor. I picked them up.

'You didn't let him in, did you?'

'Shackleton was going to be a doctor – did you know that? But he joined the navy instead.'

'I don't give a shit about Shackleton.'

'Well, you should . . . That's the trouble with your generation—'

'For fuck's sake, Edward, the doctor?'

He reached over, snatching the glasses from my grip. 'I don't need to see a doctor . . . I'm absolutely fine.'

My hands reached for the top of my head and I paced the only clutter-free area in the room. 'Oh my God . . . you promised. You promised Maxine.'

'The only thing that's making me ill is your interrogation. And as for Maxine . . . it turns out she's highly irritating.'

And suddenly I was swathed in that feeling. The fear of him leaving me. Loathing the selfishness. Of him not caring if he did.

'I can't do this,' I said, and left to put his shepherd's pie in the oven.

I remained in the lounge while his dinner cooked.

When I lifted the window to smoke, I turned my body inwards to face the room, not you. Extending my arm outside into the harsh, dark air. Focusing on Ursula, wishing I could be as calm and cold as I flitted between anger at you, Edward, Mum. But my will was weak and I glanced towards you for a split second. You were laughing at something on the TV. My rage intensified and I slammed the window shut.

I hovered next to the bed as Edward pushed food around the plate. 'It's not as good as the Sainsbury's one.'

'It is the Sainsbury's one. Let me get you something else, then—'

'No . . . no . . . I had a big lunch, that's all.'

I perched on the chair, watching as he laboriously carried forkfuls of mince towards his lips. His crooked hand tremored so violently only tiny amounts made it into his mouth.

'If you're no better by tomorrow, I'm calling the doctor myself.'

His fork dropped to the plate. Gravy splashed the sheets.

'For Christ's sake. Let me tell you about doctors, shall I? The doctor came out to Amy. Doubled with stomach ache she was. Fever. We'd been up all night with her crying . . . screaming. "A tummy bug," he said. "Drink lots of water. Be a brave girl. You'll be right as rain in a couple of days." I didn't think it was right . . . knew it was worse. "You must listen to the doctor," Irene kept saying. "The doctor knows best. She'll be fine in a couple of days." Well, she was dead in a couple of days.' He placed his plate on the bedside table.

I dropped my head. We remained silent for a few seconds, until I said, 'It's awful about Amy, Edward. But if you're no better by tomorrow, I'm still calling a doctor.'

'You will not. You bloody well will not.'

I could sense arguing was futile so turned to leave the room. Stabbed in the back with 'You're not my daughter, you know.'

When I left Edward's, I didn't look up towards your flat. My eyes avoided your building completely. I lit another fag and coughed as the beautiful vile smoke entered my lungs. When I dropped the lighter and packet back into my bag,

I checked my phone. No missed calls. No messages. None of the usual questioning from Dale as to when I'd be home. Thankful at least for this small blessing, I hoisted my bag onto my shoulder and set off for the Tube.

It began to spit with rain.

Brolly-less, I flipped up my collar to shield my face from the droplets, which rapidly increased in size and frequency. My ears ached under the biting shower and I retracted into the neck of my coat like a threatened tortoise.

I hadn't gone far before I sensed something wasn't right.

Through the now pelting rain, I could hear my footsteps slap against the wet pavement. But the rhythm was off. Additional beats interspersed my own.

I walked faster.

Uncertain whether to look round or carry on. Initially I chose the latter. But the speed of my follower increased too. Once again I played out the police interview in my mind. This time, Gary Oldman was the officer. And Sir Alec Guinness was Edward, the last person to see me alive. Again I played myself, this time with a wooden cross lying upon my chest.

I'd made it to the end of the road. My sight blurred with water, I could just make out the Tesco Express sign, guiding me to safety. With the relief brought by the presence of other people, I briefly turned back.

Rain distorted the image, but there was a figure submerged in the darkness. A man. Sporting a dark anorak. His face concealed by an oversized hood. But he didn't appear to register me. Which led me to conclude that I was being paranoid.

* * *

I treated myself to a minicab from the station. Although it was only a five-minute walk away, the incident had left me edgy, so I called Dale to see if he'd come and meet me, but he wasn't answering. I was desperate to be safe and cosy. For him to listen to my neurotic ramblings and make me a cup of tea.

Entering the house, it was unlit and felt no warmer than outside. I expected to see the line of light under Dale's door, but it was absent. As was the comforting sound of shooting and zombie deaths.

I hadn't been using my room much and it felt unlived in, abandoned. Cold air laced with mustiness. I removed some crisp, dried knickers from the radiator. The ridged metal was lukewarm at best, so I dragged out the small electric fan heater from under the bed. Blocking the image of the suitcase from my mind.

Once plugged in, the warm stream smelt of burning dust. But I didn't switch it off. I was too wet and cold to worry about fire hazards. Shivering as I climbed out of my sodden clothes, the contrast of the now hot blast made every hair on my skin stand to attention.

I collected my dressing gown from the floor, wrapped myself up and sat on the bed, wondering where Dale had got to. I called him again. This time he picked up.

'Hey. Where are you? I'm home now . . . I've been trying to get hold of you.'

I could barely hear his response. The combination of broken signal and pounding rain meant I could only catch snippets, such as 'shop', 'pizzas', 'couldn't', 'nearly'. After a prolonged silence, I realized the call had dropped.

I remained still, just enjoying the warmth against my legs. Momentarily pushing away all the shitty events of the day. But as Mum would say, I was cold to the bone, so was contemplating getting up to make a cuppa when I heard a key in the door and the weather forcing its way into the hallway, stopping dead with a slam.

'Bloody hell, it's mental out there,' came Dale's voice.

'Where've you been?' I shouted back.

He mumbled something about putting the stuff in the kitchen. I left my room and followed the sound.

'They had a two-for-one on pizzas, so thought we could have that tonight.' I could hear him in the kitchen.

My bare feet suffered shocks with each step along the vinyl hallway floor. I stopped at the doorway. The tiles in there would be even worse.

I couldn't see Dale. He was behind the door, putting stuff away in the fridge. But I could hear the persistent crinkle of plastic bags.

'They only had margherita, though, so I bought mushrooms separately for us to add.'

'Perfect,' I said against the sound of the fridge sealing shut.

'How soon do you want to eat?' He pulled the door back to show himself. Dripping wet. Wearing a navy anorak. Pushing a large hood from his head.

*

I rocked back onto my heels as his icy lips kissed mine.

'Are you OK?' he said.

'Yes . . . yes, I'm fine. You're soaked. We could've had something else to eat. Saved you going out.'

'There wasn't anything.' He unzipped the anorak. Particles of water flicked onto the floor.

'Is that new? I've never seen you in it before.'

'Kind of – someone left it at work ages ago, and it was pissing down, so . . .'

'Oh right . . . Well, it looks good.'

He removed it and placed it on a kitchen chair. Ruffling his hair back to life. 'Don't you fancy pizza?'

'Yes . . . yes, pizza sounds great . . . I'm just going to put some clothes on.'

He came closer. 'Please don't.' His cold, damp hands circled my waist and pulled me towards him.

'Dale . . . you're making me all wet.'

'Already? Blimey.'

'Dale, I'm serious. Please . . .' I pressed his hands away.

He remained in front of me. Dropped his head for a moment, then returned to look directly into my eyes. 'Sure,' he said, repositioning an unruly strand of my hair to behind my ear. 'It'll be ready in about fifteen.'

I barely saw you the following morning. The one time I brought you a tea, my coldness must have been apparent.

'Are you OK, Constance? You're very quiet today.'

'Am I? I really don't think I am,' I said, and left, stony-faced.

You were then on house calls for the afternoon, and I was thankful it was a Friday and I'd have a couple of days' break from seeing you.

Although, the whole weekend I was barely present. Thoughts of you and her, whoever she was, tortured me, along with a nagging feeling about Dale and the anorak. To the point where I felt unable to be around him and feigned a migraine as an excuse to migrate to my own room. But after a cold, rainy trip into Ealing on the Sunday, where everyone seemed to be wearing dark hooded anoraks, I realized I was being paranoid. And if I was being paranoid about Dale, then I was probably being paranoid about you.

By Monday I was calmer about the whole situation. And by Tuesday I'd convinced myself I'd been fretting unnecessarily. That it was probably an old friend that you'd been speaking to. Perhaps from university. Possibly not even female. And I was relieved I hadn't let my imagination ruin things. Taint what I'd looked forward to all week.

Peculiarly tired, I clock-watched the entire day. Culminating in me willing the big hand to complete the extra ten minutes to bring it to five o'clock.

'Are you doing anything nice this evening, Dr Stevens?' I asked as you said your goodbyes.

'Just poker with the boys. Need to recoup my losses from last week.'

Alison giggled like an imbecile, and Linda smiled with a disapproving moralistic air.

'Oh, well, good luck,' I said.

'Thanks. I'll need it. I'm a much better doctor than poker player.' You winked at me, then left. Once again releasing the butterflies from their chrysalises.

Edward was fully dressed and sat in his chair, listening to a book-reading on Radio Four when I arrived. I was so relieved he'd returned to his original dapper self.

'Constance, thank Christ you're here. This book is utter tripe. Tell me, what do you like to read?'

'Me? Well, I . . . I don't really . . .' I took my seat. 'Reading wasn't really a thing in my house. How are you feeling today?'

'Well, you must read, darling girl. You'd love it. Being completely absorbed in other worlds, lives . . . Are there any books you've ever fancied reading?'

I shook my head, then remembered the card I bought you. 'Oh . . . well, *Wuthering Heights*, I guess.'

'Really? Well, I must have a copy somewhere.' He pushed himself up, stopping halfway. Wheezing.

'There's no need to look now—'

'You know, Constance, I was a journalist for many years, among other things. Worked for a few of the rags.' His breathing got the better of him and he stopped in his tracks, then returned to his chair. 'I'll have a look for you later . . . if that's OK, darling girl? I'd better have a think first, where it would be . . . Anyway, what I really wanted to do was write a novel. Not the sensationalized claptrap I was churning out every day for the papers but something with depth – something people would remember me for. So I got up every day, wrote before work. Sat at my typewriter and bled, as Hemingway would say. *An Explanation of Love*, it was called. But sadly I never finished it.'

'Oh no, why not?'

'Because I realized, there really isn't an explanation of love. And of course, it also turned out to be sensationalized clap-trap. Just longer.'

I laughed. 'You're looking good today, Edward. Nice to see you dressed. Are you feeling brighter?'

'Of course, look at me.' He spread his arms to show off his navy jumper and paisley cravat with pride.

Ashamed as I am to say it, the truth is it felt better to believe him.

I stayed while he ate a sandwich and supped on a cup of extra-sweet tea. Happy as I was to see him eating, sitting there with me, it made it almost impossible to watch your movements. And after another mini-debate about vege-tarianism – 'That's why you always look like a Victorian ghost, dear girl' – I turned to check on you, but your car had already gone.

Outside, I came alive. The warmth of anticipation made me immune to the freezing temperature. Leaning against the pillar at the top of the steps, I smoked a cigarette to mentally prepare. The streetlamp in front of your building flickered annoyingly, so I averted my eyes. But in doing so, I noticed a movement in the adjacent hedge. Presuming it was a cat, I winced as headlights approached, then firmly shut my eyes, praying for its safety as the car sped past. When I reopened them there was no dead cat, thank God, but it happened again. The rustling. I licked my finger and put out the fag, returned it to the packet, then crossed over.

The image of Dale's anorak reared its head again. The paranoia of prying eyes. I pulled out my phone and dialled him. It rang once, twice. Then, 'Hey, Connie. I was just about to call you. You on your way back?'

'Yes . . . well, in about half an hour. I'm just seeing him into bed.'

'OK, well, hurry up. I'm starving.'

'I will. I promise.' As he rattled off a shopping list of stuff to get from Costcutter, I separated the leaves of the bush with my free hand. There was nothing there. Not even a cat.

With the call finished, I was preparing to walk up your steps when I noticed Tippi Hedren and her dog approaching. Minus sunglasses but headscarf still in place, she didn't exchange pleasantries. Didn't even acknowledge me as the dog lunged towards my thighs, whining for attention.

I lit up again, forced to hang back as she entered. Allowing time for her to settle in her flat. I didn't know which floor she lived on but gave her the duration of a whole cigarette before letting myself in.

I didn't enter blackness this time. The hall light was on. Far from calming me, my fear increased and I froze, listened, until I was certain of your absence.

It's hard to describe the feeling I had being in there alone.

A conflicting mix of danger and safety. Your lack of presence was loud, yet you were everywhere. Not like the house after she'd gone. It didn't scream death and torment and guilt. It was gentle. Magical. Romantic. I sensed you in every room, around every corner. Smelt you. My stresses dissolved. I was at home there. Both with and without you.

I headed straight for the bedroom. There was so much I wanted to touch, see, after being cut short last time. I followed the scent of your aftershave. Then stopped before entering. Worried there would be something in there I didn't want to see. Know. But the truth is, there was nothing about you I didn't want to know. However much it may have hurt.

I exhaled loudly when all appeared comfortingly unchanged. No strewn posh slut's knickers. No discarded condoms.

The bed was unmade. Duvet thrown back. I patted the sheet for signs of wetness. All was dry and soft, and I crumpled onto it like a marionette. You, my unknowing puppeteer. I pulled your pillow around my head, over my ears, inhaling so deeply my eyes watered. It was all you. No cheap perfume or woman's sex. Just you.

I closed my eyes. Only for a moment. Yet I could feel my body float away. It would have been so easy to drift into a dream, so I forced myself to sit up, and once again having forgotten to take a photo, I attempted to return the bedding and pillows as before.

Still perched on the edge of the softened mattress, I opened your side drawer. My sweating hands slid over the handle. Eyes closed, I pulled. Prepared myself. But inside were only the familiar things. The copy of *Great Expectations*. The bookmark no further. An old mobile, ibuprofen, a phone charger, a tin of boiled sweets, a half-finished pack of fags with a lighter stuffed inside, a comb, weaved with strands of your hair, which I brushed against my cheek, then popped into my bag. And finally, the thing that brought me to look there, the box of condoms. My mouth dried as I lifted the flap of the packet. Counted the contents. There were seven. It was a pack of ten. One had been used with me. I convinced myself you must have bought them when you were seeing Fiona and shut the drawer.

En route to the en suite, I passed Laura's cupboard. Clicked it open. It remained untouched from the first time. I found comfort in that. The fact you weren't dwelling on what was in there, touching, smelling, like I needed to do. I pushed aside the hangers. The finery mocked me. I hated her and her privilege and had the urge to remove my key and make a hole in the black lace dress, hung like an elegant ballroom dancer. But it was so expensive, pretty, I couldn't bring myself to do it.

My eyes lowered to below the delicate hem.

The box. Your mother's box.

Unsealed, the folds were merely placed to conceal the contents. Begging me to look. Despite the wintery weather, the flat seemed excessively hot and I wiped my perspiring hands on my trousers before touching. My first finger slipped beneath the nearest section and I lifted the cardboard. A glimpse of white. I opened it fully. Taffeta, lace, beading. It was beautiful. Your mother was no doubt an enchanting bride. I imagined how sad it must have been for you to look at it. I understood. It was like the diaries. Locked away. Avoided.

I lifted the heavy dress. It was so long and voluminous that even with my arms stretched, part of the skirt remained inside the box. I held the bodice against me. The embroidery delicate, fine. The tiny beaded flowers only visible on close inspection. I imagined myself wearing it. Standing next to you.

The tinkle of something falling to the floor broke my daydream. A pearl had removed itself and rolled across the parquet.

Panicked, I shoved the dress back in its home. Closed the box. Once again draped the clothes over it and shut the cupboard before getting on my hands and knees to find the runaway bead. Finally I glimpsed it under your Ercol drawers. Once I had it in my palm, I went over to my bag and dropped it in. Another souvenir.

I kept my bag with me from that point on, placing the strap across my body so my arms were free. I checked the clock. It was already nearly seven. I envisaged Dale pissed off, fretting, and I resented him for rushing me.

You'd left the bathroom in a mess. I smiled at our similarities. You must have showered in a rush. The cubicle was damp with condensation. The sink spattered with a mix of minute hairs and shaving foam. The smell overwhelming: your soap, aftershave, sweat.

Your swanky toothbrush stood, boasting, on the glass shelf above the sink. I picked it up and pressed the button. It vibrated so hard that I dropped it in the basin with shock. Fingers fumbling, I scooped it out and switched it off again, placing a hand on my chest to calm myself before inspecting it. Still damp, minty like your breath. When not contaminated with booze or sex. I know I shouldn't have. But the urge was too great. I placed the head in my mouth and gently brushed my teeth. No water, no paste, just you. Transferring you onto me. Me onto you.

It was now ten past. I didn't want to leave, though knew I had to soon. Before doing so, I needed a few more minutes on your bed, to soak up the last molecules of you. I melted once again into your pillow. Pulled my legs up slowly so as not to disturb the sheets. And lay in the foetal position, remembering what had happened in that very spot. How your skin felt when touching mine. The sensation of you inside me. And I couldn't help it. I placed my hand down my trousers, inside my pants. Kept it there. Moved it there. Thinking of us.

I woke. Hot, shivering. Sweating in my coat. My chin wet with saliva, my body filled with fear. I sat up, looked over at the clock. Five past ten. My fingers trembled as I scrambled through my bag for my phone. I pressed the home button. Twelve missed calls.

Initially, so panicked about Dale, I didn't think about the possibility of you coming back. But once I did, I became light-headed. Standing in the middle of the room with my hands clasped at the back of my neck. Seeing if everything was back how it should be. Incapable of clarity, calmness. I thought the pillows looked right but couldn't remember. I couldn't remember anything. I wasn't even fully awake and shook my head to bring me round.

Accepting that everything was as good as I could get it in the bedroom, I inspected the bathroom. I wanted to go on checking, checking, but had to get out of there as quickly as possible. I switched off the lights and headed for the door. My mouth was so dry I could barely swallow and it felt like I was suffocating. My phone flashed again in my bag. I checked the time – quarter past. Then ran into the kitchen, switched on the light and turned on the tap. Unable to use a glass, I placed my mouth under the gently running stream and lapped like a cat. My hair got wet and I tried not to flick the drips anywhere by carefully tucking it into my collar. Once finished, my hand poised over the light switch, I caught sight of the fridge door. That same milk note. Your calendar. All the entries as before. With a new addition. In red pen. Circled for the extra importance. Friday the 9th: *5.30. Vini Italiani. Laura.*

*

The sweating, the sleepiness, had been the prelude to an illness that had taken hold, and I wondered if it was perhaps payback for Ms Kemple's mug, even though you'd escaped the effects entirely. Regardless of the cause, by the time I'd made it home, my throat felt skinned and my body emanated a heat that mirrored my fury.

I'd told Dale that I'd fallen asleep at Edward's. He bought it. At least, at first. Unable not to, as I stood in his room shivering, barely able to speak. But later, after I'd slept, my dreams repetitive, long, stretched like elastic – appearances made by you, Laura, Mum, other people I'd forgotten existed – I woke, dripping wet, my heart trying to escape my chest.

Dale was sitting on the edge of the bed. 'I couldn't sleep. I was worried . . . You haven't shut up the whole time.'

After pulling myself up, I switched on the lamp and checked my phone. It was coming up to 2 a.m. Gulping some much-needed water, I noticed my throat had eased marginally. Excess liquid cascaded down my chin, but I welcomed the cold against my skin. 'What was I saying?'

'Just ramblings. Who's Laura?' He watched me for an answer and I shrugged. 'Anyway, you feeling any better?'

'I'm not sure.' I swiped my hand across my upper chest

and behind my neck, then squeezed the duvet to rid the sweat I'd collected.

Dale offered me a towel he'd picked up from the floor. 'You should take your pyjamas off too. They're all wet.' He gently pulled me forward. 'Lift your arms.'

I complied as he reached down my back for the fleecy edge and pulled the top up over my head. I felt awkward, exposed, yet happy to be free of clothes. I inched up the duvet to conceal myself.

'Lie down.'

Again I did as I was told. He threw the covers off me and I stiffened as he tucked his fingers into the waistband of the bottoms, pulling them down, removing my knickers at the same time. I lifted myself to help. But didn't want to. I sensed him watching my body. On full display. Sticky and rancid.

'Where were you really last night?' he said.

I tensed further. My eyes fixating on the swirled Artex above. 'What do you mean? I've told you.'

'You fell asleep at Edward's?'

'Yes.'

He screwed the bottoms into a ball and threw them onto the pile of dirty clothes spilling out of my washing basket in the corner. 'OK.' He held up the towel. 'I'll go and wet this.'

Once he'd left, my limbs relaxed, but it wasn't long before he was back, the towel now heavy with water. Drips falling to the carpet.

'Here.' Beginning with my neck, he smoothed the freezing cloth over me.

'It's too cold, Dale.'

'It'll reduce your fever.' He wiped it over my chest, under each breast.

I was a statue. A ceiling-gazer.

'It doesn't make sense, Constance . . . doesn't add up.'

'What doesn't?'

'Last night . . . you were about to make him a sandwich, then – what, you suddenly just fell asleep?'

'Yes . . . I really don't feel well, Dale—'

'So how? How do you go from buttering bread to sleeping for hours?'

'Please, Dale.' The towel slapped my stomach. 'It's freezing.'

'But how can that even be? It doesn't make sense to—'

'Because I'm fucking ill.' I pushed his hand away and pulled the duvet up to my face. 'I made him a sandwich. He was in bed. I sat in the lounge while he ate it and I was overcome with tiredness. And now I know why.' My voice cracked towards the end. The last few words barely audible and punctuated with a raw cough.

Dale dropped the towel to the floor as he sat on the bed. 'Where does he live?'

I rolled to face the wall. 'Edward?'

'Yes. Who else could I possibly mean, Constance?'

An icy fear washed over my burning skin. 'In Kensington. I've told you—'

'Where in Kensington?'

'You want his address?'

'Yes.'

The peeking rainbow of wallpaper gone by stared at me. 'Flat six, 25 Gregory Place.'

'So if I went there tomorrow . . . instead of you, I'd find

poor old man Edward, would I? And he'd tell me you visit him almost every day, would he?'

I sat up. My head throbbed. 'No . . . you can't do that.'

'Why?'

'Because he'd hate it, that's why.'

'That's not why.'

His red-rimmed eyes bulged. A raised vein on his shiny temple. The worm that had burrowed into his head.

'Fine. I'll call him in the morning. Tell him you're dropping off some food because I'm ill.' I winced at the pain of creating so many words.

He covered his face with his hands and with a broken voice mumbled, 'Thank you.'

Neither of us moved for some time. We were a tableau. Until he stood and pressed two paracetamols from the blister pack and handed them to me.

'You're due these. I'll leave you to sleep. I need to get some myself or I'll feel like shit tomorrow.'

He turned off the lamp, stroked my head. Then became a vague form within the black as he walked towards the door. The sound of the handle turning brought with it a wedge of light from the hall.

'I love you, Constance. I don't know what I'd do if I lost you.'

As I was thinking of a reply, the door shut and I was once again in darkness.

In the morning, after I'd rung twattish Linda ('Not again? You've been most unfortunate with your health, haven't you, Constance?'), I reluctantly called Edward, as agreed.

'I'm not having some bloody stranger in my flat.'

'He's not a stranger, and he's only dropping off shopping, then he'll go. Think of him as the man from Sainsbury's.'

A coughing fit erupted, and I was unable to speak through the beeping of his dying handset.

'I wouldn't permit the bloody man from Sainsbury's to be in my flat either. And for goodness' sake, just get off the phone and get better.'

The rattle in his voice perturbed me, but before I could say anything or request that he cover for me should Dale ask about me falling asleep, I was halted by the dialling tone. I rang again. No answer. I imagined him presuming I'd taken his advice, oblivious to the defunct phone perched on his chair.

I remained in bed. Sore, lifeless, as the virus radiated through my body. Concentrating in my chest. So much so that for the first time since I was fifteen, I couldn't inhale the cigarette I'd foolishly lit.

I slipped, feverishly, fluidly, in and out of sleep. A carousel of thoughts. You and Laura. Dale meeting Edward. You and Laura. Dale meeting Edward. Round and round and round.

'How are you feeling?'

Confused, I pushed myself up. It was dark outside. My lamp was switched on and Dale was standing next to the bed, bags of shopping in his hands.

'Sorry. I should've let you sleep.'

'What time is it?' I said, my hand scrambling around the bed in search of my phone.

'Nearly six thirty. You were fast asleep. Anyway, I dropped the stuff at Edward's.'

To prevent him detecting the fear in my face, I continued looking for the phone even though I could see where it was. 'Oh . . . oh good. How was he?'

'He seemed OK . . . but, Constance, his flat is off the scale. That diving helmet is fucking awesome.' As he excitedly talked about how Edward had worn it when he'd supposedly been a deep-sea diver, my body relaxed.

My sins were still my own.

I was back in work on the Friday. I had to, you see.

Phlegm-throated, husky-voiced, weak on standing, yet determined.

Dale was too busy with his morning routine to notice my waxen complexion and ice-pick breaths. I must admit his lack of caring was disappointing.

I was so monstrous in appearance that even Linda was uncharacteristically pleasant to me. Not for my benefit but because she'd been so embarrassingly unsympathetic when I'd called in sick.

'You shouldn't have come in, Constance.'

'Well, I wasn't sure if you believed me, Linda, and I didn't want to let you down.' I coughed until I heaved behind the reception desk and she ran to the kitchen for water.

Admittedly, I enjoyed her squirming. Thinking it was her doing. My suffering. When really it was yours.

To compensate, throughout the day she topped up my fluids with a constant stream of hot lemon and honey after sending Alison out for the ingredients, and also got me some more paracetamol from the on-duty Ratched. Alison seemed oblivious to my state, prattling on about the yoghurt-making kit she'd bought the night before on QVC. Perhaps she was being kind, thinking death by boredom would put me out of my misery.

As for you, I expected you not to notice either. Not with your approaching date and rekindled love to keep you occupied. I hadn't seen you all morning, as you were with patients and Alison took in your coffee to save me getting up. I was desperate to know if you'd asked after me, but she never said, so I presumed not. But in the afternoon, when you entered reception with a file to copy, you appeared taken aback.

'You look terrible. Why did you come in?'

Linda reddened. Sipped her coffee.

'Alison, can you copy that, please, while I check on Constance.'

Once again we were alone in your room.

'Take a seat.' You spoke as Dr Stevens. Not Samuel. Didn't you realize it was too late for professionalism?

As you felt around my neck, for once I wasn't concentrating on your scent. Or your heated breath fluttering across my face. Or our lips, kissing distance apart. Instead, I imagined how soon your soft hands would be touching her. Your mouth on hers. Your heart, which visibly pumped under your shirt, would be beating for her.

You pressed my tongue with a lolly stick, then shone a light down my throat.

'It's inflamed, but there's no infection.'

The thermometer double-beeped in my ear.

'It's a nasty virus. Possibly flu. When people say they've got the flu, they usually haven't got the real deal, but it's fairly prevalent at the moment. Ms Kemple came in with it. You really should get a flu jab next year, like I do. I'm surprised Dr Harris didn't mention. The nurse would have done it. If you'll just remove your top, I'll check your chest.' I didn't respond. You thought I was quiet because I was ill. You were wrong.

It amuses me to remember what happened next. You were over at the cupboard getting your stethoscope, and I undressed, as you'd asked. Removed my jumper then blouse. But as I'd been unable to bear anything tight against my battered body that morning, I hadn't worn a bra. And once you'd turned around, stethoscope in hand, you were faced with my nakedness.

'What are you doing?'

'I thought you were listening to my chest?'

'Yes . . . but . . . you should have kept your bra on.'

'I didn't put one on this morning. It's nothing you haven't seen before.'

'No . . . no, I know . . . but it's inappropriate.' You marched back towards me and grabbed my blouse from the chair before gesturing for me to put it on. Turning around until I was less embarrassing to you. As if you could rewrite history. Wipe me away.

I pulled my hair from beneath the neckline. 'More inappropriate than fucking me on your desk?'

You spun back around. Furrowed-faced. Cheeks bruised. Could you not believe I'd dared say such a thing? To speak the truth.

'That's . . . Don't say it like that, Constance . . . You know that was different.'

We remained suspended in time. Until finally, you pressed the cold metal disc against my furious heart. Both of us knowing that for that moment I'd won. Disclosed you for what you were.

'There's a definite crackle – a chest infection.' You appeared relieved that there'd been a valid reason for you to have seen me topless and wrapped up the appointment like I was one of your patients. Prescribed me antibiotics. Told me that I mustn't stay in work. That I needed to go home and rest.

Back in reception, Linda called me a cab and within half an hour I'd left the surgery.

But I had no intention of going home.

*

The small hipster cafe was directly opposite your chosen wine bar.

. I grabbed a window seat and prepared to hunker down. Tell me, was it somewhere special to you? Vini Italiani? Somewhere significant for you both? Did it hold romantic memories? It's a shame we never had a place like that. I'm not sure the alley behind the Wheatsheaf counts.

The frosted lettering that spelt out the word *Cafe* across the window hampered my view a little, but your lovers' venue was ideal. Glass. Ceiling to floor. Ensuring its rich-prick punters could be clearly seen by the poor and miserable rough sleepers.

I ordered tea rather than coffee. It was more soothing. Although in hindsight perhaps additional caffeine would have been helpful. And a plain muffin to pick fluff from, to line my stomach for the paracetamol that I hoped I'd keep down.

A young waitress with a Spanish accent and Kate Bush hair served me.

'It's so cold,' she said coincidentally, then placed down the pot and cup.

'It is,' I said.

The truth was, I couldn't wait to rid myself of my coat, unravel the scarf from my neck. I felt nothing but burning heat.

When paying Kate, I noticed the prescription folded in my purse. But I assured myself that a couple of hours wouldn't make much difference and I'd go to the chemist on the way home.

After taking the painkillers and eating crumbs, I rolled my scarf into a ball to use as a pillow and draped myself with my coat. A blanket to counteract the intense cold I now felt. The battered leather club chair creaked with each attempt at comfort, but I eventually managed to find a good position and surrendered.

'Are you OK, miss?'

'Samuel?' I opened my eyes.

'Is everything all right?' Kate was standing over me, her face strained with concern.

I wiped the dribble from my chin. 'Yes . . . Sorry . . . I just . . .'

She retrieved the cup of cold tea and put it on a tray. 'Would you like me to order you a cab or something?'

It was now dark outside. For a moment I was confused. Unsure where I was. Then I glimpsed the red-and-green neon of the Vini Italiani sign through the window. 'No . . . thank you. I'm waiting for someone. Can I get another tea, please?'

When she left to make my order, I looked up at the giant clock on the wall. No matter how hard I stared, I couldn't work out the time. Blinking over and over before finally registering it was five twenty. Somehow an hour had passed since I'd arrived. *You'd be here soon.* I massaged my temples. Then remembered it wasn't me you were meeting.

Kate placed a fresh steaming pot and clean cup on the table. When paying, I missed her hand and one of the pound coins fell to the floor. She retrieved it, once again mentioning a cab.

'No . . . I've told you I'm waiting for someone. I just want to drink my tea.' She'd pissed me off at that point. I didn't understand why she kept asking. She didn't seem to be asking anyone else. But at last she got the message and left me alone.

My sweaty hands slipped around the large, overfilled cup. As I brought it to my mouth, droplets of tea fell from beneath it onto my chest. I winced as I felt the burn. Quickly wiping away the scalding liquid.

When I'd finished and my eyes returned to the window, focusing beyond the letter 'F', I was faced with you. The back of you. Jumping from foot to foot. Kidding your body that it was warmer than it was. Or perhaps it was nerves. The excitement of meeting your love.

My fingers weakened. The cup escaped me. Crashing to the table and falling onto its side. Hot, sticky tea penetrated my trousers, through to the flesh of my thighs. You'd think I'd have jumped up. Shouted out. Sworn. But I sat there. Calm and still. Separate from the acute pain on my lap.

Kate flew over with a wad of blue kitchen roll. Wiped. Dabbed. Asked if I was OK.

'I'm . . . I'm sorry . . . I don't know what's . . .'

'I'll get you another tea . . .' She spoke more, but I didn't listen.

You were running across the road, narrowly avoiding a speeding car.

'No, no, it's OK, Kate . . . I've got to go . . . thank you.'

Outside, with my scarf draped loosely around my neck and my coat hung over my bag, I took my position at the bus shelter adjacent to the cafe. Perched, among the Normals, against the cold tilted plastic seat that wasn't a seat at all.

You were inside the bar then, being shown to a window table by a tall, blonde waitress dressed in black with a white apron longer than my whole body. You probably fancied her too. Would've tried to fuck her if it wasn't for your beloved's arrival.

You said something that made her laugh. Then cracked up at your own joke. Even after she left, you continued smiling. How hilarious you were.

A double-decker bus pulled in, blocking my view.

Ant-like, the people arranged themselves into single file. Marched aboard. The lucky ones winning a seat. The losers hanging from straps. Bus gallows.

All the shelter-dwellers got on, apart from a young lad cradling a KFC bucket. The aroma of battered battery chickens made me want to gag. I covered my mouth with my scarf to filter the smell, then removed it again immediately to release heat. I didn't understand why the paracetamol hadn't kicked in. I was suffocating. KFC Kid inserted headphones into his ears. The tinny tin-tin permeated my head. Severed my nerves. I was desperate to say something, tell him to shut the fuck up. But thankfully I was distracted by the departure of the heaving bus.

I rubbed my eyes to refocus. Clarity returned. It wasn't just you sat in the window.

It was you *and* her.

She was pretty, I'll give you that. I was too distant to decipher the intricacies of her face, but I could see it better than the first time. It worked perfectly. Long, dark hair. Like mine. But she was a grown-up. Elegant. She placed her expensive bag on the floor. You kissed her. Cheek only. As serious lovers do. No back-alley rendezvous. You were treating her with the utmost respect. You appeared nervous. Running your fingers repeatedly through your hair as the waitress took your order.

I couldn't blame you for picking her. She was the polar of me.

Blame you? No.

Resent you? Hate you? Absolutely.

As I watched you both talking, she removed her coat smoothly, like a model on the catwalk, and appeared far removed from the nut-job you'd painted. Then, all women were crazy to you, weren't they? Just for being women. Having feelings. Wants. Needs. Expectations of you. Crazy fucking bitches. All of us.

The waitress returned with your drinks. Interrupted you both laughing. Had you churned out the same joke? You instantly cupped the beer you were handed, like you were relieved you finally had a prop to help with your nerves. She remained cool, took a sip from her tall glass of clear liquid.

After watching you both for a while, attempting to lip-read to no avail, a couple more people arrived at the bus stop. But only KFC Kid leant against the seats. *Pst, pst, pst, pst.*

He nodded in time to the beat. *Pst, pst, pst, pst.* I pressed my hands against my ears and closed my eyes to shut it out. My hair was soaked, but it wasn't raining. It seems impossible as I say it, but I think I must have dropped off for a moment. Because when I reopened them, KFC Kid was holding my bag. I thought he was robbing me at first, then realized it had dropped to the floor and he was handing it to me.

'You all right, lady?' *Pst, pst, pst.*

'Yes . . . yes . . . I'm fine. Thank you.' I held on to the bag like Blusha. And as I hugged it/her, I had a shot of reality. What I was doing. The pathetic act of watching the person I loved, loving someone else.

Focusing on you both once more, the atmosphere between you had changed. You were now leaning in. Close to her. Listening intently. She was wiping beneath her eyes. I presumed tears. Which you gently brushed away with your thumb, then in a continuous movement placed some wayward hair behind her ears. A look between you. A look that had never passed between us. Which only ended when you opened your arms and beckoned her for a hug.

I folded in two with the pain you were causing me. My chest so tight I could hardly breathe. Once I'd straightened, I closed my eyes again. Blocked you out. I couldn't look. I stayed there. Still. Blind and oblivious to what else was going on. Bracing myself for seeing the kiss. Envisaging it in my head, so it would hurt less when witnessed. Your mouth tenderly touching hers. Fingers entangled in her silky hair.

With a deep breath I reopened my eyes slowly.

Nothing was as imagined. You were both back to talking normally. Had stopped the torturous display of love. Whatever had caused that intensity had now made way for a lighter mood. The tears had been replaced with smiles and animated chat.

Relieved, I pushed back my damp hair. I could smell body odour fermenting under my arms. At least it would deter anyone from sitting next to me. Especially the loud cockernee builder attempting to chat up a girl around my age. *She just wants to get home. Leave her alone, you prick.* She was trapped between the prick and the stink. It was only the four of us at the stop by then. The worst-ever double date. Thank Christ another bus came and all three of them boarded it. Then with a blast of compressed air, it moved off.

You were still talking pleasantly. Your glass near empty. She used a straw to stab what was presumably a slice of lemon. Bitter, like me.

My teeth began to chatter and I reached for my coat, which had slipped to the floor. As I bent down, the ground moved with me and I put my hand on the seat to steady myself. Determined to keep my balance, I slowly slid on the sleeves, then wrapped the sides around me. Blocked out the iced air. And when I looked back up, you were gone.

I focused beyond the window to see if you'd moved, but realized you were now in front of it. On the pavement right ahead of me. Both enveloped in your luxurious coats. A real-life John Lewis advertisement.

You hugged again.

Unable to pull myself away, I waited for the kiss to destroy me. But it was small and placed upon her forehead. Initially I was surprised, then not, as it really was the ultimate show of love, caring. Like Dad did to me that day.

There was another embrace. Then you walked in opposite directions.

Squinting with confusion at your parting, I should have been grateful. Thankful of not witnessing the whole show, as I did with Fiona. I know I should have left. But for once it wasn't you who drew me like a magnet. I didn't want you that night. I didn't need to know where you were going or what you were doing. That night it was all about her. The compulsion to view her up close. Her eyes. See what you saw. What you loved.

Traffic was at peak London insanity. Making it difficult to cross the road, and easy to lose her. A woman in a BMW stopped to let me pass. I remained in the middle. Stood on the broken white line. A skittle buffeted by vehicles in both lanes. When a gap emerged, I bolted. Barely able to breathe when I hit the pavement on the other side. I pressed my fist into my chest to subdue the stabbing. Coughed until I heaved. My wet hair sticking to my face as I doubled over.

I looked up. Luckily, along with her other perfect qualities, her model height meant she was still visible. There she was. Calmly bobbing along. No concept of what she was doing to me. I ran to catch up with her. When a few metres away, I stopped. Heaved again. Covered my mouth with my scarf to muffle the noise. No sick. No time for sick. I carried on.

Oblivious to my presence, she turned the corner into a residential street. Though we battled the same wind, my hair resembled Medusa's, whereas hers blew gracefully behind like Diana Ross's.

This road was quieter. I crossed to the pavement opposite.

Walking as fast as I could to get in front. I planned to return to her side. Pass her. Stare at her.

As I sped up, I couldn't maintain a straight line. Blaming my sways on the gusts.

She slowed. I crossed the road. Changed direction. Flowed against her. Towards her. Talking on my phone to an imaginary person. Laughing. Playing the part. Supposedly unaware of her coming towards me. Of our nearing each other. Within an instant I altered the plan. I'd knock her. Just enough to make her stop, look at me. I'd apologize. And in true British style she'd apologize back.

The moment came. My shoulder was in line with her chest. I did it.

But it went wrong. It was too hard. I'd gone too far.

She was on the floor.

I dropped the phone into my bag and held out my slippery hand for her to grab on to. 'Sorry . . . I . . . I didn't see you . . . I was on the phone . . . I'm so sorry.'

If she was angry, she didn't show it. I'd say she was more upset, fearful.

'I really am sorry,' I said. I was. I am. For the monsters you created inside me. The things they made me do.

She didn't respond. I no longer expected the quintessential Brit apology, of course. She attempted to stand. Making it hard for herself by only using one hand. The other remained on her abdomen as her coat flew open. I pulled her up off the ground.

'Thank you,' she said, once upright. But then she folded. Winced. Her palm made circular motions over her stomach. Her stomach that didn't match her elongated, lithe body. Her stomach that protruded slightly.

Her pregnant stomach.

'You should watch where you're going.' Her eyes were heavy with tears. She bent forward again, pain-faced.

I was disgusted at what I'd done, what you'd made me do. It became impossible to suppress. I was crying.

'I'm so sorry . . . Are you OK . . . ? Please tell me you're OK.'

She appeared taken aback by my anguish.

'I'm . . . I'm sure I'm fine . . . Please don't get upset.' It was then she looked at me with those huge brown eyes and I realized what you must have fallen in love with. The same eyes you would have stared lovingly into when you came inside her, made this baby, this thing I instantly hated, this thing I was terrified I'd hurt.

'How . . . how far gone are you?' I tried to appear normal. Conversational. But she was perturbed by me, I could tell. Humouring me.

'Nearly four months,' she said.

Four months. I stepped back. Dizzy. *More lies.*

'I'm fine,' she continued. 'It was a shock, that's all. Please . . . you really don't have to worry.'

Did she have to be so bloody nice? Perfect and nice and pregnant.

'Have . . . have you got far to go?' I asked.

'No, not really, but I should probably get a lift, I think.' She reached in her Mulberry bag for her phone.

I didn't speak. Couldn't. Merely stood, wide-eyed as she made the call.

'Hey, sweetheart . . . Look, I'm on Tilbury Terrace. Are you far? You couldn't come and get me, could you? I had a bit of a fall . . . No, no, I'm fine . . . A little shaken, that's all.'

I couldn't hear your voice, but I imagined it. Loving. Caring. Like I'd experienced once. Almost.

'It was an accident . . . I wasn't looking where I was going . . . I'm with a lady . . . What's your name, sorry?'

'Angie,' I said.

'OK . . . OK . . . Thank you . . . Love you too.' She returned the phone to her bag. 'He's only round the corner. He'll be here in a few minutes.'

'I have to go. I'm . . . I'm sorry. You will be OK, won't you?'

She nodded. Utterly confused.

A bead of sweat fell from my nose.

'Are you OK, yourself?' she said.

'Yes . . . I . . . I have to go, though. I'm sorry. I'm so sorry.' I turned and walked away, jelly-legged, spinning with vertigo.

I stopped at the main road. People everywhere. But I was in a different world to the one they inhabited. In and out of focus, they scurried past. My scarf hung loose to the floor, asymmetric. I swayed on the edge of the pavement. Looked across the road.

It was then I saw her.

Beautiful and smiling.

Just as I remembered, in real life, not photographs. She looked just like me. I waved. She beckoned me across with her hand. I didn't question it. I couldn't wait. To see her. To hold her. I missed her. Oh God, I missed her.

My foot dropped from the kerb. My other joined it. A car

307

sped by. I stood in the road. Horns beeped. I didn't care. I didn't care if they hit me, because I just wanted to be with her. I glided across. Vehicles sliced around me. I was so near. Almost on the other side. A man shouted from his van window, but he didn't understand that I didn't care. I stepped up onto the pavement. Carried on until I was right in front of her. I lifted my hand to touch her face, her warm face, which had already faded from my mind. I was crying. Happy tears. She cried too. Smiling.

Then everything turned cold.

My hand was touching the glass of a shop window. She was nowhere. There was only me, staring back at myself.

*

According to Dale, a kindly cab driver named Mohammed walked me, ghost-like and clutching my prescription, to the door.

Though I have no recollection, Dale saw me into bed and went off in search of a late-night chemist. After taking an antibiotic, I slipped into a delirious slumber, in which I apparently stayed, aside from being woken for sips of water and additional tablets, until the Saturday evening.

With my fever broken, I found the energy to sit up and gaze blankly at an old episode of *Lewis* on TV. I had no idea what was going on, who'd been murdered or why. It was just nice to feel relatively normal.

But with consciousness came memories. The baby. The fall. The kiss. Imagining the family photograph that I'd soon endure every time I'd bring you coffee.

Dale didn't leave my room. It stank of illness, but was at least tidier, as he'd picked stuff off the floor while tutting and saying things like 'Why don't you hang your clothes up when you take them off?' and 'When we get our own flat, you can't be like this, you know.'

Though thankful for his care, I found his presence claustrophobic. I craved solitude. To cry. Scream. Hurt. But I

309

couldn't do anything except pretend I was fully there. Listening to him. Watching *Lewis*.

There was at least some respite on the Sunday. Dale had to go to his parents' anniversary dinner. Thirty years. Imagine that. I wonder how I'll feel about you in thirty years.

I'd been invited along, but he insisted I was too ill and should rest. As Mum would say, *Silver linings. Always silver linings.*

He'd convinced me to have a shower, rinse away the disease that oozed from every pore. As I scrubbed at my greasy hair and sticky body, thoughts of you swilled down the plughole with the grubby froth.

Afterwards he sat next to me on the bed as I dried my hair. 'Mum's disappointed you're not coming . . . Here, make sure you dry it properly.' He leant down to the floor and stretched the hairdryer and cord towards me, smirking in an unfamiliar way.

'Yeah . . . I'm disappointed too.' The dryer felt heavy in my weak hands.

'Anyway, it may be for the best. I can kill two birds with one stone, Birthday Girl.' Wink.

'What do you mean?'

He tapped his nose, then left. I didn't know what he was referring to. He was happy: it was obviously something nice. Yet it perturbed me, and my insides twisted.

Before settling down, I called Edward. 'Well, when are you going to be better? I've run out of prunes, and Maxine is horrendous. She's arranged for a doctor to come out on Wednesday. Says she's staying to make sure I let him in.'

'Well, thank fuck for Maxine, I say.'

Calmed by this news, I temporarily avoided thoughts about you and her by watching *Vertigo*, which had just started on TV. The ending had always made me sad. I wonder if it would make me more or less so now. The way he watches her fall to her death. Knowing it was his fault. I've always imagined my dad as James Stewart. Not only because I can't remember him properly, but what better father to invent than Jimmy Stewart?

Is there a syndrome, Doctor? Where the stricken obsessively loves a person they despise? And if it exists, what's the cure? Was your mother cursed with the same illness? Was I inconvenient to you in the same way she was to your father?

On the Monday, thankfully feeling well again, I sat in reception, which was now adorned with silver and blue Christmas decorations. Desperately hoping your presence would somehow ease my internal agony. That being near you would calm me as it had done in the past. But I was mistaken.

You arrived, carefree, smiling at us 'girls', saying, 'So glad you're feeling better, Constance. I'd love a coffee,' and an entity formed inside my belly. Again created by you. But not a perfect baby. An eroding, acidic rage.

In your room, we talked about the forecast of snow. You said it turned you into a big kid and that being able to go sledging was a valid reason to have children. I smiled and agreed. How did you not sense? A doctor. An intelligent man afflicted with such fucking stupidity.

When my fake-laughing at your accidentally-throwing-asnowball-at-a-policeman story had stopped, I turned to leave.

Then you said, 'Oh, before you go – my friend's coming in for a consultation at about one. It's during lunch, so she's not on the appointments. Tall, pregnant. Can you send her straight through?'

Returning to the reception, I swallowed hard to keep down the porridge Dale had made me eat. Not only because of the unimaginable fear of seeing her, being found out, but her coming to the surgery at all. Needing to have the baby checked. The harm I must have done. Such concern you couldn't set her mind at rest, as you'd probably spent the weekend delighting in each other's company.

My pulse was so fast it felt devoid of gaps between each beat. I stood in front of Linda, waiting for her to finish her call with Mr Jacobson. She was taking her time. Flirting in the most inappropriate fashion as she rearranged his appoint-ment, explaining that Dr Short had left for the day as his little girl had fallen at school and hit her head. Finally the receiver went down.

'Can I go to lunch a bit earlier today, please, Linda? I have to take my medication at a specific time and need to have it with food.'

I cannot adequately explain the terror that enveloped me for the rest of the morning. As I awaited my escape, trips to the toilet increased. Lunchtime loomed and I remained so quiet I had to announce to Linda and Alison, 'I'm sorry for being strange. I . . . I still don't feel a hundred per cent.'

At twelve forty the danger was so close I stood and said,

'I'll be going now, Linda—' but I'd barely spoken her name when the phone rang.

While picking up the receiver, she held out her arm to signal me to wait. I gathered my bag and put on my coat and scarf to prevent her stopping me. I could barely use my shaking fingers. They had a life of their own as I urgently worked on each button. I stood there. Claustrophobic. Sandwiched between Linda's faux concern for the patient she was speaking to and Alison's prattling.

'I hope it comes tonight. I love snow, you know . . . Hey – snow, you know. I'm a poet and I don't know it . . . Kevin and I had our first kiss when it was snowing. He was walking me home from the party that we—'

'It's not snowing, Alison,' I said as Linda put down the phone. 'I'm heading off now, Linda, if that's OK?'

'Did you call Miss Keller to tell her about Dr Short?'

'No . . . Sorry. I—'

'Well, you can't go without doing it, Constance.'

I slapped my bag onto the desk and pressed the digits into the phone with the same force I wished I could apply to Linda's face.

'Yes . . . yes . . . Thank you, Miss Keller . . . Apologies once again . . . We'll see you tomorrow at three, then.' It took two slams to replace the receiver. The noise resonated around reception.

'Happy now, Linda?' It was five to one. I didn't ask her permission, just grabbed my bag and stomped towards the door.

As I pulled the handle, there was a push from the other side.

Only her shoe was visible at first.

Patent. Perfect height. Not slutty, not frumpy.

The gap widened. Camel wool and the smell of jasmine spilt into the room. Head dropped, I pulled my scarf up to my eyes. Violently coughing, to make her turn away in disgust. She raised her arm high to open the door for me. I dipped under.

'Hello. I'm here to see Dr Stevens.'

The door slipped between us, then slammed shut.

The rest took place only in my mind as I walked to Edward's. Your excitement at seeing her. Touching her belly. The child you now loved and feared for so much. The slipping of her wrist under her sheet of hair to manoeuvre it out of her perfect face. The kiss. Introductions. The love that emanated from you both that everyone would say was so romantic.

It was hard to tell if it was the gift of tinned prunes and posh cheese or seeing me that made Edward so elated. But as we scoffed our sandwiches with a cup of tea, which he complained was cold, he paused, placed his butty down onto the Sixties brown crockery and pulled out a paisley hanky. I presumed it was to wipe off the mustard paint-brushed across his cheek, but he pressed the crumpled silk into his face and said, 'I didn't realize how lonely I'd been for so long until you stopped visiting last week.' He did one final press onto his eyes before returning the now darkened square to his pocket, saying, 'You've gone a bit overboard on the mustard.'

'I missed you too, Edward' – we simultaneously took bites from our bread – 'but listen, I can only pop in at lunch again tomorrow. It's my birthday and Dale reckons he's making me a dinner.'

He looked confused. 'But it's not your birthday.' Before I could ask what he meant, he spoke again. 'Oh . . . sorry . . . I . . . It's your birthday? My goodness, how marvellous. You must bring cake. We shall wear hats. No, I'll wear a hat. For you, I have a tiara.'

Being with Edward meant I forgot everything for a while. I even managed a laugh at his story about Maxine catching him giving her the finger behind her back.

'That's the problem with being so old, Constance. One's reflexes aren't what they were.'

But as soon as his front door shut behind me, my mood returned to its darkened state.

Knowing you had an appointment at one thirty with Mrs Towers, I waited until ten minutes after that before returning to ensure Laura's departure.

In the staffroom, I encountered Linda, a can of SlimFast and a Double Decker wrapper laid before her on the table.

'I'm sorry about before, Linda. I just really needed to take my medication.'

She hauled herself up, dropped the foil and can into the bin. 'Dr Stevens asked to see you after his patients this afternoon.'

Once she'd left, the cheese of my sandwich tickled the back of my throat, forcing me to retch into the sink.

The atmosphere in reception was as if I'd turned up to the funeral of a person I'd murdered. Not that I'd do that. Linda misguidedly thought ignoring me was a punishment. Alison was scared to talk, which, again, was a result. But within the stilled hush, it was difficult for me to disguise my fear. My mouth had stopped producing saliva, so I nursed a glass of water. Sipping, sipping, sipping, going over why you'd want to see me. There was no relief. None of the options was good. All of them boiled down to the same origin. The bad things I'd done.

I gathered the papers I'd copied for Dr Short in his absence and told Linda I was taking them to his room. Diverting to the toilet, I closed the door and pushed two fingers down my throat to empty myself of whatever was sitting there making me swim. The relief wasn't as profound as I'd hoped as I wiped the specks off my chin and splashed my face with water.

Dr Short's office was different to the rest of you doctors'. Especially yours. It looked barely used. Sterile. He usually brought his mug to the staffroom at the end of each day and washed it. The only non-arsehole. Though that day it was still there. Cold black coffee with a white swirling film.

When placing the file on his desk, I noticed a cupboard hadn't been closed properly. As I went to press it shut, I was faced with packs of needles and blood test tubes. A memory punched me. Of Mum. Her visible upset whenever they brought the tray. How they failed to penetrate her collapsing veins with the needle. Her no-fuss silent tears as they tried the second time. Third. Fourth. The different nurse brought over to help. The false bonhomie.

I reached inside. Took one of the needle-tip packs between

my fingers. Recalled the suspended bags. *Drip, drip, drip.* The chatting, flicking magazine pages, eating biscuits. A normal day out. The most abnormal day out. And before I knew it, I'd tucked the needle under my cardigan sleeve and was walking back towards the toilet.

Door bolted, I pulled down the seat, sat and rolled up my sleeve. My white flesh, delicate, glaring. The wrapper crinkled as it tore. I hadn't done it since I was a teen. But I needed to feel something else, to release the tension. Feel what she went through. Punish myself in the same way. For her, the baby. To be honest, I didn't think I could do it. The tip glistened under the harsh strip light. I pinched it between the fingers on my right hand. Brought it down onto the soft skin. Watched the dimple it created first. Like the buttons on her pink velour headboard. Then in it went. Pierced the surface. My eyes screwed. Bit my lip at the immense pain as I scraped down. Straight line. Amateur surgeon. The blood came. A parting sea. Not gushing, emerging. I watched, yet it didn't scare me. I'd faced it.

I pulled and pulled toilet roll off to soak up the blood. Pressing hard to stop it coming. It was shallow but stung, throbbed. I put the needle back in the wrapper, rolled it in toilet roll and dropped it into the sanitary bin. When I removed the wad from my arm, its remnants stuck to the coagulated sections. Like Dad's shaving cuts. I peeled off the remaining scraps, wincing. Flushed the soiled tissues. It was the shame that made me cry. Not the pain. I pulled more off the roll. The blood was stopping now. Clotting. I ran the wound under the tap.

Aware I'd been so long, I gathered paper towels this time

and patted it dry. Wrapping one around my forearm, before rolling down my sleeve, scanning the room for evidence. The only thing that remained was the arm itself, burning under my cardigan.

By the time Mr Franks, your last patient, had left, the warm, sticky blood had seeped through my sleeve. But I decided not to prolong my fate any further and went to your room.

After calling me in, you finished writing in your diary. Letting me stand there, until eventually, you said, 'I still haven't found my bloody pen. You couldn't ring Mrs Carter and Mrs Johnson, could you? Check if I left it there during house calls?' You turned, looked up.

I nodded. 'Sure.'

Your eyes were flat. They didn't knock me off balance, make my stomach swirl. Not now they connected to someone else.

'Are you still ill, Constance? You look very pale.'

'No . . . no, I'm fine, thank you.' I squeezed my arm to stop the sting. 'Linda said you wanted to see me?'

'Oh right . . . yes . . . I made it sound formal to her, but I just wanted a chat – see how you were feeling?' You swivelled round and chewed on your biro. Not the portrait of a man worried about his unborn child. 'Shall I check your chest?'

'No . . . no, there's really no need. I'm just a bit drained, that's all. How are you?'

'Me? Yes, I'm good, actually . . . Yes.' You smirked.

I pinched my arm, ensuring it hurt. To distract me from the worse pain that you were about to inflict.

I smiled. 'That's good.'

You dropped your head and shook it. Forced a laugh. 'To be honest with you, I've had a strange day.'

I swallowed hard. 'Oh really? Why's that?'

'Oh, nothing . . . nothing. It's just funny, life, isn't it? How things work out.'

'So funny.'

'I shouldn't really . . . Oh, you know what . . . ? I trust you completely, Constance. You won't gossip, I know . . . So that woman that I said was coming in before—'

'Sorry. I'm a bit tired. Do you mind if I sit?' I grasped on to the nearest chair to steady myself and lowered my body.

'Of course. Look, it doesn't matter . . . I don't wish to bore you, anyway.'

'I'm . . . I'm not bored. Go ahead.'

You twisted and dropped the biro onto the desk. 'OK . . . Well, it's nothing, really. It was just that it was Laura – you know, my ex.'

I gripped the wooden arms of the chair. Were you truly that oblivious to someone crumbling before your eyes? 'Oh right . . . I thought you hated each other? I mean . . . that's what you told me.'

'Well, we do . . . did, I guess.' You turned and wrote in your diary again. Didn't even have enough respect to look as you destroyed me. 'And . . . well, basically she's pregnant.'

I shut my eyes and dropped my head. Listening to the pen scratch the page.

You turned again. 'And her fella came to collect her . . . the one I took her from in the first place – not that he knows – and I met him. He actually seems a decent guy . . . a bit of a dick, but you know, OK . . . and it's just so . . . I don't know, funny . . . how things turn out.'

'He's the father?'

You laughed. 'Yes, well, at least I hope so or the poor guy's being well and truly shafted. I must confess I did wonder when she first told me, but it's definitely his. Thank God she's ruining someone else's life, not mine. No . . . no, that's unfair. It's just everything was so, you know . . . intense all those months ago and now . . .' You leant forward. 'He doesn't know, but we met up last week. She wanted to tell me in person . . . I thought that was nice. Don't you think?'

I nodded.

You continued. 'It's just strange, life. How you can love someone so much and then not even care they're having some other man's baby.'

'The baby? Is it OK?'

'The baby? Oh yes . . . She had a little fall last week and had been fretting. All is OK. I wouldn't be surprised if she asked me to be the bloody godfather now or something. Jesus, I hope not.'

I felt faint, bent forward, whispering, 'Thank God.'

'Are you OK, Constance?'

'Yes . . . I'm fine. It's been a bit much today, I think. My first day back and that. I should go.'

'Of course. Sorry. Do you want a lift somewhere?'

I shook my head. I couldn't bear it. What I'd put myself through for nothing. The person I'd become.

In reception, Linda and Alison were putting on their coats and shutting down their computers. I too dressed to leave and gathered my belongings. The heaviness of the coat material scraped against my wounded arm. It was clear I needed to apply ointment and a dressing, though ironically I had to leave the doctor's surgery in order to do it.

The girls left me behind. I was alone. Aware. Not just of the throb of my cut but why I'd done it. It wasn't right. I wasn't right. And I knew it was time. To say it. Confess.

'Is everything all right, Constance?' Dr Franco had on his coat and scarf, and was standing in the middle of his room, briefcase in hand, which he slowly placed down onto the rug. 'Come . . . sit down. What's happened?'

I allowed him to guide me to the chair, gently pressing my shoulders, giving me no option but to lower myself. I was aware of my thumbs circling each other, round and round. Unable to stop.

'Take your time.' He sat himself, pulled his chair closer.

I remained silent. Felt stifled. He must have sensed this as he moved further away from me once again.

'Has something happened?' He handed me the box of tissues. I presume I must have been crying.

I shook my head.

'Then what is it?' He leant back, allowed me the freedom to talk.

The clock tick-tocked slower than time itself. The wind rattled against the window.

'I killed her,' I said.

*

The pollen was high, and the trees candied.

The bus ride from our house to the Christie was long, requiring two changes: one in the overwhelming bustle of Piccadilly, the other in Fallowfield. So near yet so far away without a car or a body strong enough to walk the additional stretch. As usual, she wasn't talkative throughout any of it. Neither was I. Never was on result days.

On the last bus, a single-decker, she sat in the window seat, staring beyond the glass etched by youths, holding her mouth to control the nausea. She'd already thrown up that morning. The same noise of retching that rung in my ears from being a kid. Except the source had changed from booze to chemotherapy.

After rubbing my hay-fevered eyes, I turned away from her to sneeze. *No germs. Must avoid the germs.* She pulled a screwed-up tissue from her bag and smoothed it out before handing it to me.

'It's clean,' she said.

She hadn't bothered to wear her wig. Too hot for it, she insisted. In the early days she wouldn't even go out into the garden without it balanced on her scalp. I'd pretend that the heavy fringe and shiny nylon bob looked natural.

We'd both pretend. But you get what you pay for and this came free with the voucher they handed over at her first treatment. Fast-forward to after her last chemo, sick, weak, pains in her feet – 'I can't bear it, Constance' – and she'd stopped wearing it at all. And scarves. 'I'm not a bloody fortune-teller.' She wasn't completely bald. Clusters remained. I told her to shave it off. 'I will. We'll do it tomorrow . . . Remind me to get the clippers from next door,' she said, every day.

The place was rammed, as usual. The cancer farm. More wigs than a fancy-dress shop. More scarves than a football match. Yet it was loud, upbeat. The powerful energy of people's determination to survive.

She took a seat, and I pulled a number from the ticket machine for those waiting for bloods. Like when we'd treat ourselves to a small wedge of our favourite Gouda from the deli instead of adding a few quid to the holiday fund.

We still didn't speak. Only exchanged knowing glances about the atrocious wig on the woman sat opposite. Telepathically knowing we were both saying, 'Dolly Parton.'

It was difficult to look at Mum at all by this point. I'd avoid it. Focus just past her like a blind person. Her teeth protruded from her skeletal face. Her sunken eyes were further away from me than ever. I'd turn away when able. Imagining I was addressing her round, ruddy cheeks and warm, tipsy, chestnut eyes.

She emerged from phlebotomy rolling down her sleeve.

'How was it?'

'That bit's easy, isn't it? It's on the bloody hand that's impossible.'

I changed the subject, to something worse. 'I think we need to get you some new leggings. The Lycra's gone in those.' It hadn't, of course. They were now just so baggy they hung like trousers.

We waited in two different seated areas before being called in by the nurse.

'Hi, Angela. Let's pop you on the scales, love.' She recorded her weight. Seven three.

Mum looked as though she hadn't even heard the diminished numbers. For me, tears surfaced and I wiped my eyes. 'This hay fever's pissing me off.'

The consultant, Mr Wallis, tall and bumbling, the type to be bullied at school, didn't start with his usual small talk.

I knew.

Mum stood to greet him as she always did, like she was meeting the Queen. He shook our hands. Sat and pulled his chair closer to the small square table. Opened the manila folder.

'I'm afraid, Angela, the markers have risen significantly despite the last course of chemo, and the thing is, we're running out of options. The next step would be to see if there are any trials running.'

Neither of us spoke.

I wanted to hold her hand. It was millimetres away from mine. But I didn't.

We left that room for the very last time. Joined the herd as we walked towards the large glass exit. My throat clenched, chest caved. But I couldn't break. Make her feel worse. Before leaving, we gelled our hands. *No germs. Must avoid the germs.*

Outside, I lit a fag. She extracted it from my fingers and had a drag.

'You can't smoke, Mum.'

She laughed. 'Constance, don't be daft. But hey, on the positive side, the diet's going well, eh?'

I smiled. Which extended to a laugh that wanted to be a cry. I turned and tapped my foot to stop it from happening.

She stamped out the ciggie and beckoned me towards her chest. Put her sharpened maternal arms around me. Comforted me. It should have been me comforting her. She felt light, as if half of her had already gone.

Tearing myself away from her bones, I said, 'The trial sounds promising, though.'

She was so weak I acted as her crutch during the walk from the bus stop. Once home, I told her to go in the lounge and I'd make us some pasta. While the kettle boiled, I went in to ask if she wanted tubes or shells. She was sat in his chair. She'd never sat in his chair.

'What are you doing?'

'Just sitting,' she said.

We ate our dinner accompanied by *Coronation Street* as always. And as always I commented on Gail Platt's irritatingly soft voice and fluttering lashes. But she didn't laugh as she usually would, or say, 'She's the most annoying thing on telly. Wish that Richard Hillman had bumped her off.' Instead she said, 'There won't be a trial.'

I placed my fork inside the bowl that rested between my legs. 'What do you mean?'

'He didn't say there would be a trial. He said he'd find out if there was one running, but he wasn't aware of one.'

'He didn't say that.'

'He did, Constance.'

I stared at Gail, hooked a tube onto the fork and slowly placed it into my mouth. Chewed and chewed and chewed. Unable to swallow.

'I don't want to drag it on,' she said.

I continued with the same mouthful until it evaporated into liquid, into air.

'For you, I mean. With Dad, it was—'

'You're not Granddad,' I shouted. The bowl dropped to the floor. Pasta jolted over the sides onto the carpet. I spat the watery mouthful into it. 'Why are you always so fucking selfish?' I said, before running up to my room.

In bed, I chain-smoked. Window open, towel under the door, so it didn't harm her. Drank half a bottle of old confiscated Martini I kept in my wardrobe. An hour later I heard her slowly climb the stairs. She knocked, whispering my name through the wood. I should have answered. Apologized. But I didn't. I just listened to her throw up in the toilet before going to bed.

Hours later I still couldn't sleep. It was nearly two in the morning. My bedroom spun and I focused on the sound of rain falling onto the guttering above my window. It intensified. Became torrential. The *blop, blop, blop* of the water a torturous punishment. Then without warning, the sky exploded into a storm.

I left my bed and hovered next to hers. Half asleep, she pulled back the covers to expose the empty side of the mattress. I slipped in next to her. Began to pray. The thunder growled, then barked. With eyes still shut, she lifted her arm. I moved under it, nestled in her pit, my hand hugging her swollen belly.

'The storm's here because of me. I'm sorry,' I cried.

She stroked away the hair stuck to my face. 'God's not angry at you, baby. You're angry at God.'

When I woke the next morning, the air smelt fresh and earthy. Everything had reset. I could hear Blondie playing downstairs, so with my boozed brain pulsating against my skull, I threw on my jeans, T-shirt, pumps and headed down.

At the bottom, I watched her beating eggs in a bowl. 'Come on, I'm making us breakfast,' she said.

'But you never make breakfast.'

'Well, today I am. Today I'm going to be a good mum, do the right thing.' She smiled and beat to the beat. As she turned towards the cooker, she paused, dropped her head to catch her breath. Perking up again to sing along to 'Heart of Glass'. 'This song reminds me of us, Constance.'

We sat and ate our scrambled eggs on toast at the kitchen table to the background of *Parallel Lines* and talked about the beautiful day that lay ahead.

'We could go for a walk in the park if you feel strong enough later? The fresh air will do you good.'

She smiled, placed her hand on top of mine. 'How the fuck did I make you?' she said.

I cleared away the dishes and thanked her for breakfast.

'That's OK,' she said. 'Sorry for not doing it more often.'

'My turn tomorrow,' I said. And as desperate as everything had been the day before, it was now hopeful, lighter. She had her fight back. More than ever.

I scraped my crusts into the bin (never wanted curly hair), and with them the fears that had clung to my every cell since we'd left the hospital. She was wrong about the trial. Never listened.

She came behind me, cocooned me. Rested her chin on my shoulder. 'Nothing could be more than us,' she said.

We stayed there, rocking, for what seemed like an eternity. What I wish was an eternity. Until she broke away from me and said, 'Can you fetch my bag from the lounge?'

I carried in the peeling PVC handbag and placed it in front of her. She didn't thank me. Just unzipped it, retrieved her purse and pulled out a twenty, then a ten.

'I want you to treat yourself to a haircut this morning.'

'But I don't need a haircut.'

'Are you kidding me? Look at the bloody state of you.'

'What about the holiday fund?'

She jerked her hand for me to take the money. I caught her eyes. Deep in their sockets they spoke. Like they did about the Dolly Parton wig woman. But this time I didn't know what they were saying. I didn't. I didn't.

'No, please, Mum, I don't want to. We can't afford it. Let's have a walk. The park will be quiet now.'

She took my hand and pressed the notes into my palm. 'You need to, sweetheart.'

For some reason I began to cry. But I wasn't sure why. I

now realize she didn't ask me why either. She didn't need to.

My hand scrunched the money like a claw. I turned away from her eyes and grabbed my keys from the side.

'OK,' I said.

No goodbyes were exchanged. We never liked goodbyes.

Outside, everything was fine once more. I nodded and said hello to Cheryl from number four, off to work in her nurse's uniform. Stopped to read the lost-cat poster on the lamp post. I told myself that my upset was nothing more than a hangover, a Martin overload, accompanied by lack of sleep. And my hair really was a fucking mess.

I'd only ever been to A Cut Above when waiting for Mum to have her roots done. And she only went there because Natasha, the owner, was the daughter of Liz, her drinking partner in the White Lion. As I approached, it dawned on me for the first time that it had once been a terraced house. It still resembled one, with its greying net curtains. The only thing differentiating it from the homes it was sandwiched between was the large black-and-white print of a woman with a perm and the signage over the window. It was then it also dawned on me that Liz hadn't visited Mum once since her diagnosis.

It was fine at first.

I sat, wet-haired, shrouded in a thin plastic robe with a green bleach-stained towel draped around my neck. A pretty girl, younger than me, with a heavily painted face and those marker-pen brows I'll never understand, presented me with a stewed tea and a dog-eared copy of *Heat* magazine before Natasha came over to ask me what I wanted.

I told her just a trim. But before I knew it, she'd talked me into layers, and as the hair fell away, all I could think of was Mum saying, 'Oh, she's made a right bugger of that. You know your hair's too fine for layers.'

'How's your mam doing?' asked Natasha, lifting strands between her fingers.

'She's OK,' I said. 'She's being put forward for a trial.'

But as I watched her replying in the mirror, only her mouth moved. I heard no words.

Because I felt it.

Understood what her eyes were telling me. I must have known all along. I saw Mum beating the eggs. *Today I'm going to be a good mum, do the right thing.* Half her allowance pressed into my hand. No goodbyes. We didn't like goodbyes. And on the countertop I saw the small, sharp knife.

The blood drained from my face.

I stood. My legs buckled. I ripped off the robe; the towel remained in place. My hair, cold, wet, slapped against my ears. I could hear Natasha's words again: 'What are you doing?'

The towel dropped onto the tarmac. I heard beeps. Felt the heat of a car bonnet inches from my body. Ignored the abuse from the driver. Had to carry on.

It took forever to reach my road. Even running, the journey stretched beyond recognition. Like one of those dreams in which you need to make a call and can't dial, or are late to be on stage in a play. But it was no dream.

Breathlessly, I turned into Cholmondeley Road. Past the houses. Fourteen, twelve, ten, eight . . .

Jamie was in next door's driveway tinkering with his car. 'I've got that hair-trimmer for your mum,' he said.

I tore open our gate. Reached the door.

Then I calmed.

Looking through the window, all was fine. The lamp glowed in the lounge. The TV flickered. My concerns transferred to the hairdresser. I was mortified. Already deciding Mum would have to call Natasha on my behalf, say I'd had a funny turn.

I unlocked the door. 'Mum,' I shouted.

No response. Only the *This Morning* theme tune coming from the lounge. I followed it. She wasn't there. I muted the volume and returned to the hall.

'Mum?'

Nothing.

Except the *drip, drip, drip* of the tap upstairs.

I followed the rhythm.

Opened the bathroom door.

To that snapshot. Cauterized on my brain forever.

I focused on her toe. Bobbing serenely in the water. But the photograph had been captured in its entirety. The glass of Martin. The ashtray. Burnt-out cigarette perched on the toilet lid. Her diary watermarked on the floor. The contrast of the red water against her blue skin.

I shut the door. Threw up on the landing. And I haven't stopped throwing up since.

When I called the ambulance, the operator told me to check if she was still breathing.

'I can't,' I said.

She told me I needed to. So they'd know if she was still alive.

The door squeaked as I pushed it open. But I couldn't look again. I couldn't. I screamed down the phone she was dead.

'I'm sorry, Constance. The ambulance will be there any minute now . . . You're being so brave.'

She thought I'd checked the pulse, but I hadn't. She may have had one. She could have still been alive.

I let her die twice.

So that was it. I'd told him. As I'm telling you now. All that time rotting me from the inside. Would anything have been different if you'd known? Would you have hated me more, loved me more?

When I'd stopped talking, I was perched on the cold windowsill on the other side of Franco's office. My thumbs still dancing partners. My cheeks chaffed from salted tears.

He'd remained in his chair throughout. Unnoticed by me, he'd removed his scarf and coat, as they were now draped on the back of his seat. He held no notes.

'Come and sit down, Constance,' he said. 'Come on.'

I followed his instruction and took the chair opposite him once more.

'How are you feeling now?' he said.

'I . . . I don't know.'

'I'd like to thank you for telling me this. It was very courageous of you. How many other people have you told? Or know?'

'That she killed herself, or that it was my fault?'

He blinked slowly with a half-smile. 'That she killed herself.'

'No one . . . I don't know . . . I think some people on the estate knew. Not from me . . . from rumours. No one here, though. I wanted to leave it there. I mean, they all probably knew, but I didn't even make it through the funeral . . . didn't speak to anyone. They didn't give a shit about her. No one did but me. How are you supposed to do that? Watch your own mother glide through a fucking curtain to be burned? Because of me. No . . . I . . . I left before the end. And I only stayed in Manchester a few days to get the ashes back. In the meantime I sold a few bits, counted up the holiday fund, scraped as much money together as I could. Pawned some of her jewellery . . . my grandma's jewellery, which I now regret. Then when I finally got the jar, filled with her. A jar. Like one of the big plastic catering mayonnaise jars they had when I worked in pubs. My mum was in that. Once I had her with me, I packed a couple of suitcases and left. Got on a coach to London.'

He pulled his chair right up. I didn't mind this time. He took my hand, his fingers grazing the cut on my forearm. I tried not to wince. His cheeks pinked. I'm not sure he was supposed to touch me like that. But his hands were warm, comforting.

'Remember you told me about your father? That you felt it was your fault because you let go?'

I nodded.

'Well, that wasn't your fault, was it?'

'I don't know.'

'He made his own decision that day. We don't know his

reasons, but sometimes people do things out of love for others, though their actions appear to show the opposite.'

I dropped my head. Tears fell onto my coat.

'Constance . . . I want you to look at me, Constance.'

I did as I was told, but it was awkward, strange.

His hand squeezed harder. 'It was the same with your mother. She was a grown woman who made her decision. And it seems that decision was based on not wanting to suffer a painful, drawn-out death. Nor for you to witness it, like she did with her father.'

'So she thought me walking in with her floating in a bloodbath was better?'

'I don't think she thought rationally about any of it. She just wanted it to end. For both your sakes. But none of it was your fault.'

I shook my head, dismissing his words, yet simultaneously gaining relief from them. I stood and collected my scarf, which had slipped to the floor.

'Dr Franco, you don't seem to understand . . . I didn't stop her. I could have stopped her.'

He shook his head. 'How?'

Unconsciously, I wrapped the scarf around my hand. 'What do you mean?'

'Tell me. How you could have stopped her?'

'Well, I . . . I wouldn't have gone to get my stupid hair cut . . . left her—'

'Ever? You were only gone a short while.'

'I never checked her pulse.'

'Because she was already dead, Constance. You knew that. She was dead.'

'I would have encouraged her to remain positive about the trial—'

'There was no trial. He said he'd see if there was anything, but, Constance, they are rare—'

'For fuck's sake, he didn't say that.' I shouted so loud the words ricocheted off the walls and slapped me across the face.

He slumped back in his chair, lowered his head.

'I'm sorry, Dr Franco . . . I shouldn't have troubled you. I get paid next week. I'll pay you for your time—'

'Constance, I don't want your—'

'I've got to go, Dr Franco . . . Thank you.' I unravelled the scarf from my hand, placed it calmly, neatly, around my neck and picked up my bag. 'Will this go any further? I mean . . . am I safe?'

'Safe?' He repeated the slow blink, half-smile, then nodded.

I sensed him watching as I walked towards the door. When I was about to shut it behind me, he said, 'I hope you start to feel better from now on, Constance. Please think about what I've said.'

I pretended I hadn't heard and pulled the door to.

Outside, I lit a cigarette. The first since I'd been ill. My adult pacifier. At the bottom of the steps, I rested my back against my usual wall. Dizzy with nicotine, I closed my eyes. Remaining tears squeezed out to mix with the freezing air, biting my cheeks. I reopened them, looked up to the clear black sky.

'Is he right?' I whispered. 'For fuck's sake, tell me somehow. Is he right?'

I waited. There was nothing. No answer. No sign. Nothing.

I gave it until I reached the filter, then wiped my face with my scarf, pulled the collar up over my ears and set off down the road.

As I did, it began to snow.

Which brings us to my birthday.

The day.

It started so well. Waking for the first time unladen, without guilt pressing against my chest, my skull.

I'd slept in my room the previous night. Told Dale I had a banging headache, enabling me to both dress my arm and compute all that had happened with Dr Franco.

Surprisingly, Dale had left before I'd woken. His only communication a card with a picture of Princess Leia on the front, slipped under my door. *Happy birthday to my own princess. Dinner at 6.30 sharp*, it said inside.

Once at the surgery, I was accosted by a grinning Alison holding out a pearly-pink gift bag with a glittery unicorn on the front. 'Happy birthday, Constance.'

'Oh . . . oh, thank you. How . . . how did you know?'

'It's on our system, silly . . . You look nice.'

She clapped her hands together with excitement and followed me behind the reception desk while I removed my coat then the lime-green tissue paper that concealed the present. White furry cat-face earmuffs. Whiskers and all.

'I made them myself,' she said. 'Try them on.'

I appeased her, attempting not to fluff up my hair, on

337

which I'd spent more time than I'd ever remembered doing. 'I love them, thank you. That's really lovely of you.' And it was the first time ever I'd not been sarcastic to Alison.

Even Linda wished me 'many happy returns' when she exited Dr Harris's room.

'We'll do something in the staffroom this afternoon,' she said. 'Nothing fancy. Some Battenberg, perhaps.'

Her pleasantness was so shocking that I was uncertain if it was genuine or merely excitement at the opportunity to eat cake.

As touching as this all was, it was only you I wanted to see. To witness my happier state. Lack of black cloud. As if I'd been wiped clean. Reset at zero.

Once Mrs Tullings and her boy brat had finished their appointment with you, I took it upon myself to make you a coffee and take it to your room.

'Hey, Constance. Goodness, you look nice. What a difference a day makes, eh?'

I turned to close the door, concealing the joy in my face at your noticing. That I'd dressed for you. Worn the same silk blouse that had turned your head in the beginning. 'I've made you a coffee. Thought you might need one after Sebastian Tullings.'

'Ah yes . . . Sebastard Tullings.'

I laughed and placed the mug on your desk. Leant forward.

'You really do look lovely today, Constance. Glowing.'

We were close to each other. Like that day. The blouse draping open as expected. You looked at me. Nothing furtive this time. Bold. Obvious.

'It's my birthday,' I said.

'Your birthday? You never mentioned. Well . . . well, we must celebrate . . . We should get a drink or something. Oh, hang on, I can't tonight . . . poker. Though I could do a quick one? After work? What do you say?'

Was that all it took? For you to see me differently? Me being less sorrowful, self-hating? I'm often nauseated by those motivational memes people share on Instagram. A picture of some perfect woman performing an impossible yoga pose on top of a mountain. *Happiness depends on your positivity of thought*, or some other bullshit. But for that moment, as you waited, wide-eyed, for me to agree to go for a drink with you, I must admit I wondered if those morons were right.

'Yes . . . yes, I'd like that,' I said.

From that point on I surfed the hours on a wave of excitement.

My elation only momentarily stained at lunch, when on my way to Edward's, I rang to warn him of my arrival and the phone rang out. It was presumably uncharged, but I endured stabs of fear until I arrived to find him snoring in his chair, oblivious to my presence. Even under the circumstances, I couldn't help but smile when I saw him dappered up in a pinstriped suit, shirt and tie. On his head, a fancy-dress gold crown encrusted with plastic rubies.

'Edward . . . it's me . . . Wake up.'

With a grunt, he jolted awake, his headwear slipping to a jaunty angle. 'Oh, bloody hell, are you trying to give me a heart attack?'

'Sorry . . . I—'

'No, no . . . it's me that's sorry,' he said, feeling his head, remembering why he was wearing a crown. 'Happy birthday, darling girl.'

'Thank you. I've got cake. I'll make us some tea.'

'Here, put this on first . . . It's just to wear for lunch, mind. It doesn't leave the flat.' He handed me an exquisite glittering tiara. Speechless, I placed it on my head. 'It was my mother's. Given to her by an Indian prince. A fan.' And I heard myself gasp when he said, 'They're real diamonds.'

I returned, feeling half-royalty, half-servant. Jewels in hair, tray in hand. The sponge lit with a lone candle. Edward sang 'Happy Birthday', breathless and weak. I joined in, giggling and tuneless. At the end he told me to make a wish, so I closed my eyes, blew and wished for you.

As I served up, he rose with difficulty. 'What is it you want, Edward? I'll get it.'

'You mind your own. And don't be stingy with the slice . . . What the hell is that? I want a piece not a wafer.'

He returned from the cabinet carrying a book-shaped item, wrapped in newspaper. 'Here,' he said, dropping it to the table.

'Is that for me?'

'No, it's for bloody Ursula. Of course it's for you.'

I handed him his tea and cake. 'Well, you shouldn't have got me anything.'

'Don't worry – I didn't.'

After shoving cake in my mouth and slurping tea, I tore off the makeshift wrapping to reveal a faded blue hardback copy of *Wuthering Heights*. I hugged it to my chest. 'That's brilliant. Thank you, Edward.'

'Look inside . . . I haven't got you a card but look inside.'

I flipped the front cover open.

Happy birthday to my best friend. Thank you for saving me, Constance. Love, Edward.

'Thank you, Edward. It's . . . I love it.' I looked at him, freeing his chin of jam and suppressing a cough with a sip of tea, and I had the overwhelming feeling that I'd wished for the wrong thing.

I stood and relit the candle, but as the air left my lips, extinguishing the flame, I heard Edward say, 'You shouldn't do that – it's bad luck.'

The rest of the day flew by.

At nearly five Linda called everyone into the kitchen for my birthday fodder. Except Dr Short, who was still at home looking after his daughter, the Ratcheds, who'd already left, and Dr Franco, who was with a client. I feigned exuberance, but as well as being all caked out, I was preoccupied by our pending rendezvous.

Alison made the teas, while you and Dr Harris hovered awkwardly in the servants' quarters.

'We need to do this room up, don't we?' said Harris, after spending a whole five minutes with the strip lights and shabby chairs.

After another ten minutes of phoney frivolity and comments about how I was 'still a baby' and that they'd 'kill to be twenty-seven', Linda presented me with a card that everyone had signed. I scanned the messages and thanked you all earnestly. Although, it was only yours I really cared about. *Happy birthday to the best coffee-maker in West London. Love, Dr Stevens x*

Love.

* * *

I wish I could end it there.

The rest is difficult for me to write. I'm sorry. But I need to get it out, you understand. Tragedy by tragedy.

As the mini-celebrations wound down, I noticed Dr Franco's client leaving so took him up some cake. He was all ready to head off but still happy to accept the offering.

'Oh, Battenberg, my favourite. How very kind. And happy birthday.' He bit into the sponge, then with a full mouth said, 'How are you feeling today?'

'Much better . . . thank you.' And I realized it was the first time I'd said such a thing in so long without it being a lie.

'Well, that pleases me even more than this cake.'

By this time I was almost bursting with anticipation. I headed to the toilet to reapply my lipstick, which I also dotted slightly on my cheeks. Not that I needed to: they were already flushed pink. You were right. I was different to the day before. I looked so much like her. When she was well and happy. Or maybe it was her who stared back at me. Visiting.

'Happy birthday,' I whispered to my reflection. Imagining it was her saying it.

You entered reception, turning up the collar of your coat, as I was buttoning mine. When Linda bent down to collect her bag, you mouthed that you had the car and for me to meet you in the car park.

'Goodbye, Dr Stevens. See you tomorrow,' I said.

Alison and Linda echoed my words as you left. We followed on. But once outside, I hung back and lit a fag.

'Constance, that should be your birthday resolution,' said Alison.

'I know . . . I know.' I smiled, attempting to maintain my goodwill towards her. 'I'll see you tomorrow. And thanks again for the present and cake.'

While smoking, I watched them disappear into the distance, before texting Dale that I was nipping in to see Edward first.

Don't be late. I've got dinner on, Birthday Girl.

Then I called Edward to check on him, immediately wishing I hadn't, as it rang out. Running down the steps, I tried him again. *Wrestles tigers, deep-sea diver, can't charge a bloody phone.*

I turned the corner, entering the car park. Away from the street, its only source of light was the glow from surrounding buildings. There were three cars still there: yours, the surgery Smart Car and a Mercedes, which I presumed belonged to Dr Harris.

My shoes crunched across the gravel as I nervously pulled so hard on my cigarette the ash crackled, then cascaded to the floor. Light-headed, I threw the rest away. You popped open the door from the inside for me to get in.

'Sorry I was a while. I had to wait for Linda and Alison to go,' I said.

It had been a long time since I'd sat in there with you. The potent scent of leather stirred memories.

You rubbed your palms together as if starting a friction fire. You were, of sorts, weren't you? You smiled at me. At least, I think that's what you did. It was dark and hard to tell as my eyes hadn't adjusted yet.

'So where do you want to go?' you asked.

'I . . . I don't know. I've not got long. I've got to be back by six thirty at the latest.'

'No worries. Me neither.'

Part of me hoped you'd object. Ask me to stay out longer. Say you'd change your plans.

'I don't mind, then,' I said. 'You pick.'

A window of one of the houses sprang into lightness, enabling me to see you more clearly. Your head dropped, deep in thought. A dog howled from the same home, making me jump.

You looked up at me. 'Are you nervous?' you said.

'No . . . no. It was just the dog.'

The house plunged back into darkness. As did we.

'I am,' you said.

'In case Dr Harris sees us?'

'Harris? No . . . No, he's catching up on paperwork. He'll be stuck in there till gone eight. It's you. You've made me feel nervous all day.'

I was glad of the anonymity within the blackness. Hiding my flushed face. 'Why would I make you nervous?'

'I don't know. I . . . I guess I forgot how much chemistry we have. How much I fancy you.'

I didn't want it to be a joke, but my mind could only presume it was. Until you said, 'Do I not get a birthday kiss?'

I can't express how unexpected the whole thing was. You spoke the words so naturally. Like I was yours. You were mine.

'What . . . what about Harris?'

'I've told you. Fuck Harris.'

You tugged at my arm to twist me towards you. I grabbed on to the cold metal gearstick to steady myself. And then, as you know, it was as it always was. More than just a kiss. Although the air was biting, your mouth was warm, soothing. Your hands weaved my hair. Hurting, pulling. Then you separated from me, your breaths heavy, white with cold.

'We could just stay here,' you said.

If I'd known that would be the last time we'd have sex, I would have treasured it more. It made me high, feeling how much you wanted me. How urgently you needed to be inside my body. But it was somewhat hindered by logistics. The awkwardness as you shuffled across to my seat and man- oeuvred me on top. My head repeatedly knocking against the car roof. How when it was over, and you'd pushed me up and pulled out, you came all over my coat. I was conscious throughout it all. Of the light going on and off in the house, the dog's barks, Dr Harris.

Once we were untangled and back in our respective seats, you leant over – I presumed for the cuddle I craved, but your arm carried on past me and flicked open the glove compartment.

'Sorry about that,' you said. 'I've got tissues in there somewhere.'

Hampered by lack of vision, I removed as many sheets as I could from the soft plastic packet and passed some of the collection to you. I could hear you wiping yourself down, zipping yourself up. Once finished, you shoved the tissues into the door pocket and I could then just make out both your hands on the steering wheel.

'So, what are you doing tonight?' Your fingers drummed against the leather.

'Nothing . . . I was just going to go home. Have some dinner.'

'With your fella?'

I nodded, furiously and blindly scrubbing the wet patch on my coat. Wanting you to make a fuss. Tell me how you didn't like it. Show your jealousy once more.

'Well, that'll be nice.' You reached for your coat, which had been thrown into the back, and retrieved your wallet. 'Look, I . . . I feel awful doing this again, but here . . .' You pulled out some notes and handed them to me. 'You make it so difficult for me to stop once we start . . . but we can't risk it, can we? I'm so sorry . . . If I could take the pill for you, I would.'

I took the money, scrunched it in my hand and pushed it into my bag. 'Sure,' I said.

'I suppose we'd better head off.'

Another house lit up. I could see from the clock that only twenty minutes had passed since I got in the car.

'I'll drop you at the station . . .' Your words seemed to trail off, distracted, as you looked in your rear-view mirror. 'Shit. Harris.'

You pushed my head down hard, causing me to knock it on the open glove compartment. I remained down in the uncomfortable position, rubbing my temple as you revved the engine and waved to Dr Harris as you drove away.

Snow fell.

You switched on your wipers as the large, delicate flakes transformed to slush on contact with the window.

We were silent for most of the journey. You didn't even bother with music. But as the flurry multiplied, I said, 'Do you feel your mum is around you when it snows? That it's saying she's with you?'

'You mean, do I think the natural process of cold clouds turning water vapours into snow is actually a message from my dead mother? No, I don't . . . You're so funny, Constance.'

As we approached the station, you pulled up on the double yellow line. 'Sorry, Constance. I don't mean to rush you . . . I just don't want to get a ticket . . . but you have a nice birthday . . . And thank you.'

The hall was filled with the aroma of spices. My salivary glands pulsed, hunger triggered. Then they were shot dead by guilt.

'Hi . . . I'm back. I'm just dropping off my coat and stuff in my room,' I shouted.

When I'd stood by the lights of High Street Kensington, watching you speed away, the contrast between the crusted white residue and the black wool of my coat was glaring. I'd purchased a bottle of water, a pack of baby wipes and the morning-after pill from Boots, then facing into a corner in the arcade, set about erasing the stain. Once home, however, I was still aware of the faint ghost that lingered.

Free of evidence, I followed the smells to the kitchen. Took a deep breath and prepared to play my role.

'Wow, this all looks amazing.' A white cloth covered the table, restaurant-like. Two unlit candles in glass candlesticks I'd never seen before were surrounded by poppadoms and ramekins filled with various coloured dips. A bottle of white wine. Matching glasses.

'Take a seat, Birthday Girl. Just on time.' He dropped a sauce-coated spoon onto the kitchen side before flicking a tea towel onto his shoulder, in that clichéd way men do.

He struck a match near the candles, then blew it out. 'Actually, shall we have the big light on? I like to see when I'm eating, don't you?'

I nodded in vague agreement. 'What is all this?'

'What does it look like? I've made dinner. My first curry from scratch, no less. Now, tell me' – he picked up the spoon and extracted some of the bubbling liquid – 'is it hot enough?' He pressed the metal to my mouth until I sipped.

'Yes . . . plenty,' I said, an octave higher than my usual voice.

I filled a glass of water, becoming fearful at the thought of eating a whole plate of the stuff. Not just because of the kick, or the layers of saccharine cake that lay heavy on my stomach, but because I had to sit opposite him, make conversation, enjoy the food he'd laboured over, after what I'd just done.

He removed two plates from the oven and spooned rice from a pan onto them. Then the curry.

'So how was Edward?'

I delayed my response by taking a swig of the water, some of which dribbled down my chin and neck. 'Yeah, good.'

He smiled.

I took my seat. 'It looks amazing, Dale. I'm really impressed. Thank you.'

He placed a plate in front of me and sat down with his.

'I . . . I thought we were just going to get a pizza or something. You shouldn't have gone to all this trouble.'

'On your birthday? A pizza isn't enough for the woman I love on her birthday. But if you don't like it—'

'No . . . no, I do. It's delicious.' As I took a proper mouthful, I realized it really was, and I at least didn't have to lie about that.

He poured us both a glass of wine. 'Believe it or not, this is courtesy of Mr Papadopoulos. I bumped into him on his way out, and when I mentioned it was your birthday, he went back up and returned with this. It's Greek. Not sure what it'll be like. But we've got this other bottle of Sauvignon Blanc if it's rank.'

'I . . . I don't deserve all this. Everyone's been so nice.' The image of you pushing up my skirt, pulling my knickers to the side trespassed my mind.

He paused, his fork suspended. Waiting, proud, for me to have more. And only when I said, 'Honestly, it's delicious. Hot . . . but really tasty,' did he begin to eat.

I dropped my head as I ate. Stared at my plate. Avoided his eyes.

'Are you OK? Is something up?' he said.

'Yes . . . No . . . I'm fine. It's just really lovely of you, that's all. I think I'm in shock at how kind everyone's been.' I told him about the cake at work and how Linda and Dr Harris weren't massive arseholes for once.

'Sounds like a good birthday.'

'Yes, it was . . . is . . . and Edward let me wear a real diamond tiara and gave me a book.'

'A book? Which book? I've never known you to read.'

'No . . . well, I don't, but he said I should start and that I'd like it . . . It's an old copy of *Wuthering Heights.*'

He gently rested his fork against the edge of his plate. 'That's nice,' he said, looking directly at me. Latching on to my eyes. '*Whatever our souls are made of, his and mine are the same.*'

Time pulsed. I dared not look away. Swallowed the rice at the back of my throat.

'It's a famous quote from the book. Sorry, Constance – I thought you'd recognize it . . . which is silly, as you've obviously not read it yet, so why would you?'

'No . . . no, I . . . I probably won't ever read it . . . It was just nice . . . I—'

'You should. Edward chose well for you. I'm sure you'll like it. Lots of themes I think you'll find interesting: intense love, betrayal, revenge . . . You've gone very red, Constance . . . Here . . . have some of this cucumber raita I made.'

Our plates were empty; the bottle Mr Papadopoulos brought us was drunk dry. My mouth was numb. So was I. The table looked like mice had been to dinner. Crumbs everywhere, splashes of luminous chutneys against the crisp white of the cloth.

'That was the best birthday present, Dale. Thank you.'

'Oh, I haven't given you your present yet.' He stood and gathered the dishes.

The food churned inside me, terrified he meant sex. 'Well, I don't deserve another present. That was perfect.' I yawned. 'I'm so tired – I don't know what's wrong with me . . . I'm sure I'll be spark out soon.'

I stood to help clear up.

'Leave that,' he said. 'In fact, go away for ten minutes. Go in mine and pick a DVD to watch. There's a few new ones I bought from the charity shop the other day. They're next to the telly.'

I knew he wanted me out of the way to prepare my birthday cake, but I was worried how I'd manage to eat any of it.

I went to my room first. Exchanged my blouse for a sweatshirt. Removing the silk released such a strong cloud of your aftershave I was amazed Dale hadn't noticed. I kept on my skirt and pants, which were damp from us both. I wasn't prepared to let go of you quite yet. Closing my eyes, without the shame of Dale staring back at me, I relived it all. Feeling you again. A wave ran from my stomach to my knickers. Were you doing the same? Smiling at your poker hand, fingers tainted with me? My scent seeping through the wool of your trousers, making you want me again?

I took *Wuthering Heights* from my bag and sat on the floor next to the bed. Bent into the dark dust, reached blindly for the case and slid it out. Once in front of me, I stared at it. Not because it seemed filthier than ever. Not because I couldn't face her diaries on my birthday, even though that thought crucified me. But because the metal clasp, the left metal clasp, which I'd so strongly pressed to lock the previous time, was up, unattached. Open.

The curry curdled in my stomach. I wiped the layer of sweat that had formed on the back of my neck and unclicked the right. Lifted the lid. They were there as usual. The worst one on top. Your allocated corner the saviour. I took our card, still refusing to believe what I knew, and inserted it inside the book as I'd looked forward to doing all day. Ignoring the tiny bulge due to the pearl I'd kept safe inside the envelope. Then I placed it neatly next to your pen, comb and T-shirt. Before lifting them all out again to find our photograph, which must have slipped underneath one of the diaries. I extracted, disturbed. Moved everything around, rummaged. It wasn't there.

'Have you found one you fancy yet?' His voice carried through the hall into my room, into my skull.

'Sorry . . . I was just having a quick ciggie. I'm going now,' I shouted back.

The wine and realization turned my legs to jelly as I negotiated the hallway to his room. Inside, I shut the door behind me. The anorak swung from the peg on the back with the motion. I didn't know where to look, but began opening his drawers as quietly as possible, my head flicking constantly towards the door, aware he could come in at any second. In the first drawer, there was nothing of note, except a pair of my knickers among his boxers. The second held his T-shirts, nothing else. The third contained tangled wires, old remotes, defunct mobile phones, packs of cheap bulbs. I went to close it, thinking where else to try when I caught sight of a small black box right at the back. I lifted it out. Removed the lid. And it was like my suitcase. Filled with souvenirs. But different. I don't know how, it just was.

There were cinema tickets of films we'd seen, another pair of my knickers that I didn't even recognize, the lipstick I'd lost, other receipts for things I didn't remember going to. And there it was. Our picture. Except you'd been cut off.

And there were other photographs. Of me sleeping in my room. They were dark, grainy. Feeling nauseous, I lifted them out. Looked through them. And as I did, I noticed the tinge of a pink feather in the corner. And I realized that the person asleep wasn't me.

'You can come in now,' he shouted. 'Constance . . . you have to close your eyes until you get here.'

With shaking hands, I returned the box, shut the drawer and grabbed one of the DVDs next to the TV.

Walking through the hall, I kept my eyes open, my eyes that were now wide open, until I neared the kitchen. Then complied. Screwed them tight. Like my insides. Feeling my way through the door frame, sensing the change from light to dark.

'OK . . . you can open them.'

I did. Looking towards the table. There was no cake. Only the two candles now flickering within the unlit room.

I couldn't see him at first. Then I could. He was next to the table. On the floor. Not collapsed. Worse. Kneeling.

He opened the tiny box that balanced within his cupped palms, like an oversized Oliver, asking for more. More of me.

'Jesus, this is harder than I . . . Constance . . .' He pulled out the ring. It was too dark to see properly and I prayed it was a Hula Hoop. That at any second, he'd point and say, 'Argghhh, your face. Gotcha.' Then I'd pretend it was a cruel thing to do to a woman. But as he held it between his fingers, I could see it glisten.

'Constance, for the past week I thought I . . . Oh God . . .' He placed the box on the floor and wiped his lip with his freed-up hand. 'I know I don't see my life without you . . . and . . . I want to look after you and make you feel safe . . . I want to be your husband. I want you to be my wife. For you to be Mrs Constance Cox.'

Constance Cox.

If only the ridiculous porn-star name was the sole reason I wanted to crumble into dust.

I don't know how I reacted. I'm not sure I did or said anything, as he added, his voice and hands tremoring in equal measure, 'I mean, you'll probably want to keep your dad's name too . . . so Constance Little-Cox.'

An eternity passed.

He returned the ring to the box. Stood and placed it on the table. 'I've asked you to marry me and you haven't said a thing.'

I remained in the doorway. Head down, a child about to be chastised. Gripped the DVD as if it was Blusha. 'I know you have . . . I'm sorry.'

I felt him move closer. Waited for him to push past me, go to his room. But instead he flicked the light switch and brought all the embarrassment into brightness.

'Well, I'll take that as a no, then.'

He moved further into the kitchen. Placed his hands upon the worktop, bending forward, then stood upright again and collected up the dirty dishes.

I flinched at the noise of a pan dropping heavily into the sink, followed by the scraping of plates.

'Dale . . . I didn't say that . . . I . . .'

He turned with a bowl held between his fingers. 'So you're saying yes?'

'I . . . No, but . . .'

He turned his back to me again. 'Do you want to wash or dry?' The noise of water flowing from the tap and the squirt of washing-up liquid filled the silence. Until he said, 'I think you should wash. I mean, I did make the fucking dinner after all.' The ceramic slipped from his fingers and dropped to the floor. Smash. White, sticky shards everywhere. He looked down. Didn't move. Until he reached for the unopened bottle of Sauvignon, unscrewed the lid, poured a huge glass and downed it like water on a hot summer's day.

I placed the DVD on the table, then knelt next to him. Collecting the smaller fragments of the crockery within the largest curved piece. He poured another glass, gesturing to ask if I wanted some. I shook my head and continued collecting the shards. Aware he was watching me, sipping. I couldn't look at him. Perturbed at what I knew. What he knew.

'Can't we talk about this, Dale? It's . . . It just took me by surprise, that's all.'

'Why? Why would you be surprised?'

I stood and walked over to the bin. The pieces rattled as they fell inside. 'Because I—'

'Is it because I tell you how much I love you and need you all the time? Because I do tell you that, don't I? You not so much, though, hey? Is it because all I do is care for you and look after you? Is that why you're so fucking surprised?'

'I just didn't think we were there.' I bent down again for the dustpan and brush. Remained on the floor, moving on my knees over to the residue and dust.

He was now sitting at the table, shuffling the box around his hand like a stress ball. 'Where are we, Constance?'

'What do you mean?'

'Well, if we're not there, where are we?'

I swept the debris into the pan, then dared to stand, resting my back against the worktop. 'I . . . I don't know.'

'It was my grandmother's. I told Mum and Dad I was going to ask you. They were so happy that I was doing something right for once. They were actually proud of me. Then she went upstairs and returned with it . . . said she wanted you to have it.' Eyes glazed, he downed the remainder of the wine left in the glass. The mottled deep pink of his cheeks spread down his neck.

'Dale . . . don't drink more. Please . . . let's just talk about it.'

'Don't tell me what to do. You're not my fucking wife, you know.' He laughed. 'Do you get it? You're not my wife?'

I emptied the pan into the bin and remained facing the wall. 'I think I should go to Edward's. It's best if I leave you be tonight.'

'No . . . No. What are you talking about? It's your birthday. We're having fun. I just made you dinner, so you can't leave – you've got to do the washing-up.' He came over to me and pulled me by the arm. 'Come here . . . Come and sit with me. Have some wine.'

His fingers gripped harder as he led me over to the chair and pressed me down. Before sitting himself, he poured us both a glass.

'Happy birthday.' He lifted his glass and brought it towards me to clink.

I tentatively raised mine to meet his. After a huge gulp he caught site of the DVD. '*Extreme Fishing*? Interesting choice.'

'I . . . I must have picked—'

'It's pretty, isn't it?' He was opening the velvet box. Removed the ring. Pinched it between his fingertips before holding it up to the candle's flame.

'Yes.'

'You should put it on.'

'I don't want to, Dale.'

'Please.' His voice flattened. My heart accelerated.

He took hold of my hand, pushed up my sleeve. 'What did you do to your arm?'

'I burned it, at work.'

'On what?'

'Coffee . . . I'd made a coffee and it spilt on my arm.'

'You didn't tell me. You don't tell me anything, do you?'

Heat overwhelmed me and I tugged the neck of my sweatshirt to allow air to flow down my chest. 'I . . . I do. I tell you everything.'

He smiled and encased his fingers around my wrist. 'Who bandaged it for you?'

I didn't move. I knew how much it would hurt.

'I did.'

'Not a doctor?' The candle sparked and I turned instinctively, causing his fingers to press against my wound.

'No . . . No one did it. I did it myself. I can show you the stuff.'

'OK.' He took hold of my hand, stroked my finger before slipping on the ring.

'Please don't,' I said, but he continued. Pushing it, hard, over my knuckle. Snagging my skin. Eventually it sat at the base, tight like a tourniquet.

'It looks pretty on you. Fits as well. Hold it up . . . Have a look.'

My hand protested. White skin bulged beyond the band. 'It's too tight. It's hurting,' I said, trying to pull it off.

'Leave it . . . Just sit with it for a while.'

'I can't.' The chair screeched as I stood and headed to the sink. Ran my hand under the cold tap. Hoping to reduce the swelling, the throb.

'Nothing I do is right, is it?'

I splashed water on the back of my neck to control the burn spreading over me.

'Is it, Constance? I'm just a joke to you. To you, Anna . . . all of you.'

'Anna . . . Is Anna the girl who lived here before? Did you . . . Were you together?'

'No, Constance . . . not together. No, you lot don't want the nice guys, do you? It's all about looks and money. Men like me never have a chance.'

'What are you talking about?' The diamond indented my other fingers as I yanked at the gold. I reached for the washing-up liquid.

'Constance, don't . . . Please don't. Try it for a bit . . . See how you feel.'

'For fuck's sake, Dale, it's killing me.' As I massaged the green gel around the metal, I sensed him behind me. The curry rose in my gullet.

He moved my hair to the side. His breath tickling my neck. 'Please just leave it.' He lowered his lips to kiss my crawling skin.

I turned to make it stop. His chest met my face, the thick wool of his jumper suffocating me. Within the free inch of space between our bodies, I twisted and twisted until I managed to prise off the ring. My hand squeezed up in front of us.

'Here,' I said.

He lifted my chin with the crook of his finger. Forced me to look at his clouded eyes. At his face, now wet with tears, to which I'd been oblivious.

'Do you have any idea what it's like? To love someone so much and for them to not love you back?' His voice was calm, low, tempered. Yet the hairs on my arms rose.

He released my chin, snatched the ring and sat back at the table. Rubbed it clean with his ribbed cuff before returning it with care to the slot inside the box. Closed it.

'I do everything for you,' he said.

'I know. I know you do.'

I wiped my wet detergent hands down my skirt, while watching him pour the dregs from the wine glass into his mouth, then start on mine, until he paused and said, 'Is there someone else?'

'No . . . No, of course not.'

He let out a short, sharp laugh. 'So there's no one else?'

'I've told you, no.' I turned to finish drying my hands on the tea towel. Not pausing, not outwardly showing how my heart had almost stopped and the majority of blood had left my head. I'd masked it successfully.

Until he said, 'The thing is, Constance . . . when you're so consumed in watching someone else, you don't notice eyes on you.'

My legs weakened. Spices burned the back of my throat.

'What about the doctor?'

We looked at each other. I knew from his stare there was no point denying it. That it would make it worse. I lowered my head, barely able to make a noise from my constricted throat, and surrendered. 'It . . . it was over before us. I swear.'

Nothing. I dared to raise my eyes to view him. He was tapping the box on the table, one, two, three, then flung it across the room like a cricket ball. It hit the wall, fell to the ground, lid splayed. Our silence highlighted by the sound of the ring tinkling against the terracotta tiles.

'Please, Dale. You're my friend. I don't want to hurt you.' As soon as the words left my mouth, I knew they were a poor choice.

'Friend?' He got up and went to the fridge. 'I'm your friend, am I?'

'I . . . I don't mean just my friend.' It was then I had a clear sense I should have run. But it was Dale. Only Dale.

He reached in for a beer, then came and stood right in front of me. With his eyes glued to mine, he slowly opened the cutlery drawer adjacent to my hip. I could hear my heart. He removed the bottle opener and popped off the top. Let it fall to the floor.

'Then lift your skirt,' he said.

'What?'

'If I'm not just a friend, then lift up your skirt.' His body swayed as he gulped the beer. Not stopping until I could see half the liquid had disappeared. Then he started to cry.

I leant heavier against the counter. 'Dale . . . you're upset . . . I understand—'

'I'm not upset. I'm just awake, Connie.'

His attempt to reach around me and put the bottle on the work surface failed and it toppled into the sink. Glass shattered against the pan. Beer sizzled into the water.

'If you don't just see me as a friend, then lift up your skirt and let's fuck.' His pained eyes leaked tears over his flaming cheeks, and white stringy froth connected his top and bottom lips as he pressed against me. My hands slipped back on the worktop and I could feel leftovers smearing my flesh. Plates clanked. My fingertip scraped the chopping-knife blade.

'Dale . . . listen, you have to get off me. You're upset, drunk.'

His face buried into my neck, while his hand reached for the hem of my skirt. The material rose between his fingers like a Roman blind, and he tried to kiss me. Our lips opposing magnets. Hot mucus and saliva slipped over my face. His free hand pulled at my hair. As I liked it. But I didn't like it. I wanted to tell him, scream, though I couldn't make words form, only pig-like squeals as his mouth overcame mine. Intruding tongue. A prelude to his hand weaving into my knickers, pulling them down and inserting his fingers inside me with force. It hurt. I cried.

Fury travelled from my toes up through the parts he was abusing and reached my head, until finally I managed to pull my mouth away long enough to shout, 'Stop. Dale, you have to stop.'

At least I thought I did. I wondered if I'd made a sound at all. Because Dale would have stopped. But he kissed harder. Pushed deeper. Breaking away only slightly to whisper, 'If you love me, then show me.'

My underwear was around my boots then, binding my ankles, my skirt gathered around my abdomen. With one hand he undid his zip. I managed to step out of the leg holes to free myself and pressed my arms up between us. Tried to hit his chest. But there wasn't gap enough to have any impact. His jeans dropped to his trainers, his boxers with them. I could feel him, hard, trying to enter me. My attempts to fight him off lasted seconds, or minutes. Then somehow, from somewhere, I heard a guttural noise escape my throat. The monster inside returned. Reminding me what I am capable of.

I pressed harder against the cupboard. Created space between us. Found the strength to pull my leg as far back as possible before swinging it forward, punching my knee violently between his legs.

The suction of his lips broke, allowing me to scream, 'You. Fucking. Disgust me.'

And it stopped.

He stepped away. Bent forward, grimacing, red, gathering himself from the pain. I dared not move when he reached down and pulled up his trousers, softly uttering, 'I know. I know I do.'

Silence reigned. Aside from our short breaths. We stood, heads lowered, deactivated. I pulled down my skirt to cover myself, closing my eyes to soak in the relief.

Then smack. His fist hit my mouth.

So hard it twisted me into a pirouette. I fell forward onto the kitchen counter. A shattering sensation seared through my face. Blood splattered the dishes. I spat red onto a plate, expecting a tooth to join it, but it remained. Loose and throbbing. I couldn't move, breathe. Paralyzed by shock. Until I saw the blade of the knife that gleamed near my eyeball and gripped on to it, tight.

He was sobbing when I turned. Pathetic.

'Oh my God, Constance . . . I'm so sorry . . . Oh shit. It's because I love you so much. Oh my God . . . I'm so sorry . . .' The words looped as he paced the kitchen. Alternating between pulling and smoothing his hair.

He didn't even notice the weapon that I held out, ready, at a right angle as I watched him, broken, pitiful.

I let it fall to the floor. Launched myself away from the counter. Pushed past him.

'No . . . Where are you going? Constance . . . I'm so sorry. I'm drunk . . . I love you so much.'

I turned to him. Dabbed the blood on my lip with my fingers. 'What just happened here, Dale, isn't love.'

Unsteady, knocking myself against the door frame, I left the kitchen. Stumbling through the hall to my room. Stuffing bits into my bag. I wasn't sure what. Phone, cigarettes. Put on my coat. Terrified, knowing I'd have to return for the rest.

He didn't follow me. Something that still surprises me to this day. Though, as I closed the front door to the words 'You can't go . . . What am I going to do? What will I tell them?' I realized his remorse was for him, not me.

*

Exiting High Street Kensington Station, I battled the heavy snow.

Numb-fingered, raw-legged and knickerless, my boots crunched into the inch-deep snow. Everywhere was Christmas-card perfect. Twinkling lights entwined in trees, strung between buildings, glittering window displays, shops open late to accommodate the frantic present-buying, the homeless man freezing outside an estate agent.

Now penniless, I poured some of the Vladimir that I'd bought before boarding the Tube into the man's empty paper cup, then stopped for a lengthy swig myself. The harshness stung my gums. Scalded my throat. But after the initial pain subsided, it warmed my organs one by one.

For my next vodka pause before turning into the side streets, I pulled into the doorway of a closed posh frock shop called Rags (rich people are so hilarious) and phoned Edward to warn him of my impending visit, so as not to give him a heart attack by turning up so late. A drunk vampire with a bloodstained chin.

It rang out.

I lit a fag, swigged more booze and called you. If ever there was a legitimate excuse to call you, turn to you, this was it. I'd be calm in your arms. Your bed. After you'd told me I deserved better, that you'd been so jealous but didn't know how to tell me, and now you could.

It rang out.

As I walked, inhaling smoke, the freezing air electrocuted the nerves of my tooth, which wobbled back and forth inside the cushion of swollen lip. I threw away the cigarette, breathed only through my nose and carried on.

I was on your road. Your car wasn't there. Snow lay in its place. I looked up to Edward's. The light was on in the lounge and I was thankful I wouldn't be waking him.

The warmth of the foyer hit me as I shook my body free of the transparent flakes. Watching them disappear into the brown, wiry mat, jealous of their invisibility.

Climbing the stairs, I concocted my story. *We split up. I left, upset, and slipped in the snow, falling on my face.* I was unsure who I was protecting: Edward, Dale or myself. But for whatever reason, the truth seemed too hard to tell. As it often is.

At the top, I bent forward out of breath. The rapidity of my pumping blood made my tooth pulse. I touched it. Red smeared my finger. All I needed was rest. That was all. To have more drink and sleep everything off. Wake to a brighter day.

As soon as my key opened the lock, I announced myself so as not to frighten him.

There was no response. Not that I expected one: the TV blasted so loudly that even the excellent of hearing would struggle.

'Edward, it's only me . . . No wonder you're going bloody deaf.' I passed his bedroom. The bed was unmade. 'Edward, it's me.'

Then I stopped. Stayed still.

Because I knew this feeling.

The hallway distorted. Not due to alcohol.

I was at the bottom of the stairs at home. The TV playing the *This Morning* theme tune. The *drip, drip, drip*.

I started up again. Continued towards the lounge. Peered in. His chair was empty. The door creaked as I pushed the crack wider. A suited man stood in front of a picture-perfect snow scene that filled the screen. 'More snow on its way, with low pressure bringing easterly winds . . .' I focused on him as he pointed to areas on a map. Because I knew he was there, you see. Edward. Slumped on the floor like a rag doll. But I couldn't look. Couldn't.

I steadied myself by holding on to the door, heaved.

My immediate thought was to run away. Bail. Let someone else deal with it. I've never admitted that before. Not even to Dr Franco.

But we'll never know if I truly was that much of a despicable person, because before I could make that decision, I noticed from my peripheral vision he was moving.

I opened the door fully, dared to look. He was breathing, albeit shallow and laboured, and I shut my eyes and thanked God.

'What's happened?' I ran over, intending to help him up. Presuming he'd fallen and that was the extent of the problem. But as I crouched on Poor Tiger next to him, his face ashen, clammy, a splat of vomit between his legs, I grabbed the phone out of his hand and pressed for a dialling tone that never sounded.

'For fuck's sake, why isn't it charged?' I scrambled in my

bag for my phone, my hands uncontrollable. 'I've told you you've got to charge it. This is why . . . This is bloody why, Edward . . . Ambulance, please . . . I'm sorry for shouting at you, Edward. I'm so sorry . . . Hello, yes . . . I think my friend's having a heart attack.'

It may as well have been the operator who dealt with Mum. She employed the identical phoney serene tones, asked practical questions to which I didn't know the answers.

'He's still alive,' I put forth unprompted.

'Good. You're doing great, Constance.' The same lies.

She asked if he had any aspirin. When I relayed the question to Edward, he lifted his hand and quietly squeezed out the word 'bed'.

Reluctant to leave him, I ran to the bedroom, searched through copious shit. Throwing things on the floor, opening drawers like a desperate burglar, until thank God I found a bottle in his bedside cabinet, then was furious at myself for not looking there first.

Back in the lounge, I placed a couple on his tongue to chew as instructed. But he could barely move his mouth and white chalk paste dribbled onto his chin.

I slid down the wall. The smell of urine hit me as I thumped to the floor next to him. A dark blot expanded down his thighs.

'Here, hold on to me,' I said, taking his damp bent hand. It was colder than the snow floating in front of the window. 'Hey, listen . . . You're going to be fine. You're a strong bugger. You wrestled this tiger, for Christ's sake.' I didn't cry. Wouldn't cry.

Inhaling sharply between each phrase, he said, 'It was . . . from a shop . . . in Holland Park.'

I held on to him tighter. 'You see. We've got stuff to talk about, you and me . . . You're not going anywhere.'

'I think . . . this . . . is the big one, Constance.'

'I'm not having you say shit like that. You can't say shit like that. It's bullshit. You sound like her. I need you now, I'm afraid. So you can't go anywhere. You need to be around, being a cantankerous arsehole. And . . . and I'm going to look after you properly from now on . . . stay here with you. Clear all this shit up and do crosswords together . . . because I got that clue, didn't I? Do you remember? And I wasn't even trying. I reckon I'll end up better at them than you. And you can give me more books to read and I'll read them. And then we can—'

'Constance . . . don't . . . give me a . . . headache as well.'

I lowered my voice. 'All I'm saying is, you can't leave me, Edward . . . or you'll be such a bastard.'

'Don't . . . make . . . me laugh. It hurts.'

'It really does,' I whispered.

I stood, useless, superfluous, as one of the paramedics attached oblong sticky pads to his torso, all wired back to a small machine, which in turn beeped erratically.

'Is it a heart attack?' I asked through my hand-covered mouth, an attempt to conceal my swollen lip that he'd already clocked. But he had more pressing issues.

'We need to get a proper diagnosis at the hospital . . . You're doing great, Edward.' Everyone spun the same old shit, it seemed.

Edward's oxygen mask clouded with each struggling breath. The other paramedic – Jamie, I think he said his name was –

neared him with a weird stretcher-cum-chair. Unable to speak, Edward's flimsy hand searched for mine.

'I'm right here with you. You're going to be just fine. Isn't he, Jamie?'

'Edward, we're going to get you into this chair and take you to the hospital,' said the big bear-like one whose name I can't remember. He then looked at me. 'Are you coming in the ambulance?'

I nodded. I'd never ridden in an ambulance before. They don't offer it up when they're dead.

I followed behind as they carried him through the flat, not mentioning the artefacts as people usually would. Oblivious to Cyril the Squirrel. They remained serious and focused as we all headed into the light of the communal stairway. It seemed more brutal than usual. Service-station break on an all-night drive kind of brutal. One minute they were talking to him as they negotiated the stairs, along with the still-attached machine and oxygen, chatting in faux-jolly tones, saying things like, 'You're doing great, Edward. We'll be at the hospital in no time,' and the next they'd sped up, rushing down the stairs with him, stopping abruptly at the bottom.

I could see Edward's eyes had now closed. 'Don't sleep . . . Please don't go to sleep, Edward,' I said as Bear-Like's enormous frame blocked my view, projecting words I didn't understand.

Jamie lowered the back of the chair and Edward's upper body was flat, his legs in the air. It would have been funny had it not been so terrifying.

'What's going on?' I asked. An irritant. A useless irritant.

'Can you keep back, please,' Bear-Like said to me.

They too stepped away from him. Their energy different. Intense.

'What's wrong? What's happening?'

A woman's robotic voice filled the foyer. 'Evaluating heart rhythm.' A loud high-pitched beep pierced my head. 'Delivering shock.'

'Why are you doing that?'

He didn't acknowledge me and was now next to Edward. Pressing down on his chest. Counting. I'd seen enough *Casualty* in my life to know what was happening. The word 'cardiac' echoed through the stairwell.

Jamie was shouting, 'Edward . . . come on. No, Edward, don't leave me . . . please.' Or perhaps it was me. I can't be sure of anything. It was probably me. Because I was screaming. I think I was screaming. It was as if I had died. I was outside of my body watching them, slow motion, pressing and pressing and pressing and pressing.

'No pulse for seventy-five seconds.'

Pressing and pressing and pressing.

And I couldn't do it. Couldn't see him dead. So it was then that I knew for sure that I was that despicable person. It was then that I ran away.

*

Then there was one.

I'd called and called you, but you weren't picking up.

I wasn't angry. Presumed you were sitting at some over-priced reclaimed kitchen table, flush in one hand and beer in the other, oblivious. But when I go over it, as I do daily, how I wish you'd answered.

I gave it about fifteen minutes. Fifteen minutes, cold in every sense, before I returned to the scene. The ambulance had left. And Edward with it.

Sipping vodka, I prepared myself for that feeling. When they're gone. The juxtaposition of the emptiness and screams of their presence. Although, nothing could be as bad as last time. It's not like in the movies: the police don't deal with everything when someone violently kills themselves. I had to arrange it all myself. When the people had left, the bathroom was cleaner, brighter than it'd ever been before. Except it wasn't. It was foul and tainted, and I continued to scrub at it every day, tile by tile. Unaware the contamination was a different kind.

The door slammed, activating the automatic light, and as I climbed the staircase, I must have looked dead myself. Like one of Dale's zombies, I stared ahead, unblinking, until I

372

noticed a crumple of colour from the corner of my eye. It was his paisley handkerchief. Creased, dirty. Fallen from his pocket as they manoeuvred the stretcher. I picked it up, immune to the usual repulsion I'd feel at such a thing, and pressed it against my heart.

Inside, I took another swig, which tipped my alcohol content and caused my vision to double, bringing with it the sound of a man's voice. Soft and gravelly like his.

I walked down the hall. 'Edward?'

It was all different. As was to be expected. Like Dr Williams's office. Like home. Devoid of life, incomplete. Cyril lacked humour. The diving helmet was now pointless.

I reached the lounge. The TV was still on. A man dressed in a chef's outfit was instructing viewers on how to make game pie. It wasn't Edward. And I relinquished the hope that perhaps I'd dreamt it all. That he'd be sitting in his chair interrogating me as to whether I'd bought his Bovril.

I turned it off. The silence boomed.

After cleaning the sick off the carpet and switching on the heating, I sat in my chair. His, though vacant, was full of him. The concave indentation he'd created over all those years. The layers of dust formed from his skin.

'He's fucking left us, Ursula,' I said, dropping back into the seat, gluing the bottle to my lips.

I know you don't believe in signs, Samuel, but when coming up for air, I glanced over to your window. And I swear the broken cuckoo, Colin, sprang from his door, causing me to jump and slosh drink from the bottle onto my skirt. Ten times it tweeted.

'Edward?' I said to it, and it retracted back inside.

The bottle was near empty, so I necked the dregs before dropping it to the floor. I don't remember feeling drunk. Though I must have been. Grief and shock internalized everything. Feelings multiplied with nowhere to escape. I may have conquered the usual slurring and falling about, but inside I was more pissed than Mum on a Saturday night.

Requiring more, I scanned the room for the likeliest place Edward would have stored some old whisky or an ancient port. The bottom cupboard in the dresser was a strong possibility.

Kneeling in front of the huge mahogany piece, I pulled on a warped and reticent door, which opened with a sudden jolt and a waft of musty air. It wasn't the cocktail bar I'd hoped for, but an abundance of photographs that avalanched onto me. Once the flow stopped, I collected them up and was forced to look. Many were so old they were backed in card, not flimsy photographic paper. Black and white. Sepia. Gnarled corners, white creases. I recognized the eyes. Even more piercing with the contrast of darkened prints. Edward as a toddler, Edward as a teen playing cricket, Edward as a pageboy, Edward as a living, vibrant, youthful being. Edward. A whole life. In a cupboard.

The images blurred. Not because of alcohol but because I was finally crying. I stood. Dropped the memories to my feet. Looked over at his chair. The ocean was here again, but I didn't have the will to swim, so I grabbed my bag and left.

Marinated in vodka, I felt invisible when I entered your flat.

I'd tried to remain on Edward's outside steps, but the snow had thickened, like the time Dad took me sledging in Heaton Park. It was so cold even the alcohol ceased to insulate me and I could feel my core temperature dropping. I'd tried to call you again, but you didn't pick up. I'm not blaming you, but if you'd just picked up . . .

When I checked my phone, I was confused that it was just turning ten again. Then I remembered that Colin was fast. I had around an hour until your return, but I wasn't stupid. I'd planned to be in there nowhere near as long as that.

Inside, I instantly calmed.

My first stop was the kitchen, in search of top-up anaesthetic. I found the bottle of brandy you'd loosened me with that night. It looked untouched since. Fiona didn't need it. I unscrewed the top and unleashed the scent of that day. Your breath as we kissed.

The calendar entry for your meeting with Laura was still stuck on the fridge, humiliating me. As I stared at it, I gulped the fiery spirit until it lodged, hot, inside my chest. Sedated, I returned the bottle to the cupboard, lax about exact positioning. When I turned to leave, the room appeared disjointed and I had to blink repeatedly to recalibrate my vision.

On the way to the bedroom, I stepped into the lounge, switched on the light. All was fine. Still. Neat. Inspecting the room, I opened the CD player. Arthur Rubinstein. Chopin. *Nocturnes*. I pushed it back in and turned to leave. It was then I noticed your phone on the coffee table. Relieved you weren't ignoring me, I pressed the home button to illuminate the screen. I forgot everything for a fleeting pleasurable moment when it displayed only my missed calls.

As I wandered back through the hall, I was losing the battle. Waves were flooding in from all directions. I needed to be closer to you, to lie on your bed, feel you cocooning me, distracting me. Was that what you'd been all along? A distraction?

In your bedroom, the tidiness both surprised and unsettled me. Clothes away. Shoes army-worthy, against the wall. Your bed made, inviting me.

Sinking onto the mattress, I closed my blurring eyes. The room spun like Dorothy's house in *The Wizard of Oz* and I was haunted by images of Edward's lifeless body, interspersed with Mum's lifeless body. A flickering snuff movie I couldn't switch off. Which culminated with her blue, blood-freckled face turning to look at me. I jolted upright, clammy, and staggered to the bathroom to splash my face.

Nauseous, yet unable to allow myself any release, leave evidence, I fearfully hung over the sink. Dizzying further by watching the water swirl the basin, I looked up to the mirror. It was her again, staring back at me. I blinked and she was gone.

I needed it all to stop. Distract myself further, immerse my brain with pleasant thoughts. Other thoughts. Which led me to the wardrobe. Inside the forbidden box.

The luxuriousness of the fabric took me elsewhere. Taffeta scraped across the cardboard as I dragged it free. I'd only intended to hold it against me, but as I did, a vision of Edward's surrendered face intruded my thoughts, so I removed my coat and jumper, and slipped my skirt over my boots. Stepped inside. Allowed the frothing, rustling ocean to envelop my body. Positioning my breasts correctly into the bodice before zipping it as high as I could manage. It fitted me so well. Made to measure. Perhaps somehow it was. That I was destined to wear it.

I clipped in the delicate veil. Brought half up over my dishevelled hair to cover my face. The rest draped my back, pulling me into the correct posture as I closed my eyes, imagined you watching me glide towards you, a bouquet of white roses in hand. Nothing garish – you wouldn't like that. Understated. The guests would gasp at my elegance. How pretty my dress was. The veil. How radiant I was beneath.

When I lifted it from my face, they were both stood, one either side of me in the mirror's reflection. Her perfect crooked grin. His watery grey eyes, which I'd remembered for the first time. Planting an unwanted seed of anger as they pierced through me.

They were both alive, there. Proud. Ready to give me away.

My mum and dad.

I raised my hands to reach for theirs, but there was only air. And in the mirror, once again, there was only me.

I stumbled backwards, knocking against the wardrobe and disrupting the perfect line of shoes. This made me hyper aware of where I was, what I was doing, and I had the sudden urge to leave. Straightening myself, I wiped my face with the back of my hand and reached behind for the zip. It was fine at first. Gliding down as required. Then it stopped. Snagged. Presumably on the veil. My initial concern was to not damage the fragile tulle. But my priorities changed as my gentle tugs achieved nothing. The force I applied increased on each attempt. I was hot, suffocating. Sweat seeped as I repeated the action again and again and again. Hindered by the voluminous sleeves that also blocked my vision as I twisted to see if the mirror could help me identify the problem. My biliousness increasing with the panic of each unsuccessful reach and grapple.

I thought I'd imagined it at first.

Froze. Blinked. Hoped that it would disappear in the same way as all the other hallucinations.

The sound of a key in the door.

The step, step, step.

My head spun like the Waltzers. My body remained a statue. The taffeta desperate to give me away. I listened as you went to the lounge. Closed my eyes and prayed you'd just come back for your phone and would rush off again.

'Yep, it's here . . . Sorry, mate. You know what I'm like. I had visions of it being on the pavement in the snow and I'd be screwed . . . Ha . . . Yeah, totally . . . Not to mention five years of totty. Cheers, pal. Sorry again . . . Yeah . . . OK . . . See you next week.'

Then there was music.

I presumed it was the Chopin playing. I must take this opportunity to thank you again for introducing me to classical music. Even then, a trapped animal, it calmed me. I closed my eyes. One, two, three, four. One, two, three, four. Perhaps my calmness was submission. Coming to terms with my fate. Which arrived within the next couple of bars.

From inside my bag, my ringtone joined in with the melody. Inharmonious, displeasing. The discord worsened by the additional step, step, step.

I turned towards the doorway.

And there you were.

Phone at your ear. Until your hand dropped to your side in shock.

*

I can't recall which of us spoke first.

Though I remember running towards the bathroom, dress hitched, bustling behind me like Cinderella leaving the ball at midnight. Before tripping, jolting forward and hoisting up an armful of material and pushing it between my legs. *You don't know what's round the corner in life, good or bad.* And finally throwing up in your sink. The veil, a fishing net catching the vile juice. I could see your reflection in the mirror. The stench of sizzling booze triggered another heave, muffling your shouts.

'Of course, of course you're being sick . . . You *are* fucking sick.'

You were uglier than I'd ever seen you before. Mouth contorting, spit accumulating in its corners. It was surprising how much you reminded me of Dale.

Regaining my breath, I managed to talk. 'I'm sorry, Samuel . . . Please, I'm so sorry.'

You paced behind me. Gripping your hair like you used to do to mine. Fury emanating from your pores, electrocuting me with your sharp words like a stun gun against the head of an animal awaiting slaughter. I sank into my own world, listened to Chopin. One, two, three, four. One, two, three, four.

'Constance. Are you even fucking listening? How the fuck did you get in? You know what, it doesn't matter . . . You can tell the police.'

Like all animals, I wanted to survive. 'Please, Samuel . . . don't . . . don't call the police . . . Just let me explain.' I turned and placed my hand on your arm, gentle proof of how harmless I was, how sorry. You flinched as if I was a leper.

'Explain? What's to fucking explain? You're in my flat . . . You're wearing my mother's wedding dress, you absolute lunatic.'

You were right, of course. I don't blame you for being so angry. But your words stabbed me and I slid down the fascia of the sink unit, onto the floor. Surrounded by taffeta and lace. My face stretched, crying.

Through the blur I noticed you lift the phone, press digits, before almost instantaneously returning it to your pocket and looking at me.

'Fuck it . . . Go on then, Constance. Explain.'

But when it came to it, I didn't know what to say. How to articulate myself. How do you explain such a thing?

All I could muster was, 'I'm sorry,' as I grabbed on to the slippery-edged sink and pulled myself up, before running past you to the bedroom, where once again I tried so hard to remove the dress.

After a delay you followed me in.

Your calmness was unsettling.

You were still. Arms loose by your sides. I mirrored you. Dropped mine from behind my back. Then you spoke. Slow, measured. 'The calls . . . the card . . . It wasn't Fiona, was it?' You edged nearer. 'The car. It was nothing to do with those lads. It was all you, wasn't it?'

I couldn't bring myself to plead guilty, but weary of the denial, I confessed with my silence, cowering my head, like the bad child I was.

All was quiet. Aside the hypnotic piano. One, two, three, four. One, two, three, four. I'd hoped it signalled the end of the confrontation, but you grabbed me by my wounded arm, twisted me to look at you, before speaking through tightened teeth.

'Take the dress off, get the fuck out of my flat and life, then get some help.'

The way you looked at me was not dissimilar to when you were fucking me, and part of me wondered if you'd lean in for a kiss. But you released me with an extra jolt to push me away, then stumbled backwards into your perfect row of shoes, which led you to bend down, pick up a brown brogue and lob it across the room.

I jumped as it thudded against the abstract black-and-white print that I never really understood.

This seemed to calm you enough to walk over to the bed, drop onto the edge and lower your head. Your hair cascading over your face in that way it did. Enticing me to run through it with my fingers.

'Why, Constance? I've only ever been nice to you . . . I thought you were my friend?'

You truly believed that, didn't you? Within your little bubble of self and wants. I wonder, do any of us grasp our effects on others, as we float through life in these bubbles, fuelled by our own desires? You looked so hurt. I was distressed I'd disappointed you, just like I'd disappointed Dad. So I spoke the words I'd regretted not saying when he went for his walk that day.

'Because I . . . I love you.'

You looked up at me. Your face lifted as if you'd waited all this time to hear me say it. You smiled. As did I. And the relief I felt after so desperately wanting to express it all that time was instantaneous. But your smile switched to a laugh. A nasty, mocking laugh. Only breaking to mimic me.

'I love you . . . I love you.'

I tried not to cry as your cackle bounced around the room. Humiliating me. And I realized that's what it had all been. Just one long humiliation.

'It's true, Samuel.' I turned to the mirror. Tugged at the zip again, trying to see in the reflection what the problem was, but it remained my trap. My frustrations grew. At you, the dress, myself. Then the scream came from me.

'Please . . . please stop it, Samuel.'

It worked.

You looked ashamed. As if you'd finally understood how hurtful you were being. You'd been. Grasped everything you'd done.

You stood, paced the room.

I used the silence to help you understand. 'Dale . . . he . . . well, he hit me tonight . . . and my dear friend died, and I . . . I just wanted to be close to you.'

You stopped and glanced at me, before closing your lids for a moment as if to show how sorry you were. The pacing began again.

I waited, watched you ruminate. 'Do you . . . Did you love me too?'

You stopped mid-movement, like in a game of musical statues, despite Chopin continuing in the background. One, two, three, four. One, two, three, four.

Slowly you turned towards me. Your face a twisted version to the one I knew.

'No. No, Constance . . . I don't. And I didn't. And I'm stunned that you'd have thought I might.'

The words echoed before infiltrating my ears, my mind, my heart.

Was it the way my stomach contracted as if you'd punched me or my tears I could no longer control that fuelled you into grabbing the tops of my arms, causing the dress sleeves to deflate like burst balloons. Shaking me.

'What's wrong with you lot? We had sex. That's all. For fuck's sake, since when does sex down an alleyway indicate love?' Blood flooded your face as you let go, walked away, then turned back, pointing your finger. 'No, you don't . . . I got my memory back of that night way afterwards . . . Don't you dare think you have any moral high ground here . . . Don't you fucking dare.'

You went to the bedside table and retrieved the pack of cigarettes from the drawer. Lit one as you walked over to the window, hoisted it up, then held your smoking hand outside the room. The influx of cold air was a welcome sensation.

'Did I make you a promise, Constance? Any promises at all? Tell me.'

'No,' I whispered.

'No . . . exactly. I mean . . . what are you, a teenager? You think because we have sex we must be in love? That I'd want something more from you?' You blew smoke towards the outside world before removing a particle of tobacco from your tongue.

'I was in love, though, Samuel.'

You laughed as you flicked ash onto the outside ledge. 'Well, Constance, that's because you're fucking nuts.'

I raised my head, stood up straight. 'You said you'd only sleep with someone if you had feelings for them.'

You took a hard drag, your words entwined with the exhaled smoke. 'You know what? I'm done . . . This is insane . . . You're insane—'

'And you knew I had feelings for you . . . yet you kept on doing it.'

'Oh, so this is all my fault now?' You stubbed the cigarette out on the ledge, dropped the window with a thud and turned. 'I should have you fucking sectioned.'

All went silent.

We looked right at each other. Your cheeks turned puce. Knowing what we were both thinking. How like your father you really were. How those apples don't fall far.

'Get out, Constance. Go on . . . get out. Or I really will call the police.'

I took you at your word. Gathered my clothes and bag, and ran out the room as best I could, hindered by the cumbersome material.

'You can't take the dress, for fuck's sake.'

As I opened the front door, you came behind, attempting to press it shut, which led to a brief pushing-and-pulling sequence, until you let go and the edge ricocheted back, smacking me in the face, knocking the already-damaged tooth.

Pain shot through me like a bullet. The metallic taste of blood burst into my mouth. I couldn't see what you were doing, or your reaction, because I'd broken free and was about to run, when I stopped at the top of the stairs, swathed in the chandelier's glow.

'Come on, Constance . . . just give me the dress. It's my mother's.'

I turned to you. Earnest. 'It won't undo, though.'

The atmosphere changed as if we'd called a truce. You came to me. Gently. As though we may kiss. Then yanked me around and tugged, hard, at the zip. Strands of my hair entwined your fingers, though it lacked the pleasure it used to, and the combined agony of my now bruised scalp and broken tooth caused me to yelp.

A droplet of red fell from my lips to the bodice. Then another. And another. I surrendered to the music once more. One, two, three, four. One, two, three, four. Waiting for it all to end.

The door of the opposite flat opened.

Tippi Hedren emerged, her excited dog circling her legs as she stared at us, phone in hand. You were oblivious to our audience. Shouting, swearing, shoving me around like a doll.

I looked directly at her. 'Samuel, you're hurting me.'

I don't think I'll ever truly know what happened next.

I frequently attempt to fill in the blanks. But each time it's different, like a game of Chinese whispers.

I had my back to you, so I'll never know for sure. But Tippi Hedren, or Mrs Jennifer Prowse, as I now know her to be called, gave the best account. The account the police believed.

'Leave her alone,' she shouted, 'or I'm calling the police.' The Labrador barked its support.

Perhaps it was the veil that slipped down my head with every jerking movement. Mrs Prowse insisted it was. That your shoe caught in the net, causing you to step back once, twice . . . We both know what happened the third time.

Forced to shift with you, I swirled beneath the tulle, as if we were dancers transported to a ballroom. One, two, three, four. One, two, three, four. Teetering on the top of the stairs, arms reaching for mine, your torso leant backwards over the sweeping marble steps. I grabbed your wrist, tight, knuckles whitening. My other hand gripped the rail, which moved, unstable, back and forth. I was your counterbalance, and we were engaged in the most intimate split-second dance.

It's funny, they say when you die your life flashes before you. But I too saw a film rush running backwards, catching moments. The day I first saw you, the *drip, drip, drip* of the tap, dancing to Blondie, searching the pubs of Salford for her, Dad kissing me goodbye.

And as we locked eyes, the familiarity of yours dawned on me. The creases at the corner; long, silky lashes; watery grey. They were just like his. And there it was again. Our beautiful connection. Everything I knew we were.

Then I let you go.

So there it is. My explanation. My explanation of love.

Dr Franco was right. It has been cathartic to write it all down. Get it off my soul. Make peace with it. I hope when we meet again that you'll find it within you to forgive me. As I have forgiven you.

I'm sorry I didn't make the funeral. You know how I don't like funerals, especially ones that . . . you know . . . But I knew you'd understand. You hate them too.

A few days afterwards Dr Franco visited me, said the crematorium was packed out with people singing your praises. So that's nice.

We lit a candle for you here instead. Said a prayer. Our own little ceremony. I light one for you every night in my room. Next to the funeral booklet Alison sent me. But you probably already know that.

I don't see anyone anymore, though, apart from Dr Franco. I still have sessions with him. Not at the surgery but at his home in Ealing. Except I pay now. Not full whack, because he still likes to think he's helping me. But he fills me in on the goings-on.

There's a new doctor apparently, a woman. Linda hasn't taken to her and keeps threatening to leave. And Alison got engaged to Kevin. I promise I'm not being facetious when I say they really are made for each other.

But we mainly talk about you. Well, I do and he listens. I wish I could tell him the truth. It may help. It feels like I'm always destined to carry a guilty secret.

We talk about Dale sometimes too. He kept calling me after that night. Asking if we can meet. Saying he needs to apologize. That he loved me, needed me. Once, I saw him standing below the flat, though I didn't let on. Then it all just stopped. Never heard a peep from him again. Except I did see him. When I collected my stuff from the house. Not face to face, thank God. I'd arranged it with Mr Papadopoulos, who was pissed off at me because he had to box everything up and put it in the kitchen in order to let the room again. I went early. Got the taxi to wait on the other side of the road. Watched, waited for Dale to leave for work. Which he did, as clockwork. Although he looked different. He had some kind of beard arrangement going on. And he wasn't alone. He was with a girl. Pretty, she was. Blonde. Didn't look anything like me. They were chatting, hands animated, but it didn't seem like they were together. It was more friendly. At least, it looked like it was from her side. And it dawned on me that she was probably the new occupant of my room.

It was weird being in the house. Familiar, yet I felt a complete disconnect to the place. It wasn't long before the strangeness became discomfort and I couldn't wait to get out.

When returning my key to Mr Papadopoulos, he made some comment – 'There's a new girl . . . nice girl . . . This one I trust' – and so I told him. What happened. About the pictures of Anna. Added that he needed to sort out proper locks, as a landlord should. Then as I was leaving, I stopped outside my room, scribbled a note on the back of a receipt I had in my bag and slipped it under the door. It was the right thing to do, yet part of me still felt bad for doing it.

Anyway . . . there is some good news. Firstly, Edward's doing great. And he told me I mustn't worry about you or Mum anymore. Because he remembers everything. Going into cardiac arrest. 'That big lump of a man' doing CPR, trying to bring him back. All of it. But most importantly he remembers being dead. He died for just over four minutes in total. Can you believe that? To be dead then not be dead? I often go over the fact that if I wasn't such a coward, if I'd stayed and seen the outcome, that all would have been different. But Dr Franco says you can't live like that. A life full of 'what if's. 'It's about what is,' he says.

Edward insists there was a light. I thought he was talking rubbish at first – 'Jesus, couldn't you come up with something a bit more original?' I said. But he swore he wasn't bullshitting. Reckons he hovered over his own body, watching them at work. Is that what happened to you? Did you see me, standing over your distorted body? Crying, before fleeing?

I started to truly believe when I saw the change in him. When he'd talk about Amy, his anger, sorrow, was replaced with what I can only describe as enlightened joy. She was there, you see. Sat on the stairs. Waiting for him, he says. But what confirmed it was that he saw me too. Praying before running away. So it must be true. He knows he'll see her again. And in turn I know I'll see you. And Mum. And possibly Dad.

Edward will never let me live it down, of course. 'You owe me at least fifty cups of tea for abandoning me.'

'As if I don't make you fifty cups of tea a week anyway,' I told him.

It's made the whole concept of death less frightening to me. Appealing even. Knowing I'll be with you again. Her. Knowing you're both there. Somewhere. Waiting for me.

I've decided I don't want her to see me sad anymore. It must have been breaking her heart watching me. I can't imagine anything worse than seeing your child suffer. I've been working with Dr Franco on it for a while, and he thinks it's about time that I read the diaries, or more specifically her last one. The last entry. He thinks it will help me move on with my life. By not avoiding it. That facing it will stop it weighing me down. So tonight's the night. I said I would, once I'd finished this letter. This exercise. I'm nervous but ready.

As you can see, things are getting better for me. Like I said at the start, I'd intended to join you both soon after that night, but I couldn't do it. I wasn't ready and didn't want to leave Edward. I hope you understand. Though he won't be here forever. I can't believe how much I enjoy looking after him. He looks after me too, in his own way. Teaches me stuff, makes me feel safe again.

And thank goodness I didn't. Because the other good news is, it's not just me now. There's a little us growing inside me. Please don't be annoyed but I never took that last pill. Though I honestly just forgot initially, with everything that went on. But then, after you'd gone, I wanted to see if part of you was meant to stay with me. And it was. It's a girl.

Eighteen weeks now. Angie I'm going to call her. But she won't have the same fate. I promise. I won't let her. I'll do it right. I'll make her right.

'This must be my last bacon butty, Constance. Only healthy stuff now, so I get to be a granddad,' says Edward all the time. Though it never is.

He can't wait for Angie to arrive. He's discovered online shopping, which is a disaster, as we have more stuff arriving constantly. A beautiful cot turned up unexpectedly this morning. And some toys. He loves me, you know. Edward. And Angie. I feel it, and it's nice. I love him too. But my God, he's a pain in the arse. I've told him he mustn't spoil her.

I've sewn a new eye onto Blusha. So that'll be her favourite toy. It's not as good as it was before, but as fixed as it can be, and Angie won't mind. She's loveable even if a bit damaged.

You'll never guess but I've become a book addict. Well, I needed something to replace the fags now I can't smoke. That and biscuits. I'm reading *Wuthering Heights* again. Did you ever read it? I'm presuming not or you wouldn't have described the card as 'psycho'. Oh, and you really should have finished *Great Expectations*. It's very good. What a shame.

I think I'll write again. It makes me feel closer to you. Helps me keep you alive for Angie. But before I go . . . Hang on. Can you hear? I'm playing it for you. I play it all the time. And I'll always play it for her, so she knows. Our song. 'At Last'.

The moment we fell in love.

*

My beautiful Constance,

I'm so sorry to leave in this way. You've no idea how much it hurts to know that when I'm gone, I won't be the one to make you feel better. My baby girl.

I fucked it all up, Constance. Everything. Apart from you. You were my one perfect thing.

You were my life, but when I'm gone, you mustn't make me yours. I know it's going to hurt. And if I could stay, I would, but the thing is, I'm holding you back, baby girl. You mustn't follow in my footsteps. I am weak and foolish, and you are not. You are strong and clever and special, and I need you to know that. To always remember that.

Yesterday, when I sat in his chair, I realized how stupid I'd been. What a waste it all was. The reason his chair was empty was because he didn't want to sit in it. If someone doesn't want to sit in your chair, Constance, you let them go and sit where the fuck they like, because you're better off without them – they don't deserve you, do you hear me? Promise me you'll never let a man take away your happiness.

Whether I'm here or not, you have all the love you need. It doesn't disappear. No one can love you as much as I do, and I'll always be there. Following you, getting on your nerves. I won't be feathers, because as you know birds terrify me, but I'll be something. I'll be snow.

Thank you, my baby. For everything. This isn't goodbye. We don't do goodbyes. But there's no need to write more because we know it all anyway. Nothing could be more than us.

Mum x

Acknowledgements

I'll start with my wonderful agent Jo Williamson of Antony Harwood. Thank you for randomly seeing a tweet, messaging me and then actually liking the book. I am so grateful for your honesty, kindness and support. I know I am blessed to have you as an agent.

Thank you to my publisher Wayne Brookes. For not only having such belief in the book, but for eradicating every fear I'd had about the publishing process by being so approachable and hilarious and warm and lovely. I lucked out big style and I can't thank you enough.

So much thanks to my editor Alex Saunders whose insight, hard work and enthusiasm helped make the book the best it could be. I suspect he's never had so many conversations with an author about contraception and car sex. But the fact those conversations weren't utterly horrendous says everything!

Much gratitude to my lovely desk editor Samantha Fletcher for all her help and hard work, Mel Four for the fantastic cover design, and Hannah Corbett in publicity, Emma Draude of EDPR and Sarah Arratoon in marketing for all the brilliant ways in which they've promoted both me and the book. Thanks also to the copy-editor Laura Collins, proofreader

Karen Whitlock and anyone else at Mantle and Pan Macmillan who has been part of getting this book out into the world.

For all the joy that having this book published has brought me, there's also huge sadness that my mum and dad never got to witness it. The last time the novel was discussed with my dad, he said, 'When's it going to be finished? It's taking longer than *Gone with the Wind*.' I hope he somehow knows that it's now complete, and that it took me one year less than Margaret Mitchell. My mum believed in me my whole life and supported everything I wanted to do, presuming that I was perfectly capable of doing it (even if I thought the opposite). They both died only months apart in 2015, and it was after my mum's death that I dug out a terrible abandoned version of the book, and rewrote it from scratch, with a totally different angle. Then when my dad died, I had no choice but to channel all my grief into writing. How bittersweet that the best thing that has happened to me has come out of the worst thing that has happened to me. I love you Mum and Dad and thank you for everything.

Huge thanks to Gavin Towers who, with the non-existent spare time he had, read the manuscript and helped enormously by highlighting its awfulness and guiding me towards improvements. The biggest accolade being when he read the final draft and said, 'It's actually pretty good. I'm genuinely surprised.'

I must also include Victoria Towers and Martin Serene. Mainly because I just must include them, but also for being family and supporting me throughout this journey.

To Edward Knight, my dearest friend and business partner, for being someone who always believed in me and shaped my creativity in my adult life. Without him allowing me the freedom to write whilst I should have been doing the day job, there would be no book and for that I am eternally grateful.

To my amazing friends, Sian Hall and Sarah Keller, for being there as support whilst both writing and negotiating grief. Especially Sarah for helping me get out of 'the wedding dress pickle'. And Angela Feely for being there throughout the rollercoaster of submissions and edits, and Grace Feely for being its first reader and making me believe that people may actually like it.

Thank you to the people who have encouraged my writing along the way. Especially, Lisa Davies et al at the West London Writing Group. To Ali Harper, my mentor-turned-friend. It's highly likely I wouldn't have finished the book had it not been for her.

A big shout-out to my Twitter friends who helped with umpteen research questions and have been a surprising but wonderful source of love and support. Especially Rob Palk for answering all my annoying queries. To the CBC and Savvies Facebook groups. The former for the support and the latter for being a guiding light during this weird process.

And last and least, my gratitude to the men throughout my life who have treated me in a less than acceptable fashion. Without them I wouldn't have been able to create such shitty male characters.

But I really must end on a more important note than that – so thank you to my cats.